TALES OF THE NIGHT

"Høeg's imagination is dazzling: he scoops up ideas, and just keeps running. He is clever without being self-conscious. He administers tiny pristine shocks. He pinpoints the divide between the intellect and the senses without ever being pious or recondite. And he conjures pictures to fix things in the reader's mind for ever"

MICHAEL POLLARD, *Financial Times*

"There is here a talent for storytelling of rare brilliance. In a controlled and almost chillingly distanced prose, what is delivered in these improbable tall stories is a criticism of civilisation which is a devastating assault on the whole of western culture"

BIRGER HAGLUND, *Allt om Böcker*

"Such is his talent for layering meanings and images, these tales take on something of the resonance of legend"

ROSEMARY GORING, *Scotland on Sunday*

"He has his own inner language which, even in translation, is well worth learning" DAVID HUGHES, *Mail on Sunday*

"A writer of arresting originality . . . [which] is very much in evidence in this collection . . . Fine, evanescent stories"

JULIA FLYNN, *Daily Telegraph*

"A veritable firework display of inventive intellectual virtuosity"

LUIGI FORTE, *La Stampa*

"Nothing more stimulating to the imagination, rich in ideas and linguistically enjoyable is being published in Sweden this spring. The reader is flung into the world of sagas, myths and violent speculation" LARS-OLF FRANZÉN, *Dagens Nyheter*

"This accomplished work is a most welcome addition to the list of Høeg's works available in English"

ANDREW RIEMER, *Sydney Morning Herald*

PETER HØEG was born in 1957 and followed various callings – dancer, actor, sailor, mountaineer – before he turned seriously to writing. After publishing the present volume of stories and his first novel, *The History of Danish Dreams*, "a vaultingly ambitious and hugely accomplished first novel" in the opinion of Peter Whittaker, *New Statesman & Society*, he went on to write the innovative crime novel, *Miss Smilla's Feeling for Snow*, which assured him an international reputation. The variety of his talent was amply demonstrated with his subsequent novels, *Borderliners*, a remarkable study of children that caused controversy within Denmark and beyond, and the recent satirical ecological fable, *The Woman and the Ape*.

BARBARA HAVELAND, a Scot married to a Norwegian and resident in Denmark, has translated Peter Høeg's *The History of Danish Dreams*, *Borderliners* and *The Woman and the Ape*. She is also translator of Solvej Balle's *According to the Law*.

"The stories in *Tales of the Night* are tragic, comic, adventurous, taut and wild. Love here again becomes enigma and torment, self-evident and incomprehensible"

RAGNAR STRÖMBERG, *Göteborg-Posten*

"These stories probably attain the highest point of brilliance and subtlety in his entire work to date"

MAURIZIO BARTOCCI, *Manifesto*

Also by Peter Høeg in English translation

THE HISTORY OF DANISH DREAMS
MISS SMILLA'S FEELING FOR SNOW
BORDERLINERS
THE WOMAN AND THE APE

Peter Høeg

TALES OF THE NIGHT

Translated from the Danish
by Barbara Haveland

THE HARVILL PRESS
LONDON

First published with the title *Fortaellinger on natten* by
Munksgaard/Rosinante, Copenhagen, 1990

First published in Great Britain in 1997 by The Harvill Press

This paperback edition first published in 1998 by The Harvill Press
2 Aztec Row, Berners Road, London N1 0PW

3 5 7 9 8 6 4 2

www.harvill-press.com

A CIP catalogue record for this book is available from the British Library

ISBN 1 86046 504 8

Designed and typeset in Sabon at Libanus Press, Marlborough, Wiltshire

Printed and bound in Great Britain by Mackays of Chatham

Half title illustration by Keith Money

For my mother and father
Karen and Erik Høeg

CONTENTS

These eight tales have a date and theme in common.
They are all concerned with love. Love and its conditions,
on the night of 19 March 1929.

Peter Høeg, Copenhagen, March 1990

TALES OF THE NIGHT

JOURNEY INTO A DARK HEART

A book is a deed . . . the writing of it is an enterprise as much as the conquest of a colony. JOSEPH CONRAD in *Last Essays*

Mathematics is the shadow of the real world projected on to the screen of the intellect. ATTRIBUTED TO ARCHIMEDES

On March 18th 1929 a young Dane, David Rehn, was in attendance when the railway line from Cabinda, near the mouth of the Congo, to Katanga in Central Africa was dedicated to integrity.

Also present were the King and Queen of Belgium, Prime Minister Smuts of the Union of South Africa and Lord Delamere of Kenya, all of whom made speeches; their words, like champagne, making David's blood sing. Later, at the dinner in the governor's palace, he mingled with black servants and white guests, deliciously giddy without having touched a drop of alcohol. Although he could not remember with any certainty who had said what he would never forget their words: had it not been the King himself who, pointing, had said, "See, ladies and gentlemen, the ocean is as blue as the Aegean, and with the bright sun hanging above us and soft sea breezes wafting around us surely it is quite evident that we are in the presence of Ancient Greece. The Greeks, too, sailed along the African coastline; they were the first to colonize this continent and have we not, in truth, fulfilled the ideals to which the ancients aspired: integrity of thought, integrity in the wielding of power, integrity in trade and commerce was their goal, in the pursuit of which no sacrifice was deemed too great. And in dedicating this railway, possibly the longest in Africa, do not our thoughts turn to the Colossus of Rhodes, is it not the temple of Artemis at Ephesus, is it not the Seven Wonders of the World that spring to mind and is this railway not the eighth? Are not these two shining rails of steel the pure lines of thought and commerce which, as the arteries of civilization, shall carry clean, oxygenated blood three thousand kilometres through the jungle, deep into the heart of the dark continent?"

Never in his life had David found himself in such close proximity to heads of state and the aristocracy of international finance and it seemed to him that their enthusiasm and forthrightness on this day helped him to see clearly for the first time in a long, long while.

One year earlier a sudden, nauseating instance of life's unpredictability had thrown him off the track he had been following since childhood and cast him out into a wilderness of uncertainty. Influential and well-meaning relatives had tried to set him back on the right path by placing him with a trading company – a global concern of Danish origin – where they had procured for him the only guaranteed key to upward mobility in this life, a good, secure position, and where one of the company's directors had promised to act as his guide. At the company's head office in Copenhagen David had endeavoured to work his way back to that vantage point from which the world acquires some semblance of coherence and order, but so far all he had gained was the sympathy of his fellow men. People liked David for his pleasant manners, his diligence, his open and trusting face and his physical gaucheness, and for something else which they could not quite put their fingers on. Even the company director had not been able fully to explain his motives for suggesting that David accompany him to the Belgian Congo for the dedication of the Katanga railway, in which the company had a certain interest.

Until a year previously and for as long as he could remember

David had been a mathematician. Not the sort who studies this discipline because he believes he is quicker on the uptake in that field than in any other, nor because one must make a career of something, nor out of curiosity. No, he became a mathematician out of a deep, burning passion for that crystal-clear, purifying algebraic science from which all earthly uncertainty has been distilled. By the time he moved up to the middle school he had a better understanding of infinitesimal calculus than any of his teachers and when, at the age of eighteen, he was interviewed about an article on Abelian groups he had had published in a German journal, he explained – blushing because the immediacy of the female journalist disturbed his concentration – that "cool mathematical reasoning is my greatest joy".

Algebra seemed to offer an obvious, exhilarating and in every respect satisfying career for David until, while studying at the University of Vienna, he met a boy a couple of years his junior, a boy who ran into David in a fog of abstraction and optimism. The boy's name was Kurt Gödel. He was a sickly individual with a thirst for knowledge that took nothing for granted and had earned him the nickname "Herr Warum". When they met he was pursuing a line of thought which would result just a few years later in a proposition destined to shake the world of mathematics to its very foundations and even though it had not as yet been perfected it shook David to *his* on the day, sitting in a café, that the boy made him privy to his cogently formulated doubts. Afterwards, David walked the streets of Vienna in a state of shock, knowing full well that after what he had heard that day nothing would ever be the same again. He had long since also learned to use mathematics as both medicine and stimulant. Whenever he felt down-hearted he could console himself with the scintillating logic of Bertrand Russell, if he were feeling cocky he would read one of the unsuccessful attempts at a geometric trisectioning of the angle and when his mind was in a turmoil he found tranquillity and stringency in Euclid's *Elements*. But on this particular day, in seeking some salve for his despair, he slipped up.

On his desk lay a beautifully bound facsimile of the notes of the French mathematician Galois and, as he had done so often before, David read the young man's hastily scrawled résumé of his momentous work on the solving of irreducible equations and of his burning faith in the future. At the end Galois – then twenty-one years of age – had written: "I have run out of time. I am off to fight a duel." Then he had risen from his papers and gone out to his death. And suddenly it occurred to David that he was reading of his own undoing.

He left Vienna that same evening, firmly resolved never again to have anything to do with mathematics, and those who, later, laughed behind his back at his despair were people who had never understood that so all-embracing is love that to a person in love the very nature of life may be revealed in the smallest details and the verity of life stand or fall on the minutest grain of truth, even that contained within a mathematical proof.

In order, nevertheless, to survive, David had withdrawn into a state of assiduous insensibility, out of which he was jolted only upon encountering the tropics. At first he felt that he had merely been awakened to fresh and unbearable confusion – their ship, the *Earnest*, one of the company's own passenger and cargo ships, having sailed, a fortnight after setting out, into a heat that rose up into the air like an invisible wall. Then came landfall in Africa and with it the blazing sun over David's head, unfamiliar vegetables and spices to assail his digestive system and dark, inscrutable faces all around him to weigh on his mind. It took a month for his initial bewilderment to give way to a feeling, if not of security, then at least of stability and the dedication of the railway brought him the first joyful sense of seeing with a clarity he had never thought to experience again.

On the day itself an unforeseen coolness in the air had eased the almost palpable pressure; the thoughts of all the people gathered outside the governor's palace ascended freely into the blue sky. The sea breeze carried the voices of the speechmakers to their audience and David saw that these speakers were happy; that, on this day, these sovereigns and statesmen of the civilized world blushed with pleasure, their hands shook with profound, inner emotion, their eyes shone and their voices faltered. To David it seemed obvious and fitting that the future of the world should rest in the hands of these particular men and for the first time he realized that with leaders such as these ordinary people need have no grasp of politics; with leaders such as these, he thought, we might never need to concern ourselves with politics at all, since not only are these men possessed of an insight deeper than the rest of us could ever hope to plumb, they can also – on a day such as this – render politics as lucid and transparent as the blue ocean out there beyond the breakers of Cabinda.

For David, absolute truth had always taken the form of numbers and this day had abounded in numbers. With reckless courage and sincerity the managing director of the railway, Sir Robert Wilson, had detailed the numerical aspects of its construction. "We have," he said, "set seven thousand men to lay two thousand seven hundred and seven kilometres of track through country where the temperature fluctuates between fourteen and one hundred and twenty degrees Fahrenheit. The sum of all its ups and downs amounts to two hundred thousand metres. The track is one metre wide and has cost two hundred and fifty thousand francs per kilometre – two hundred and seventy million seven hundred and fifty thousand francs in all. It follows the river Congo through Leopoldville to Llebo, then on to Bukama and the Katanga copper mines, where it joins the Benguela line from Angola, the Rhodesia–Katanga railway, and in a few years' time it will link up with Tanganyika's central railway network, thus penetrating and opening up Africa from the Indian Ocean to the Atlantic, from Cape Town to the Sahara."

"Opening and penetrating," thought David later, bewildered and blissful, and heard himself telling the wife of the Belgian colonial minister how the great Kronecker, one of those upon whom he had modelled his own life, had once said that "God created the natural numbers – the rest is the work of man". "And what a work," he declared rapturously to the minister's lady.

For the occasion a number of partitioning walls in the palace had been removed to create a reception room running the entire length of the building and here, at a table that seemed to stretch into infinity, down the length of which a miniature model of the railway had been set up, a place had been set for every one of them. The dinner service was Crown Derby, the wine was Chambertin-Clos de Bèze and the saddle of venison tasted to David just like the red deer at home. For once the sudden tropical nightfall did not seem to him like an assault, for the chandeliers had been lit and only the white tropical suits, the suntanned men and the black servants in their livery and white gloves betrayed the fact that this was not Europe.

A powerful air of kinship pervaded that dinner. Each and every guest was filled with the sense of a tough job well done. Their limbs ached slightly, as though they personally had shovelled earth and hauled sleepers into place, and their concerted efforts had eradicated all differences in rank, everybody was forthright, everyone talking at the tops of their voices. The minister's wife playfully teased David who, for his part, felt that their presence in such sterling company increased the worth of every single one of them, himself included. "Here," he thought, "we all have our natural place and a part to play in the scheme of things, none of us need languish in a corner like some indefinable quantity."

During the dessert a message was delivered to the banquet, a message which erased the last stiff traces of formality. At one point the King of Belgium was called away and when, minutes later, he returned his face was so pale that no one had wit enough to get to their feet as he positioned himself behind his chair. He struck his glass and raised his voice slightly. "I have just received some good news," he said, "from an English journalist who arrived here on the Sankuru steamer twenty minutes ago; a man who, as a guest of the Belgian government, is to represent the world's press on the maiden run along our railway line tomorrow. He brings us word, ladies and gentlemen, that yesterday at Kamina a joint Belgian, British and Portugese force led by General Machado defeated the native rebel bands which have posed the greatest problem to construction work in recent years. The Ugandan rebel leader, Lueni, was killed in the fighting. His body is to be brought downriver to Cabinda." The King clicked his heels together. "Ladies and gentlemen, a toast to our gallant armed forces!"

For a second not a breath stirred. Then everyone stood up and gravely raised their glasses, there being times when a happy event may be so overwhelming that it can only be digested gradually and in silence. To new arrivals like David the name Lueni had an exotic ring to it, as menacing as the dense jungle that surrounded the town. But to the permanent residents it constituted the essence of fear, it represented death as precipitate as cerebral malaria, it meant cut supply lines and hunger, steamships drifting downriver with no trace of their crew. A name from the innermost chamber of Africa's murky hell.

Fleetingly and amid total silence, as in a vision they all saw the body, black as polished wood, laid out on a canvas stretcher. Then joy swelled like a river, the cry went up for champagne, the King lost his composure and hugged Sir Robert to his chest and tears could be seen glistening in the monarch's eyes. Old Lord Delamere who, as everyone knew, had trekked across the Rift Valley from Mombasa with an oxcart and more than once had fought, rifle in hand, for the lives of his wife and his children, sat slumped in his chair with his hands resting on the edge of the table, muttering, "Can it be, can it be?" A few voices broke into the Belgian national anthem, "La Brabanconne", people were slapping one another on the back and at one point David discovered to his consternation that he was holding the wife of the colonial minister by the hand. He gazed happily on the flushed faces, the glinting medals, the shimmering gowns and the servants' livery; he sensed a mood of unrestrained camaraderie flowing through the room buoyed up by these mighty feats of engineering and military prowess and with the lady's hand in his, suddenly sensitive to symbols, he realized that this was like a celebration in a barracks, a gay carnival behind which lay the most perfect form of justice.

Later, wanting to be alone for a moment, he went out into the garden. He felt that the tropics, like a young Negress, were laughing to him. Strange and enticing sounds and scents swirled around him, the gramophone music carried to his ears through the open doors – inside they were dancing to Strauss waltzes. With its white pillars the governor's palace looked for all the world like a floodlit Greek temple and above its ridgepole rose the constellation of Libra, that great, celestial square. "Perhaps," thought David, "as a sign not to give up where Galois did."

The following afternoon when, with the first ever train from Cabinda to Katanga, the railway was officially declared open; when the rejoicing of the previous day had been reinforced by the prospect of the journey; when the military band had played; when the King had shaken the travellers by the hand in farewell; when everyone's thoughts were quite plainly running with the railway tracks all the way up to the distant blue mountains, on the platform, unnoticed by anyone other than a handful of servants and stewards, in the grey area between the shade of the platform canopy and the dazzling sunlight, there arose a moment's doubt. The previous day the colonial minister – carried away by the elated atmosphere and the news of the rebels' defeat – had announced that he too intended to make the trip. As regards this man, his wife had confided to David that for every new position of authority he had attained he had gained two pounds in weight, and once this colossal figure had eased his way into the leading Pullman, which was to have carried all of the invited guests, it became immediately apparent that the coach was full.

At that moment came the hiss of the train's pressure valves being checked and in the cloud of steam that enveloped the platform four remaining figures gravitated towards one another, as though springing straight out of the ground. While round about them arrangements were being made for yet another carriage to be coupled to the train they stared at one another, eye to eye. Over the past few days David's attention had been caught by a good number of faces but he was certain that he had never seen these three before. They appeared, standing there before him, to have crystallized around this distressing little breach in the otherwise faultless arrangements, so silent and strange that it seemed they would never make contact, that they shared nothing other than just this: that they were on the outside.

Directly opposite David stood a soldier, a short, stiff-necked, thickset and forbidding individual with a black eye-patch over one eye and a uniform bedecked with so many tokens of imperishable military glory that, thought David, one would have had a hard job finding room enough to scribble the tiniest *Quod erat demonstrandum* in pencil on that impossibly white dress uniform. David knew nothing of military matters but among the gleaming symbols he recognized the German eagle and he was struck by a vague sense of surprise at meeting this ruffled bird from the losing side here, among the representatives of those nations which had won the World War.

Out in the sunshine stood a slim black servant girl in a white dress. She carried a large leather suitcase belonging to the fourth and eldest member of the party, a ruddy-faced man with doleful eyes, a coarse and unhealthy-looking complexion and a flamboyant waxed moustache. He wore an expensive tweed suit, complete with waistcoat and stock, an outfit which seemed tantamount to suicide in the tropical heat.

Just when David could bear the silence no longer and had put out his hand, meaning to introduce himself, the party were shrouded in yet another cloud of steam. Solicitous hands took hold of David and his luggage and led him past the soldiers in the personnel carriers, past the goods wagons – which were, for the first time, to carry a goodly quantity of the boons of the Western world to the mines at Katanga and return bearing copper and gold – and up to and into the newly coupled Pullman. From the running board he watched their Majesties and the Belgian district commissioner waving them off while behind the station building the sun was setting so fast that it seemed to drop straight down on to the horizon. Through the carriage windows the soldiers saluted with fixed bayonets and, thought David, here we are driving into the heart of Africa bristling with rifles – like a hedgehog, a belligerent hedgehog on rails. In that selfsame instant he was consumed with embarrassment at his own unbridled imagination and at all of the people on the platform waving and shouting "Hurrah!". Cheeks flaming, he lurched into the little cloakroom at his back.

Here he paused for a moment and straightened his light-coloured jacket. Then he opened the door into the carriage.

After a month in the tropics David believed himself to be more or less inured to the sudden shifts between darkness to light, to the violent contrasts which had, during the first few weeks, made his head ache. Even so, he remained in the doorway for one stunned moment trying to work out how it could possibly have come about that he had stepped out of Africa and into the most extreme and yet classic example of European comfort. A thick, deep red Persian rug was spread on the floor, curtains of heavy cream silk covered the windows, some leather-upholstered chairs encircled a table, the walls were hung with paintings of cool oak forests, the ceiling was adorned with gilded stuccowork, at the far end of the room stood an open marble fireplace and the whole of this unlikely tableau was lit by two tall, slender oil lamps set on the table.

His two travelling companions were still on their feet, as though they had been waiting for him, and as he eyed the man in uniform and the gentleman in tweeds the word that occurred to David was "theatre". "This is a stage set," he thought, "that is why everything is juddering and swaying, we are being lowered from the flies on to the stage."

Into the narrow void of doubt and irresponsibility which had opened up between them the man in tweeds now stepped, bowed stiffly, waited for a series of nervous twitches originating in his left shoulder to run across his face and away, then began to speak, courteously and with authority.

"Gentlemen," he said, "allow me to introduce myself. I am a reporter. I had the honour yesterday of bringing His Majesty the news of our troops' victory. So you see, I came this way only yesterday by river, a journey I made once before, many years ago. Bearing in mind my somewhat wider, relatively speaking, experience and the – how shall I put it – *responsabilité sociale* accorded by age, I therefore offer my services as your host." He tapped two of the broad leather chairs lightly, David and the military man took their seats and the thought crossed David's mind that this was no invitation but a command, and that beneath the old man's politesse, from his first words of welcome, there had lurked something which David – if he had not known how well dressed and how respectable in every respect his host was –

might privately have considered calling lugubrious impudence.

Unasked, the girl settled herself on a stool in one corner where she remained quite motionless.

"I have been given to understand," continued the man who was now their host, "that yesterday this expedition was dedicated to integrity and that it is therefore the intention that it should be no ordinary railway journey at the end of which one is every bit as much a stranger to one's fellow passengers as at the outset. On the contrary, it is up to us to fulfil His Majesty's wish by making this an open and honest journey, and to this end it goes without saying that we must begin by making one another's acquaintance. My name is Joseph Korzeniowski but my friends, among whom I am sure by the end of our journey I will be able to number your good selves, call me Joseph K."

Just then a black waiter entered carrying a bottle of champagne in a large silver ice-bucket. Having placed this on the table he proceeded to light a fire in the grate. At that very moment a gentle shudder ran along the length of the train as the locomotive commenced its ascent towards the distant mountains and David found himself thinking that even here, on the equator, it could well be a cold night.

Then he realized that the others were waiting for him and he drew himself up to his full height. "My name is David Rehn," he said, "and I am a mathematician."

This last was a quite involuntary addition. He ought to have introduced himself as a secretary with the Danish delegation but had their host not said that they were all travelling into a night of integrity?

And Joseph K. was in fact now rubbing his hands together with satisfaction. "A mathematician," he said, "how fitting, how . . . symbolic, after all would you not say that mathematics is the sincerest of all disciplines, and the one which most closely approaches the concept of the universe?"

"Yes, indeed!" blurted David and, blushing but nonetheless with some pride, he added: "A great mathematician once said that when God created Heaven and Earth and separated light from dark and water from land and above from below he showed himself to be a mathematician, since such actions presuppose a knowledge of binary opposites. So, to the question of what was there in the beginning we can reply: 'In the beginning was mathematics'."

"What a brilliant aphorism," said Joseph K., and attempted to open the champagne. In this he was unsuccessful and David noted that his right wrist was badly swollen. The soldier then took the bottle from him and in those expert and powerful hands the cork slid out with only the faintest whisper of carbonic acid, then – with the napkin held between the warmth of his hands and the cold bottle – he poured the champagne, leaned back in his chair and said, in a thick German accent: "I am von Lettow. General Paul von Lettow Voerbeck."

Even to David, who prided himself somewhat on his ignorance of that part of the world not featured in mathematical journals, this name as it was uttered seemed to fill the air with all the weight of an equestrian statue suddenly materializing in the room. In the eyes of Europe at that time General von Lettow Voerbeck represented the very quintessence of courage, he was a hero and as far as that fact was concerned it made not the slightest difference that he had fought on the losing, German, side. On the contrary, in East Africa during the Great War von Lettow Voerbeck had fought with all the courage of a lion, the wisdom of an elephant and the venom of a snake for the legitimate German colonies against a devastatingly superior force. Among those English and Indians who had been shipped to the African continent to take part in the European war he had become a legend on whom they never laid eyes but whose presence they could always sense. With the white troops and black "askaris" under his command he had developed and refined his own hit-and-run strategy, a form of guerrilla warfare that put off the inevitable confrontation and the inevitable defeat, thus earning him the same nickname as the wily Roman consul Quintus Fabius Maximus: "The Procrastinator". On Germany's surrender, having received orders from Berlin to down arms at Kasama, he returned home to a hero's welcome and a number of honorary military and political posts all of which carried with them a fine though never overstated air of martyrdom together with the implication that, had General von Lettow Voerbeck not received orders to capitulate, somewhere along the banks of Lake Tanganyika he would be fighting yet.

And here was this giant, of whom everyone had heard but whom so few had seen, sitting in the capacious leather armchair like some comfortably ensconced phantom from the jungle.

"General," said Joseph K., spreading his hands palms upward in a gesture of impotence, "I do not know what to say. The god of war's chosen one here in our midst! I must tell you, General, sir – having now learned who you are – that I take the liberty of feeling I already know you, since I have of course read your *Memoirs of East Africa* and your unforgettable *Rallying Cry to the German People*, in which you remind us all that we must keep an iron grip on our colonies and never let them go. Mr Rehn, come and stand beside me so that we two, as representatives of both the victorious and the more . . . circumspect powers, may drink a toast to this gallant son of Germany and of Europe, the Cunctator of German East Africa," and with one swift and practised flick of his unswollen left wrist Joseph K. drained his glass, then refilled it.

"General," he said, after a moment's thought, "you too are, of course, an apostle of the truth. In your *Rallying Cry*, I remember quite clearly, you also described how it was in fact the war which prompted Africa to reveal its true face. 'The humane war', as you so elegantly put it, and I hope that during this night of integrity you will elaborate upon that interesting viewpoint to enable the two of us here to defend it against the evil – and mainly Bolshevik – voices throughout Europe which rail against war, claiming that no matter where or when it occurs it is invariably inhumane."

The general's one good eye had been fixed unwaveringly on the speaker. Now, without the powerful features, which put David in mind of heavy cast-iron mouldings, losing any of their concentration, he lifted his eye-patch away from his face and, using a snowy-white handkerchief, dabbed his eye socket with the same leisurely thoroughness with which he had uncorked the champagne.

"The war," he then said, calmly, "has proved the potential within our colonies for the founding of a new Germany. It has revealed that Africa possesses undreamed-of resources, that this continent represents the perfect territory for the coming German expansion."

"As a matter of fact," said Joseph K., smiling affably, "I have always thought of you as Paul, Our Lord's commander-in-chief, preaching the gospel on his missionary travels. Have you ever wondered whether you are preaching to heathens who listen or to Jews who turn their backs on the truth?"

"In my life," said the general guardedly, "I have never found much time for Bible reading."

"How wise," Joseph K. answered warmly. "The practical side of life ought always to go hand in hand with the spiritual side. Was it not your colleague, Cromwell, who said: 'Trust in God, lads, but keep your tinder dry'?"

Joseph K. turned to David. "And you, my young friend," he said, "while we are on the subject of Christian names and their symbolism, you must of course be the boy David, newly anointed, unaware that the world awaits him, so meanwhile he tends . . ." – and here the speaker judiciously pondered his metaphors – "tends his mathematical sheep."

As he said this, David was suddenly convinced that their host's bluff courtesy was a front for something else, something sinister. He leaned towards him.

"And who might you be?" he asked Joseph K.

"I," replied the old man, and his face beamed with triumph, "I am Joseph, cast out by his brothers among men, thrown into a well out of which he will nonetheless manage to drag himself. I am, of course, Joseph the interpreter of dreams and no one has ever understood the dream of Africa as well as I."

Speaking of himself all irony vanished from his voice to be replaced by a note of tremendous pride. Cloaked in this he stood up and stepped into the centre of the room, where the lamps on the table lit his pallid face from beneath and cast his shadow up behind him as though he had summoned a witness to testify to his stature.

Prior to this David had been, in all ways, an amiable soul. Indeed it is likely that if one had asked those who knew him the majority would have said there was no other side to his character, that this unreserved friendliness said all there was to say about David Rehn.

In which case those same people were forgetting his desire for truth. All those who are searching for something must learn to separate what is false from what is true and must therefore be just as familiar with downright lies as with reason. So now, when David spoke to the old man, his polite question masked a tremor of something that was at one and the same time curious, provocative and impertinent.

"Then perhaps," he said, "you can explain to me why in Europe pictures of Africa always seem so inaccessible. It seems to me that those pictures of Africa which find their way to us always show the dark fringes of a forest, from which sudden death strikes in the form of a wild animal or a poisoned dart. And it has crossed my mind that this might not be anything like the whole truth. One would expect a theory to be free of contradiction, exhaustive and as simple as possible. As far as I can see, this cannot be said of the 'forest-fringe' theory."

The smile left Joseph K.'s face and when he answered his voice was quiet and cold.

"The dream of which you speak was created by me," he said, "and it is dark because Africa is dark."

He gave one sharp tug on a cord, the pale curtains slid back and there on the other side of the window was the tropical night, black and impenetrable.

"Out there," said Joseph K., "lies Africa, out there the dark lies waiting to . . . tear every one of us to shreds. Out there is the river Congo, a mighty serpent, coiled up with its head in the sea and its body in a fever-ridden hell. And if it seems reasonable to dedicate this journey to integrity that is only because there are no clear-cut lines out there. Out there, there is nothing but utter oblivion. Ah, yes, in encountering this blackness, certain stripes are scored into our souls and out of these wounds, for some of us, wells an awareness of our true selves and of the fact that loneliness is, as it were, built in to life, that we live as we dream – which is to say, quite alone."

Even though he had, with this last sentence, regained control of his voice, the carriage was now filled with a hypersensitive silence, such as comes in the wake of any sudden exposé.

Without warning, David leaned forward and blew out the oil lamps. At first the carriage was plunged into pitch darkness. Then, out of the gloom, the moonlit landscape outside emerged, glittering whitely, as if the treetops were covered with an endless carpet of snow.

"The trouble with the light of learning," said David quietly, "is that we can end up believing both the world and ourselves to be already charted when in fact we have been blinded by the light source itself, with the result that our surroundings seem dark and unfathomable while our own noses are brilliantly illuminated. Anyone who travels through Africa in a brightly lit railway carriage is bound, on his return home, to tell everyone that Africa is a lowering forest fringe."

They sat for a while in silence. In the moonlight streaming in from outside the faces of the general and Joseph K. were pale and smooth, of the servant girl only her dress was visible, the light did not penetrate to her dark face. Then Joseph K. struck a match and lit the lamps on the table. In the glow his features seemed at first set and hard, then they relaxed.

"You," he said, as if noting with interest some delightful surprise, "are an . . . intelligent young man. And I am sure that you are also, to some extent . . . on the track of the truth. But what you say would not sound too . . . good to European ears, would it, it lacks – am I not right, General – any real . . . punch."

"I am not interested in punch," said David, with a new dryness in his voice. "As a mathematician, as a logician, I am only interested in the truth."

Joseph K. got slowly to his feet and walked over to the window, and for a moment he stood there looking into the black glass surface in which the carriage, the lamps and the general's medals showed up as duplicated, glittering, golden reflections. Then he drew the curtains and turned to face the table.

"The truth is an excellent thing," he said softly, "an excellent thing. I take some interest in it myself, as it happens. There is just one thing wrong with it and that is that it is so . . . bloody poorly paid! And I know what I am talking about since, as yet another contribution towards our pool of integrity, I will let you into a secret. I am here not so much in my capacity as a journalist but because I am a writer, and a famous one at that. I have had a long and full life in which to familiarize myself with the difference between reality and fantasy and for you, Professor," said he, addressing David, "I am prepared to lift the lid on what I have gleaned from experience – namely that for those of us who, like the Field Marshal here and myself, earn our living as travellers, there is no bloody way we could survive on the truth."

For a moment the general just sat there, saying nothing, then he leaned towards Joseph K.

"You consider yourself then," he said, "to be a man without honour."

The writer poured the last of the champagne into his glass and downed it with relish. Then he smiled at the general.

"Even at my great age," he said, "life never ceases to amaze me. To think that I should be lectured on pride by a man who won his gongs" – pointing at the decorated chest in front of him – "for beating a retreat."

Von Lettow's eye never left his antagonist's face. "I have always believed," he said, "that I could serve my country better by going on fighting on my knees than by dying on my feet."

"And I," replied Joseph K., "as a human being and a writer, prefer to stand with both feet firmly planted on the bottom rather than flounder about, out of my depth, with my arse in the air. As an old sailor I can tell you a thing or two about the sweetness of knowing one cannot sink any lower. I once wrote . . ." he said, throwing himself back in his chair in exasperation, ". . . I tell you, gentlemen, I once wrote a book about a trip I made over the very stretch of country through which we are now travelling. I put my heart and soul into that book, it was a valid expression of myself as a person and consequently it quite naturally contained both lies and truth. For the truth the public threatened to stew me with onions and sweet potatoes while, for the lies, they were prepared to fête me. Ever since then I have taken great care to emphasize that my books are works of fiction. That way I can always refute the truth by saying that it is all make-believe and, with the lies, claim that they have a solid foundation in reality. But, General, I am in fact standing upright on the bottom,

I would not sink so low as to call my lies 'memoirs' or 'rallying cries'."

Even when, as now, the general grabbed hold of the old man by the lapels, hauled him out of the chair and pulled him to his chest, his face remained expressionless and his voice soft. "What lies?" he asked.

Displaying not the slightest hint of fear Joseph K. supported himself on the table, to allow some breathing space in the iron grip from which he hung. "The actual basis of your . . . writings, Field Marshal, is formed not by the modest and meticulous . . . Teutonic accounts of how you, by virtue of your beliefs, have conquered countries, administered justice, gagged the lion, quenched the power of fire, evaded the sword point and emerged a war hero. No, most telling of all is your assertion that the niggers love us, that – proudly, happily and with a song in their hearts – they fought against us and their own kind and died like flies fighting our, and more especially Germany's, glorious World War, when the truth is that they walked into that war on the point of a German bayonet with their heads in a cloud of promises and religious hot air. In your history of the willing and eager black men and their voluntary colonial war you, General, have exposed yourself as the biggest liar of us all."

For a split second David was afraid that von Lettow was about to break the old man's neck, sensing as he did the blind rage beneath the soldier's outward semblance of self-control. But the general merely looked Joseph K. straight in the eye. Then he released the old man, allowing him to drop back into his chair.

"A military mask may be necessary," said von Lettow – and David detected a new note in his voice, the timbre of age-old weariness, "if one is to arrive at a deeper political truth."

"And your uniform, General?" Joseph K. persisted, gloating with triumph, "That imposing piece of . . . *Weihnachtsbaum* frippery. Here, among the subjects of the very nations that dealt

Germany the final blow, rubbing shoulders with people who will only tolerate a German uniform as long as it is behind bars, does that also serve as a mask of sorts? I believe you owe our young friend here, our . . . mathematical ewe lamb, some kind of explanation for this."

At first it seemed that von Lettow would never answer, as if he had withdrawn from the company in disgust and hidden himself in some inner foxhole. Then, slowly, as though reading aloud from an apologia which he had had ready prepared, he said: "A number of German banks have a stake in this railway. And the Belgians requested my presence here. I have been accorded diplomatic immunity and I wear my uniform because I was asked to do so. All of the formalities are thus observed."

Joseph K. stared straight ahead with something resembling ecstasy in his eyes. "How wonderfully cunning," he said. "To reassure the shareholders, obviously. The soothing presence of the old lion. And to Hell with the fact that it has no troops, no authority, no teeth, just so long as it can roar and remind everyone of the Maasai massacred at Mara, the Chinks butchered in China – you have also been to China, haven't you, General? – of the Somalis at Dar es Salaam, of all those bodies in reassuring colours. Gentlemen, I give you integrity. Boy, more champagne!"

A fresh bottle was brought in. Brought in as promptly and silently as one would expect, with only David noticing that the waiter who brought it was not the same one as before and that he wore a uniform which was far, far too small for him. And that he carried the bottle cork downwards.

The general opened the bottle and poured the wine and in the silence that then ensued David looked at the girl. His eyes met hers and he realized that she had been watching them all this time. And, too, he had the strange feeling that she, who could have understood nothing, had been taking in everything that had been said and done in the room and that everything he had said had actually been aimed at her – or at any rate said with her in mind. Then, for the first time in his life, it occurred to David that even when talking to other men or to a lecture hall or to himself or into thin air he had perhaps always, in some corner of his consciousness, had an unseen woman in mind.

The atmosphere in the railway carriage had grown hostile but even in that hostility there lay a strange sense of all being in the same boat, as though these three men had something else, something as yet undisclosed, in common – over and above this journey. It was Joseph K., the writer, who put this air of intimacy into words.

"We are now," he said, "in the process of complying with His Majesty's request, insofar as we have reached a new and enlightened position, thereby confirming what I myself said a lifetime ago, namely that this expedition into the heart of darkness may also be a journey into the light. Now, it has just been revealed that I am not some unknown journalist with a passion for the truth but a famous writer and an expert . . . editor. And von Lettow Voerbeck turns out to be, not an invincible Teuton, but a prisoner of war enjoying diplomatic immunity, a kind of military sweetener for the shareholders. And our young David has proved not to be a blank page with a few algebraic curlicues in the topmost corner but a young and questing warrior who has no fear of the Goliath of . . . falsehood when brought face to face with him."

"I," said the general as though, for a moment, he too were more agreeably disposed, "have a lady friend who maintains that one can learn the truth about a person by the mask he or she wears. By this she means," he went on to explain – and suddenly David could picture him, just before a battle, outlining his strategy clearly and concisely – "that by their choice of mask people betray the truth behind their tactics."

"Your friend," said Joseph K., "ought to write a book, for she speaks more truly than she knows. The mask actually represents the ultimate truth. Not because it reveals anything of what lies behind it, but because there is nothing behind it. This holds true for everything in life. It holds true for you and for me. And, of course, it holds true for literature. I," he said – and here, with a flash of the same intuition which could on occasion produce the solution to a mathematical problem, the thought crossed David's mind that the greatest truth about their host, a man who had told them that he earned his living as an illusionist, might be that he himself harboured no illusions – "I myself put it most accurately and succinctly when I wrote that the point of a story lies not in the story itself but outside of it, so to speak, in its form. Hence the greatest truth about this journey is the train itself and the three thousand kilometres of track. The greatest truth about you, General, is your medals and the greatest truth about our young David is his undisguised naïveté."

"And you, Joseph K., sir," David asked, "what is the greatest truth about you?"

"The greatest truth about me is . . . my face," replied the old man. "These days an artist must also sell himself on his personal appearance and it strikes me as a cruel trick of Fate, although a most apt reflection of my life, that now, after sixty-seven years of hard work and unimaginable difficulties and a deal of . . . artistic drinking, all to sculpt this face, this . . . intriguing, self-promoting physiognomy, a face which, in the theatre of life, projects all the way to the very back row, I have become" – and his voice dropped to a hiss – "too senile to remember my lines."

"I find it surprising," said David thoughtfully, "that the truth, if it lies on the surface, should only come to light when people offend one another, or fight a world war or build a three-thousand-kilometre-long railway. I mean: if it is indeed there, on the surface, it should be immediately apparent.

"And I also find it surprising that we – or at any rate you, gentlemen – appear to have been wearing several masks, one on top of the other, while Africa, which your servant girl, sir, seems to me to represent, says not one word and yet remains exactly what she has purported to be all along. I am beginning," said David, aware that he was becoming strangely moved and his voice growing hoarse, "to believe that this continent, unlike Europe, has nothing to hide."

At this, von Lettow got to his feet. "Gentlemen," he said, "I regret to say that I feel I have fallen into bad company. I have seen and experienced too much in my life to waste any more time with pacifists and men without honour. I shall take my leave of you. I see now that I ought never to have left the personnel carrier." And the general clicked his heels together and executed a slight bow, first to Joseph K. and then to David.

At that moment the girl in the corner moved for the first time. She straightened her shoulders, stretched her feet out in front of her and said: "That way is closed, General."

At the sound of her dark and faultless English the three men froze. As far as two of them were concerned, until now the carriage had contained no fourth person, the Negress had been indistinguishable from the fireplace or the curtains or the paintings or, perhaps more accurately, from the darkness outside. Now here she was, materializing in the room, and no spirit from any dark forest fringe could have come as more of a surprise.

"The doors," she said, "are locked. And the gangway to the next coach has been removed." And as David glanced over his shoulder she added pensively: "The attendants have left the train."

The general had been staring fixedly at the girl while she spoke. And he was looking at her still as he said, to no one in particular and seeming not to have heard one word of what she had said: "She speaks English."

Joseph K. shook his head slowly as if in denial of something, or as if there were something he did not understand.

Then the general turned the full force of his power to command on the girl, like the beam of a searchlight.

"Stand up," he told her. He did not raise his voice but it was now heavy with menace, "stand up when a white man is talking to you. Who are you?"

The girl now looked at the general alone. With an air of supreme self-confidence she settled herself more comfortably on her stool.

"I am Lueni of Uganda," she said.

David was glad to be sitting down just then, with a sudden dizzy spell causing the room slowly to spin as he relived his vision from the day before of the prone body while being bombarded by recollections of the horrific tales he had heard about that name during his month in the Congo.

"But surely Lueni is a man," said von Lettow.

"I," said the girl, "am Lueni."

The three men did not look at one another, nor did they need to. The girl on the stool in the corner exuded an air of authority which rendered any shred of doubt and all questions useless.

Then von Lettow moved into the attack, as soundlessly as a big cat. One long, lithe bound and he was almost upon the African – his hands raised, taut and white – and in that fraction of a second David caught a glimpse, beneath his age and his military honours, of this Prussian warhorse's astounding swiftness.

But the girl was swifter still. She did not so much as blink but something glinted in the light and a snub-nosed revolver appeared in her outstretched hands, pointing straight at the bridge of the general's nose.

"This too has only one eye," she said, "but it is very clear-sighted."

Von Lettow had never understood Africans. But he had no trouble identifying death and so, never taking his one eye off her, he stepped back and dropped down into his chair – a gesture embodying all of his personal fearlessness and his talent for postponing the final rout.

"We won't have to wait too long," said the girl. "Soon we will reach the summit and then start the descent. At that point the track crosses a bridge running high above a deep, narrow valley. You are all in search of the truth? Well, you will find it at that bridge, or at least the truth about the next life, because we have removed most of the bridge supports."

David tried fleetingly to picture the bridge ahead of them, the loosened bolts, the slowly spiralling plunge and the impact. Then he looked at the faces of his fellow passengers, only to find a wide range of emotions: shock, anger, determination and cynicism, but no fear. Whatever else they may be, he thought, they are certainly not afraid; and at that very moment he too became aware of a strange and unnatural sense of hope and a new warmth, as though the fire in the grate had flared up once again. Coolly and deliberately von Lettow filled the three glasses on the table, Joseph K. produced some pince-nez from his waistcoat pocket, polished them and put them on and the girl lowered the revolver and rested it in her lap.

"A toast to Fortune," said Joseph K., "Fortune which has not as yet failed us," and solemnly they raised their glasses. "*Fortuna*," said Joseph K., "*morituri te salutant*," and they regarded one another with a new gravity which in some inexplicable way also took in the African and her revolver. And all at once David understood where it came from, this feeling of kinship. "This," he thought, "is the intimacy of people about to die together. It is that insane, bourgeois gentility, so overweening that it also embraces the executioner and her victims, as it will continue to do till death them do part. What is more, so familiar with death are these three lunatics that now, when it proves to be the fifth, stowaway, member of our party, they actually consider themselves to be in excellent company," and it was with some difficulty that he stifled the urge to scream.

Joseph K. studied him through his pince-nez, then leaned towards him and said heartily: "I believe, my boy, that this is your chance to take yet another step across the shadowy line separating youth from real life. By which I mean that perhaps now you can see what I am getting at when I talk of standing on the bottom and knowing that one can sink no lower."

"Not sink, perhaps," snarled the general, "but fall two hundred feet, certainly."

"If my former housegirl is speaking of the valley to which I think she is referring," said Joseph K. pleasantly, "then it will be more like seven hundred feet."

"You are all quite mad," thought David to himself, while the scientific scholar in him felt duty-bound, nevertheless, to correct them. "That five hundred feet of a difference is neither here nor there, gentlemen," he said, "two hundred feet is far enough, all other things being equal, for the falling train to reach something approaching the maximum rate of descent."

There was a momentary hush in which the truncated span of David's young life appeared to him like the brief, cold stretch of track lying ahead of the train.

Then Joseph K. raised his arm, as if calling a large gathering to order. "Gentlemen, the events of the last few minutes caused me momentarily to lose my presence of mind. Now, however, I feel quite recovered and while I would remind you that the need for integrity is now more pressing than ever, since" – and he pulled a gold watch from his waistcoat pocket – "since, if it is indeed the valley of which I am thinking, we have scarcely more than three-quarters of an hour until the . . . moment of truth, I would ask you, young David – considering that we know nothing about you except that you have an honest face and an . . . easily aroused sense of right and wrong – to tell us who you are."

David stared at his fellow passengers in disbelief, but it was obvious that their composure was not feigned but genuine. He shook his head. "I am afraid," he said, "that I find it difficult to think clearly, knowing as I do what lies ahead of us. I believe we should use what time we have to come up with some means of escape – jumping off, for example," and he looked appealingly at the general.

But von Lettow turned his head away in disgust. "First of all," he said, "we would never survive jumping in this terrain and at such a speed. Secondly, Mr Korzeniowski's Negress would shoot us down like dogs before we could so much as open the window. And lastly, I would not subject myself to the humiliation of attempting to run away from a blackamoor."

"Listen to the experts," said Joseph K. amiably, "and let us use this time to truly . . . live on our knees. You, young David, may perhaps take courage from observing the general and myself."

David looked at the speaker and noted, to his great dismay, that the author had a manic, somewhat elated look about him; the look of a man who has spent his whole life being humiliated, but who has now thrown all caution to the winds, delved down into the depths of his soul and found a liberating insolence.

"The general," said Joseph K. ebulliently, "has lived his whole life on the brink of the descent into Hell and I, at my advanced age and in my state of health, have for many years greeted with surprise each new day on which I have awoken to find myself still alive. Think of the general and myself, my young friend, or of something else just as enduring. Mathematics for instance."

David gazed hopelessly into space. "In actual fact," he said, "at those times in my life when I have been truly afraid I *have* studied one especially beautiful mathematical theorem, and this has generally brought me some comfort. It has occurred to me that logic seems to contain the very essence of life and indeed that if one were trying to discover the divine plan behind the universe then it is more likely to be found in arithmetic than in the Bible."

He was aware that his fellow passengers were regarding him with interest and under the pressure of knowing that he had only a few minutes left to live he heard himself rambling on to no one in particular. "And yet I am here because I turned my back on mathematics," he said, "I gave it up because I had a dream. I have been thinking over what you said, Joseph K., sir, about how we live and dream alone and I think I believe that to be wrong. You see, this dream that I had was one I shared with an entire world. It was the dream of perfect simplicity. I have the feeling that there is, in a way, something wrong with telling you this now, but I will tell you anyway: we dreamed that the world was utterly coherent and simple. Our hoping this was the case had something to do with the fact that," – David struggled to find the right words – "that mathematics was beginning to resemble the Leaning Tower of Pisa. An enormous structure which is very gradually starting to list to one side, so that there is no telling what one should do. But one goes on hoping."

He stared straight ahead with sadness in his eyes. "It isn't just in mathematics, it's the sciences too. It is names such as Boole and Hilbert and Maxwell and Planck, names that mean nothing to you, but all of which have added a few bricks to the pile. And it keeps getting taller and listing further and further. Perhaps it is not only science but the whole world. Just think of the war. So perhaps the Tower of Pisa is not the best metaphor. It is all more like Venice, it is all slowly sinking. So we create a dream, a dream of making sense of this confusion, one coherent theory which might enable us to check the slide into the mud. Not that anyone dares to say it in so many words, but we all know what it is: a longing akin to that which raised the Tower of Babel, a longing to reach all the way to God."

David swayed back and forth in desperation. Before the eyes of his companions the openness of his features dissolved and they beheld a man who had adopted the listing action of the world in which he lived and who now seemed, in his own despair, about to imitate that selfsame slide.

"We thought," he went on, "that the neurologists and psychiatrists would prove that the human soul is also biological in form. The biologists and physicists would reduce this biological form to chemistry and physics and the mathematicians would break the chemistry and physics down into arithmetic. It would then be up to us to reduce this mathematical exercise to a logical equation.

"Human beings," said David, and for an instant his voice rang with all the unshakeable conviction of European science, "would be thoroughly accounted for by means of a handful of signs and the rules governing their various permutations."

At this point Joseph K. leaned across the table and for the first time that evening the old man seemed to have been drawn out of himself. "It is just as I have always known," he said. "It is what I predicted in my books. And it will come true. To a visionary writer it is quite obvious. There is something . . . predictable about the human race. If one unearths its background, its . . . brooding urges, if one charts its shadowy inner landscape, at the end of the day everything appears so very, very simple."

He got to his feet with a jolt, propelled out of his chair by some powerful surge of emotion, and proceeded to limp back and forth across the floor. "As a boy I used to look at maps, I was . . . obsessed with maps, the white areas most of all. They denote those places of which we know nothing, dark spots in the universe that exert a . . . savage attraction. That is why I went to sea. I had to visit those places. So one travels and travels, through Asia, through South America, up the river Congo, and it is . . . it is . . . a journey into one's self, the drawing up of a vast map. One becomes a . . . psychological geodesist. And then a landscape looms up which is so terrifying and dark that it takes . . . a real man to set foot in it, and one learns something, something or other. And there comes a day when one has seen it all, when one comes up against . . . a wall in the universe, one can go no further, there is nothing new under the sun, no more blank spots on the map. And yet there is still something that one does not understand. Inside human beings there are still some blank spots and one . . ." At this point he fell silent, staring vacantly through his pince-nez with brimming eyes. "This is where," he said when he had once more gained control of his voice, "science has to step in. Once the artists and explorers among us have shown the public all that there is to be seen it is up to science to prove that those last blank spots, guilt and religion and morality and . . . love, are a . . . what was it you called it?"

"A logical equation," said David.

"Just so, a logical equation proving that we are all, you and I, General, and this young man here, in fact, one."

"I feel no kinship with you, chemically or in any other way," said the general in a voice cold as ice and for a moment the girl was forgotten, this seeming to be a more crucial matter than the question of life and death. "This evening has shown me that you are an unscrupulous civilian and a coward, driven by the impertinence of an inferior race!"

For a moment Joseph K. just stood there blinking disconcertedly in the face of this first verbal broadside from the self-possessed military man. Then his moustaches turned upwards in an infinitely compliant smile. "Ah," he said, "you arouse my curiosity. By what noble and complex motives is our son of the Fatherland driven, then?"

"Till the day I die," the general had no hesitation in replying, "in all that I do I shall serve the spirit of Teutonic brotherhood as expressed by our great poet, Goethe, when he says:

nimmer sich beugen, kräftig sich zeigen
rufet die Arme der Götter herbei

"Well, as far as the day you die is concerned," said Joseph K. thoughtfully, "that would appear to be taken care of. As regards Goethe, I must say that once again you surprise me by turning out to be . . . a man of letters. But when it comes to the bond between you and me, General, there is no way round it." Propping himself up against the table he brought his face down to the soldier's. "A few years from now our young friend will have united us in a . . . logical equation. A few years from now some young orderly will click his heels together and pass a bundle of papers bearing a handful of signs and the rules for combining them across the counter in some dingy Prussian army camp and say: 'Here – down to the last detail – you have General Paul von Lettow Voerbeck!'"

"I seem to remember you saying earlier," the general said blandly, "that you had invested your entire being in a book about a journey through Africa. That being the case, then day after day a bundle of papers bearing a handful of signs and the rules for combining them must also be being passed across British bookshop counters, with the words: 'Here – down to the last detail – you have that great writer Joseph K.'"

For the first time on this journey the old man appeared to be lost for words and in the pause that then ensued, David cleared his throat.

"I am afraid," he said, "that is most unlikely," and he felt all eyes upon him. He surveyed the company, then his eyes met the girl's and stayed there.

"In Vienna," he continued hesitantly, "I met . . . someone with a very clear view of things. He is working on a particular theorem, a proposition. When I saw this proposition it seemed to me to shatter my dream. Of course he is not the only one. There have, as I have said, been various indications of what was afoot. But he showed me Venice, he showed me that it is the foundations that are unsound. He has proved – no, he intends to prove that when one is dealing with complex systems, and we humans *are* complex" – and here he felt himself reddening under the girl's gaze – "within any complex system there are certain elements which cannot be deduced from its basic characteristics. This may mean that even if we had known every particular of the circumstances surrounding this journey, we would still have been unable to guard against the unpredictable.

"This proposition also suggests," he continued, "that, even when fully aware of our own circumstances, we cannot be certain of avoiding contradictions at a later date. And," he said, and had to lower his gaze, "life is, as we know, full of contradictory emotions."

He lifted his head again. "At the end of the day," he said, "it will be established that it will never be possible, as we had thought, to determine in advance what shape a logical theorem may take. At any rate not in mathematics and possibly in no other area of life. We cannot," – and here he found himself searching for words – "do without . . . ingenuity and . . . emotion in mathematics."

He fell silent for a moment, then: "Until tonight," he said, "I had always thought it dreadful that there was nothing in this life, nothing at all, that was not, right from its inception, subject to uncertainty. Now, however, I have the idea . . . I have the idea that perhaps it doesn't really matter anyway, that one could perhaps do some work. And now it is too late . . ."

Using both hands, and with some difficulty, Joseph K. filled their glasses, as if preparing to toast whatever it was that was too late.

"And yet," said David slowly, "it is odd that tonight it should be we, the Europeans, who have taken the wrong turning. Each of us has left his native land. You, Joseph K., have left your writing behind, the general his soldiers and I mathematics. We seem to be on the wrong track. You, Miss, on the other hand, appear to be" – David groped after a suitable expression – "in your proper place."

"You fool," the girl said, almost kindly, "I am four thousand kilometres from my home."

"But perhaps only for the time being," suggested David.

"I was educated in England," said the girl. "In my tribe we have a saying: 'He who wishes to dream like *otoyo*, the hyena, must learn to eat corpses.'" David looked at her blankly. She bent forward. "The European languages," she said, "are good for large numbers. In English, for example, the seven thousand slaves who built this railway are easily counted."

"Slavery," said von Lettow, "has been abolished."

The girl regarded him thoughtfully. "We also say that *omuga*, the rhinoceros, runs faster than it thinks, with the result that on the savannah one encounters little gusts of wind – those being the little thoughts from which the big beast has fled. In order to build this railway Belgian troops rounded up four thousand Africans from the Gold Coast and Angola. Some were drawn by the promise of what was a very low wage but the majority came because it is hard to say no to a rifle barrel. They worked under armed surveillance, under the lash, and with steel rings around their necks so they would be easily recognizable should they run away. But we must finish our sum: the final three thousand were made up mainly of European convicts, most of them from Portugal. Of these seven thousand workers, five thousand died of ill-treatment, blackwater fever, sleeping sickness and overwork. In my tribe we say that the railroads across Africa run not over railway track but over African bones. What would you call slavery, if not that, General?"

Just then a shudder ran through the train and with a squeal of brakes the locomotive went into a sharp turn. The girl straightened up. "It is time," she said, getting to her feet, and without so much as a glance at them she crossed the carriage floor and went out of the door.

Feeling slightly sick, David went limp. The girl had been the power source which had held them all in a quivering, watchful state of suspense. As soon as she was gone they collapsed.

Then the focus within the room shifted as Joseph K. produced a flat, dully gleaming pistol. "Gentlemen," he said, "five minutes from now the train will brake as it goes into the third, very tight turn. That is where we get off."

David had noted how the general's face when he saw the weapon stiffened into a suspicious mask, a sign that on this night his credibility had been stretched to its limits and that he would now meet everything that came his way with the most profound distrust.

"General," said Joseph K., "I have yet another mask: that of businessman. One of the goods wagons trundling on ahead of us contains a number of boxes stamped with my name. These contain a consignment of excellent Webley rifles which I sold to that young lady. From my sailing days I have retained a taste for certain . . . enterprises more profitable than writing."

"So you are on the side of the Negroes?" said the general.

"I am on my own side, General," said Joseph K., "and in this century, that, I believe, is the only possible side to be on."

"Words fail me," said the general.

"That I can well believe," replied Joseph K. "It's not as though the spirit of Teutonic brotherhood has any long story to relate. But I," he said, taking out his pocket watch and considering it for a moment, "I have one last tale to tell, before we jump. And it is only fitting, don't you think, that the writer should have the last word."

Only now, so near the end, was David coming to understand the old man. He realized that throughout his life Joseph K. must have kept himself on a very tight leash. And yet all that time a fuse must have been burning away inside him. And now, just as he was about to meet his end, this hissing ember had reached the secret powder-magazine of his soul. What they had been witnessing tonight was the great writer's swan song which, in his case, was bound to consist of one long series of explosions.

"In Dar es Salaam," said Joseph K., "on Biashara Street, there is a little shop. It is run by an Indian who was once tremendously fat but who had, over the years, cast off the burdens of this life and by the time of this story had already grown lean. This shop is possibly the only place in the African continent where genuine articles can be bought: the heavy silk *kente* cloth of the Ashanti tribe, interwoven with symbols whose significance was forgotten two hundred years ago; bronze statuettes from the vanished kingdoms of Central Africa; gold ornaments from Zanzibar.

"And on the wall of this shop hangs the rarest piece of all: a green dancing mask from the Maconde tribe, a crude, upward-slanting face with an impassivity that makes it seem continually to be shifting expression.

"One day, a couple of years before war broke out, an army officer visited the shop. A colleague of yours, General. As soon as he saw the mask he felt the need to buy it. When told that during a dance it took possession of its wearer and foretold the future he insisted upon having it, as only a German officer in pre-war Dar es Salaam could insist. The Indian explained to him that the masks of the Maconde people can neither be bought nor sold.

"At that, the officer donned the mask, danced a few steps in his riding boots and bellowed from behind the carved wood: 'And if I buy you, where will that lead'? And a voice replied: 'To Hell.'

"At this the officer flew into a Teutonic rage and, service revolver in hand, forced the Indian to sell him the mask, that he might prove it to be harmless. Because, wherever it has come across it, the European – and perhaps most especially the German – race has always encountered the primitive African idea of a mask and its bearer being one, with their guns cocked.

"Soon after this the officer left on a tour of duty, first to Arusha and then on to Bismarcksburg and Lake Tanganyika, and wherever he went he would put on the mask and dance for the white officers, who were thoroughly entertained, and the black soldiers and native inhabitants, who were not at all amused, but the mask never spoke again and its silence bored into the officer's flesh like *loa-loa*, the worm that causes river blindness. Eventually he took to drink and one day in Ngorongoro he danced himself into a seizure from which he did not emerge until his death three months later. His belongings were either given away or put on sale in the garrison at Bagamoyo – I bought a razor with a tortoiseshell handle myself – and no objections were made when the Indian came for the mask.

"The funeral took place the next day. It was during the monsoon, the funeral procession was coming down Biashara Street and, just as the blue urn drew level with the shop window, the carriage bearing the officer's ashes drove into a mudhole. The mask and the Indian looked at the urn and then the mask said: 'To Hell.'"

At that moment the locomotive emitted a long-drawn-out whistle and with a bow their host invited them to step into the cloakroom. Then he kicked the carriage door open and the mountain air came rushing to meet them, cold and clear. The sky was milky with stars and ahead of them ran the train, taking the bend like a long, glittering worm.

"Jump, gentlemen," said Joseph K. and brandished his weapon persuasively. "Jump and let us see whether Africa will cremate us or glorify us."

Soon afterwards the same four people were standing facing one another just as they had once stood on the railway platform. On the track a group of Africans waited in silence. Off in the distance the train – no more than a string of twinkling pinpoints and a faint rumble – headed, on collision course, into the heart of darkness.

The general made an attempt to brush the dust from his uniform with a tuft of grass.

"I assume you will allow me a minute or two, that I can be sure to die looking spruce," he said.

Joseph K. looked at him benignly. "You are not going to die, General," he said. "You are a free man, free to set out on the return journey." He pointed back along the track. "I am sure that once you have walked the two hundred kilometres back to His Majesty you will have discovered new meaning in the phrase 'to live on one's knees'."

The writer stuck his gun into his jacket pocket, turned on his heel and started walking towards the waiting Africans. He was limping and in a flash David saw that this man must indeed greet every prolongation of his life with surprise.

A moment later the general faced about and, with a spring in his step, began to walk back along the track in the direction from which they had come.

For the first time David and the girl were alone. They eyed one another warily for a while. Then the girl said: "In my own language my name means 'war'."

David nodded. "Europeans," he said, unaware that he spoke as though this were a class in which he no longer formed a subset, "Europeans are experts when it comes to waging war."

"In my tribe," said the girl, "we say: 'The croaking of the little frogs will not stop the cattle from quenching their thirst.'" Then she shook David briefly by the hand, turned and walked over to the men who stood waiting for her.

David did not watch her go. Instead he sat down and buried his head in his hands. Above him Libra crossed the zenith of the night sky and dropped towards the horizon. European justice descending over tropical Africa.

HOMAGE TO BOURNONVILLE

> The height of artistry lies in concealing mechanical action and effort behind harmonious serenity.
>
> AUGUST ANTOINE BOURNONVILLE
> in *My Life in the Theatre*

It was March 19th 1929; the beginning of the twenty-sixth night of Ramadan, the night on which Allah sent the Koran from Heaven to Earth; and in Lisbon harbour, just down from the Alfama district, two young men had, in all respects, reached the end of the road.

They were sitting on the deck of a small sailing boat, of a kind known south of the Horn of Africa as a *meli*, a craft which has no business in Lisbon, her sails being designed for another sort of wind and her hull for another type of swell, in addition to which she leaked slightly and sagged at her moorings as though drunk on the salt water she had taken in, or as though sinking to the bottom in despair over the two who sailed her.

They were lit by a small charcoal fire which glowed on a metal sheet set between them. They had gone without food for a long time and one of them, sitting straight-backed and cross-legged, was by now so emaciated that his naked torso seemed to consist solely of the levers of its bones and the fine cords of muscle that allow these to move. He wore a turban of white wool and in his face African and Oriental features and a number of individually mordant and volatile qualities blended into a harmonious whole. His name was Rumi and he was a monk of the Islamic Mawlawiyah order.

His travelling companion had clearly at one time been strong, but starvation had also taken its toll of him, so that even when, as now, he reclined at his ease, he frequently had to shift position to take the weight off his own protruding bones. His name was Jakob Natten and he had once been a dancer at the Royal Theatre in Copenhagen.

There was something natural about the tranquillity of the two men; an observer might easily have overlooked the dilapidated barque, imagining that here were two mariners enjoying some peace and quiet, with time on their hands and obvious reasons for being where they were. While the truth of the matter was, neither of the two was capable of setting sail or plotting a course, both knew that on this night they were living on borrowed time, and so amazed were they by the fact of their own existence that they had no idea – not even the Mohammedan – whether they had wound up in Lisbon because it was in their own and the world's best interest, or whether somewhere in the universe an angel happened to have mislaid their papers.

They had met one another six months previously in Sardinia, in Oloroso. When the fascist Italian *carabinieri* descended upon that town they could have taken to the *maquis* with the resistance but instead they chose to sail on. It was at this point that they had been struck by the thought that they might be displaced not in space but in time. That they perhaps belonged in a century other than that into which they had been born. Together, since then, they had travelled so far out on to the fringes of society that they had now reached the point where life leaves off and something else begins. But even here it was clear to see that they had once been at the centre of things; over their undernourishment both wore the same flaking dignity; no one could have been in any doubt that the glow of the embers played upon two down-and-out child prodigies.

Accounts of Rumi and his childhood and youth are still subject to exaggeration even though, then as now, the truth more than suffices. He was raised in Konya in Turkey, capital of the Mawlawiyah order. At the age of five he knew the Koran by heart. He was taken to Mecca and there, in the square in front of the Kaaba, for five days and five nights, he recited the Holy Book to the faithful twice running, with nothing but a very short break for something to drink; and by the age of twenty he had attained such a degree of contact with Allah in the holy whirling dance that he was expecting to be raised up to Paradise any day. Two years later Atatürk banned the order and closed the monastery, and Rumi was cast into a state of insecurity the like of which he had heard of but had never really imagined possible. By then he had for some time been something of a celebrity and, like other homeless religious leaders of the day, he would undoubtedly have found a welcome in some European capital, there to be given a foretaste of that Paradise of which Allah promises in the Koran (in the seventy-sixth surah) that we shall all sit on soft cushions in the shade of the trees. But this Rumi would not have. The Mawlawiyah call themselves "dervishes", a Persian word meaning "poor", and they have dedicated their lives to seeking Allah through faith, poverty, dancing and music, and not in Paris. This unwavering standpoint had first led Rumi to take to the road and later it had caused him to sin ever so slightly against the Koran when, in order to stay alive, somewhere near Port Said he stole a boat. It had then swept him across the Mediterranean to Sardinia, where he had met Jakob, and from there it had carried him as far as Lisbon.

Rumi knew nothing about Jakob Natten other than that he had once been a ballet dancer and that he was possessed of an obstinacy which now looked likely to be the death of him. Rumi had once asked his travelling companion what had prompted him to leave his dancing and his native land and all Jakob had said in reply was that circumstances had taken such a turn that had he gone on dancing in Denmark then it would have been in prison.

They both knew that this evening a hunt was on for them. Somewhere, a detachment of gendarmes was methodically combing the docks and now and again the baying of the dogs carried across the water to the two on the deck. One of the harbour police's low, dark launches moved slowly – drifting almost – downriver, scanning the vessels riding at anchor.

Neither of the two now questioned what they were wanted for. The day before, in a bar, a man in uniform had asked to see their passports and Jakob had butted him in the face, not for any political reason – so hazy were Jakob's ideas on politics that they could never have been the cause of his hurting anyone – but out of the panic-stricken paranoia that builds up inside those who are sinking to the bottom. They had managed to shake off their pursuers somewhere in Lisbon's maze of narrow streets and squares, but only by the skin of their teeth, and both of them had sensed the approach of the end, because behind this escape bid lay the memory of all the other times they had fled from those places where they had stolen things, or from the harbour police or customs officers, and although neither one of them (nor yet both of them together) had any extensive knowledge of society, nonetheless they were beginning to understand that for anyone without a passport or papers or an occupation, anyone who has not been married or at least engaged or run off to join the Foreign Legion, simply staying alive, staying afloat and at liberty for any length of time is an impossible task.

So now they were waiting for the finish, and perhaps it denotes some act of mercy on the part of Nature that, when exhaustion is so great that one needs must stop and turn to face one's pursuers, one can do so with the sort of composure that comes from knowing that one has no choice. It was this composure which moved these two men to make themselves comfortable on the brink of the abyss.

Now, when they had ceased to expect anything of the world, their surroundings granted them everything. The sun had gone down; it was that hour when the importance of friendship and love, punishment and reward, thirst and justice fades and disappears, as Allah reveals that he is blue. The Tagus was a mirror of congealed silver, against the purple hillsides the houses of the city showed as delicate boxes of white marble, and the last light of the setting sun was a sliver of flame, fired gold against the blue-black clouds in the west.

Occasionally the two men drank from a kettle set on the coals, containing milk spiced with cinnamon – the seething liquid sending a mildly delirious exhilaration coursing through their veins. Though no words passed between them their thoughts turned on to the same path and fell into step. They reflected on the art of survival, on the squares where they had thieved and the houses at which they had begged and on the fact that they, who had once danced for Allah and the patrons of the Royal Theatre, now danced for passers-by. Only at that point did their thoughts elect each to go their own way and only then did speech become necessary.

"Rumi," said Jakob, "have you given any thought to the fact that until not long before we met I believed that I was going to dance my way into everlasting, or at any rate very long-lasting, fame? And you were under the impression that you were going to dance your way into Paradise. In a way we had the idea that we were moving, in time with the music, towards eternal life. And now it turns out that the place for which we were headed was a Lisbon jail." "That will be no more than a transition." "It could end up lasting a lifetime," said Jakob and in a flash of despondency saw the face of the Portugese dictator pass before his eyes. "Even then it will be but a transition," said Rumi. "And there is no guarantee that it will last that long." "Do you never think, Rumi, that you might have ended up somewhere other than where you now find yourself?" asked Jakob. "The Koran commands us to consider each day how we shall spend eternity," the Mohammedan replied. "But what about where we will be tomorrow?" Jakob persisted. "I laugh at tomorrow," said Rumi. "But you never laugh," objected Jakob. "I laugh to myself. Since coming to Europe I only laugh to myself," answered the Mohammedan. "You Europeans could put up a gateway at Gibraltar and on it could be inscribed: 'Only those who are absolutely serious may enter here'. Because the countries of Europe are the most serious places I have ever seen." "The Arabic songs you sing are like one long lament," said Jakob. "We Muslims," said Rumi, "yearn for Paradise, realize that we cannot attain it and weep and wail. And then we laugh. You Europeans yearn like us and weep like us. But then you whine, hoping that perhaps even so you can move your God to put an end to all earthly suffering. I have no desire to be anywhere but where I find myself, I am not about to plague Allah with my whining." "I don't ask anyone for help," said Jakob earnestly. "But shortly before I met you someone asked me something and that question has been ringing in my ears ever since. It is the question as to whether we should stay or run away." "That is for Allah to decide," said the Mohammedan serenely. "That may be," said Jakob, "but I have the feeling that he wouldn't mind hearing, in passing as it were, my thoughts on the matter. Would you care to hear," he continued, "how the question of staying or fleeing came into my life?" And without waiting for a reply he straightened up and drew closer to the embers. On the other side of the fire, he knew, sat a curiosity as patient and boundless as his own, and as he settled himself more comfortably he unwittingly mirrored the Mohammedan's own posture, with the result that he who spoke and he who listened became one.

"In this story I too have a part to play. But the central character was a friend of mine. The one to whom these things befell was Andreas.

"In order to understand what I am about to tell you, Rumi, you have to know that in my country the rich have stopped propping themselves up against the five pillars of duty upon which you say that Islam rests. They have discovered that they can get by on a day-to-day basis without faith and prayer and fasting and pilgrimage and charity."

"They will burn in Hell," said the Mohammedan.

"Not necessarily," said Jakob. "Because they have instead raised a temple of sorts to these five pillars. And the temple in which the first four are worshipped is a grand theatre in Copenhagen."

"What about the fifth, charity?" asked Rumi.

"Charity," said Jakob, "is dispensed from another theatre. It is known as the State. But that is another story."

"That one you can tell me in prison," said the Mohammedan.

"Which would in a way be the proper place in which to tell it," replied Jakob. "But the theatre tale is so confined that it had best be told out in the open.

"The theatre in question is the Royal Theatre. On the outside it has the columns and staircases of a temple, and the form and gravity of a castle; inside it possesses all the grandeur of a palace and the intimate alcoves and corridors and faded plush carpeting of a bordello. I tell you, so unfathomable a place is it that I know that whatever I have picked up about it amounts to no more than snatches. It resembles some vast machine and anyone else who, like me, has passed through it would have a different tale to tell from me. If they told it, that is. But the strange thing is that they do not. Those who describe the machine are still part of it, are themselves cogs, and the tale a cog in motion tells *has* to be a muddled tale.

"One of the things I never understood was the audience. But this much I did grasp: that for our spectators – who were few in number, so few that I have wondered whether the public for which we danced did not in fact consist of the same thousand or so people, filling the theatre day in, day out – to them that place was a temple. They made a sort of pilgrimage to it. They came to see people on the stage who *have faith*, perhaps because they themselves did not trust anyone, not even God. And they came to hear how it sounds when someone *prays* to something or other, perhaps because they themselves did not know of anyone or anything they believed would listen to them. And they came to see *fasting*, and I am convinced that this had something to do with the fact that in their daily lives they were so busy accumulating things that they *had* to come and see people who willingly practised self-denial in order to catch a glimpse of God.

"Obviously there must have been other reasons, too, for their turning up. But right now, this evening, I cannot think what.

"Andreas and I joined the theatre ballet school as small children. What brings parents to enrol their children in such a school? The belief that children can act as some sort of straw through which the adults may drink in real life. And don't ask me for any better answer to that question because just the thought of these parents incenses me and this is not meant to be a bitter tale, or at any rate not solely a bitter tale.

"There was no inscription over the school door. But I see now that there might have been one that read: 'Only those who have hung their independence in the cloakroom admitted here.' Because as soon as one stepped through that door every and any form of free will became an impediment, a kind of lead in one's shoes, because at this school one entered into a freedom so great that it ruled out everything else: freedom from having to think about one's own life.

"We were taught to jump by a teacher whose experience and love of the dance rested in a short switch with which he hit us across the legs if we didn't jump high enough. After a while we began to believe that the world was ordered in such a way that somewhere in the universe there sat a God with a switch."

"That God was not Allah," said the Mohammedan.

"No," said Jakob. "And I'm not at all certain that there was any God. I'm not blaming anyone. I am merely trying to come up with a metaphor for it. And you're right, the God metaphor is no good. More than for any other reason we worked because we ourselves wanted to. In Denmark everyone agrees that the greatest mystery is that of *diversity*. In our society the incomprehensible individuals are those who are out of step, who keep tripping over their own feet or who have raced on ahead because they feel something burning at their back, or who cannot catch up with the rest of us because they happen to have a wooden leg or to weigh three hundred pounds. Trying to understand these people has become an art. With me, Rumi, it's different. Or at least it has become different. For me the great secret is why so many stay in line; my mystery is the *mystery of discipline*.

"I'm no longer sure how things stand regarding *suffering* in the world. Having seen that one can be in need of nigh on everything and still be as happy as a sandboy, I tend to think twice before classing people as suffering. But this much I will say, that most people had a hard time of it at the theatre. And it may not even have been the one or two from each class who were thrown out each year because they weren't good enough who were the most unhappy.

"They were always telling us that the ballet school had flourished like a plant. It had been a seed, and a tender but promising shoot and then, last century, it had been taken over by a great gardener and ballet master, a born general who danced a military polka by his father's deathbed and who swore that he would construct his theatre like a barracks and train his dancers like soldiers. During his time the school and the dancing produced a large rose that has been blooming ever since, and the reason it has succeeded in lasting so long is that it is made of stucco. In those days, for a while at least, the dancing must have been soft, and it has then been moulded to imitate life, after which it has hardened, like the plants adorning the theatre itself, into a stiff, white and everlasting instruction to posterity as to how to envisage the living.

"Maybe that's why we did as we were told, maybe the theatre explained itself, as it were. Maybe we put up with the pain because everything around us vouched for the fact that, now and for evermore, there would never be any real life but this.

"For a long while my friend Andreas was a vital component in this machine.

"If he were sitting across from you this evening you would be thinking to yourself that he, like me, was ready for the knacker's yard; like me he would remind you of something that was to be carted off this very night by the bin men. But until not that long ago his body constituted the perfect instrument for a God who bows his violin with a switch. And I use the word 'body' deliberately. I know there are those who believe there is no way we can dissociate the soul from the body but that is because they have not seen what Andreas and I saw. He and I, we know now that it is possible to dance without your soul and with your head under your arm and still persuade the world at large that dead things live.

"Our hours are numbered, Rumi, and they are too few for modesty on others' behalf. When Andreas danced, the audience out there in the darkness saw their dreams come true. I don't know how such things come about. Perhaps it was his technique. His pirouettes, his cool-headed preparation, his centring and his sharp and yet perfectly poised turns. Or his slightly premature take-off in the jumps, the culmination of his leap just before the first beat and the way he hung there until, when everyone expected him to land, to come back down to earth and the rest of us, he would stretch out and continue to soar. And at that moment those of us in the wings and the two thousand people in the auditorium held our breath and could not have said whether it was the angel of life or of death that had blown on the back of the neck of every one of us.

"That is how Andreas danced, so effortless in his balancing feats that he might simply have been taking a stroll. And yet that was not the key factor; his technique is no more than incidental to this story. The important thing here, and for everyone else who will remember and understand Andreas, was his way of becoming one with the dances he performed, how he could mingle with the rest of us, smiling and hardworking and of his time, and yet like something forgotten and left behind in the theatre a century earlier. How he, more than any other dancer before him, was filled with the stucco of which the ballet is formed.

"The master's ballets deal with many things. With how right and proper it is that there should be a difference between rich and poor, and with how wonderful it is to be out in the countryside, but above all they are about love, about love being all around us and being overwhelmingly beautiful or overwhelmingly sad, but always something to do with over, with above, and never anything to do with below and most definitely never, ever anything below the waist.

"These dances quite naturally lent a distinct tone to our collective madness, and naturally we all routinely went around, even on the way home from the theatre, with our toes turned out and a swagger in our step and traces of greasepaint on our faces to show people that love clung to us, that in each of us there resided something of a prince, a princess, a peasant girl or a devil, that in us, at any rate, the precious metals were to be found.

"But with Andreas it was different, with him it was not powder and paint. He did not play a prince, he *was* a prince. Offstage, of course, I mainly saw him practising, always with the wild intensity that stems from knowing one is doing the only right thing in this life; since the suspicion harboured by some of our number, that the theatre was actually a spur track that ran off at a tangent, never occurred to Andreas. He was convinced that every glissade brought him closer to the essence of life. But when he was not practising I think that his life revolved around women, indeed I am certain that it revolved around women. Not around any one woman in particular though – more like the opposite: it revolved around women as an ideal. Above all else, I recall him as being a proper gentleman; when I call my image of him to mind I see him holding doors for the ballerinas, and carrying their bags and helping them with technical problems, but first and foremost I see him dancing with them, not as a dancer playing the part of a romantic hero, but as the romantic hero himself; like some balletically brilliant and thoroughly compelling relic of the last century.

"Who could ever understand it, who has not seen it with their own eyes? Suffice to say that when he suffered agonies on stage his pain reached out into the auditorium, so that people wept. And when he strode round a woodland lake of painted cardboard I would have sworn I heard nightingales sing. And there have been times, when he has raised his dagger to commit an unlikely histrionic suicide, that a female member of the audience has rushed on to the stage and stayed his arm, and everyone in that theatre, even I, who knew the ins and outs of the cardboard knife and all the other illusions, even I believed – some evenings at any rate – that I was about to see someone die. Let me put it this way: Andreas' romanticism was such that it was perfect, apart from the fact that it was a hundred years out of date. At the time I thought: he's never going to have any sort of ordinary life, he'll never have a woman or a family or an old age, he is only capable of coming alive on the stage and so there he will have to live for ever. In fact it was not inconceivable that he, who broke the law of gravity every evening, might go on dancing for ever. And, thought I, if he cannot, then he will just have to die onstage, at the height of his career.

"I got it all wrong, Rumi, which is just as it should be. When one sleeps and dreams that something here on Earth is going to last for ever I think one ought to be woken and be told about it.

"I was there when he laid eyes on the girl for the first time and so I know what took place, as far as one can understand something one witnesses but is not actually a part of.

"There had been a get-together somewhere in Copenhagen, in a flat high above the city. The party was over by this time; I seem to remember there were people slumped in chairs and on sofas, sound asleep. Only two were awake, Andreas and I. I don't know why he was still there, he was usually one of the first to leave, but that night – or it might have been early morning – he was still around. Perhaps he cherished some hope, perhaps he had been seized by a longing for something or other and now felt that if only he waited the world would draw him to its bosom and free him of some of the stucco inside him.

"I am not one of those who think there's much to be gained by waiting and hoping so I woke the violinist. He was a small boy with a club foot and coarse hands, a country bumpkin who had played at dances in village halls until someone discovered that with his violin he drew the music through the air like a flawless silver thread. Andreas and I were very young but he must have been even younger, so in a way he too, Rumi, was a child prodigy. But, still and all, a runty shepherd boy, a cowherd – that there was no denying – and yet we took him everywhere with us. When I walk, behind my own steps I can still hear the lopsided, lumbering thud of his shoe. We didn't have much time for ugly people at the theatre, the last thing we wanted to be reminded of was wretchedness. As far as we were concerned cripples, and especially cripples from the provinces, were an affront to the grand and sacred delicacy of the theatre. Nevertheless, we took the boy with us wherever we went and this we did because of his music. For from the first time you heard him play you knew that half of this boy's soul had been left with the gods of music while the other rested with the composers of today, whence it whispered its burning inspiration to the gimp. Added to which, he was happy. How do I know he was happy? I cannot say. I can't recall ever speaking to him. I don't even remember ever having seen him smile. And yet I know that he was happy. He – a cripple, a person who seemed to us born not even to tragedy but to the most abject misery – he glowed, when he played and when he dragged his foot after us, with an unnatural zest for life. And I have an idea that we took him around with us much as one walks around with an unanswered question that will not leave one alone.

"So I woke him. We had given him wine, I remember; it was the first time he'd ever had anything to drink and the alcohol had had an extremely stimulating and, later, a brutally stupefying effect on him. But now he played anyway – a song; a disjointed, stuttering, gleeful, plaintive and yet nonchalant refrain. I heard it for the first time that night, I now know it by heart. It was written by a man called Stravinsky and then, as now, the music acted as a provocation. I have since learned that it tells of a young man who plays the violin, and who then sells his violin to the Devil, but even at that time I had the feeling I was listening to something drawn from the abyss.

"Then the girl danced. I don't know where she appeared from, I hadn't noticed her earlier, but suddenly there she was on the vast, bare floor. She danced barefoot and she lifted the gimp and me out of our alcoholic haze and into a wild and quiet rapture. And Andreas she lifted into a mad infatuation.

"Eventually she stopped, then disappeared, and after that I went home. When I left the room Andreas was sitting stock-still in a chair, as if poleaxed, gazing at the spot where the soles of her feet had kissed the floor. I said not a word to him, partly because I was loath to spoil the moment and partly because, as I'm sure you will agree, one should never speak to anyone into whose brain the Lord has, as it were, injected an extra dose of oxygen.

"Something like six months must have passed before we saw her again and though we never spoke of her it was not because we had forgotten her but because we knew of course that somehow she was waiting just around the corner. And one morning there she was in class, standing at the barre working along with everyone else as if that were her rightful place. I have no idea how she got in, normally there would have been no question of the theatre taking on an unknown nineteen-year-old, but even a mausoleum finds it hard to say no to a thing of wonder. And it may be that in the first instance they had rejected her, who am I to say, but she was the type who, even if it were a strong-room door that was being slammed in her face, she would stop it with her foot and slip through the gap as if they had been begging her to enter.

"So now I had the chance to see her dance, not only her own indefinable movements but the eternal, meticulously laid down steps of classical ballet. I have been in the same room as her and on the same stage more times than I can count and I have never so much as come close to understanding how she could possibly have learned so fast and danced so beautifully. I tried guessing her past from her movements and the nearest I can come to describing what I observed then is to say that she had definitely, quite definitely, spent a lot of time out playing with the boys.

"In fact I was well aware that it was not so much her that I understood when I watched her dance, as God. To be quite honest I don't know what to think about the existence of God – I make no bones about that, even to you, Rumi – but if he does exist and did create the Earth then, having seen that girl, I can see why he created the fish and the birds and the wild animals first. Because, I said to myself, obviously he had to practise, obviously he had to train himself up to the point where he was capable of combining the suppleness of the eel, the streamlined precision of the sparrowhawk and the panther-like spring of the cat in such a person as this girl.

"When she left her first morning class at the theatre Andreas was holding the door open for her; he had been standing there waiting for quite a while, wanting to be in good time, and when she had gone he stood on, propped up against the door handle, staring at the empty space in the air that she had left in her wake; and I was glad. It was good, thought I, to see a statue come down from its pedestal to stand swaying sheepishly in its adoration, particularly when the statue happened to be one's friend.

"Right from the outset I hoped that she would pick him up and dust him down, and when she had been at the theatre for a year and danced with him for the first time I felt quite sure that she would. And in that hope I was proved both right and wrong.

"What I am now about to tell you, I learned from Andreas. I saw what went on from a distance only, but what happened in fact was that his chivalry was stretched to the limit. As a couple, onstage, they made everyone believe that love is undying and that it is possible to love the soul without lusting after the body. Offstage they were the best of friends, but no more than that. The one time when I took the bull by the horns and asked Andreas about their relationship he smiled at me, coyly and politely, and said how much he respected her and how women were superior beings, while I saw right through his smile and into the ice-cold loneliness out of which he knew only the girl could raise him.

"Until one particular day he bit back his feelings then swallowed them, to save them attracting notice and intimidating the superior being who lay in his arms every evening in the sight of two thousand people. But there came a day when he threw discretion to the winds and told her how things stood.

"I'm almost thankful that I did not personally have to hear his explanation. Andreas was a dancer, *words* did not exactly trip off his tongue, and it is difficult to be in love in Denmark, things that ought to fall so beautifully on the ear can so easily end up sounding as if they have been dredged up from a different age, as if they have been buried underground. Nevertheless, he managed it and he told me that it had come as a relief. At one point, as he was talking and confessing everything, something had seemed to give way and he had dropped down on to one knee and kissed her hand and out of him there poured a hotchpotch of stage directions from ballets in which he had danced, along with huge chunks of stucco and clichés he had picked up as a child, and something else, too – a stream of pure gold.

"He told me that the girl heard him out without interrupting. Then, after a moment's deliberation, she told him who she really was.

"She began by saying that, since he felt as he did, she would have to tell him the truth. And this she had done, matter-of-factly, almost as if she were reading out a newspaper report, as if it were all something she stood outside.

"She was born in Germany not long before war broke out, to a mother who for some reason was Danish, in a town whose name she did not care to recall but which had been engulfed by the front line. Her mother worked in one of the brothels in the town, establishments which were later appropriated by the State and presented to the army. She was the only child living in this place and she had no idea how her mother had contrived to hold on to her; she told Andreas that she had no explanations to give, nor did she seek any, all she knew was that ever since she had been old enough to remember what she saw her mother had been a skinny, hardworking little whore feared by all and sundry, even her customers. She had entangled the long succession of men who passed through her door each day in long garlands of brazen behaviour. The girl told Andreas that somewhere inside themselves men always hate a whore and that her mother was hated more than any other, and that she knew that all of the countless men who returned to her – until they were sent away and never returned to anyone ever again – came in the hope that the sperm they squirted into her would somehow make her shut up.

"By now Andreas was already begging to be spared hearing more, but the girl stuck her foot in the gap and asked whether he hadn't just asked for her confidence, and then she had continued.

"From when she was very small her mother had had tuberculosis and the girl had always felt that this woman, her only mainstay in life, ought actually to have been dead. 'Children can sense these things', she had remarked to Andreas, 'children know when someone is living at odds with the natural order of things. I had this picture of Death as a man with a scythe,' she went on, 'and I fancied that the reason he did not show up, was that he was scared of what would come out when Mother saw him and opened her mouth.'

"From the age of four, the girl had washed the soldiers' penises over a tin basin bearing, beneath the imperial eagle, the legend: 'Pure in faith'.

"Again, at this point, Andreas had begged to be let off. 'But that's life,' the girl had said.

"'Then I don't want to go on living,' said Andreas.

"'That's what they all say,' said the girl. That's what the soldiers had said, what her mother had said, what she herself had said. But just look at the soldiers whom she washed. They had been shells. The insides of every one of them drained of all humanity, and all filled with the same abysmal horror and misery, which never left them. Even when they took off all their clothes they held on to their rifles, placing them on the floor next to the bed, within arm's reach; and even when they came, squinting, inside her mother, it was the rifle they were squinting at. Yet even such shells as these struggled to stay alive, though they said they couldn't care less whether they died or not. Even they visited the girl's mother to have the chance, for a moment, of despising a woman, and to obtain a kind of picture, a postcard of sorts, of a tenderness that might have been, if it hadn't been for the war.

"The girl thought she must have been nine years old when her mother judged her old enough to sleep with a man. Nine was of course rather young, but she did not blame her mother. She was dying, so for them both it was a matter of life and death, and when it comes down to life and death there isn't a great deal to be said, so there's no point in blaming one another. And it hadn't hurt as much as one might have thought. She was not even angry at the men any longer, she said. Them she had forgiven.

"'When did it stop?' Andreas had asked, meaning of course when was she going to stop telling him all this and spare him this unwished-for encounter with reality, hearing himself ask in a hoarse, unrecognizable voice, the voice of a stranger, the stranger he had become in the short time it had taken her to tell her story.

"There came a day when her mother was dead and shortly afterwards, on what she thought must have been her fourteenth birthday, a man had tried to harm her. She had lain beneath him and felt her body being hurt and thought, 'No, I *will* live,' and then she had clammed up around his penis so he could not pull out and then she had cut him loose with a razor blade, and it was at that moment that she had ceased to hate men, at that moment she saw what the army chaplain had been getting at. She had laid her hand on this man's head and sent him out into the desert to atone for what the others had done to her mother and herself.

"What happened thereafter was not something she told Andreas about at that point, revealing it instead a little at a time, and it was a story of surviving on the street, of crossing borders to get back to her mother's old homeland, of finding foster parents and at long last stepping into the sunlight.

"What she told Andreas at the time was that he was not to look at her like that, she was happy now, she was strong and healthy, she never thought about those days now. She had only told him about it so that he would understand. Understand that never again could any man touch her in that way.

"'But I touch you, onstage,' Andreas had said.

"'Yes,' she had replied, 'onstage, when the lights are lit and the theatre is packed with people and we are dancing exactly as we know we are supposed to dance, I can rest assured that nothing unexpected is going to happen, so it's perfectly all right for us to show love for one another up there. When the men wanted to switch off the lamp my mother kept next to her bed she would say no. I want it left on, she would say, because I'm a lamplight whore. And that's just how it is with me, Andreas, I'm a lamplight whore, it is only possible when the stage is lit.'"

Here Jakob took a momentary pause from his storytelling to sip from the kettle. Night had fallen. Somewhere in space, one could tell, the moon was waiting, but as yet the sky was overcast as if the world (that is to say, Allah the learned, the wise, the merciful) would draw a veil over the two men and their tale.

"I wonder, Rumi," said Jakob, "what I can give you by telling you this story."

"A journey," the Mohammedan solemnly replied. "Right now, I am with you on the stage of which you speak."

"But how can I be sure that it is the same stage?" asked Jakob.

"Let us not expend our energies on questions to which there is no answer," said the Mohammedan, "especially when we are in the middle of a story."

"You're right," said Jakob. "And that is what I told myself, wondering back then whether Andreas had actually grasped what she had told him. But as time went on, he proved to have a better, more profound grasp of it than anyone else could have had.

"One of the best-loved ballets in Denmark is *La Sylphide*. It was also one of those pieces which Danish audiences flocked to see because it presented them with *all four* pillars of faith at one go. It is a ballet about a man in love with a woman he cannot touch, because she is an angel of sorts who stands to lose both her life and her wings should any man attempt to make inroads upon her person.

"It is the quintessential ballet and Andreas was tailor-made for the part of the young hero. *La Sylphide* was one hundred years old, but when he danced anyone could see that it had been choreographed for him. There was only one thing wrong with it: its age. Even when they tarted it up and presented it as something fresh and topical, still there was something hopelessly old-fashioned about it, still it was obvious that it had had its day. When the girl entered our and Andreas' life, the years evaporated from this piece like mist before the sun, because the girl *was* just such an ethereal creature, lithe as a cat, benign as an angel, virtuous as the Virgin Mary and, above all, totally unapproachable.

"From then on, Andreas danced only for her. When you, Rumi, tell me that it is possible to live without women, I believe you, I know you are right. But only because I have seen Andreas and the girl dance.

"I wouldn't say that, up until then, I'd had much knowledge of love, but if nothing else I was quite convinced that at some point a fusion of the two sexes would have to occur; that one way or another, sooner or later, they would have to sleep together. As the years went by I realized that I was mistaken and I am grateful for having been set straight on this point. As time went by Andreas and the girl explored, for themselves and for the rest of us, including myself, the love that flourishes in the space between two people who never conjoin.

"Now it so happens that, in his ballets, the Maestro had availed himself of set pieces and stereotypes from other lands. Andreas and the girl filled these empty landscapes with genuine emotions. Seeing them dance I understood the Catholic stringency of the Spanish flamenco that threatens at any minute to seethe with blood, and the blithe chastity of the Italian tarantella, that is only waiting for the first unguarded moment before throwing itself into the mire. Of course it was all a performance, to an extent that was beyond my ken at the time and which only became clear to me later; and in a way it *was* all an act, all faked. I can only say how it seemed to me back then: I watched them dance and I understood the nature of love. And not only that between two young lovers. Because, when the music softened, becoming slow and mournful, Andreas' steps grew more ponderous, dragging him earthwards, until I could see suffering like a huge stack of years on his shoulders, and then he danced out of time and into that which was to come; then he showed us old age. And when the girl glided into his arms, when he supported her with a serene composure that has seen and endured everything, what I saw were two people who have borne their love over an endless succession of years and who are now fearlessly staring death in the face. And until I saw them wiping off the greasepaint in their dressing rooms I would have sworn that that evening must have given them grey hairs.

"At the time I did ask myself whether we have the right to ask more of love than this, and I have not yet come up with a definite answer to that question.

"She was promoted to prima ballerina, then the theatre created a special position just for her; within a few years she had become the first ever dancer in the company who could have everything exactly as she pleased. I'm sure everyone felt that the entire theatre was bound up in her person. She had presented herself and stepped into the light never again to forsake it.

"Anyone else would have excited a great deal of envy. But not she, who won praise from everyone, and never anything but praise. It had something to do with the fact that the story of her past had become common knowledge. I didn't understand then how this could have come about, since Andreas was in such a state of stunned panic and loved her too much for one word of it to have escaped his lips. And I was giving nothing away. Nonetheless, that was the way of it in the theatre; from the day the girl started rising through the ranks and being given solo roles and attracting attention everyone knew she was a lost soul.

"Why was she lost? How can I explain our way of thinking, particularly to someone like yourself, Rumi, who has opted for a life without women? Maybe there will never be any explaining it, perhaps I should stop trying, but what I *will* say is that for us, for us dancers, from the youngest pupils in the school to the oldest members of the company, now retired, who roamed the corridors, acting as the corps de ballet's memory and helping with the job of reproducing the Maestro's ballets correct down to the merest crook of a finger – for all of us, physical love represented the sixth pillar of duty, if you take my meaning, and as far as we were concerned anyone who could never sleep with a fellow human being was beyond saving.

"Envy calls for some sort of affinity. For us to have envied the girl her dancing and her roles and her fame we would have had to have felt somehow connected to her. But one doesn't envy a cat its spring, does one? One doesn't envy a statue for being beautifully put together. And no one would dream of envying Jesus his fine words on the cross, would they? And that is, of course, because – in a way – neither the cat nor the statue nor the Saviour are of this world, each in their own way they are in fact tragically unreal – the cat because it lacks any insight into the way of the world, the statue because it is inanimate and the

Saviour because he had to go through so much as God's soloist that no one could seriously envy him his role.

"Now, looking back on it, I can see that the girl's life fused with the theatre. Her dancing could bring tears to the eyes, out of sheer joy and confusion at the very fact of her existence, while at the same time one had the feeling that her tragic fate extended beyond her to take in all of us; that she danced to heal an incurable wound of the soul. In so doing she gave the Maestro's ballets the ring of truth, she revived the last century; up on the stage she smiled and all the stucco rose from the grave and advanced, weeping, upon us; we grew dizzy; we sensed the way in which the theatre became filled with meaning, and with the Holy Spirit; sensed that one true, all-embracing art did indeed exist, and that the girl was its prophet.

"Prophets are above envy, paying as they do a terrible price for their exalted state. I gazed upon the girl with tear-filled eyes, I might as well admit it; I wept and caught myself observing her own resemblance to a desecrated temple: a sort of divine ruin.

"There were so many evenings when I stayed behind in the auditorium to watch them rehearse. Around me the dark, empty theatre. On the stage, light and three figures. The girl, Andreas and the boy with the club foot, whom she had lifted out of the orchestra pit and into life. What did they have in common? I asked myself. Dancing and music, the world replied, and I dare say that's right. But I sensed that there was something else too, and sitting out there in the darkness I realized what it was: imperfection. They shared the knowledge of what it is like to live as damaged goods among sound human beings.

"The boy also had a talent for modelling. Often he could be found working with a lump of clay on a wooden board rather than with his violin, making models of her. At one point they had a number of these little statuettes fired and put on display in one of the corridors off the foyer, but even here they drew the audiences to them during the intervals and after a while they were taken down because they were thought to lower the tone. Now of course at that time everyone at the theatre looked upon the girl as being some ethereal creature. But in the gimp's statuettes I caught a glimpse of something else, the quality that occasioned their being taken down, a distant memory of the time when she had danced barefoot high above Copenhagen.

"But first and foremost he played. He plays, and the girl and Andreas dance, or they rehearse a tricky lift from the long pas de deux in *The Corsair* over and over again, with a patience that knows no bounds, until the manoeuvre is as effortless and self-evident as – how shall I put it – as a caress. They are in what seems to be a cavern of light, a warm pool of light and art and goodwill. No one gives any thought to time, no one knows what hour of the day it is, time no longer exists, there is only the music and these two dancing, as proof that there is a place beyond war, desire, resentment, everyday life; a place where art and dancing rear up like a promise of a pure, an unbesmirched eternity.

"And I sit there in the stalls, my body in darkness. But in my heart the house lights are lit and I am very happy.

"I don't need to tell you, Rumi, how rare a thing it is for God to breathe on us when we dance. And you and I both know the cost of longing to be breathed on, of begging for it and being ignored, of having to bide one's time. But let's not talk of that misery this evening. You have said that we must not whine. So instead I will tell you about the last time God breathed on Andreas.

"Of the experience itself there isn't a great deal to be said. It is, after all, divine and hence inexplicable. But the theatre was celebrating the centenary of the first ballet created by the Maestro in his capacity as newly appointed director of the company. Naturally, Andreas and the girl performed *La Sylphide*, that quintessential ballet on the impossibility and the necessity of love, and God breathed on them, and when Andreas came off into the wings after the last curtain call, he stopped in front of me, clasped his hands and said, as slowly and fervently as if he were praying: 'May it always be thus,' and at that moment neither he nor I was in any doubt that his prayer would be answered.

"We sat and talked while the theatre emptied, until the dancers, too, had gone home and the footsteps of the last watchman had faded away, and then it was that I asked him what it was like to love someone from afar as he did, whether it was enough, and Andreas eyed me gravely for a second before saying: 'It is heavenly, and shouldn't heavenly be enough?'

"At that moment we understood one another perfectly, we both knew that he was sacrificing his life and romantic happiness for art and for the dance and for this girl and I was filled with quiet joy for being able to be with him this evening and listen to him and support him as he bore his cross. In silence we walked side by side through the theatre, across the deserted stage and along darkened corridors; and that we eventually found ourselves approaching the girl's dressing room was due, we sensed, to the tendency of the female sex to draw us to itself even in its absence.

"Even while still some way off we could hear her singing, an exquisite chant which we both took to be a psalm. We moved closer: quietly, cautiously, and yet irresistibly drawn by the divine service we expected to come upon. Never before had we heard her sing and yet it seemed to go without saying that we would peep through the keyhole and find her engrossed in some form of prayer.

"The keyhole proved not to be necessary, because the door was open. We popped our heads round it, reverently, fearful of committing sacrilege.

"On the dressing table a candle had all but burned away, the wick caught in the wax, its light no more than a spark that did not penetrate the darkness of the room. In this darkness all we could make out was something snow-white coming into view then vanishing, coming into view then vanishing. At that moment, Andreas seized my hand and squeezed it hard, and I sensed what he was thinking and that his thoughts echoed my own. For one staggering instant we were convinced that the girl had shed her human form and was now in the act, in the darkness, of unfolding a pair of immense angel's wings. In all its mad improbability this notion was perfectly beautiful and perfectly dreadful – beautiful inasmuch as it was at one and the same time so right that she should dance straight into Heaven and so dreadful that she was about to leave us.

"Just then the draught caused the light to gutter, the wick broke free of the wax and flared up, and a ray of light was cast from the dressing table on to the big, tilted wardrobe mirror, whence it was bounced on to the girl's face. This was thrown backwards, her head hanging over the back of a large armchair, and its being the wrong way up in relation to ourselves gave it an enigmatic expression. But the divine whiteness now stood out sharply. Not angel's wings but the clubfooted violinist's white backside rising and falling, coming into view then vanishing, as it pumped up and down above the girl's upward-tilted pelvis. And as we stood there, frozen to the spot, her expression became quite clear, even to Andreas. It was distorted by the desire both to press on and to hold back."

At this point Jakob took a lengthy break and gazed out into the night as if watching the images of that other night roll past his eyes. After a while Rumi said: "I know the next part of this story. Outside the door God breathed on you and filled you with divine fury. You presented your friend with a flame-wreathed sword and with a strength increased sevenfold by rage he kicked down the door, charged into the room and nailed the girl and her whoremonger to the chair as one would stick a pin through two insects mating. Then you both sat by the double corpse until dawn, talking of life and death."

"That," said Jakob, "would have been a very un-Danish ending. We have to respect the fact that this story takes place in Denmark."

"True enough," said Rumi. "And as it is written – in the forty-second surah, verse thirty-seven – 'Though we be provoked, we must try to forgive.' So did your friend forgive the whoremonger?"

"Not that either," said Jakob, "for that too would have been very un-Danish. The next part of this story involves a conversation between the girl and Andreas, a conversation to which I was not privy but which he told me about. I don't know exactly when it took place, but I fancy that it must have been that same evening. I think Andreas must have waited. Even though he must have known that between him and the girl there now gaped a black hole that no one could bridge, I think he probably waited."

"Where were you, Jakob?" Rumi enquired.

"Sometimes," said Jakob, "the cross of life is so hard to bear that one cannot even help one's best friend.

"At some point the girl was left alone and Andreas went in to her and she looked him straight in the eye for a long time. And then she said: 'I just felt like it.' 'I see,' said Andreas. 'So it wasn't true, what you told me before?' 'No,' said the girl, 'not much of it was true.' 'Then why did you tell me all that?' he asked. 'I don't know,' she said. 'I just felt like it. Afterwards not a day went by when I did not want to tell you the truth.' 'So why didn't you?' asked Andreas. 'Because I saw how beautifully you danced,' she said, 'and I realized that my falsehood had been a great work of art. That I had told you what you needed to hear in order to dance your very best.' 'I think,' said Andreas, 'that back then I would rather have heard more of the truth.'

"Then the girl sat back, as if withdrawing into another world and, thought Andreas, perhaps that was indeed what she was doing. From there she said: 'The world is not geared for the truth,

Andreas dear, and nor are you, and even though you probably cannot understand it, nonetheless I will try to explain it to you: the people in this world, and especially those in this theatre, *must suffer*, and this they must do because they spend every second of their lives pulling in two opposing directions. When you dance, Andreas, you create an image of effortlessness. Evening after evening audiences watch you dance across the green meadow as the carefree young prince or the birdcatcher or the nobleman under no obligation to anyone and with not a care in the world. You are the living image of nonchalant freedom. But you and I and the audience know that in order to form this image of freedom you have willingly cloistered yourself and dedicated your life to the toughest, most monotonous work the world has ever known. Each evening in the theatre you demonstrate that in the universe obligation and freedom are kept poles apart.

"'Each evening, onstage, you dance the role of the virtuous, chivalrous young man who goes out of his way not to offend womanly modesty, and you dance the part of the saint in trousers so tight that everyone in the hall can see what you have between your legs, and that is one reason for their coming to the theatre. Each evening, onstage, you show that in the universe lust and virtue are kept poles apart.'

"'I don't want to hear any more,' said Andreas.

"'No,' said the girl. 'Of course you don't want to hear any more. Each evening on the stage you offer glimpses of happiness. You show the world that happiness is wine and women and the countryside and being able to do whatever comes into your head, while everyone knows very well that your life does not allow for alcohol or women or freedom of choice; that only by turning your back on such temptations is it possible for you to create this image. You do not wish to hear the truth and that you shall be spared. What you need is a tale such as the one I told you, the tale of a tragic soul in a beautiful body. Do you know the story of Moses parting the waters so that his people could walk across dryshod?'

"'Yes,' said Andreas.

"'You are Moses,' said the girl. 'You hold two opposing forces in abeyance so that the audience can cross dryshod and find their way home.'

"'If I am Moses,' he said, 'who are you?'

"The girl took but a second to consider this. 'I,' she said, 'am God.'

"Andreas regarded the slender, chignoned figure in the tulle skirt. 'That's not how God looks,' he said softly.

"'It was brought home to me,' the girl said, as if talking to herself – and, thought Andreas, perhaps she was, 'when I resisted the temptation to tell you the truth. I understood then that I was standing on the outside. And that is how one can know God, by the fact that he stands on the outside.'

"'For Christ's sake!' Andreas groaned. 'You're a human being just like the rest of us.'

"'In one way, Andreas,' said the girl, 'I am just like all of you, but in another way I am different, alone. And that's what it's like to be God. You understand everything, but you are always alone, and so you are free to do what has to be done.'

"'And what is it that has to be done?' he asked.

"'There has to be dancing, here, in this theatre,' said the girl.

"'Even if, as you say, the truth about this theatre amounts to two lies held in abeyance?' he asked.

"'In that case,' she said, 'it is more important than ever that you all feel you are working for something that is greater and more in tune than yourselves.'

"'And what about you?' Andreas enquired. 'What are you working for?'

"'Ten years from now,' she said, 'I will be ballet master, the first woman ever to become ballet master at this theatre. And people will say of me: "She was once a great dancer. Now she is a great ballet master." When that day comes I will be rich, I will be famed throughout Europe and the dancers of this company will fear me in a way they could never dream of today.'

"'I believe I have some inkling of it,' said Andreas.

"'And yet,' she continued, 'the power, the money, the acclaim will be merely incidental; the real reason will be something quite different: you all do your best, you all work like horses. But the one who gives Moses the strength to part the waters and keep them apart, even though she knows that in so doing she must set herself above the truth, she more than anyone else must be capable of acting under the pressure both of the deluge and of the falsehoods. Acting under pressure is what is known as doing one's duty, and that is what I do. And that is what the Maestro was doing when he created his ballets.'

"By now she was out of her chair, her face right up against Andreas', and he saw that she was no longer far away and that at that moment she was displaying an honesty he had only remarked in her twice before: when she had danced alone in that room high above the city and when her head had been hanging over the back of that chair.

"'I do my duty. I do it for the only thing that is greater than I am, greater than all of us put together,' she said. 'I do it for *the dance*, to ensure that here, at our feet, the dancing will be of the finest.'

"That was as much of this conversation as Andreas could recall, or as much as he chose to tell me," said Jakob. "And there are now two possible endings to this story.

"The next day Andreas did not show his face. But the day after that, there was a message lying at the theatre from his parents, to say that their son, whom they had expected to provide them with their entrée into life, had instead taken them with him to Hell, by bracing a hunting rifle against the floor, putting its two barrels in his mouth and standing on the trigger.

"I cannot say how we reacted to this. For my part, all I can remember is the picture that came into my mind just as the news hit me, as I hung there, numbed and weightless, waiting for grief to wash over me: Andreas stood before me, hunched over the black holes of the barrel as if in the act of calling down to the underworld that he was on his way, and I thought to myself what a terribly messy way of death he had chosen, and that his fine feeling for beauty certainly seemed to have failed him at the last; he, who could have made such a beautiful corpse.

"Much later I came to see that suicide had been the only decent way to end it. Because time would of course have caught up with him, he too would of course have grown old. Instead he had now entered upon that eternal youth in which the memory of the theatre and its audiences would preserve him. His had been the perfect end, turning his life, as it did, into a romantic ballet.

"That, Rumi, is one possible ending."

For a while they sat there, saying nothing.

Then, "No," said Rumi, "it was not a perfect end, because it does not provide any explanation for how you come to be sitting here tonight telling this story. There should always be some explanation of the storyteller's part in the tale. In Arabic this night is known as *alilet*, the fateful night; the night on which Mohammed recites the Koran. But only because Allah passed this tale to him through the Archangel Gabriel. So in the Koran the storyteller's role is clearly defined. Which is how it should be."

"Why?" asked Jakob.

"So we can be sure that what we are hearing is the honest truth," said the Mohammedan. "A story may be untrue. But both the story and its narrator are always truthful."

"You're right," said Jakob. "What this story needs is a sequel. And in a way this sequel is Andreas' funeral, because on the evening of the day on which he was to be buried, we gave a performance of *La Sylphide* in his memory.

"It was the girl's idea. I see now that for some time she must have wielded a much greater influence at the theatre than any of us dancers realized and now here she was, wanting to dance this ballet as a memorial to her partner. Everyone else felt that such enterprise was to her credit. I don't really know what I felt. But I do remember thinking that she could even make use of death to impart life to the dance.

"I am at a loss to know why she wanted me to dance the young man's, Andreas', role. She may, by then, have been working on a new story, a dance of death designed to turn me into a new Andreas. But I think not. I believe she chose me in order to bind me more closely to herself. I believe she already sensed that I knew something, that I was already standing slightly on the outside. Naturally I tried to get out of it, saying that I was in mourning, but she stepped right up to me and said that the dance was bigger than the grief of the individual, said it in such a way that – even had I not known what I knew about her – I would have sensed that this was no human being but the theatre itself that addressed me.

"I cannot claim to have been seeing very clearly that evening. But I'm sure I remember there being a very beautiful atmosphere in the theatre, because his suicide had been such a consummate act. I said earlier that I did not know what to make of the audiences. But that evening I did in fact gain some glimmer of understanding. And what I perceived was that all of them must occasionally have wished that real life could be like the life portrayed on the stage. And that in some inexplicable way they knew the story which the girl had told Andreas, that she had managed to leak this tragic lie about her life to the public, so that the audience now knew that Andreas, when he stepped on the trigger and the buckshot vaporized his head, wedded life with art.

"The young man in *La Sylphide* dies of grief over the death of the untouchable sylph. As a ballet it represents a cry to the gods on the beauty and the tragedy of purely spiritual love and now they all sat there in the auditorium, knowing that this was the cry which Andreas had yelled down the rifle barrels.

"In the minutes remaining before the curtain went up I tried to empty my mind of sorrow and anger, to leave these feelings behind in the dressing room, but to no avail. I danced the first act of the ballet, but I danced it with feet that seemed glued to the boards and during the short break I had while the girl danced her grand, languorous solo, I walked past all the people standing weeping with emotion in the wings and retreated to my dressing room, wanting a brief moment of peace and quiet.

"When I leaned forward and gazed in the mirror at my vacant eyes, a white face loomed up behind me in the darkness. Even before I turned round I knew it was Andreas and for one cold, cold instant I thought that he had come down from Heaven to Earth to take me to task for being weak. But then I remembered the gimp's white arse in the darkened room and decided that there had been more than enough bloody angels. Besides which, I could see that the reason Andreas' face was white was because he was in make-up. Made up and dressed to dance my, or rather his, own role.

"What did I say to him? 'So you're not dead then?' 'No,' he said. 'She has taught me that there can be a great and essential art in lying. But now I am going on in your place.' 'Is that such a good idea?' I asked. 'D'you think you can deny a pal the chance to take part in his own funeral?' he asked, and then he was gone.

"I watched their meeting from the wings. She was quite sure that he was me. Until he touched her she was bursting with tear-stained, peacockish triumph, but the minute he put out a hand to support her and she turned to face him and recognized him she turned to ice. And then she began to moult.

"Frozen inside though she was, the most stupendous force of habit drove her on, so that to begin with I was the only one who *saw*. Saw how Andreas supported her, confidently, casually, considerately, while all the time speaking to her in a whisper. I can guess what he was saying: 'The dance is greater than the individual, greater even than you, and if you do not carry on, if you do not see this ballet through to the end with me, I will lead you down to the footlights and tell everyone the truth about the two of us. After all, it's not as if I have anything to lose, I'm as good as dead if you see what I mean, and the dead stand on the outside, and for those who stand on the outside certain very special rules do, of course, apply.'

"I cannot say how long they danced, perhaps a few minutes, and during those few minutes he exerted a terrible power over her, during those minutes he held her transfixed in a vacuum, and if there is any justice in this world then in that vacuum she came face to face with the difference between truth and lies.

"Then her legs gave way and someone behind the scenes must have recognized Andreas because they brought down the curtain. But before it could drop as far as the stage he ducked underneath it to stand alone before the audience. They tried to get me to go on and bring him off but I wouldn't do it, I just stood there and listened.

"'Ladies and gentlemen,' he said, 'I really am Andreas, that Andreas whom you believed to be dead, and indeed I *was* dead, but I have now been resurrected and if you will open your eyes and die and, in a small way, be resurrected together with me, then I promise you that this evening you will be with me in Paradise.'

"At that point they dragged him away and threw him in the clink for a short term, then they let him out, whereupon he promptly disappeared. I had no chance to talk to him, I never saw him again. But after the events recounted here I found it very hard to stay on at the theatre, I no longer felt comfortable there and one day I left. That, Rumi, is how I come to be telling you this story."

They sat in silence for a long time, watching the moon now breaking through to shine down on the sleeping city.

"You," said Rumi with conviction, "are Andreas."

"It's a far cry," the other replied, "from the Andreas who danced in Copenhagen to the Jakob sitting opposite you now."

"But," said Rumi, "it's quite possible that, somewhere in the world, Andreas too is sitting on the deck of a boat, looking at the moon."

"Yes," replied Jakob. "It's possible."

"Did anyone learn anything from Andreas' fate?" asked the Mohammedan. "Did any members of the audience follow him to Paradise?"

"No," said Jakob. "He made that journey alone."

"So who *did* learn anything from it?" asked Rumi.

"I did," said Jakob. "I learned that it may be necessary to stand on the outside if one is to see things clearly. But I cannot say which of the characters in this story taught me this.

"Recently it has occurred to me that I also learned something else. These past weeks there have been times when I have ceased to be upset, when I have viewed the theatre and the girl and Andreas without anger, as if I have become capable of seeing it all through someone else's eyes, as if there might still be a chance of being on the inside."

"Whose eyes?" asked Rumi.

"The gimp's," replied Jakob. "And at those moments, I forgive them all."

"Forgiveness is a beautiful thing," said Rumi. And in a crystal-clear, hushed and yet powerful voice, a voice that had been created for and accustomed to a large audience, he recited:

To those who have faith
you must say
that they must forgive those
who long not for the kingdom of Allah.
Allah alone will reward
with goodness and with evil
the deeds that man performs.

Slowly, Jakob got to his feet, stretched, and leaned back against the rigging. The moonlight filtered through the chequered pattern of the ropes and cast an illusory Harlequin suit over his torso. The two men gazed pensively into the night and, without a word passing between them, their thoughts turned on to the same track and fell into step, as they pondered how their own story now had two possible endings. At this moment there was no way of telling whether they would stay where they were and wait for whatever would befall, or whether they would shove off, hoist the sail and endeavour to transport their mutual obstinacy downriver and out to sea.

☾

THE VERDICT ON THE RIGHT HONOURABLE IGNATIO LANDSTAD RASKER, LORD CHIEF JUSTICE

Anyone wishing to understand the history of Europe in the nineteenth and twentieth centuries should turn to its civil servants. To their enigmatic, monotonous, dogged industry, their talent for self-denial, its sequestered and yet overweening sensibility.

Planning entails generating a certain tension. Realizing one's plans entails sustaining this tension. In the history of Europe the art of planning was brought to perfection among the civil servants. And with it: the art of creating and withstanding stress.

Seismology is the study of surface tremors caused by tension built up below the earth's crust. The study of love represents the seismology of the individual and of togetherness. Which is why – when seeking some intimation of the future – the world and the family will always, in the first instance, look at the love life of their children.

Being a fellow human being entails being able to bottle up one's urge to love. Being a pillar of society entails being able both to bottle up and to channel this urge. Anyone who is capable of devoting his whole life to this piece of erotic engineering has the potential to become a great civil servant. Anyone who is incapable either of channelling or of devoting his life in such a way has the potential to become a tragic figure. Or an artist. Or something else again, something unpredictable.

On March 19th 1929, Thomas Landstad Rasker married Charlotte Rømer in Holmens Kirke in Copenhagen.

On the afternoon of that same day, each from their own tall window in Thomas' father's apartments overlooking Frederiksholms Kanal, the newlyweds watched the sun setting over the capital. In the room's third window bay stood Thomas' mother, Eline Landstad Rasker.

The day had been hazy, but now the mist caught the sunlight and a voluminous golden veil settled over the palace church, the royal stables and the Supreme Court; and, further up, above the Church, the Army and the Civil Service, hung a sky of clearest blue.

Eline gazed up at the bright sky. She seemed to see a long, radiant procession of other sunsets and in her heart the years of her life merged into one single point filled with joy, sadness, a pressure that was close to bursting point and the certainty that up ahead the night awaits. She looked at her son and her daughter-in-law, trying to divine their thoughts, and, as so often before, she was struck by how little parents knew about their children and indeed how little human beings comprehended what they themselves had had a part in creating.

Then the door behind them opened and Hektor Landstad Rasker entered the room.

At no time would Rasker, barrister-at-law, ever be alone. Wherever he went he would always be attended by a shadowy train of men, now deceased, whose deeds in the service of Danish society nevertheless lived on. For eight generations, at the university, in the ministries and the courts, the Landstad Rasker family had formed the backbone of the Danish judicial system; and the energies invested by them in the service of justice had accumulated and been passed on from father to son as an obvious duty.

To all that he had thus inherited Hektor Landstad Rasker had added his own meteoric rise, his doctoral thesis, his victories at the Academic Boxing Club, his travels abroad, his command of foreign languages and seats on various boards; and his own merits as well as those of others had consolidated around his tall figure into a corona of magnetic energy. This power appeared never to leave him, was with him even now. When he closed the inner set of padded leather double doors and motioned to the three people facing him to take their seats around a low, circular table, he was in every respect shutting out the outside world. Later that same evening these spacious apartments would be filled with guests and, later still, with music, but right at this moment, for these four people, nothing existed outside of themselves.

In church the barrister had been dressed in the uniform of the Supreme Court which, with its military cut, its dress sword and the Grand Cross pinned high on his left breast, had served to accentuate his athletic figure and innate dignity. Now he had changed into an elegant dark suit, but no matter what he would wear, thought Eline, he is a stranger to me.

Her marriage to the man now standing opposite her had lasted one year. Shortly before Thomas' birth he had obtained a divorce from her and moved her out of his own apartments and into others on Gammel Strand. Every day since then she had looked across at his windows, where they stared out from the white-washed façade like blind and darkened eyes in a pallid face, and every Sunday afternoon she and Thomas had walked the few hundred metres along the canals to the heavy portal and, in the salon in which tables were now being laid for the wedding guests, they had drunk chocolate with Hektor Landstad Rasker, who had chatted distantly but politely with his former wife, while Thomas in his sailor suit sat on the edge of his chair, sucking on his silver whistle, and observed this man who was his father.

So powerful was the force that emanated from Hektor Landstad Rasker, so great the air of dignity that hung round Eline, and so few details did they vouchsafe that the dissolution of their marriage was only ever discussed in strictest confidence and then only with the utmost caution, and never with the couple themselves. One of the men who had passed through Eline's life had once – in a wild and desperate attempt to occupy and raise his standard in the very deepest recesses of her life – demanded an explanation. She had walked over to the window and looked down at the canal.

"They do say," she said, "that during the Ice Age, some of the big cats actually succeeded, contrary to the laws of nature, in surviving on the ice. That is how I see him. Like a sabre-toothed tiger on a glacier."

"You mean like some admirable and tragic figure," concluded the man behind her bitterly.

"No," said Eline, "like a fellow creature with cold feet."

That was as much as she ever let slip. Thomas never asked her, but when she judged him old enough to be curious she told him: "Your father will explain it to you. He is a barrister. He can describe how it was."

As Hektor Landstad Rasker closed the door and turned to face them and motioned them to their seats, she realized that – after twenty years – the time had come for him to present his case, and she thought to herself: "The court is in session."

Then the barrister raised his right hand so all could see that with him he had brought a long carving knife, smiled at their expectant faces as if at some unspoken, private joke, and stepped up to the table. On its polished surface stood a dusty, black, high-shouldered wine bottle.

"This," he said, "is a bottle of vintage port. Quinta do Noval, harvested the year that you, Thomas, were born. To my mind, the greatness of this wine consists, first and foremost, not in its alcoholic effect, nor its taste and colour, nor even its price. For me the value of this bottle lies in its ability to harness memories and, later, to unleash them. It has aged in the bottle and has preserved and heightened a certain evanescent but profound truth about its birth. Do not misunderstand me. I, too, look upon intoxication as a gift from God to us mortals, to enable us to see clearly, and I too have learned all that I know of the colour red by regarding a candle flame through a glass of burgundy. But above all a wine must cause me to hark back to the year when those grapes were picked.

"So too with this bottle. It presents us with the answer to many questions and poses, to begin with, just one: how are we to open it? This is, after all, a delicate wine, bottled after only a handful of years in the cask. It has deposited a layer of sediment at the bottom of the bottle, a worthless clump, an acrid dust composed of grape skins, pips and stalks, the leavings of the chemical storm that has swept through this bottle in order that, today, it may permit us to remember with perfect clarity.

"I could use a corkscrew, you will say. But in that case I would first have to remove the lead seal, and then perform a number of other disturbing operations. I would have to manhandle the bottle, conscious all the while of how it has stood untouched on this table for three days, so that the wine should be absolutely clear. With a corkscrew, I could not help but stir up the lees.

"This is merely a bottle, but the point about this wine – and now I speak to you as a lawyer – is also the point about society: how to keep the sediment separate, how to isolate the lees from the pure wine? My whole life revolves around this question."

The barrister placed his left hand on the shoulder of the bottle and in one swift, sharp movement brought the knife down in a sweeping curve towards it. With a brittle crack the neck of the bottle seemed to disintegrate and vanish. And as the echo of powdered glass scattering across the parquet floor died away, the eyes of everyone in the room were fixed on the clean cut that had exposed the wine while leaving it unsullied.

"I have taken the liberty of staging this little demonstration," said the barrister, "as an argument in support of the theory that the harshest solution is often the kindest."

Turning his back on them he removed a carafe and four glasses from a cupboard. He then raised the bottle and slowly poured its contents into the glasses. As the first drops began to flow the wine seemed to wake from its sleep, its bouquet spreading like a huge, invisible blossom over the table top, filling the air like some torrid memory of parched, terracotta slopes along the banks of a slow-running river. Hektor Landstad Rasker nosed the wine. "Here," he said, "you have the scent of a winter of twenty-two years ago."

"The letter from my father was delivered to me here, in this room," he began.

Hands behind his back the barrister crossed to the wall and gazed intently for a moment at the dark, oval portrait of his father – of the Right Honourable Ignatio Landstad Rasker, Lord Chief Justice – and when he turned back to the three at the table the resemblance between the two was seen to be striking. In the painting the judge was lit from the side, the light catching his white hair and the finely chiselled cascade of tiny wrinkles running from his eyes. Beneath him, the barrister's face was smooth, his hair thick and dark and yet, as so often before, Eline was conscious of a dryness in her mouth and a faint tightening around the heart at the melancholy, feline beauty of the two men. And as so often before she found herself thinking that it was inexplicable and strangely reticent, as if those slanting eyes, those long eyelashes and those vulnerable lips drew onlookers to them, drew them through the skin and into a core of mysterious grief. "And even I," thought Eline, "even I, after all that has happened and after all these years, even I have to grip the arms of the chair to save myself from being sucked down and away."

"You know," the barrister said to Thomas, seeming now to be speaking to him alone, "what your grandfather has meant to Denmark. You know that in his day and age he was regarded as the definitive symbol of the Supreme Court, the highest court in the land, whose judgements were absolutely final. Know, too, that he resigned from his post under circumstances that have never been made public.

"But you still do not know what he was and what he became to me. It is for this that I have summoned you all here. To tell you, Thomas; to tell you that even in his private life, even to me, he represented the highest, the ultimate authority in this life.

"I believe that parents have the right to expect the respect of their children, but not their admiration. Admiration is something that must be earned, it cannot be demanded of anyone. Your grandfather won and accepted my admiration with the same assurance with which he had won that of the public at large and this he did by being a man of flawless character.

"You know that modern man bears the head of Janus. That he looks outwards at the world with features that are fixed and tense, and inwards at his private life with a calm, relaxed countenance; and so be it. Society is a flimsy structure, constantly threatened by chaos and upheld only by a boundless, hard-won self-control which the majority, by far the majority, lay aside – nay, cast off – the minute they turn their attention towards their nearest and dearest.

"But there are exceptions to this rule, people for whom self-control is not an effort, but a deep, inalienable and integral part of their character, and such a man was your grandfather.

"Note that I do not say he was inhuman. I have seen other solid citizens whose spirits are imprisoned in tombs of propriety and who go to and from court day in, day out without ever displaying a trace of humanity, without ever being alive. Your grandfather's character was of another order, a type which it takes centuries to form, a man whose nature happens to coincide with the course of history. If you were to ask me who reared your grandfather, I could reply that his parents and nursemaids had done so. But I could, with as much – no, greater – right, say: Time reared him, Denmark reared him, or even better: Justice – the justice of Anders Sandøe Ørsted and Carl Goos – reared him. Nowadays, we are undergoing so many changes that a character as pure as his is already fading into the mists of the general process of disintegration. But this much I can tell you: so amazingly, so effortlessly just was your grandfather, so uncompromisingly upright, that Alberti, the Minister of Justice – who had a long lifetime of experience in gently bending and adapting the law – had once commented irritably that it was impossible to slip even an item as thin as a hundred-rigsaler note between Ignatio Landstad Rasker and Justice.

"When I was about ten years old, J. F. Willumsen the great painter asked my father to pose for his painting *Justice wrestling with Injustice* and I still remember so clearly the long sunlit days in the painter's atelier, with my father standing in the middle of the room, naked, doubled up in his fight against black Injustice. I remember how his energy radiated towards me, sitting quietly on the floor, and the young painter working frantically, inspired; and even then, years before I was capable of formulating the thought for myself, I could sense that my father's power was inextricably bound up with his public office, his judge's cape and uniform.

"I was standing at my father's side when Willumsen unveiled the finished painting, revealing also that, contrary to what had been agreed, he had endowed the figure's face with my father's features. Without raising his voice my father drew this mistake to the painter's attention, but Willumsen brushed aside his objection, telling him how difficult it would be to repaint the face and how it was an honour to be thus portrayed as Justice. At that my father opened a door into his inner self, just a chink, to afford the painter a glimpse of a willpower that was quite unshakeable. 'Be so kind,' he said, 'as to replace my features with some others. You do, of course, understand that this sort of personality cult is irreconcilable with my position as a judge in the highest court in the land.'

"Willumsen took a step backwards, I recall, as if he had been struck by something, which indeed he had – one man's sense of justice having collided with the artist's moral uncertainty – and we knew that his face would be replaced by another. I stood bolt upright next to my father, very young, incapable of understanding all of this and yet very much aware that even as a private individual, standing there facing the artist, my father was a paragon; even naked, not for one second did he lose his sense of propriety.

"I will not dwell on the years that lie between this incident and the events I am about to relate. All I will say is that there has never been one moment when he did not shine like a star in my eyes. I grew up with the sort of distance between father and son which is almost non-existent in our own day, but which seems to me to be a good thing, indeed – all things considered – a necessity. I have never cared much for the sentimental aspect of our society, have never seen the need for individuals to cling to one another like blind men, feeling their way and trying to drag others down into their own darkness. I believe in light and my father was such a light. Human beings need role models; it is of the utmost importance that there should be someone with the courage and the stature to stand forth and say that this, *this*, is the way life must be faced. For most young people, their first experience of life is as a wilderness of loathing, at the moment when they discover their parents' frailty. And at that moment it is difficult or even impossible for them to believe in the ideal. I myself recall with the most profound sadness the first time my mother lied to me, and, since then, have seen her frailty and that of other women as a long succession of reminders that up ahead, grey death awaits us all. I believe that when Death comes it will come in the shape of a woman standing by my side and assuring me that I will live for ever.

"With my father it was a different story. As far as he was concerned, I knew that he had a good grip on life. Not only those parts of it which fall in with our wishes, but life as a whole, that creature with the cool, smooth skin that wriggles and squirms when we try to pin it down; he had a good grip on that and he held it out at arm's length from himself and looked it straight in the eye.

"I am not much given to dreaming, but I will confess to you that I have had a dream about old age. I have no idea when it first appeared but I think it must have been when I was about twenty years old. One day I looked in the mirror and caught sight of a shadow, a wrinkle running like a tiny, threadlike worm down across my cheek. I laughed at it and noticed that it simply grew deeper and I realized that this was the worm of time, a small and sensitive reptile, a sign of something that had just begun and that would not come to an end until everything came to an end. I think that prior to this I must have been looking down, I think I had been walking around with my eyes fixed on the ground. But at that moment I looked up and forward, at that which awaits us all, and then I saw my father in a new light. No longer as Olympus, as some distant peak, but as what lay in store for me, and it was then that I formed a vision of his old age.

"Ever since that day I have been aware of how we humans have risen out of the dust and derided it, as though never again would we lie down. I believe the reason we sleep in beds is that we wish to keep our distance from the earth; to convince each other and ourselves that sleep is but a temporary state.

"But the earth is waiting for us, and this I have known since the age of twenty. You must know that every morning since then I have woken with a distinct sense of being buried; over me hang gravity and the knowledge that the obligatory objective of all life is six feet of sod, and I think to myself that above my head they have nailed down my coffin lid. And then I realize it is too soon, realize that death is a sinecure, a retirement which I have not yet earned, a reprieve on false grounds, so I shove the shroud aside and hack my way up through the earth and greet the new day, and this I say with no bitterness but also with no illusions.

"To summon the strength each day to pull oneself out of one's own grave one needs help, and this I drew from my father.

"I formed a picture of him as an old man in his library, a picture which was pieced together, I dare say, in protest against decay. Against that old age that is all around us every day, as a burned-out state, as old people who forget to put on their shoes when they go out, and judges who have to ask me to approach the bench because they cannot hear what I am saying and who interrupt court proceedings by getting to their feet and saying the court is temporarily adjourned, the court needs to stretch its legs because the court has varicose veins! And who, when I have said my piece, stare at me with vacant eyes full of senile shadows and all the things they no longer understand.

"As a counterweight to this darkness that had begun to drag me down, even before I came of age, I formed an image of my father. He is in his library, silver-haired as in this portrait here, wrinkled, straight-backed and crystal clear and deep as a well. He is sitting there reading, I come in and I note our resemblance to one another; two people who hold themselves upright, both physically and spiritually. I ask him a question and he gives me an answer, a clear, concise answer which is like a gleaming capsule of crystalline experience, of the salt of life, and I nod and take my leave of him. That is how I pictured him and at that time there was nothing, nothing whatsoever to suggest that this dream would not come true. Until I received his letter.

"He had never written to me before. Well, fathers never did write to their sons much, and besides, he had a lawyer's wariness of the written word. And what would he have written to me about, anyway? On the one occasion, while I was at Herlufsholm, that the school contacted him and asked him to give me a written reprimand for having spurned a schoolfellow's sexual advances by knocking out two of his teeth and suspending him under the cold shower for half an hour to give him a glimpse of a masculine view of things, he got into his Mercedes, drove up to the school and into the quadrangle, parked it amongst the rose bushes and marched up to the headmaster's office, placed himself before this gentleman and said: 'I am here to advise you that my son's predilections are none of my concern.'

"His letter arrived one winter's day and I read it in this room. Your mother was also here, she was expecting you at the time, and outside it was bitterly cold. He had written: 'I ask you all to come. It is more important and more urgent than any of you can imagine.'

"I remember being stunned. Never before had I heard him ask anyone for anything, not even at the dinner table. There, as in life, he reached for things himself. He would draw attention to an error, he set life straight, but never before had he asked anyone for anything.

"I was thirty years old, I had a wife, an apartment, a practice, I was soon to become a father and yet we went. Not the next morning, not that same evening but that very hour, such was the nature of your grandfather's power to command even when, as here, it was disguised as an entreaty, and not for one second did

I doubt that he had summoned us because he had found out that he was dying.

"I cannot tell you why I was so sure of this, but just think what he had done. With his letter he had reached out and intruded on my work and all my instincts told me both he and I knew full well that only someone calling from their deathbed has the right to call the living away from their work.

"He had gone out to an island owned by our family which lies at the point where the Kattegat strait becomes the Skagerrak, forming one of the last outposts of Denmark. He would go there whenever he had some important written suit to review and that was where he had gone this time, too.

"The island had been in our family for five generations. Its northern end was a desert, if such a word makes any sense in this context; depending on the season, an ice-bound or a sun-baked expanse of hard sand over which the north wind forced the lyme grass to fight for every inch of ground. And it was here that my father had built his house. A mansion, I would call it – built out of wood to be sure, but still a mansion; a white house on two storeys with pillars, glazed tiles and a tall fence enclosing a garden in which a gardener cultivated roses. I suspect that it had to be this plant and none other because my father wished to demonstrate that a man should not let anything get the better of him, not even the forces of nature.

"We set off at night and arrived there in the morning, on a day yellow with sunlight but with a piercing, intense, keen chill to it. The sea was perfectly calm, not a breath of wind stirred and the water was coated with a film of transparent, paper-thin ice that sang tremulously as the ferry cut through it. And as transparently and gently as this ice, I thought, is death closing around my father.

"There were twelve of us on board the ferry and as soon as I laid eyes on them I knew that before the day was over I would sit down to table with them. I found myself thinking: how typical of my father, with his meticulous disposition, to see to it that we should number thirteen, just as there were thirteen at the Last Supper and just as thirteen judges sit in the Supreme Court.

"Whom did I recognize? My mother, of course, two judges, the head of the vice squad, a professor of law and the Bishop of Zealand who, I knew, had gone to school with my father. We were picked up at the landing stage by two landaus and on the short drive to the house I experienced something that was, for me, quite unusual. You know that, without being misanthropic, I do tend to regard my fellow men with the scepticism of an advocate. For as long as I can recall I have seen through people; always, behind the cordiality and politeness, I can see the underside, and such perception makes it impossible to hold on to one's illusions. I am a person who harbours no preconceived ideas, but no expectations either. I have felt attached to only a very few people in my life and then only once they have produced full and final proof of their worth.

"Nonetheless, on this short drive I found myself conceiving an instinctive sympathy with my travelling companions; experiencing a sudden rush of fellow feeling. These, I thought to myself, are people who have been close to my father, these are the ones to whom he intends to deliver his last will and testament, these are the people who can testify that his life has come as close as any human life can do to the ideal. The bishop knew him as a boy, I reasoned, the judges and the professor have known him in his official capacity and even my mother would admit, particularly if we were lucky enough to catch her in one of her rare rational moments, that both before and after the dissolution of their marriage he had always displayed an unstinting and irreproachable sense of responsibility.

"The presence of the four other women puzzled me rather, but also for this some satisfactory explanation would doubtless be forthcoming. For them, too, on this carriage ride, I surprised myself by entertaining warm feelings.

"Let there be no doubt that inside I was as numbed by the cold as the landscape through which we drove; that from the moment I laid aside my father's letter I had been unable to see any way back to life for me, once my father was gone. I sat there, being jolted back and forth in the carriage, with my heart encased in a transparent, paper-thin film of ice. And yet, at the same time I was filled – understand it he who can – with a new vitality, a strange elation, and believed I felt that way because it was what my father would have wanted of me. In that life which he held at a distance and in full view Death also had its place and was now, in the worst form imaginable, breathing down my neck, and I was conscious of facing up to the chill of it, its threat of a kind of inner permafrost that sears everything away, with stiff-necked defiance.

"I thought I detected this same defiance in my travelling companions, certainly among the men, every one of whom radiated a powerful, all-embracing air of distinction. Even sitting there on the hard wooden seats, in their furs and travelling capes, and swathed in rugs, there was nothing helpless, nothing hidebound or comical about them, but rather a common, boundless if latent dynamism. There are those whose station in life is all bound up with objects and places; with the drill room, with flasks and cathode-ray tubes, with ebonite pens and cartridge paper. The power of these men, like my father's, was bound up with history, with the mother country, and it never left them; even in the jolting, swaying carriage it was there with them, in the form of a composure that enabled them to put up with this temporary lack of comfort, knowing as they did that eventually they would reach their destination, just as they always had done. I had the feeling that I was not travelling with any random group of strangers. I was travelling with a period in my country's history, a period of which my father was an indivisible part.

"Sure in this belief, I nodded politely at Death; the frozen expanse of sand seemed to me to be covered in crosses and it occurred to me that only when we depart without leaving any trace do we truly disappear. When one has made history, as my father had done, and carved out an era; when one has friends of such consequence; when one has erected a house in a desert and an even greater edifice of words in the courts of Denmark then one leaves behind a full life, a body of work, great achievements; then whatever dies is minimal compared to what will live on for ever. In this state of euphoria I felt up to anything, even to carrying on a polite conversation with my mother, and so we arrived at the house which looked, bathed in sunlight as it was, as if it were expecting us for a celebration and not for a leavetaking.

"He welcomed us on the terrace and I was the last one he greeted. He clasped my hand in his and held it there. We looked into each other's eyes, and it dawned on me that I had arrived at the last outpost of life; the land of old age and the ultimate clarification.

"He had hired a cook to prepare the food and we spent the time until dinner in the room overlooking the sea. As the sun went down, we sat and he stood before us, as I now stand before you three, and it was then that I first noticed his absence of gravity. He showed off his ships. All his life he had built ships in bottles and these creations filled the room in a way which, even as a small boy, I never could fathom. To me, putting ships in bottles is and always will be a hobby for the lower classes; odd, solidified bubbles surrounding something flighty and tawdry. And how these homespun dreams could hold any fascination for my father was something I had never understood. But in the past he had kept quiet about his pastime, only in this house on the island had he allowed his fancy free rein; here, he, who never touched alcohol himself, had poured countless bottles of Barzac into the soil because the clear, high-shouldered bottles appealed to him. But he had done it in private.

"Now here he was showing them off, now here he was bringing them down, one after another, from their stands, and sailing them past our eyes like some tasteless convoy. I do not know how the other guests felt but I must have turned away, wanting to hide my mortification at his careless levity, because suddenly he was standing beside my chair.

'Hektor,' he said, 'I see that this bothers you. Nonetheless, I insist that you look at this ship.'

"I looked at it.

"'This is the yacht *Spray*,' he said, 'in which Captain Joshua Slocum sailed single-handed around Cape Horn.'

"'Indeed, father,' I said.

"'I fear,' he said, 'that you have never really understood this passion of mine. And yet the explanation is so simple. As a boy I read seafaring tales. Without exaggerating, I can say that I spent a large part of my childhood and youth at sea, without ever leaving dry land. But as with so many others, my life has been less windswept, less variable than I could have wished for or imagined. And so it has become vitally important to me that I should be able to keep my tropical dreams encapsulated in a bottle. Do you understand that, my son?'

"'Yes, father,' I replied.

"'And then,' he added, 'there is something I doubt you will ever understand: what it can mean to a man to channel all of his conscientiously curbed passion into coaxing such an expansive dream through such a narrow opening.'

"After that we went in to dinner.

"What I can tell you about that meal is that it was the Paschal feast, the Last Supper; I believe we all knew that we were performing a religious act. The cook must have served the food, but I never saw him; from that meal I remember only fleeting glimpses of his white uniform and powerful hands and the rich voice introducing the various courses, none of which I remember either. Was there pâté de foie gras, was there saddle of lamb, were there exotic fruits? I do not recall, for all of that was secondary to the company itself, all our senses focused on drinking in Ignatio Landstad Rasker for one last time. It was an ice skater's meal. Weightlessly we glided across a paper-thin film of transparent ice and the manner in which we satisfied our hunger and the aplomb with which we paced our intoxication was all calculated to heighten our receptivity to him who was about to die.

"He got to his feet and said, 'Drink up and make room for my ships,' and 'Eat up, for everything must grow, are we not all growing boys and girls?' And we laughed at him, a laughter dazzled by his radiance and by the sorrow lurking beneath the ice. The bishop made a speech, stood up without knowing why he did so, out of sheer emotion, and told us that this meal of which we were partaking was a Paschal feast, the Last Supper, and even this he managed to utter with a surprising jollity that was, in some way, determined by my father's manner. Then the men paid their tribute to him, with deep genuflections masquerading as amusing anecdotes in which they saluted him as a past-master of the well-turned phrase. I remember the professor recounting how my father had had in his employ a gardener who was sacked for having, for years, lined his own pocket through the sale of flowers and vegetables from his employer's garden, and who had then had the cheek to ask for a reference. My father had looked him civilly in the eye and then written, 'Of this man I can honestly say that he has got out of my garden everything that could possibly be got out of it.' But these superficially light-hearted anecdotes were underlaid by the deepest solemnity, every man there fell on his knees before my father, who accepted their tributes with a tolerant smile, and I thought to myself how good and how necessary it is now and again to encounter an individual who happens to be divine; and tonight, thought I, tonight no one shall betray or deny my father.

"Then he raised his hand and ran his eyes over us. 'You are mistaken,' he said, 'you are all mistaken, and if I might have your attention I will explain why I asked you to come here, though I fear that what I have to say is likely to lead to an *Umwertung aller Werte* and that, when I have said what I have to say, the greatest among us will be the least and the least, the greatest.' And we stared at him, the men composed but pale, the women with tears in their eyes.

"'I invited you here,' he said, 'because I have discovered that I cannot go on living, that my life is on the brink of its final collapse. And now, at the eleventh hour so to speak, there is something I wish to tell you, a matter for which I do not crave understanding, only attentiveness.'

"We all looked at him as one looks at a person one is seeing for the last time, and I knew what he was going to say. He was going to tell us of some fatal illness, something he might have been labouring under for years, but which had now flared up, leaving him no choice but to deliver his last will and testament to us and say farewell. I speculated as to what this illness might be, and came down in favour of a tumour, a rapidly accelerating cancerous growth that allowed no time for deterioration, for the diminishing of the great man before us. Instead he would suddenly and swiftly dwindle and fade before our very eyes, and then he would be gone, struck down by blind absurdity.

"But before that he intended to present his summing up, he intended to favour us, and especially me, with all his experience of life as naturally and harmoniously as the countryside around us; purified and perfect as a crystal of snow glinting in the sunset.

"'I asked you all here,' he said, 'to tell you of the Supreme Court's handling of the case against the writer Morten Ross, a case in which – as you will all know – judgement was passed three weeks ago.

"'That this case should have gone all the way to the Supreme Court, that the Ministry of Justice should have granted it a third-instance hearing, was due solely to the author's standing in the public eye and to the fundamental nature of the case. You may recall that the young man stood accused of offending public decency in his novel *A Daring Exploit* and also – in the grammar school at which he taught – of having had intimate relations with a sixteen-year-old boy.

"'On the matter of the book, the municipal court had sentenced him under section 184 of the penal code, which dates from the Freedom of the Press Act of 1799. The High Court confirmed this judgement and increased the sentence, the court being backed up by a long and distinguished legal tradition. If I might just mention the verdict on Moses Levin for his translation from the French of "The Sofa"; the verdict on Gustav Johannes Wied for *The Young and the Old*, and on Herman Bang for *Hopeless Generations*. And in a society with a judicial system closely akin to our own: the trial for blasphemy of August Strindberg.

"'On top of this came the damning relationship with a pupil, a relationship in which the boy had, to be sure, been a willing partner – indeed, in all probability, the instigating partner – but for which, nevertheless, the boy being under age and his consent therefore carrying no legal weight, sentence was passed according to section 185 of the penal code of 1866, relating to unnatural intercourse.

"'The Crown had originally also preferred charges under, among other things, the law of libel, the novel having been deemed to contain an attack against the very pillars of our society as well as exhortations to rebel against the established social order, but these charges had been dropped.

"'This left Morten Ross sentenced to three years' hard labour, with the entire print-run of his book being confiscated and Ross himself having to pay all the legal costs.

"'I have, in my life, had the opportunity to become acquainted with many different sides of life. Even so, I was shocked when I read this writer's novel in the weeks preceding the first sitting of the court. I worked my way through it, only a couple of pages at a time, having to lay it aside every minute or so and ask myself: what prompts such a young man to depict the refinements of sensual love with such coarseness and such insatiable lust?

"'Naturally I always approach any defendant with as open a mind as possible. But where this man was concerned, I knew from the very first time I faced him across the courtroom that he would have to be severely punished.

"'I know the newspaper men have been at great pains to describe the insolence of this young man. Let me just add that in his case even the constitutional mendacity of the press fell short of the truth.

''He appeared before the High Court without a defending counsel, intending to present his own case, and when he entered the courtroom for the first time, waved to the spectators, looked out of the window and grinned at us thirteen judges, I was put in mind of the trial of Oscar Wilde, while realizing that even yon roué's notorious, arrogant vanity would have seemed both polite and refined when set alongside the crude conceit of this man of the people.

"'The spectators' gallery was packed to the gunnels with the curious and the public prosecutor was rather on edge. I read his thoughts, I knew he was afraid that in the eyes of the common folk this was going to seem like the crowning with thorns of a martyr to the socialist cause; and he did, in fact, ask permission to speak.

"'"Your Honours," he said, "the law of the land sanctions the right to close the doors of the Supreme Court in special cases. Bearing in mind the delicate nature of this case I would ask that the doors be closed in the interests of moral wellbeing."

"'I looked across at the accused. I think I had been expecting some sort of protest or perhaps a sneer, but the young man merely adjusted his canary-coloured jacket, smiled graciously and leaned forward.

"'"Is the public prosecutor thinking," he enquired facetiously, "of his own or the public's moral wellbeing?"

"'"You," I told him, "will have respect for this court!"

"'He looked straight at me for the first time, sending me an intense blue look that spirited away everything except him and me.

"'"No, Your Honour," he said, "I will *show* respect for this court."

"'His eyes held me captive for just an instant, then I turned to the public prosecutor and denied his request.

"'"The trying of cases in open court is written into the constitution," I said, "and should only be prohibited under the most exceptional circumstances. Whatever takes place here must take place in the full view of all."

"'Very few of those present here have ever seen the offices of the Supreme Court in the Bernstorff Mansion House on Bredgade, but I can tell you that they are by no means spacious and at the second sitting of the court in the case of the State versus Morten Ross the hordes of spectators made them seem positively minuscule. They crowded right up to the bench, to the point where our court officers were growing uneasy.

"'While the clerk of the court was reading out the sentence of the High Court I observed the accused. On this occasion he was clad in a royal blue coat with a grey waistcoat and red stock and I was struck by the thought that such is youth, even at those moments when his fate drops its mask to smile at him like a death's-head, still he hangs on to the hope and the delight of being the one at whom it is smiling. As with his book, I thought, that naïve blend of prurient moments and lascivious, guiltless memories. Then he looked at me and all at once it dawned on me that those blue eyes could see every bit as far as my own, which is to say right through the walls of the court and across Denmark and into Horsens Prison, which would close around him then systematically break down his resistance, whittle him down to a gnome and spit him out again, a shadow of this creature now standing opposite me, listening to the catalogue of his own misdeeds. Now he is afraid, I thought, which is just as it should be, the court shall and must inspire fear, and as the recitation was drawing to a close, I envisaged that his sang-froid would have deserted him and he would have lost his tongue, thus bearing out the common conception that a defendant should always be represented by a lawyer and should not conduct his own defence; that he who is his own lawyer has a fool for a client.

"'The clerk of the court broke off, then called on the author, the defendant, Morten Ross, to proceed with his plea, and I saw that I had underestimated him, for at that moment he lifted himself out of his reverie as if from a deep well and, as if his atoms had been spread to the winds but had now returned and reassembled, he straightened up, glowing with impertinence.

"'"Your Honours," he said, "may I begin by saying of my opponent who, as everyone knows, if he had any more brains would be a half-wit . . ."

"'The public prosecutor was out of his chair, the courtroom was in an uproar and I was obliged to quieten everyone down.

"'"For this show of insubordination the accused is hereby fined two hundred kroner for contempt of court," I said. "Should he repeat this behaviour he will be expelled from the court."

"'Morten Ross lowered his head momentarily, as if swallowing a bitter mouthful. Then he lifted his face, cast a searching glance around the room and continued, slowly and clearly.

"'"May it please Your Honours. Of my honourable opponent, who now has the Supreme Court's ruling for the fact that he is indeed a half-wit, I would like to say . . ." and here the outcry from the body of the court drowned out his words. At that point we decided to postpone the rest of the proceedings until the following day.

"'Only under loud protest did the public deign to be herded out of the courtroom that afternoon and it may have been all this confusion that led the accused to leave behind a file containing some papers. At any rate they were lying there when the court officials cleared the room and they could have been put away in a cupboard; one might consider that they ought to have been put away in a cupboard but since my daily stroll took me, as a matter of course, past Nytorv and the jail I decided to deliver them to him in person. I thought to myself that whatever an author – even an author branded as immoral – has committed to paper should be handled with especial care.

"'In the Supreme Court burden of proof does not apply; no witnesses are called, the court sees defendants only in those rare cases where they present their own defence and so my visit to the jail was somewhat unusual. You should not, however, blame the officer who admitted me to the cell. You must understand that, no matter where I go, I am never alone; even when I divest myself of my judge's cape I remain cloaked in the authority of the court. Which is precisely why the Supreme Court is self-elective; why its judges may not simultaneously occupy other official or directorial posts. The life we live outside of the court can be no different from that led inside it, wherever we go we must uphold the principle of *juris immaculatio*, unblemished justice, and even on this little detour past the jail I considered myself well within my rights.

"'Morten Ross was sitting on a bench built in to the wall. He thanked me for bringing the manuscript. "It is the story," he said, "of a court case."

"'"I hope," I said, "that in this story you have endeavoured not to outrage public opinion."

"'He then asked if he might read this story to me and even now I have to ask myself what it was that moved me to stay. Of the moment itself I recall only the sun shining through the window set high up in the wall and the regal elegance of this young man in the midst of his degradation.

"'And he read me the tale of a young woman who stands accused of a crime and who, during her trial, conceives of the notion that all of the protagonists in the case, herself excluded, are mechanical dummies. Filled with horror and circumspection she mounts an offensive in which she diverges more and more often from the due process of law in order, by dint of her unpredictability, to uncover an area in which these automatons are not on their guard. This she succeeds in doing, and finally, sure in her belief, she steps down from the dock without anyone making a move and circles round behind the judge, who is staring blankly at the spot where she has been sitting, and she sees that every one of them has a key in their backs for winding them up.

"'More frightened, far more frightened than if they had been real, she walks towards the spectators and they too are of clockwork. But on coming face to face with a young man whom she had noticed earlier she stops, looks into his eyes and realizes that he is alive.

"'Here Morten Ross paused and I must have looked enquiringly at him because he then told me that this was as far as he had got, but that if I would visit him again he would have it finished.

"'At this I perceived the gravity of the situation: a judge paying a call on the accused and instigating a private conversation.

"'"I must leave," I said.

"'"It would give me great pleasure," he said, "if you were to call again."

"'"Mr Ross," I said, "I am not here to give pleasure, but to do my duty," and with that I left the cell.

"'The third sitting of the court opened with the defendant's statement. Deliberately, diffidently almost, he recounted the details of his affair with his pupil and despite the matter-of-fact tone of this account I noted how the court burned with a bright red flame of disgust and indignation at such insouciant forthrightness in the description of a subject as fraught with responsibility as sexuality; at how casually this character viewed the danger of corrupting the morals of the young.

"'Only in the gallery did I detect sympathy and good cheer, something I could not understand.

"'When the public prosecutor took the floor to make his rejoinder his voice was hoarse with repugnance. He said the State requested that the defendant's sentence be increased, for was not this punishable and perverse liaison, was not the accused's vulgar explanation, was not his sensually deliriant work a massive, concentrated attack on the chastity of youth?

"'At this Morten Ross stood up.

"'"Sir," he said, "your concern for the youth of today does you credit, but are you certain that you are not setting too much store by my influence and putting too little faith in the morality of the young? I should like to ask you: did you yourself feel overwhelmed by sensual delirium when you read my book?"

"'At this point I deemed it necessary to interrupt. "Mr Ross," I said, "the public prosecutor does not speak here for himself or his own private experiences. He appears in this court on behalf of the Crown."

"'"Ah, I see," said Ross. "Then in that case I should like to ask you, Mr Public Prosecutor, sir, whether during the reading of my book, you were filled with delirious sensuality on behalf of the Crown?"

"'And so it went on. And the public laughed. Never before had I found it necessary to raise my voice in court. Never before had I wished so heartily that I had listened to others and left it to justice to tame this character behind closed doors. When I announced that the court would now adjourn for the dinner hour he stood up, turned to the gallery and shouted to them that he would feed them all, "wait for me and my constable in the anteroom," he cried, "and we'll eat our fill and drink a toast to the Crown for having, through this trial, assured my novel of sales on which I have made a pretty packet!"

"'I spent that hour strolling along the city ramparts, his words having spoiled my appetite, and it occurred to me that he was turning the court into a playhouse. A book such as his ought to be met with a chastening hush, a liaison of the sort into which he had entered ought to be punished severely but in silence, the whole point being, after all, to eliminate an infection, to stamp out a sickness that thrives on publicity. Such a rake ought to be surrounded by emptiness and loathing, I told the wind; ought to hang in a dreadful vacuum. But look what has happened. Thanks to the court's insistence upon exactitude, upon the presentation of all the facts, thanks to all the weighing up of *pro et contra* we have instead stirred up the mud, we have spread the infection, we have stuck our heads into a hornets' nest. Now the book is selling like hot cakes, the public is laughing its head off, the newspapers are printing stories about him. We wanted to hush things up, to bury, to amputate, and instead we have aroused curiosity, given rise to titillation, we have fanned the embers of public prurience into a Saturnalian bonfire.

"'And doubt came and went by my side, and questioned me on the nature of justice. Is this what it amounts to? it asked. Is it not, then, clear justice that you serve but some obscure ritual? Is the Supreme Court not the ultimate seat of justice but simply the most grandiose of public brothels?

"'Not until I stopped in my tracks, straightened up and realized that I was feeling to see whether I had an aperture for a key between my shoulder blades, did I tumble to the fact that I had veered off course, that I was the one person in this country who must not entertain any doubts and when I raised my eyes the doubt was gone and I was once more utterly alone.

"'During the concluding stage of the proceedings that day we met the accused with new and crushing precision.

"'The prosecutor for the Crown read out appraisals of the book by a number of literary critics. Their findings were quite conclusive: "A defence of licentiousness masquerading as literature."

"'"Our critics," said the public prosecutor, "have cultivated and refined their faculty for judging literary merit. Consequently, their scholarly and psychological insight now makes it possible to determine that the artistic worth of this work ought to be rewarded by imprisonment in an institution for the criminally insane. If, that is, its author had not, with his profligate behaviour, proved how admirably suited he is for a spell in an ordinary Danish state prison.

"'The accused had nothing to say in reply to this. I sensed that he was on the verge of collapse and thought, now his soul is hovering speculatively above the inner wall of Horsens Prison, where it belongs. But this was not enough for me, I had to look him in the eye, had to see him attest to his defeat in this room, so I called him back.

"'"It is vital, Mr Ross," I told him, "that you understand the question here is whether your aim in writing this book was to produce a work of literary excellence or simply a piece of pure pornography."

"'He gazed at me from a great distance then slowly turned around.

"'"Who is to say, Your Honour," he asked, "that being pornographic might not be a literary merit?"

"'"There is a long and historic precedent for differentiating between art and what is simply sybaritic," I replied.

"'"Oh, I see," he said, "I think I understand. This exalted court is thinking of how Ovid was run out of Rome for *The Art of Love*, and how the erotic element in *Romeo and Juliet* was omitted from the Danish translation, and how Flaubert was tried for *Madame Bovary*."

"'Then he fell silent and after that he said no more.

"'But his last words remained with me long after the court had risen; it rankled with me that he had thus succeeded in firing off an impudent sally while, at the same time, heaping glowing coals on my head; it pained me physically and as I made my way through the city in this migrainous fog I composed a short speech to deliver to him, a speech the main substance of which was that of course the decision of the court does not simply reflect current tastes, of course an enduring standard does exist for the evaluation of fine and morally sound works of art and of course there are abiding ethical and religious reasons for considering love between persons of the same sex abhorrent; and this, I thought, I must tell him in person. Now that the court case is, strictly speaking, over, this responsibility rests with me alone. Who else could be expected do it, is it not the case that I *am* the supreme court?

"'"There was no surprise in the look he gave me when I entered his cell; and impassively he listened to what I had to say. He invited me to take a seat on his cot, but I remained standing; I had come only to deliver a message, history's and morality's message to an immoral writer.

"'When I was done he nodded.

"'"You came here to tell me this?" he asked.

"'"It wasn't as if it was out of my way," I said.

"'"He had risen to his feet and standing there before me he seemed to regain the fighting spirit of that first court sitting.

"'"I see, Your Honour," he said, "that you are a man who never takes the roundabout way; a man who on his deathbed will be able to say: I went *straight* from the cradle to the grave."

"'I have the idea that we were circling around one another like two contenders in a boxing ring.

"'"Yes," I said, "but at least I make progress, which is more than you will be able to say of yourself in Horsens Prison."

"'He smiled bleakly. "You have already passed sentence on me," he said. "So the court really did have a key sticking out of its back."

"'"What became of that story?" I asked.

"'"It won't ever be finished," he replied. "But I envisaged the man and the woman running away together, off into a brief burst of optimism that would come to an end when the girl's hands found the keyhole in his back. And they raise their eyes, having gone – so to speak – behind the back of the city, and see that this too is a stage set, a vast, soulless, mechanical conspiracy, a fabrication of façades and delusions."

"'"And where does this unlikely story end?" I asked.

"'"Having made her discovery the girl returns to the courtroom and takes her place in the middle of a new court case, without anyone noticing. The case runs its course and she is convicted of a crime other than the one with which she had previously been charged, and she accepts this sentence, since it is better to take part in a senseless mechanical ritual than to float around in a vacuum. So the story ends, Your Honour, where it always ends: in court."

"'"I was seized by a powerful urge to lash out at him. By rights, all of the centrifugal forces should have hurled us away from one another, but this was not what happened. Instead, we must have drawn a little too close to one another because suddenly, standing there before me in the sunshine, he seemed the most beautiful, the most naked person I had ever seen and I was drawn towards him like a meteor destined on impact with the surface of the planet to turn into a crater and a ridge of dust. But this was not what happened. What happened instead was that I kissed him.'

"At this point," said Hektor Landstad Rasker, "my father paused for a moment and gazed straight ahead. But he was seeing not us, his guests, but something else. 'And the only odd thing about it,' he said, dreamily, 'the only thing that was different and surprising was the gentle scrape of beard stubble.'

"Then he pulled himself together once more. 'The following morning we considered our verdict,' he said, 'all of us well aware that we were conducting this debate on the brink of a new century. We knew the future held a relaxation of the Freedom of the Press Act and a new outlook on the physical side of love. But more than this awareness of a new age, far more than this, that morning in court I was conscious of the presence of something else: of the defendant's arresting charm.

"'In the Supreme Court the youngest judge is the first to make his pronouncement, and the first six votes would have scaled down the sentence to the point of insignificance. I recall one of these six judges saying that what had been said during this trial had sown doubt in his mind as to the appropriateness of judging art and should this doubt not be turned to the defendant's advantage?

"'The next six cast dissenting votes, they wanted to uphold or to increase the sentence. They had not much liked what they had seen and heard in this case and they were now looking for this to be defused. The votes tied, just as I had guessed they would, a tied vote was what I had calculated upon.

"'I remembered the events of the previous day quite clearly, you must not think that I had banished what had happened to the deepest recesses of my mind; you must not think that I had been shattered against the surface of this young man. Quite clearly I saw my own fall, and I understood that I did not fall alone, taking with me as I did the entire judicial system; and with me, I thought, it shall rise up again, without anyone's being the wiser. And I spoke out lucidly and with feeling for the need to increase the sentence; I reminded them that the maximum penalty prescribed was six years' imprisonment with hard labour, and we cannot give less than four, I said. And so judgement was passed that afternoon and when it was read out I looked him in the eye and by then my equilibrium had been restored.

"'That night I found it impossible to sleep, so I got up and went out into the streets. It had been snowing and even though the heavens were black, the city gave off a muted, white light for all the world as if somewhere in a nearby but out-of-the-way street the moon, waiting to rise, were caught for a moment in the city's frosted glass bottle.

"'I walked the streets and on each corner fragments of my life awaited me. Silently we greeted one another and the snow muffled my steps. But outside all of your windows I stopped. In the course of that night I stood outside the windows of the public prosecutor, and outside yours, Chief Superintendent, and yours, ladies, and for a good while I stood outside yours, my son, and thought: behind those windows slumbers my life; and I tore myself away and continued, meeting no one and nothing but my own visions until finally I found myself outside the courthouse and I let myself in.

"'Just then the moon rose and bathed the room in a cool blue light, like liquid slowly infiltrating an aquarium, and in that instant it was borne in upon me that on this night I was to be put on trial, that the Supreme Court was about to ask me whether I actually had lived.

"'The counsel for the defence was the first to speak, I myself being said counsel, and on this particular night the court took the extraordinary step of allowing witnesses to be called and I called you, my boy. See, I told the court, I have had a son. And I called you, my dear ladies, the loves of my youth – ah, you seem surprised, you never knew, may not have had the slightest suspicion, but it was so; I called all of you and my wife as witnesses and said to the court: "See, these are the women in my life.

"'"And finally," I said, "I would like to conclude my defence by saying: I have to the best of my ability fulfilled my civic duty by diligently performing the duties of my office."

"'Then it was the turn of the prosecutor, he too being myself, and in his own singular fashion he seemed kindly disposed. "There is just one point in the indictment," he said, "which I should like to pursue: have you, Mr Landstad Rasker, ever been in love? Is it not true that you have never been fond of children? Is it not true that, shortly after your marriage and out of an aversion you yourself could not explain, you had your wife move out of the bedroom you shared and into a remote part of the house?

"'"And your youthful infatuations. Is it not true that you never returned the affections of these five women? That only with reluctance did you agree to trysts in empty apartments from which these women had been at great pains to banish their parents; empty apartments in which these women had made all the preparations for their own seduction, and no sooner did you feel the hands of these women on your skin than you were overwhelmed by an inexplicable nausea, by a sense of claustrophobic wrongness?

"'"And yet, Mr Landstad Rasker, you are a man full of love, a man driven by a fierce longing for sensuality. Is it not the case that these unfortunate trysts threw you into the depths of despair, in which state you sought out apothecaries who sold you aphrodisiacs whose want of efficacy led you to believe that you lacked the natural predisposition?

"'"And yet you know, Mr Landstad Rasker, and yet you know that you are a man possessed of an all-engulfing passion. But you have imprisoned it in a bottle. You have encapsulated it and labelled it and tucked it away to ensure that no one may rub the bottle and call up uncontrollable forces. And therefore the prosecution must ask: is it in accordance with the laws of life to act thus? Have you, Mr Landstad Rasker, lived? Have you truly lived?"

"'And I looked up at the panel of judges and they reached their verdict and sentence was passed.

"'Very early the following morning I went along to the Ministry of Justice, to see the permanent undersecretary, and requested the temporary release of the prisoner. It was an extraordinary situation, I no longer remember what I said but I do recall thinking: does lying really feel this easy? With the certificate of release in my hand I picked up Morten Ross at the prison, thereby contravening section 131 of the penal code, which carries the penalty of a standard spell of imprisonment or loss of office for anyone abusing their position in such a manner. The warden was surprised, but not as surprised as he would have been had he known that I was in the act of helping a prisoner to escape and thereby contravening section 108 of the penal code.

"'What, you might ask, was the prisoner's reaction' There was none. He was sleeping when I entered his cell and when I gently shook him he opened his eyes and I could see that he was wide awake.

"'"I have gone a roundabout way in order to fetch you, Mr Ross," I said, and I showed him the certificate of release. He looked at them, then stood up and dressed in front of me, and then left with me, all without saying a word.'

"Here my father paused," said Hektor Landstad Rasker.

All the time he had been speaking, the barrister had been standing up, as if he were in court. Now he was reminded for an instant of the fact that the three people facing him were his family and not his legal opponent and he looked around for a chair. Then his recollections took possession of him once more and his eyes gazed back into the past like those of a blind man.

"At that moment," he said, "those of us who were seated around the table could not look one another in the face. Then the cook stepped up to stand by my father's side and when he took off his white chef's hat I recognized him. It was the writer, Morten Ross, on whom sentence had been passed and who ought to have been wearing prison clothes, ought to have had close-cropped hair and a shovel in his hand but who stood before us with long hair, dressed as a cook.

"My anger was like the pounding of blood behind my eyes and I had to speak very slowly, so my voice would not fail me. 'You have committed an unlawful act,' I said.

"My father looked me straight in the eye. Then, 'I love him,' he said, and I felt as though loathing was about to make me take leave of my senses.

"'One cannot,' I said, 'love a man.'

"Then my mother spoke up. 'You are wrong, Hektor,' she said. 'It is quite possible. I have done it myself many a time.'

"'You shut your mouth, mother,' I said. Looking round at my table companions I saw that they were all in a state of paralysis.

"'What now?' I asked.

"'We are going to sail away from here,' my father said. 'An hour from now a fishing boat will be picking us up to take us to Frederikshavn.' And he added softly: 'We are leaving Denmark.'

"'And you, mother?' I said. 'What have you to say to all this?' And she, who had for as long as I could remember rattled off her replies, now took time to think. Then she looked at my father,

her husband. 'Ignatio,' she said, 'as far as I can see this is what you have always needed.'

"For a second or so my father looked directly at her and I suspect that at that moment they squared an account that had never previously balanced.

"Then he turned to the rest of us. 'I asked you all to come here this evening because, all unknown to yourselves, everyone of you was there, *in absentia*, on the night that an inappellable sentence was pronounced on me.

"'It was a sentence of death. The Right Honourable Ignatio Landstad Rasker, Lord Chief Justice, shall die and disappear, in order as it were to be born again. I longed for, I needed, you all to be in attendance here, at my funeral and my birth, these two moments being those at which a person must be surrounded by those he loves.

"'I know, of course, that from dust I have come, but at some point I must have turned away from the living. And yet it was my fate to turn my back on life only, nonetheless – from behind as it were – to be invaded by and filled with love.'

"At this I stood up.

"'Father,' I said, 'you will have ample opportunity to bemoan life and death and love in the Western Prison while serving your two years for abuse of office and two years for unnatural intercourse.'

"My eyes took in the others and in their faces I could detect nothing but doubt, the national sickness of Denmark. 'Chief Superintendent,' I said, 'would you be so kind as to do the necessary,' and slowly, as if moving through mud, the chief of the vice squad got to his feet.

"'Your Honour,' he said, 'you have unlawfully set free a convicted criminal. Naturally, you will have to accompany me to Copenhagen so that this whole affair can be straightened out,' and he moved towards the head of the table.

"At that moment my father put his arm around the cook in a gesture that was both protective and caressing. It was the first time in my life I had ever seen one man caress another and God willing it will be the last. For a second everything went black and I thought I was going to throw up, and during that momentary lapse of concentration it happened. When I opened my eyes once more the superintendent uttered a gurgling cry, reeled back to his place, sat down and laid his head, face down, on the table.

"Behind him my mother straightened up, both her hands gripping the handle of a heavy copper frying-pan that prior to this had been hanging on the wall.

"'Men,' she said, 'have fragile skulls and tiny brains.'

"There and then I realized that I was going to see both of my parents brought before the court and that I would have to testify against them, and it may have been as this was brought home to me that I grew up. I raised my hands. 'We need to talk about this,' I said, and my words soothed them, everyone relaxed their shoulders and I walked over to my father and his lover and delivered a short, sharp blow to the little cook's chin. He crumpled up as if his skeleton had dissolved into india rubber. Then I grabbed my father by the collar. I knew he would fight back and I knew I would have to knock him down and that I would do it, too; that this set-to was every bit as simple as those evenings in the Academic Boxing Club, apart from the fact that here there was so much more at stake. But first I wanted to talk to him, I wanted to give him the benefit of my unqualified opinion on what it means for a son to lose his father, because I had lost him this evening, and the words were on the tip of my tongue, I can remember them to this day. But I never had the chance to voice them. I opened my mouth, my tongue exploded in a white flash of pain and the next moment I found myself on the floor. Behind me stood my wife, your mother, Thomas – Eline Landstad Rasker, who is sitting right there – and in her hand she gripped a large green *bouteille* containing one of my father's ships.

"I eased myself into a sitting position and she hit me again. Lying on my back on the floor I said, 'You're hitting me, Eline,' but she made no reply and then I saw that all the other women were on their feet and all clutching frying-pans and heavy ladles and my father's bottles. Again I tried to rise but they hit me again and Eline's face swam down towards me and I remember what she said. 'Men,' she said, 'have to be shielded from themselves.'

"But I still had some strength left. 'Don't you see what you are doing?' I cried. 'He's a traitor and it is not only I, his son, who is hurt by this, but my mother too, and you, Eline, it is the whole of the female sex.' But they did not answer me and I have to admit that I wept, that I lost control. 'You bastard,' I yelled at my father, 'you pederast,' and then they must have struck me again because I remember nothing more, other than that they rolled me up in a rug without my offering any resistance and possibly they hit me, possibly I fell asleep, for when I returned to my senses it was all over.

"My father was gone, of course, and the little cook was gone and all the others were sitting here and there around the room in silence. And drinking; they had found the bottles in which he would have built his ships and now they sat there drinking – the women, my mother, my wife Eline, the bishop, the superintendent, the professors.

"I extricated myself from the rug and looked round at them but they avoided my gaze; even the superintendent, now sporting a white bandage round his head, avoided my gaze, and I realized that from these people there was no help at all to be had.

"One by one they left the room until at last only Eline was left. She sat with her arms resting on the table top, looking out over the black sea, and I will not deny that at that moment I was still hoping fervently, insanely for some explanation of or some excuse for all the things I did not understand. But she took no note of me, she merely gazed out into the night and then she murmured softly to herself: 'To have turned one's back on life only, nonetheless – from behind – to be invaded by and filled with love.'"

Hektor Landstad Rasker buried his face in his hands for a second and by the time he pulled them away he had himself once more under control. Then he turned to his wife, who had kept her eyes fixed on him throughout his narrative.

"Eline," he asked, "have I described it the way it happened?

"You have described it just exactly as it happened," she replied.

"As I am sure you will understand, Thomas," said the barrister, "I have found it very unpleasant but also very necessary to tell you this story. All that remains to be said is that I had myself divorced from your mother immediately upon our return to Copenhagen."

"Have you ever heard from my grandfather?" asked Thomas.

"Letters have been received from foreign parts," the barrister replied, "and I have returned them unopened. The last letter was received ten years ago."

Hektor Landstad Rasker regarded his father's portrait. "This story does not seem to me in itself to contain any moral," he said. "But it is my hope and my belief that it might be possible to come up with a moral here, at its ending. Thank you for hearing me out."

With these words he walked out of the room. For a split second his former wife sat on, not moving a muscle. Then she cast a fleeting glance at the newlyweds and left them, without saying a word.

Thomas rose and crossed to the window. Behind him in her

chair the girl curled herself into a ball like a cat. "Night has fallen, and we didn't even notice," she said.

Thomas walked over to the table and poured the last inky dregs of the port bottle into his glass. This he then raised and drained and his mouth filled with acrid dust and, too, with a tart, piquant suspicion of the substance of the earth.

"Yes," he said, "sometimes the night seems to creep up, as it were – from behind."

Then he walked across to one of the windows, pressed his forehead against the window pane and stared out into the night.

AN EXPERIMENT ON THE CONSTANCY OF LOVE

One of the most comprehensive linguistic exercises undertaken in this century has been the reflection of everyday life in the world of physics.

This story constitutes a warning against any such exercise.

It is also the story of just such a reflection.

It may be that this contradiction is not mine alone. It may be that it has become a condition of existence.

I am a theoretical physicist and in any linguistic field more complex than first-order formal logic I feel myself to be on unsafe ground. If I now, nonetheless, venture into the vernacular it is because I am hounded by my love for a woman. Or perhaps it is *I* who am hounding *it*.

There is only one thing I love as much as her: language. I worship it for its ability to surpass itself by pointing out its own limitations. With language I can say: "Thus far and no further my world extends" – and once this sentence has been uttered I find myself in a landscape of whose existence I had had not so much as an inkling. Perhaps that is where I will meet her.

I am said to be young (I am thirty-two years old), but that is not the case. There is no such thing as youth or childhood or age.

There are only those years when we have faith in and fight for the ultimate answer and those years when we endeavour to accept that we are always going to have to live with the questions. I myself crossed this shadowy boundary long ago. Long ago I resigned myself to the fact that all I can do is to pose the same few unanswerable questions over and over again in new ways.

Here – again – we have the riddle of why there seem to be women who move through life like salmon forging their way up a waterfall: in a glinting, opalescent arc of light and with a take-off so effortless that they appear always to be hovering and never in touch with those layers of existence that drag the rest of us downwards.

Charlotte Gabel was born in 1906, the daughter of the Danish ambassador to Paris and Lene Gabel, one of the first female Danish physicists and the first foreigner to be invited to work with Marie and Pierre Curie at their laboratory in the Rue Lhomond.

In 1921 Charlotte graduated from the École Marie Vierge which at that time lay in the Place de la Chapelle in Paris. In 1926 she took her doctorate in physics from the Sorbonne with a thesis entitled *On the term "past" in quantum mechanical measurements*. In 1926 she joined the Institute for Theoretical Physics in Copenhagen. In 1929 she returned to Paris to conduct her major experiment, of which only a handful of scientists in Denmark and Germany had any knowledge.

There she vanished from the face of the earth.

For some years the results of this experiment were eagerly awaited in Copenhagen and in Leipzig, but no word came. It was during these years that Paul Dirac formulated the equation which was to prove of such estimable significance to the development of the hydrogen bomb, Fermi made great strides in the production of enriched uranium and Niels Bohr was occupied with the principle of duality. In this futuristic current, Charlotte's theories about the past were forgotten and Bohr was the only one who, for years, at longer and longer intervals, would suddenly raise his head, stare somewhat fearfully into space and say: "We must remember Charlotte Gabel's experiment on the constancy of love."

The inertia of history will always work against visionary discoveries. But time is on their side. The day before he died, Bohr drew something on the blackboard in the study of his grace-and-favour residence in the Copenhagen suburb of Valby. For some time it was supposed that what he had drawn was Einstein's photon box and that the great physicist's last thoughts had been of his unfinished dialogue with his renowned colleague. As it turned out, this was quite wrong. We now know the box Bohr drew to have been the rectangular room in which Charlotte Gabel summoned up the past memory of elementary particles.

This is the story of Charlotte Gabel's experiment.

Since Bohr and Einstein we have all had to accept that every narrative invariably involves the narrator. I would, therefore, like to point out that this is – in the first place – the story of the Gabel sisters' life, as it appeared to the men who loved them. Viewed, that is to say, by solitary nightwatchmen standing under street lights, through wrought-iron gates and opera glasses, and clouded by the desperate ineptitude that always strikes those of us who love in the most inane fashion of all: from afar.

Charlotte and her sisters grew up surrounded by a social force field consisting of prosperity, *joie de vivre*, learning and refinement; bearing in the opposite direction from gravity and, hence, lifting up to the stars instead of dragging down to the earth.

They spent their holidays with uncles and aunts in Denmark, swooping through the long, light evenings on swings of Manila rope, beneath the dark-green foliage of the beech trees; on all sides of them stretched rosebeds and emerald lawns that sloped down to clear, blue water, and below them patient hands waited to pick them up and comfort them and put them into clean dresses of white, freshly ironed Swiss batiste, with the result that, to the boys who peered longingly from under the tall hedges, they always seemed like distant but pure-white butterflies fluttering against the backdrop of the verdant Danish summer.

In other seasons they adorned Paris. By their parents' sides they made an endless succession of entrances into rooms filled with gaily dressed guests, among whom the men, even when they were twenty years older than the girls, gazed at them as if they could not believe their eyes, then had to press their fevered brows against cool doorframes and remind themselves of the laws against such things and of the fact that they were family men and that there was nothing to be done about it because, faced with women – or even, as here, with little girls – who act as if life is nothing but one long, uplifting wave of crème Chantilly, men have always been seized by an enfeebled, defenceless, impotent awareness of being marsh frogs.

Any man meeting the sisters for the first time recognized two things on the instant and with absolute certainty: that in the company of any one of them he would find perfect happiness and that in their eyes he was of no interest whatsoever.

Such were the feelings aroused by the girls that men did not discuss them with one another, but if they had done so they would have discovered that they all felt the same: that any one of these sisters would have understood them as no one else ever had. Furthermore, from a very early age the girls were well versed in a wide range of subjects and adopted a soft, teasing conversational tone that caused the cynical diplomats and zealous scientists seated next to them at the dinner table to develop, within the space of a few minutes, a faint stammer. And so freely and easily did they dance that even the terpsichorean wolves of the dance floor found themselves, to their surprise, with two left feet.

When Albert Einstein encountered the sisters for the first time, at a dinner for the Académie des Sciences held at Colbert's palace near Robinson, the great scholar – as always when reality struck him as being at its most unfathomable – took refuge in religion. He shook his head at their mother and smiled his brilliant, childlike smile.

"Lene," he said, "Our Lord is a man, so not even he can be impartial. He has made an inconceivable exception and exempted your daughters from the acceleration of gravity."

This interpretation became widely accepted. How else to explain that no man, no place and no conversation ever managed to captivate these girls; that they glided into a conversation and out on to the dance floor, a moment later to be off, over by the door where a servant was helping them on with their cloaks, after which they sent the company one last, dazzling smile that revealed in a flash what might have come of all this? Then they turned their backs on the ballroom and the last that was seen of them was a toss of curls that in summertime took on the colour of heather honey and, in the winter, that of dark sherry. And then they were gone, beyond recall.

Throughout their childhood and youth each of the girls received a steady stream of letters from young men who had met them for the first time the previous day and who wrote to say that after a sleepless night they had been seized by a revelation of the two of them on a ranch in Australia, far from the madding crowd, with the lowing of the cattle all around them and a flaming sunset playing over their love, and they sent these letters in the full awareness that they would never receive a reply and with the suicidal conviction that they were pouring their love into a bottomless well.

Only a few went any farther than this and those who did so were offered a glimpse of landscapes out of which reared fresh and insurmountable obstacles. At the dinner during which Einstein dropped his rapturous remark, a famous German professor and gynaecologist tried his luck with the youngest sister, Charlotte Gabel. Having spent the main course giving her a detailed account of his research into the female sex drive and feeling certain, by the time they reached dessert, that the ground must be well prepared, with all the assurance of an expert he lifted her dress and placed his right hand on her thigh. Without the smile or the attentive expression leaving Charlotte's face she slid her hand down over the professor's and, with the stone in her only ring, laid open the back of his hand in one long, adamant slash. As he discreetly bound up his hand with a napkin as white as his face, Charlotte looked him straight in the face.

"Professor," she said, "you must also remember, in your next dissertation, to mention those unyielding parts of the female anatomy."

Many years later, when all the men who felt that the Gabel sisters had left them standing heard of the discovery of what were described as black holes in the universe, spots at which light and matter are sucked down into a mysterious centre and which give nothing in return, every one of them was struck, quite independently, by the thought that the Gabel sisters had been just such black holes.

It is my hypothesis that in this they were quite mistaken. Here you have another interpretation of Charlotte Gabel's early years. Bohr believed that opposites complement one another. It may be that there is something to be said for both versions.

Until the age of seven Charlotte Gabel lived her life in the belief that the universe had reached that stage in its evolution where every phenomenon constituted a promise and that she embodied the greatest promise of all.

As far as she was concerned it went without saying that the world was gravitating, in a sense, towards a point at which she and it would keep the promises they had made to one another.

There are some people who see love as one long string of minor exchanges and adjustments. Charlotte Gabel saw it as the one great and quite conclusive experiment. She kept boys and men at arm's length for the first seven years of her life, only opening up to them under sterile, social conditions, not because she was afraid or immune, but because she was waiting for the moment she knew would come, when the right experimental conditions would be present and she would have the opportunity, under unequivocal circumstances, to study the effects of love on her own system.

Her parents thought the little girl must be sick. The ambassador was a liberal-minded man, much taken by contemporary ideas on existential freedom and by psychoanalytical theories on a liberal approach to child-rearing. And so it was in a grudging and perplexed frame of mind that he bowed to Charlotte's demand that she and her sisters be sent to a Catholic girls' school.

Their mother, Lene Gabel, considered man an entity on a par with this century's major discoveries in the world of physics, and the masculine force no less strong than the radiation from Madame Curie's radium salts, which had left Lene Gabel with large, brown spots on her hands and a radioactivity in her spirit which she gave off in the form of an unquenchable passion for research. This woman found her daughters, and especially the youngest, incomprehensible. But she was forced to give in. She had the feeling that in Charlotte she was faced with some sort of natural law and, shaking her head and biting her lip in vexation, she accepted the fact that the sisters seemed only to play with one another, had a preference for enclosed, manageable surroundings and insisted on being driven to and from school, to and from parties, to and from the family's *maison de la campagne*, in the dark, closed embassy cars.

* * *

On the day of her seventh birthday Charlotte carried out her first experiment.

It happened at St Cloud, a rural suburb of Paris where Charlotte's parents owned a clutch of fieldstone buildings encircling six labyrinthine gardens and a well, not to mention reminders of the leading French poet Jean-Luc Torreau who, during the first half of the eighteenth century – at which time the house was still a *maison forte*, a miniature feudal fortress – was raised here, experienced the great and ill-starred love of his life here and finally, one day, vanished without trace together with his sweetheart.

It was a warm, clear day with a gentle breeze that seemed to be generated quite spontaneously at the heart of the garden and drew in its wake unseen clouds of flowery fragrance which had a stupefyingly euphoric, yet most illuminating effect of the sort which coffee and tobacco have been having on scientists since Descartes' day.

Over by the well, the ambassador was painting a portrait of his wife, whose pastel-coloured silk dress absorbed the sun so that she seemed to be clad in pure light. When she could tell by the sound of the girls' voices that they were far enough off she pulled her dress up higher and spread her legs dazzlingly at her husband. From outside, not a sound penetrated the garden and, all things being equal, the Gabel family and their surroundings could, at that moment, have been regarded as a closed, contented and harmonious system.

Then suddenly, on the top of the wall, high above the playing girls, a boy appeared.

At this point, the girls had not yet made their debut into society and they had never before been anywhere near boys under uncontrolled conditions. Through a hole in the fence surrounding their school they had a view of another school playground that was overrun several times a day by boys. But since only one girl at a time could peep through the hole they had wound up, not least thanks to Charlotte's theories, picturing the other sex as one swiftly rolling wave of noise, glimpsed only briefly and intermittently.

The boy on the wall, on the other hand, was sitting perfectly still. He had red hair and freckles and since the wall was extremely high it occurred to them that he must be a bird of some kind.

Then he dropped down into their midst and his voice when he opened his mouth was indeed as hoarse as a crow's.

"My name's Pierre," he said, "and I'm seven years old. Anyone got a fag?"

Then it was that Charlotte determined to carry out her first experiment and what followed was provoked not by the boy's intrusion into the four girls' Eden, but by something already present in Charlotte; by that combination of curiosity and hysteria that goes by the name of the enquiring mind.

First, the girls closed in around their visitor – children never stay surprised for very long – and thereafter they were all led into the farthest-flung of the gardens, seemingly by their play and the sum of a number of small coincidences, in reality by Charlotte.

In one corner of this garden stood an enormous Danish beer barrel. This had been done up as a playhouse with a door and a window, benches and a table and there, with her back to the warm curves of the wood, stood Charlotte, pencil and paper in hand. Gravely she eyed the boy.

"We're going to draw you," she said.

The barrel was so large that the boy could stand upright inside it, while the girls sat on the benches.

The best experiments grow out of the force field that exists between preparation and improvisation and at this juncture Charlotte was reminded of something her father – who attended life classes at the École des Beaux Arts – had said.

"When you're having your picture drawn," said she, "you have to take off your clothes."

The essence of play lies in acceptance, so the boy took off his clothes.

"All your clothes," said Charlotte.

The barrel was dark and cool, a giddy aroma of malt, oak wood, vanilla and alcohol hung in the air.

"But then I'll be stark naked in front of all of you," the boy objected.

Charlotte had another opportune recollection of something her mother had once said at the opening of an art exhibition.

"Before the artist we are all naked," she replied.

So the boy removed all of his clothes and the barrel was filled with a feverish concentration, as if the light-hearted game of a moment before had been but a thin layer of fabric masking the stark reality. The room began to expand, the walls soared up like the vaulting of a church towards a distant Heaven, as if the barrel had retained some proud but fiendish memory of this particular brewery's special knowledge of how to combine art, science and befuddling alcohol.

Pale-faced, the boy raised his arms towards the ceiling and began slowly to pivot on his heel.

At this Charlotte, the head of research, got to her feet. Her schooldays and the times in which she lived appeared to her in a flash, as images of the woman who reaches out towards the resurrected Christ, and then she wiped away the pallid Saviour and his *Noli me tangere*, for religion must not stand in the way of science, and tentatively she reached out for the white body shining in the gloom and placed her hand on one buttock. The boy's eyes were focused on the ceiling in rapt concentration and Charlotte Gabel felt each tiny, fair hair on her brown skin rising, felt an overwhelming multitude of promises being fulfilled, felt her hand on the boy putting her in touch with the fundamental meaning of life.

For a second or two she floated in that state of utter happiness that unites perfect harmony with the keenest alertness.

And then she had a scientific vision. Down along a never-ending procession of causes and effects Charlotte Gabel saw into the future and what she saw was that the happiness she had at this moment succeeded in isolating in the laboratory could never last. With overpowering certainty she realized that only like this, with her hand on the boy and this close to him, could she be happy. But outside the world was moving on, in a little while from now life would call them out into the sunlight and the boy would look at her with an interest that was already fading, for that is how it is with men and perhaps also with most women. She could call him back to her, but it would only be temporary, happening in spite of the forces which, moments later, would sweep him away again. With a sense of gazing into Hell, Charlotte perceived that the Eden towards which her whole life was orientated could never be anything but a fleeting state of order in an escalating state of chaos; that it would never be possible for her to abandon herself to the happiness she held in her hand right now and which she had always imagined, once she had attained it, would last for ever, because such is the way of the world that love is bound automatically to decay.

She stood there stock-still and her thoughts, maddened by grief, launched themselves off into space. And although she could not have put this flash of insight into words she discerned that the universe was elastic, that everything was expanding, that each and every human being was distancing themself from every other human being at an unbelievable rate of knots and that the spaces between the random particle collisions known as love were filled with nothing but the emptiness within which the sun will eventually burn out and crumble into a cloud of ash, while lifeless Earth, cooled to zero degrees on the Kelvin scale, subsides into the eternal winter of outer space.

This recognition of an all-embracing decline afforded Charlotte the chilling comfort that comes from seeing that it is only because one knows more than others that one is more unhappy and in that instant she understood that she would become a great physicist and show the world that the truth about love is that there comes a day when it is over.

Slowly she drew back her hand and walked out into the garden, and the others followed her with the heedful silence which children always accord one of their number who experiences a great hurt.

That evening, Charlotte went into the garden with the gardener and pointed to the high wall.

"I'd like something put up there," she said.

The old man knew of the little girl's fondness for flowers.

"Geraniums," he suggested with a smile.

The girl stared impassively at the top of the wall.

"Barbed wire," she said.

The next fourteen years served to confirm for Charlotte her theory that life is not worth living. When she turned twenty-one she conceived of the idea which would enable her to prove that this was in fact the case.

She had just reached the end of her studies in theoretical physics, a young woman surrounded by other young women who followed her fearfully and doubtfully with their eyes and men who would have given her everything, if they had dared and if they had not been convinced that she already had everything. Fourteen years of profound inner despair had left no external mark other than a forthrightness that never made detours and which a number of men over the years had interpreted as an invitation to them alone. In fact it represented a universal rejection.

Her idea came to her on the day on which the last people in

whom she had any trust let her down. On a morning as sunny as that of her birthday fourteen years earlier her sisters told her that they had given up being promises floating in thin air and had promised themselves to young men and had long since kept their promises. The ambassador embraced them and told them that he and their mother were thinking of retiring; told them of a little house by the water where they intended to paint one another.

Although she had had no clearly formulated plans Charlotte had always imagined that her sisters would carry on impressing an ever greater proportion of the world. She had never dreamt that they might, one by one, sink so low as to try to make just one other person happy. She had had the vague idea that her father could surely rise still further and return to Denmark and become, at the very least, prime minister. Now she saw that these people, her last allies, had dropped down to the lower energy levels where the rest of the human race was to be found and that whatever expectations she had had of them were gone, disappearing into space like a ray of spilt and useless energy.

So she turned around and walked away, determined never to set eyes on them again.

That day, Charlotte took a stroll along the banks of the Seine. To those who choose to believe that they have been born with an intrinsic amount of love unequalled outside of themselves, sooner or later the thought of suicide occurs. That day it occurred to Charlotte, and from death her thoughts turned to literature.

She had always read a great deal; in her mind the worlds of literature and physics ran side by side like two fields between which she could move with ease. In books, over the past fourteen years, she had found countless verifications of her bitter knowledge of life and so now she thought of death, of writers and of Paris.

She thought of Balzac, hounded by his creditors, with a bundle of manuscripts under his arm, making his way across the Place de l'Opéra, where he had had his young men lose their illusions and commence the descent into Hell. In her mind's eye she saw Émile Zola, talking and gesticulating wildly in the Café Trapp, doubled up with indignation and afflicted, like his characters, by equal measures of political repression and want of affection. And she thought of Charles Baudelaire, lonely and spastic in a brothel, burned away to a cinder by his attempts, through the agency of morphine, to replace the natural Hell of love with a mock Paradise.

Looking back across history, Charlotte felt that these men would have understood her as she had never been understood. People who feel with such intensity no longer exist, she thought.

At that moment she became aware of an inner concentration of energy, a sudden rise in pressure that told her she was about to have a wonderful idea, one which had not as yet taken shape. In this mood of impending, spiritual pregnancy she walked across the Pont Neuf. At the midpoint of the bridge where it passes the Île de la Cité the carriageway had been dug up because of road works and a boy was walking towards Charlotte. On a yoke round his neck he carried two buckets full of steaming tar and his naked torso, his hair and his face were black as coal. Only his eyes shone, as if just there the soot had been scraped away to reveal two slivers of blue enamel.

Charlotte was never able, later, to explain why she stopped in front of the boy. On the contrary, she freely admitted – to the one person with whom she subsequently analysed these events – that this was perhaps just the sort of incident which physics would never be capable of explaining.

With half her mind she abandoned her inner deliberations and looked at the boy, who pulled up short in confusion. Charlotte's apparatus was thus put in place and she proceeded to carry out the latest in a long line of control experiments which she had conducted over the past fourteen years. She carried it out in her head, because ever since Einstein theoretical physicists work primarily with intellectual experiments; besides which, Charlotte was convinced that love was best dealt with in theory.

With a simple sleight of hand she dismissed her surroundings and the onlookers in order to operate with as few variables as possible. Then she imagined that she approached the boy, reached up and kissed him. In one single, smooth action, of a sort which unfortunately is only possible in the laboratory, she slipped out of her dress, her shoes and her underthings. She pictured his astonishment, his trembling, his desperation and she leaned against him and dragged her nails slowly from his navel down to the waistband of his trousers. She unbuttoned his fly, pulled his trousers away from his penis, raised one leg, stood on her toes and slowly eased herself down over him.

Up to this point, this and all the other experiments she had so far conducted held the intense feeling of happiness she remembered from that first experiment in St Cloud, and from this point on it held the same apprehension of death. She knew how, even now, after the first time, his eyes would contain a glimmer of the future, of the indifference he was already starting to feel, and beyond that other images, until the last one of all in which he went away and she was left with her unrequited passion.

In that instant everything ran together to form a pattern in her mind. With a start she pulled herself together and smartly and purposefully she carried on across the bridge towards the other bank, with comprehension and calculations rumbling through her like an earthquake.

For one concentrated moment she reviewed her empirical material, all the boys and men who unwittingly had loved and failed her in imaginary laboratory tests, and she visualized all of this squandered love as a massive ray of infra-red heat being beamed out into space, or as a golden stream of effluent running into the sewer, and it was then that she formulated the first principle of love.

"Only someone," Charlotte said to herself, "who constitutes a closed system, can keep her love constant."

She lifted her face to the sun, drank in its warmth and was filled with a tremendous sense of power at the thought that her loneliness was supported by a law of Nature.

"As far as the exploitation level of love is concerned," she continued, "the fact is that only that first time do people love with all their might. Every instance thereafter is feebler than the first."

It struck her that her own, still-swelling passion did not quite tally with this model, "but then," she said, "I have never loved and hence no claims have been made on my energy. And so it shall remain, because," – and here she formulated the third principle – "because the only love worth striving for is one which lasts, and that is impossible since, in every system that opens up to another, energy is lost. There is no such thing," thought Charlotte, "there can never be any such thing as *perpetuum mobile* of love."

Never before had she come up with such an exhaustive explanation of her experiences over the past twenty-one years, but she did not stop there. Instead, with a great flick of the tail her thoughts took off from the surface and soared upwards into the blue sky.

"Whatever happened," she wondered, "to the stream of energy that people throughout history have lost in their vain attempts to get through to one another; where is Balzac's love for a hundred women – one for each novel in the *Human Comedy*; where is the inconsolable weeping that always sounded beneath Baudelaire's cynical veneer, and where are Zola's infinite reserves of sympathy?

"And where," she asked herself, and tears welled in her eyes, "where are the magnetic storms in which I was attracted to boys and men, and where is the strength with which I resisted?" And she answered this question herself: "They must still be there. There must be some trace of them, energy can be dispersed but it cannot ever disappear completely."

As Charlotte strolled through the Parisian springtime – past men who turned to look after her and thought that if it were possible to imagine the sun on two legs, then that was her – she was to all intents and purposes blind to the world. But in her mind she was travelling through a landscape full of momentous facts.

Behind her on the Pont Neuf she left the boy, having forgotten him the minute she walked past him. But the observer always has an effect on an experimental situation and behind her the boy stood as if paralysed, because Charlotte Gabel's gaze had administered an invisible injection of curare to his heart and because he had never before seen young women in the street in sleeveless dresses without their armpits being shaven, while from Charlotte's there had sprouted thick tufts of hair. But mainly the boy stood there, rooted to the spot, because in Charlotte he had recognized a little girl from a distant past whom he had seen once and never again.

By the time he regained the use of his limbs his wooden-soled boots had set solid in the fresh cement. They had to be hacked free with a chisel but on the road surface there remained a run of inexplicable footprints which stopped abruptly, as if just here someone had been lifted out of their life and into Heaven. Or possibly as an indication that Charlotte had the right of it in her crazy idea that whatever passion has existed will always leave its mark. In the years that followed it often happened that, from a cab, through a restaurant window or from a balcony, Charlotte would spy a young man standing on the other side of the road, seemingly waiting his chance to bridge the gap that cut her off from the rest of the world. It never led to a meeting and Charlotte was never sure whether it was always the same young man.

She became a doctor of physics amid an awestruck hush. By this time the modern physical world view consisted of a bewildering number of esoteric books and articles written by fewer than one hundred individuals.

Since Charlotte's principal was a personal friend of Niels Bohr, she asked him for a testimonial in support of the application she was sending to the University of Copenhagen's Institute for Theoretical Physics and one day, not long after she had formally been awarded her doctorate, the old man sent for her.

It was the first time these two had met in private and both had the sense of two eras being brought face to face. Charlotte knew that the eminent scientist still defended the modified Newtonian view of things and that he had spent the greater part of his life attempting to provide electromagnetism with an adequate formulation within the bounds of classical mechanics.

In front of him he had Charlotte's thesis. "Mademoiselle Gabel," he said, "I am too old to make any pretence. I confess that, as with your thesis, so with your application: there are whole passages where I have not the faintest idea what you are talking about."

"I am convinced," said Charlotte, somewhat testily, "that certain emotions automatically decay. In the lives of individuals and also down through the ages. That people in earlier periods of history have felt things far more intensely than do people today."

"This theory about the past being preferable," the old man said, "is more commonly paid homage to by people of my age."

"I am now certain," continued Charlotte, choosing to ignore this irrelevant objection, "that every emotion leaves some trace of itself, in people themselves and in the world around them. Every atom receives an energy impulse that is felt as a spin, a vibration; as a tremor within the particles, if you like. My thesis represents the theoretical foundation for these traces. I would like to develop this theory further in Copenhagen in order that it may form the basis for an experimental situation in which the traces can be registered."

The old man looked at her blankly. "Where will it all end?" he asked.

"It will all end with us being able to reconstruct the past," said Charlotte. "Just imagine that every wall might be regarded as a very delicate, light-sensitive film. That one day we would be able to call up every conceivable image that has ever passed over it. Picture the Louvre as an immense laboratory where we could elicit fragments of antique scenes drawn from the Parthenon frieze. Where every archway would still form a resonant cavity oscillating microscopically to the music of a far-off age. And where we can place a gramophone needle against the huge vase depicting Perseus and the Gorgons and perhaps hear the voice of the potter, laid down as a sound track by way of his fingers, like a lacquer disc from the sixth century BC."

Charlotte turned on her heel and left, and for a long while the scientist sat there, staring into space. Then he read through his letter one more time. In it he recommended Charlotte Gabel most heartily to his old friend. He dipped his pen in the ink once more and added one sentence. "Dear Niels," he wrote, "believe me, this girl is the most gifted physicist to attend the Sorbonne during my time as principal."

He stared for some time at what he had written. Then, with what was for him quite uncharacteristic spontaneity, he added: "But she is a psychopath."

The long string of scientists who in the course of time wrote their memoirs of their days at the Institute for Theoretical Physics in

Copenhagen remembered Charlotte for the light she shed on the place. The light of keen, intellectual thought with which she made her contribution to the common questions in a mutual atmosphere of delight in progress, ascetic stringency and wild fantasies. Her serene and engaging acuity during these discussions is referred to more than once in these biographies. But there was another side of Charlotte's light, her incidental radiance, which all of them omitted to mention.

In all probability, this radiance inspired the male physicists to improve upon professional achievements that were already considerable, but for many of them it was also to darken their memories of their time in Copenhagen.

In these men, surrounded only by other men, with their whole lives invested in physics and with a working rhythm that did not know the difference between night and day, Charlotte's presence evoked violent, breakdown-style chain reactions. Many were the evenings in the Institute library which ought to have revolved around atomic nuclei or the universe, around the minutest of entities or the most vast, but which instead wound up somewhere in between, namely with Charlotte having to turn down some unfortunate soul. Despondently she observed how these men, who counted among their number representatives of most of the nations of Europe, fell headlong and at speed from that position to which, to her mind, they ought to be raised by the lofty cause they served; how they hit the ground and, faced with her polite but steely touch-me-not air, slid backwards through the ages of their lives, from reason to outrage to fury until finally they wept like infants.

At this point Charlotte usually took her leave, sad and sick at heart because she could not help them. Only once did she allow herself to be stayed by pity, took an elderly Nobel prizewinner by the arm and presented him with the one great observation of his own life distilled into a single sentence.

"Go home and work," she said. "In physics there is solace to be found."

The majority of those papers on particle physics written in Copenhagen in the year of 1928 benefited from Charlotte's obliging generosity, penetrating insight and superb bilingual overview. But on the subject of her own project she maintained absolute silence. Niels Bohr alone was made privy to the problem in a brief conversation which took place the day after her arrival.

At the idea that every single particle should contain total recall of its past in the form of an infinitesimally small pattern of energy, Bohr had shaken his head.

"It will be very difficult to prove," he said.

"It has been proved," said Charlotte. "Now it has to be measured. It is time for me to reconstruct the past in the laboratory."

At this the renowned man of science had risen abruptly and, having made sure that the door from his office into the corridor was securely closed, with a strangely moved and distrait warmth he took Charlotte's hands in his own and whispered: "I want to play too."

He had spread his arms in a vague gesture that seemed to embrace all of the Institute buildings. "One big playground," he whispered. "One of the most expensive in the history of the world." He released his grip on Charlotte's hands and sank down into a chair, but his voice still did not rise above a husky murmur.

"I have a theory much akin to yours," he said. "The opposite of, but still, almost – complementary – to your own."

He leaned towards her. "I have this notion that the stars can burn for ever."

Charlotte was well aware that what she was witnessing here was one of the gurus of modern physics renouncing one of his gods and she said nothing.

"And another theory," whispered Bohr and Charlotte could

barely catch his voice. "Have you come across Rutherford? Can't add up. When he puts two and two together he gets five. But still seems to have an instinct about it all. Has a theory about the compound nucleus. Believes it would be possible to start a chain reaction. Wants to unleash the forces inside the nucleus. No way of telling which. It would be – the biggest bang in the history of the world. Has to be handled with care. But even so, just imagine. Like when we were boys. Gunpowder in a piece of iron piping, a stopper in each end. A little hole for the fuse. The most enormous bang. Blew tiled stoves to bits down on Gammelholm." Bohr looked straight at her. "We all play games," he said gleefully.

Charlotte sensed that the conversation was at an end, that the master's thoughts were slipping away, either inwards or outwards, but at any rate away from normality. She got to her feet and left. Of what the man she left behind had said she had understood virtually nothing, but she felt that she had his interest, his sympathy and his permission to do whatever she deemed necessary.

Niels Bohr did not mention Charlotte Gabel's ideas to anyone, but the following evening while taking a stroll with Heisenberg on the common behind the Institute he seemed quieter than usual and before they parted he stood for a while stock-still, as if he had something on his mind. Then he looked up at the dark-blue night sky, where at that very moment the first stars in the constellation of Lyra, the heavenly harp, were appearing.

"The way to the stars," he said suddenly, and seemingly à propos of nothing other than the celestial canopy, "takes the oddest detours."

That year scientists were invited to the Institute who brought with them mysterious news from the outer fringes of physics.

One day a famous German doctor and psychoanalyst gave a lecture in which he related how, relatively late in life, he had undergone a sort of conversion which had prompted him to leave his original field, the strictly physio-scientific study of the female pelvic region, in order, as he put it, "to penetrate still deeper".

As he underlined the exceptional objectivity of psychoanalytical theories with eloquent gestures, Charlotte's eye was caught by a fine white scar on the back of his right hand and she recognized her erstwhile dinner companion and expert in female sensuality.

For anyone else such a memory might well have affected their grasp of the lecture but as far as Charlotte was concerned the influence of the past on the present was an objective and not a personal state. She knew, long before the lecture was over, that she had found the collaborator she had always known she would, sooner or later, need.

With conviction and clarity the great scientist told the astonished company that the crux of his discovery was that when it came to their sex drive, human beings were of the same order as balloons. The more desire is bottled up, the more the pressure rises, and one was therefore under a scientific and humanitarian obligation to introduce the people of the world to the regular venting of this pressure; and he stretched out his hands to the audience as if the manual side of this venting was also something he intended attending to personally. "I have," he said, "learned a great deal from quantum mechanics. There is no doubt that a person who is subject to such an overload of sexual energy is in a situation similar to that of the atom, whose electrons – under duress, as it were – are held in energy-rich bands far from the nucleus and dream of leaping farther in still and discharging their excess energy into the universe. Ah yes, there is good reason for believing that pent-up sexual energy makes itself felt in the form of a kind of quantifiable electrical tension in every single atom.

I predict, ladies and gentlemen, that a term such as 'particle sex drive' will one day have its place in quantum mechanics."

Here, Niels Bohr put up a hand in enquiry, sensing instinctively as he did so that he was here faced with the first of a series of phenomena which could have incalculable consequences in the years to come.

"I would like," he said, "to warn against drawing inferences from the particle level and applying them to something as complex as affairs of the heart."

The doctor eyed him indulgently, then gave the physicist the answer which the majority of psychotherapists from that day on would employ to sweep aside all petty misgivings. "As a psychoanalyst," he said, "I have remarked that the objections people raise are almost always projections of their own personal problems."

That said, he carried on and Charlotte realized that this man's belief in his own infallibility encased him in the very armour necessary to render him stubborn enough to carry out what she intended to suggest to him.

That night she and the doctor sat talking in the Institute library until both felt that, by way of a number of new and promising detours, they had reached the stars now growing pale in the sky over Blegdamsvej.

That spring yet another person from Charlotte's past turned up at the Institute, someone who was to bulk large in her experiment. One day at a morning meeting Bohr introduced her to a Frenchman, the Institute's new gardener, and when Charlotte extricated herself from the young man's all too prolonged handshake and looked into a pair of blue eyes surrounded by freckles and red curls, a remote but persistent alarm bell sounded in her head. That same day she saw the new arrival working at a flower tub just across from her study. To Charlotte every kind of tension – other than the great, tragic, inevitable sort – was a waste of energy, so she came right up behind the gardener.

"What are you doing?" she asked.

"Weeding," he replied.

"Those aren't weeds," said Charlotte, "they're tulips."

He looked at the pile of torn green shoots.

"Even an expert can make a mistake," he said.

"Where have I seen you before?" asked Charlotte.

The boy met her gaze. "In a barrel once," he said, "then on the Pont Neuf. And then around and about."

Without any effort and without altering her expression Charlotte called up her memories of Pierre and set them up side by side.

Any other woman would have been lost in wonder at the coincidences at play here. But Charlotte had never reckoned with coincidences. She accepted them as an intriguing branch of mathematics and she did not discount the possibility that elements of unpredictability might be lodged inside the nucleus of the atom. But she knew beyond a shadow of a doubt and from her own undeniable experience that if a man kept putting himself within her line of sight then there had to be some underlying, far-reaching design.

"You've been following me," she declared.

He made no reply and, full of bitterness and vexation, Charlotte found herself thinking that here was yet another one who had wasted vast amounts of time and energy on a cause which she would soon prove to be quite absurd.

"You are a clown!" she snapped.

"Before the one we love we are all clowns," said the boy.

"Why didn't you speak to me?" asked Charlotte.

"The answer would have been 'no'," said the gardener.

Charlotte nodded thoughtfully. Then she turned and went

back to work and so expressive had her silence become over the years that behind her she left not the faintest doubt that the answer, now and for ever, would always be 'no'.

Charlotte Gabel and the doctor who became her scientific collaborator gave just one year of their time to Copenhagen and number 15 Blegdamsvej, a period of time not long enough for either the city or the Institute to become accustomed to them. But perhaps no random length of time would have been enough, since it was quite evident that in these two people an intense and unfathomable chemistry was at work.

Charlotte always arrived at the Institute early in the morning, before everyone else, having taken the tram from the outskirts of the city, from the boarding house for young ladies where she rented a narrow room containing a bed, a table and a chair. And she invariably looked slim – thin, almost – and pale as a very beautiful nun.

The doctor would put in an appearance late in the forenoon, coming possibly from his suite at the Hotel Konig Frederik, where he stayed for the whole of his sojourn in Copenhagen and in which he received his well-to-do female clients. And he invariably showed up in what was, even for such an informal establishment as the Institute, extremely casual attire – which is to say, in a white shirt unbuttoned far enough to expose the brawny pectorals and wiry, black mat of hair that were supposed to help his clients drop their defences and let themselves go, to slide down into the mangrove swamp of therapeutic transference. On this dark, hairy background hung a heavy gold medallion, as a reminder that in psychotherapy payment is important, a most essential part of the treatment, and perhaps also as a sign that spiritual alchemy is an objective, refined science that can never tarnish.

There was, in the mere sight of these two people together, something almost indecent, something which has been captured more precisely and more tactfully than here by the German mathematician Streichmann, in the little book he wrote about his time at Blegdamsvej. "Bohr said," he writes, "that it was the sight of these two people – the tall, perpetually sun-tanned doctor and the pale and slender girl – entering her study and locking the door behind them which led him to the final formulation of the principle of duality; the fact that opposites are complementary."

The doctor had once offered to give her a course of therapy free of charge. She did not answer him, but shot him a glance both fleeting and eloquent which moved him to run his finger slowly and tentatively along his scar. Never again did he make her such an offer.

Apart from the doctor, Charlotte enlisted the help of just one other person, a toolmaker who had been largely responsible for most of the Institute's experimental setups but whose energies Charlotte now commandeered completely. In the basement she had him build a small, windowless workshop. This was always kept locked and here he worked under Charlotte's supervision for nine months, during which time his face took on an increasingly hunted look. At the end of that time, he handed in his notice. Bohr could not summon up the courage or the presence of mind to ask for an explanation, but the craftsman himself read the question in the physicist's eyes. "I've built a machine for Miss Gabel," he said. "She says it's a big secret. But this much I can say – it's called a 'histometric discharger'. I know that Miss Gabel is going to demonstrate it for you some day. And when that day comes I want to be quite sure that I am far, far away from here."

Around this time Charlotte advised the staff of the Institute that she was looking for a guinea pig. Any other scientist would have been asked to provide some sort of explanation but no questions were asked of Charlotte.

No one volunteered. Under normal circumstances Charlotte

attracted everything, especially her victims, but the personnel at Blegdamsvej sensed instinctively and with unease that the pills which she and the doctor had been rolling in private were most likely too strong a medicine for anyone wishing to maintain their good health long enough to make their name in scientific circles, and to become engaged. Everyone smiled encouragingly, but no one came forward.

As it happened, Charlotte Gabel could not have used them anyway. During her last few months in Copenhagen it had become clear to her that what she was seeking was a very rare commodity and until she could ascertain whether it was at all to be had, she lost no sleep over her colleagues' reluctance.

And then the gardener volunteered. He called on her one day when she was alone in her study, the first time they had been alone together since their talk by the flower tub. Face to face with this boy she was conscious of an inexplicable shyness which, she told herself, could be put down to his stupidity's being so great that she could not help but be just a mite upset on his behalf.

When he had said his piece, she asked him:

"Have you heard of Marcel Proust?"

"Is he the one?" the boy asked with a snarl, as if willing, were that the case, to knock out this rival's teeth so as to assume his place in Charlotte's laboratory.

"He's dead," said Charlotte coldly. "He was a writer. To begin with he couldn't remember a thing. But when he caught the scent of a certain cake he was swamped by a torrent of memories that filled three thousand pages."

"Hand me a cake," said the boy, "and I'll remember enough for four thousand."

Charlotte stood up. "That," she said, "is the problem. What I need is someone who, even in the baker's shop of the town in which they were born, wouldn't be able to come up with two lines. I'm looking for someone with no memories."

She walked out of the room and along the corridor. The boy stood forlornly in the doorway, following her with his eyes. "Christ Almighty," he yelled, "in that case, what you need is some sort of turnip that can talk."

Charlotte did not look back. "Then that's what I'll get," she said.

That evening Charlotte was filled for the first time ever with a clear sense of having given Copenhagen as much as she could and having received as much in return as that city had to offer. A fortnight later she and the doctor left Copenhagen for Paris.

During those last fourteen days she drew up an outline of her experiment. This outline is very, very concise and couched in such general terms that today it has to be said that, with only this to go by, it must have been impossible to form any image of what she actually had in mind.

Nonetheless, this outline formed the basis of those applications for funding by means of which she succeeded in drumming up the extraordinarily large sum that enabled her to do what she did.

Her applications did not meet with an altogether unreserved response. Even though Bohr had recommended her to the free-flowing source which financed the heady years at Blegdamsvej and even though this source did also pay up, Charlotte had the feeling that the hand which had written the cheque had shaken with barely explicable reluctance.

In Paris she applied to the Chambre de Commerce et de l'Industrie and along with her grant she received a missive which voiced certain misgivings. "There is," it read, "a noble and conservative idea which says that society is a tree, politicians its gardeners and foresters and science their advisors. With this in mind, the Chamber views with concern a theory such as yours which regards the future as an emotively debilitated offshoot of the present.

"That the Chamber nevertheless has decided to approve your application is due to the fact that there is another great conservative idea which says that the past contains feelings and forces which, consolidated and refined, should be passed down through the ages."

No other person in the world was better placed than Charlotte to understand why these grant authorizations were so unusual and so obviously at odds with themselves. No one else could have had such a comprehensive understanding of the celibacy of science, of how it had struggled to turn its back on importunate reality. And knowing this, she also knew that they dished out with the one hand while making warding-off signs with the other, sensing as they did that the theory she advanced was one from which the world of physics had turned away, not wanting to have its sleep disturbed, but which it had nonetheless gone on dreaming of, all through the night.

Only once she reached Paris did Charlotte announce that her experiment was to be conducted in St Cloud, a suburb of Paris, in the Gabel family's gardens. The doctor would have pointed out the risk involved in experimenting with love in the place where one has grown up, but with her goal in sight Charlotte's patience grew shorter and her imperiousness increased, to the point where now, even with the doctor, she acted as if she were the representative of all of the natural sciences that had flourished since the Renaissance and no longer countenanced any objections. And it was this imperiousness which made it possible for her to explain to her parents and her sisters that she had come back not to ask for forgiveness but to persuade them to move out of the houses in St Cloud and leave them in her hands.

They moved out and, as with the doctor, refrained from asking any questions. Throughout this century it has seemed reasonable to refrain from asking questions and to abandon house and home in the name of scientific progress. Besides which, they were grateful to have had their prodigal daughter and sister returned to them.

Then Charlotte moved in and while she was in the process of setting up her laboratory even the doctor was banished from the place.

It later transpired, from bills sent to the Chambre de Commerce, that ten craftsmen had worked for three months under the direction of a museum curator whom Charlotte had unearthed in some far corner of the Louvre to which no visitor ever found their way, simply because they would never have been able to find their way back out again, but which contains a complete collection of French interiors from the past four hundred years.

One afternoon, after all the work had been completed, the doctor arrived at St Cloud. He too had been kept in relative ignorance by Charlotte so not even he could have been prepared for the sight that met his eyes.

He had never had any interest in the past. As a doctor his attention had always been channelled forward and as a psychoanalyst it was his belief that modern science had begun with the publication at the beginning of the century of Dr Freud's book on the interpretation of dreams. The fact that he had instantly tuned in to Charlotte Gabel's scientific wavelength could be put down to his having caught a whiff, beyond the history of his own century – which to his mind was the era of psychic and, in particular, neurotic damage – of a red-hot, seething past, a long ruttish extension of the Middle Ages. And, in this, his theory of the past was a variant of Charlotte Gabel's. What he was hoping to find was sheer, exuberant, uninhibited, historical sexuality.

He was, to begin with, somewhat disconcerted, because the room into which Charlotte ushered him was a most austere apartment. The walls were white and divided up into tall, rectangular, blank sections by narrow gold lines. The furniture too was white, upright, expectant. But over this concentrated simplicity fell a prodigal light, breaking through the leaded windows as if through a prism, to send a broad rainbow pouring across the floor of the room. The doctor looked out on to a soulful garden with a lawn soft as velvet, on which some low shrubbery half concealed, half threw into relief a sandstone monument. At the base of a column, beneath a statue of Rousseau, a child could be seen holding a pitcher from which a thin stream of water meandered downwards through the sunshine.

"That," said Charlotte, "is how the outside world looked to the writer Jean-Luc Torreau."

She then proceeded to tell her colleague and confederate about the famous artist, the story of his love affair and his mysterious disappearance.

The doctor's eyes fell on the desk, on the fresh goose-quills, the slivers of metal set into notches in the feathers to hold the ink, the sheets of paper covered in writing, the blank sheets, the penknives, a water jug, a tin mug, all without any of the museum exhibit's dull film of desolation, looking instead as fresh and bright as if someone, some person of whose proximity the doctor was suddenly very much aware, had just this minute put them down, and he realized that here, at this point in space, Charlotte Gabel had recreated an atom of the eighteenth century.

"This," said Charlotte, "is our laboratory."

The doctor leaned his head back and surveyed the twelve ceiling panels in which an itinerant artist had depicted the Sermon on the Mount, beginning with the calling of the apostle Peter, in pigments that were scarcely dry.

"Dr Bohr," he said, smiling, "would have seen this as an attack on science."

"I am not come to destroy," quoted Charlotte gravely, "but to fulfil."

"It surprises me," the doctor said in an attempt to keep things light, "that you should have chosen to have this room overlook the garden and not the street. With such enterprise as you possess it would surely have been possible to take St Cloud a couple of hundred years back in time."

"I did consider it," said Charlotte, "but it would have raised some difficult questions regarding the ethical responsibilities of science. I elected to leave the answering of those questions to Bohr."

She thought of the conversation she had had with Bohr in his office over a year ago now. "The future," she said, "will not only bring up the matter of shifting a village of one thousand five hundred inhabitants. It will point to the cities of the world and ask whether they ought to exist at all."

"Fräulein Gabel," said the analyst, regarding the paintings on the ceiling, "you have a religious streak."

"The Sermon on the Mount," said Charlotte with satisfaction, "contains a radical theory on love. In it the Saviour presents himself as one who brings mankind word of the nature of love, that once existed but has since been lost. It represents the first, intuitive formulation in history of what we are here to prove: that love decays."

"It would have been interesting to hear the Saviour's views on such an interpretation," remarked the doctor.

"Some day," said Charlotte ominously, "we'll summon him up in the laboratory and ask him."

That night, for the first time, Charlotte Gabel presented her colleague with a detailed description of her experiment and, overcome by emotion, the doctor heard her out. At a small table in the garden they sat and talked the night away, and across the heavens travelled the same constellations that had shone down on their working nights in Denmark. The change in the seasons had now pushed these further west, the journey south had shifted them further to the north and something else, something hard to explain, seemed to have brought them closer and made them more accessible. When Charlotte reached the end of her exposition the doctor, who had not laid a finger on her since that painful evening ten years earlier in Colbert's palace, clasped her hand, but this time his touch was humble, beseeching and ecstatic.

"You are an explorer," he said, "discovering a narrow and perilous strait running from science to art and venturing into it, setting aside all thought of personal safety."

With an air of modesty, Charlotte leaned back in her chair and gazed into the darkness, at the outline of what, to the doctor, looked like a huge barrel.

"Seek, and ye shall find," she said.

During the winter of 1928, Charlotte Gabel and her partner conducted six experiments using six different people. All carried out in greatest secrecy. At no time thereafter did Charlotte ever speak of these first experiments. Each one lasted two days and for the rest of their lives the test subjects maintained a strict silence on the forty-eight hours they had spent inside those high walls.

There seems to be no doubt that these first attempts proved fruitless and that by January 1929 the doctor at any rate was beginning to fear that they would never achieve a breakthrough.

At the end of February, Charlotte caught sight of Pierre, the clown, the gardener from Blegdamsvej, in Paris. She had resumed her girlhood habit of walking along the banks of the Seine when she needed to think, since her thoughts seemed then to flow as smoothly and freely as the river, and on one of these walks, while crossing the Pont Neuf, her attention was drawn by a commotion of some sort in a little square behind the Tabac Henri Quatre.

What the people were watching was the gardener. Initially,

Charlotte was filled with a powerful rage that would have washed her away had not a surprising flash of insight told her that the young man had changed.

He was on his own, and giving a curious performance in which, out of little incidents taking place round about him, he fashioned an edifice in the here and now. A lady came by holding a child by the hand and, all unbeknown to her, with a single sleight of hand he removed the child's hand and replaced it with his own. Knees akimbo he walked along beside the woman until the laughter of the onlookers prompted her to look down and then race back screaming to fetch her child. Then Pierre's eye fell on a man walking past with two greyhounds. He growled so realistically that the greyhounds lost their heads and in a trice were at each other's throats. Charlotte was drawn irresistibly closer. There was an element of supreme ruthlessness about the gardener's inventive energy and also, where he himself was concerned, no fear whatsoever for the consequences. "For him, right now," thought Charlotte, "there is neither past nor future."

She was standing in the very front rank of the crowd when she saw him keel over on to the paving stones. For a split second she feared for his life, until she, along with everyone else, tumbled to the fact that he was feigning a heart attack in order, from his prone position, to look up her dress. This last trick lost him the sympathy of his audience, however, and irate gentlemen began to close in around him. Alarmed but unrepentant he got to his feet and just for a second he looked Charlotte in the eye. And she realized that something must have happened to him, because there was no flash of recognition in his gaze, the blue eyes were blank and desolate as an untenanted room. And yet in the set of his shoulders as he ran off, thought Charlotte later, there had been something of the dullard's glee at having drawn attention to himself.

That evening, Charlotte wrote to Bohr, and at the end of her letter she enquired about his gardener.

Three weeks later she received a reply. Bohr's letter was a disjointed epistle, rambling for the most part around a discussion he was carrying on with Einstein, but in closing he wrote sadly and in all innocence that he had lost his gardener. Immediately upon Charlotte's departure the young man had shot himself in the head. He had, however, survived and some months later had been able to leave the hospital. But he had not been able to return to his old job, the bullet having ploughed its way through the *lobi frontales*, short-circuiting in the process the billions of little electrical currents which go to make up the sum total of our experience of life. As Bohr understood it the boy had suffered a total loss of memory.

Charlotte showed this letter to the doctor, while telling him about the gardener's antics near the Pont Neuf. And then she announced that this man with no history, this person who lived only in the present was just what they had hitherto sought in vain.

At this, the vague and awkward inkling of a conscience stirred inside the doctor. He recalled the way in which the young gardener's eyes had gazed over and beyond his lawn mower and through the laboratory window, at Charlotte's bowed head.

"I think perhaps you have made him suffer enough," he said.

Charlotte stepped up to within an inch of him. "What's this I hear?" she said. "A psychoanalyst appealing to a neurotic twinge of remorse?"

She went down to the Pont Neuf every day after that. It took her a week to locate the youth. After the show she walked up to him and held his gaze as she dropped a coin into his cap, her seasoned, girlish mind constituting at that moment an infinitely sensitive voltmeter which would have detected the faintest spark of recognition. But there was none. Senseless love and a bullet, one of European physics' most far-reaching advances, had discharged this young man's batteries once and for all, leaving him all alone with what Charlotte had been seeking for so long; a life with no past, lived only in the present.

When he left she followed him, keeping her distance; along the Seine and then northward, towards Père Lachaise cemetery, where Paris grows dark, impenetrable and dangerous. Outside the building into which he disappeared, Charlotte stood for a minute, pondering the fact that any experiment which transcends the bounds of science will also have to cross certain social barriers. Then she went after him.

He was living in a basement room barely large enough to allow them both to sit down. Even in the feeble glow of a hurricane lamp he recognized her.

"I saw you on the street today," he said.

"Have I seen you before?" asked Charlotte, watching him intently.

He shook his head dejectedly. "I don't rightly remember," he said.

"I came to ask you to do your act. Three days running. In St Cloud," said Charlotte.

"Five hundred francs," said the youth.

Charlotte could have wept for joy, but still she did not feel altogether sure.

"Five hundred francs is a lot of money," she said.

"Olga, the woman who cooks my meals for me, says that people like us, the poor in spirit, shall inherit the Kingdom of Heaven. The five hundred is by way of being an advance." Still Charlotte felt a vague sense of unease and for one last time she studied the face across from hers, but it was smooth and almost childlike, as if life had run across it, leaving not the slightest trace. She asked him if he could read, wrote down the address clearly and deliberately on a piece of paper, added some francs for his fare, wished him *au revoir* until the morrow and left.

* * *

The next day, March 18th, Charlotte Gabel and the doctor briefed the young man who had lost his memory on their experiment. It was the first time they had fully and frankly let a third party into their secret. "Two hundred years ago," Charlotte explained, "a young poet by the name of Jean-Luc Torreau lived in this house. In the house you can see on the other side of the garden lived the girl he loved."

"That was a nice arrangement," said the gardener.

"They never went so far as to touch one another," said Charlotte. "For two years they lived here, separated by a wall of convention, and during these two years he wrote two collections of poetry which sensitive souls say they still cannot read without being moved to tears."

"What sort of wall was that again?" asked the gardener, looking out of the window.

"Not a real wall," explained Charlotte patiently. "An invisible wall built out of their parents' mutual hatred and out of her wealth and his poverty and out of the circumstance that he held no office and out of a promise her parents had made to each other."

"It never occurred to them to climb over it?" asked the gardener.

"That is what we wish to discover," said Charlotte. "The young couple are known to have met now and again, well-chaperoned, in this room. On the night of March 19th 1731 a family party was held here. At some point this came to an end and the two young people were left alone with an elderly uncle. Everyone else had gone to bed. The next morning they found the uncle in this chair" – Charlotte motioned towards the chair in which the doctor was sitting. "He was dead. Apparently the victim of a heart attack. The young couple were gone. Since then all sorts of ideas have been put forward: kidnapping, foul play, theories involving the supernatural. What we are looking for is proof positive. We believe that this room and these walls must still retain some memory of that night."

The gardener was silent now, and attentive; and, thought Charlotte, this is one of the fortes of science: the ability always, in the end, to capture the attention of the world.

"The theoretical explanation on which this is based is not something you would ever be able to understand," she said. "But here we have transported this room and this garden back to March 1731. In the room next door there is a spinet on which a musician will play an arrangement of Telemann's French overtures. To help you attain the right level of susceptibility the doctor here will hypnotize you. In the deeply relaxed state which this will induce in you I will first connect you to an instrument called a histometric discharger and then walk you through this room. I will also read aloud to you from Jean-Luc's own diaries in which he described the two years during which his love filled these rooms."

"And what then?" asked the gardener.

"If we knew that," replied Charlotte, "then this would not be necessary." And she went on to tell him about the three principles of love, about the memory of particles and the natural decay of love.

That evening, the night of March 18th, the doctor got the young man to swallow a spoonful of a bitter drug, a mixture of cola nuts, poppy seeds, the red stalks known in East Africa as *Mira* and a small, conical mushroom he had picked with his own hand the autumn before, just after the first frost, on sloping Danish meadows, all pounded to a paste in a glass mortar. This the gardener meekly gulped down, it being the way with medicine in this century that people take it without question. Thereafter, this eminent expert on the human mind – clad on this solemn occasion in a white coat – bent over the youth, plunging him first of all into a deep sleep, then raising him to the surface of the hypnotic state's vast, mirror-like sea of as-yet-unformed awareness.

At this point Charlotte took over, helped the gardener up out of his deep armchair and led him into the room which was to form his arena.

Outside it was pitch-black night, and with the cogent scientific mind's covert delight in mysterious parallels and synchronisms Charlotte noted that the storm which the young Jean-Luc had heard blowing up two hundred years before, and preserved for posterity in his diary, was once more beating against the windows and making the willow branches whiplash menacingly over the monument bearing Rousseau's sensitive features.

The room was lit by stout wax candles in heavy pewter candlesticks. The warm, flickering light accentuated the gardener's elegant and authentic costume: the tight knee-breeches, the silk stockings, the thigh-length redingote of pleated German linen and the white lace stock. At the same time, the light hid – or rather, rendered invisible – those tenuous threads leading back to the twentieth century: the rubber tubes running from the cuff around his wrist to the sphygmomanometer sitting on the table in front of the doctor, the wires from the little electrodes for measuring the potential difference around his rectum and the coiled cable that ran from a cannula in the gardener's thigh to the histometric discharger.

The young man's eyes were open but his face was devoid of expression and white as a sheet of paper that is only now to be written on. And behind him stood Charlotte Gabel, erect and alert with the poet's diary open in her hands. Gently and adroitly she guided the man standing in the middle of the room back to the eighteenth century, to a time when love still burned full force.

For two hours she walked him around the room, her concentration not flagging for an instant, while she read the poet's descriptions of a day-to-day life in which the smallest things had absorbed the weighty significance of the loved one's proximity, and at midnight, just as she was considering stopping, they made contact for the first time. Charlotte had been describing a social gathering, an inconsequential courtesy call made by people almost unknown to the poet. Even so, in his diary he had held up this social gathering like a huge cut diamond which he allowed to sparkle, letting its light pour over his fingers like molten gold, because his beloved had been among the callers.

A shudder ran through the gardener and he began to speak to the empty room, conversing with people visible only to him. In his chair, the doctor – a man with a lifetime's experience of looking down into the abyss without flinching – went rigid and Charlotte felt every single fine, blond hair on her skin rising. And still she read on, deliberately and unwaveringly, until even that became unnecessary and she let go of the gardener, Jean-Luc, and left him free to float into the past.

For some time – though later neither of them could say how long or short a time – the two scientists watched the young poet chatting and bowing and laughing genteelly and yet boyishly, until all at once he staggered and all but fell. Together they eased him down on to a sofa, and the doctor closed his eyes, removed the cuff, the electrodes and the cannula, and brought him out of hypnosis and into a deep sleep.

The following day they plied him with questions and were treated to a strangely fascinating depiction of those visitors who had, two hundred years before, circulated around the poet. Only one portrait was hazy to the point of invisibility: that of a young woman. Speaking of her, the gardener said it was as if he could not get a fix on her.

"That's odd," said Charlotte, "when we're talking here about the most powerful emotion he had ever felt."

"Maybe he wrote it out of his system in his books," the gardener suggested.

"Impossible," said Charlotte. "To a man of passion, love is a maze. Every path looks like a way out, but all lead back to the centre."

"And how, if I might ask," said the gardener, "does Mademoiselle know this?"

"I read it somewhere," replied Charlotte dismissively, and once more she felt a tiny twinge of unease that she could not pin down.

At 10 p.m. the doctor checked his instruments one last time and gave Pierre his medicine. Then he hypnotized him. At 11 p.m. Charlotte started reading aloud from the diary.

An hour later contact was made. A jolt ran through Pierre, as if an invisible hand had reached back through time and dragged him back with it into the party marking the last occasion on which Jean-Luc and Marie-Claude were seen together.

Outside, the storm had intensified, and it crossed Charlotte's mind that the garden was no more than a flimsy, newly planted backdrop and that, in the event of thunder and lightning, the electrical instruments might short-circuit. But the doctor was beside himself with excitement. He had spent his life groping his way, more or less blindly, through gynaecology and subsequently through the psyche, but only now had he stepped out into the light; confidently his hands now manipulated the instruments and the mortar with its blend of hallucinogens; his temples pulsated and he had the feeling that the wind that howled across the roof was the overwhelming, primordial, pagan lust that he had unleashed.

In the room, this blast manifested itself as a faint keening and a flicker of the candle flames, and against this background the gardener peopled the room. Graciously he mingled with his unseen guests, who stood in window bays or sat on chairs and chaises longues, drinking the tea with rum and sugar that had been brought in. There was a touch of the savoir-faire of a bygone time about him, even while his cheeks were suffused with a perpetual, delicate blush as in growing anticipation of what was to come. Directly behind him stood Charlotte, sometimes silent, sometimes reading from the diary in a soft, penetrating voice; reading not of that night two hundred years before, since no record had been kept of that, but of previous functions akin to this one, and before her eyes the gardener moved around the empty room, making contact with people who had been dead for two hundred years.

He acquired an air of particularly bashful courtesy when speaking to young ladies and at such moments the doctor and Charlotte inclined their heads in order to catch every word. They noticed how the curve on the cylinder graph peaked and the needle on the voltmeter jumped, giving the objective, physical correlatives of the young poet's emotions and interest level. And yet these fluctuations were far too slight for Charlotte, because the gardener was still acting as if the girl he loved were not in the room.

Then, suddenly, the doctor was on his feet. Stirred to the depths of his being by the atmosphere, elated by the howling of the wind outside, backed up and vindicated by the dials in front of him, he had stuck his finger into the mortar and popped a gobbet of the bitter mixture into his mouth, there to melt on his tongue. No sooner had he done this than he heard the gardener chatting to two young sisters of whose sensual nature the doctor knew from the diary, and with a fresh sensibility all at once he saw history being played out before his eyes. Out of the white, dimly lit room there suddenly appeared a scintillating, almost chaotic gathering and with thoughts only for this, and most especially for the two women in yellow satin dresses seated on a low, firmly upholstered sofa just opposite him, he got up from his control panel and trod, unsteadily but totally engrossed, into the eighteenth century.

In the adjoining room Telemann's French overtures, dedicated to the memory of René Descartes, fell away towards their keynote as lightly and unconcernedly as a leaf falling to earth, before ascending once more to the painted ceilings. Now Charlotte lifted a large bundle out of a wooden chest and stepped behind a screen. Although, strictly speaking, such discretion was quite unnecessary, the two men in the centre of the room having quite forgotten that she existed. She stayed behind the screen for some time and when at last she came out from behind it, and when she walked straight up to the gardener and tapped him lightly on the shoulder with her fan and he turned round, all of the instruments went haywire, because there stood the answer to the riddle of the universe: the young woman from whom he had been separated by a wall but who was now standing right next to him.

Charlotte was wearing a ruffled crinoline dress with a tight bodice and a huge, bell-shaped whalebone skirt. Her hair was plaited into a coiffure referred to during the first half of the eighteenth century as *hongrois* – a style in which one long plait is wound like a coronet around the top of the head. She had been holding this change of clothes and these accoutrements in readiness, in order that she might, at this crucial moment, assume the part of the poet's young sweetheart, thus giving her guinea pig the final shove backwards.

She drew close, close as could be, to the gardener, noting with triumph how he now seemed, for the first time, to be receiving a broad, unimpeded stream of particles from the past. Incapable of movement he whispered her name and Charlotte raised her lips to his ear.

"Remember," she said, "you have promised to write a poem for me."

A slow and mischievous smile spread across his face, seeming to come from a long way off.

"Remember, Mademoiselle," he said in the rather antiquated French which he seemed to have absorbed from his surroundings, "that you have held out to me the prospect of a kiss."

For a split second this claim seemed to threaten Charlotte's command of the situation. For a split second her thoughts turned to the great traitors of history, who brought annihilation down upon their heads with a kiss: of the wedding night of the Danaides, of Judas' kiss, of Brutus' lethal embrace and of the kiss bestowed by the princess on the swineherd. And she reeled.

Then she recalled the great self-sacrificing figures: the dogs which kissed Lazarus, the kiss with which Juliet threw away her life, Saint Birgitta of Vadstena who sucked the poison out of the lepers' boils, and Marie Curie who held the lethal radium chloride up to her cracked lips with her bare hands. Seek, and ye shall find, she thought, and plunged forward, slipping neatly between the wires her guinea pig trailed in his wake, and kissed him.

As she did so, before her wondering eyes the room filled with people, with a new light from all the glittering gowns and with the clamour of voices. At one end of the room, amid much laughter and gaiety, a little group was practising some dance steps in time to the music and over against the opposite wall her colleague, Monsieur le Docteur, was deep in conversation with two young girls, their bodies inclining towards his. He was now dressed in a long coat and narrow trousers which set off his perfectly formed calves and, just as Charlotte caught sight of him, with all the assurance of an expert he lifted up one girl's dress and placed his hand on her thigh and she laughed, enchanted. With that rare, transcendental sensation of being at one and the same time part of all this and outside it, Charlotte steered Jean-Luc over to the upright desk and in a whisper begged him for just the first line. And with his back to her, thus shielding whatever he wrote on the paper, the young man proceeded to write slowly and with great concentration. This done, he closed the book and took her in his arms once more. Never once taking her eyes from his she went with him, backwards, through the room and, all smiles, the party guests made way for them, as if for a couple trying out a tricky gavotte. Out through the door they went and the music increased in volume. They were now standing in the adjoining room behind the pianist, hunched over the spinet and so wrapped up in his playing that he did not once turn his head. With her face an inch away from the poet's Charlotte allowed him to lift up her dress. As he propped up her thigh she thought fleetingly of what Bohr had said about the scientist at all times being both actor and audience and then she yielded, for had she not always been willing to sacrifice anything for the truth, and as he slid inside her, she was bombarded by a storm of images and feelings and she understood that, from a physiological point of view, she must now be linked up to the histometric discharger which had – through this boy, her medium – put her in touch with this bygone age; and, just before desire washed over her, gurgling and ecstatic, she realized that she had been right, that modern love was but a shadow of the love of times past, that emotions decay, that her theories had been borne out in every detail.

That night the storm tore up the freshly planted saplings, toppled Rousseau's monument and in a sense, in so doing, swept the garden back into an earlier condition. It also blew in several windows in the laboratory and gusted a lake of water across the scrubbed floorboards. Then it went on its way, and the next morning when Charlotte entered the laboratory the white sun and blue sky could be seen reflected in the flood waters as perfectly as in a mirror with not a single refractive fault.

That morning Charlotte had woken instantaneously. She had

fallen, so to speak, into the shimmering morning without warning to find herself alone in the white-lacquered bed, one of the props from the Louvre that had been put to one side.

She woke up bereft of memory and with no thought of the future; with the stunned notion that all laws of Nature had been declared null and void; that she was now faced with a life that could go any way. Then she opened the door into the salon and, in a desperate attempt at self-irony, thought to herself that this was how the chosen women would feel on the morning after the Day of Judgement, when they came to take stock of the devastation and realized that this truly was the end of all things and that ahead of them lay the big clear-up, and nothing but that.

The gardener lay on his back, snoring, in the shallow layer of water. In his fall the wires had pulled the control panel over on to its side and smashed the instruments. Charlotte stood for a moment or two looking down at him. Then she bent over him, not to caress him but to brush the hair back first from one temple and then from the other. She found no trace of scarring.

She waded through the mirror-like water towards the doctor. He was sitting in a chair, and he was dead. On the floor next to him sat the empty mortar. Charlotte looked at him long and hard and understood that there was no talk here either of an accident or of suicide. As surely as if he had advised her of his decision she knew that the great psychotherapist had turned his back on his neurotic age and taken the big step backwards into the free and uninhibited eighteenth century.

As a reminder of the massive surge in blood pressure at the moment of death, out of his unbuttoned trousers jutted a rampant white erection, preserved by a physiologically unaccountable, but undeniably lustful rigor mortis.

Stiffly, Charlotte pressed on to the desk and opened the book in which the previous evening the young man had written something for her. In a clumsy and unpractised hand there stood:

"No one journeys this far for a love that will decay."

A week later, as Charlotte came out of the doorway leading to the offices of the special court of inquiry in the Palais de Justice on the Quai des Orfèvres, a figure on the stairway at her back stood up and slowly followed her down the front steps.

"I've been thinking about the principles of love," said the gardener.

Charlotte did not turn.

"I don't believe there is any such thing as a closed system when it comes to us humans," he said.

She kept going and even the faint tap of her heels on the marble tiles was amplified in the resonance chamber formed by the huge courtyard.

"Through love, energy increases," said the gardener.

Charlotte's back remained deaf to him.

"Perpetual motion," the youth called out, "can be reached in one leap!"

At this, Charlotte stopped dead and turned to face him. Though this may only have been in order to contradict him.

☽

PORTRAIT OF THE AVANT-GARDE

On an October day in 1939, the painter Simon Bering and his friend, Nina, sailed out to the island of Christiansø. They sailed from Svaneke harbour on his twenty-eighth birthday; by which time six years had elapsed since the major exhibition at which his paintings had first made a wide public catch their breath the way one does when stepping out into the cold, then caused their eyes to water as if in a stiff headwind, and thereafter and ever since moved them to part with money for a stake in his faith in the future.

Simon painted large-scale canvases across which the twentieth century progressed as an unrelenting cavalcade of machines and horses and military detachments and forest fires. Back then these had raised a storm which had not yet died down and which had gone so far as to blow him into the *Reichskammer der bildenden Künste* to which only very few foreigners of immaculate racial pedigree were ever admitted.

One March night ten years earlier, as if in a fever Simon had painted the first of these pictures, works which did not close up to form flat planes but instead opened up like gateways into the future and on this day in October he felt as though what was now happening to him came as a direct result of that night a decade before; that – on a new and higher plane so to speak – he was reliving that first breakthrough to himself.

A weaker character might have been knocked for six by such fame, but not Simon, who believed that he belonged to a generation and a race healthier than any before them had ever been. With the money that all at once began to pour in he placed a hard-nosed agent between himself and the public and bought a property in the centre of Copenhagen, an old yellow-washed house with a garden surrounded by high walls. Here he found the relative peace at the eye of the typhoon, here he was able to work and here the gale that howled around his pictures and his person filtered through to him as no more than a gentle tailwind bringing congratulations and a soft rain of gold.

He could have chosen to live and work as a recluse. He could have had his vast paintings carted off through the gates of the yellow house and watched from a safe distance as they detonated like shells in the capital cities of Europe, but he did not. For Simon was also a speechmaker. He felt a powerful urge to speed the truths contained in his paintings on their way with words, for the word is also a brush and with it he wished to stand up in front of an assembly, to feel the crowd seething, to look upon these weaker brethren as a white canvas set before him, to make electrifying contact, create awareness and then lean forward and apply his own hectic flush of colour to the white faces upturned to his like so many blank pages. Hence the fact that the huge locomotives which thundered across his pictures also conveyed him all over Europe like a young prophet of a new age and a new truth. To begin with he addressed art lovers only, but later he also made speeches at political rallies, and in Berlin on August 2nd 1934 he assured his listeners that the young artists of Europe were right behind Germany's new leader and Chancellor. He told them there is only one God, and that is progress. His celebrity earned him a hearing and because he was so young he got away with saying more than many another and thus Simon succeeded in giving clear and crystallized expression to ideas which at that time were still vague and diffuse, speaking always with the same fresh and forthright power as when in Berlin – at the joint opening of the Olympiad and the art exhibition in 1936 – he had raised his strong, pale face to a public gathering, looked out across that sea of humanity and said fiercely, straight into the microphone, that while we are waiting for the great war we so fervently desire, we must arm ourselves with art that can cut to the quick of our souls, and this art must be painting. Books and music are for people beset by doubts, the war and the future decree that we must march and observe, not moulder away in theatres and reading rooms.

Nina came to him as simply as his fame or an idea for a picture. He advertised for a housekeeper, having need of a helpmate, and one day there she was, standing before him, younger than he but steady-voiced as she assured him that she was up to the job. She spoke a dialect new to him, but true to his theories that the past is of no consequence he did not question her further. To his own surprise there came a day when he realized that he enjoyed having her around. Later he began to feel homesick for her when out travelling. And in the end he dreaded leaving her.

One day, when things had reached this stage, he was standing behind her in a bright room. The sun dissolved her contours into a yellow haze and condensed her figure into a black silhouette. Rooted to the spot by some obscure expectation, Simon tried out an exercise he had resorted to on previous occasions when – faced with a white expanse of canvas – he had been overcome by doubt. He closed his eyes and made his mind go blank, then slowly opened his eyes once more, imagining as he did so that until then the world had not existed, but that it was being created, like a painting, in the moment that he laid eyes on it.

Now, too, this method brought relief. With eyes screwed up against the light, he could see that another figure now stood alongside that of the girl, and by stretching his creative faculty slightly he saw that it was himself.

And then he kissed her.

In keeping with his conviction that all ancient rituals were absurd, marriage was never an option for Simon and he was secretly proud of the fact that he never presented his declarations of love to Nina as anything but throwaway remarks. He had long since told the public at large that the true essence of love lies in there being no strings attached and he had an agreeable feeling that this put him, historically speaking, in good company with the long string of artistic movements which, since the middle of the previous century, had underlined their own particular brand of avant-gardism by proclaiming the virtues of free love.

Between himself and Nina, therefore, he had insisted on a distance befitting two modern individuals. Since he travelled a great deal and worked even more, this distance was something that grew up all unbidden and they had been living together for a year before he learned that she had been born on Christiansø, an island which, as far as the map of Denmark is concerned, is near enough the end of the world. On this same occasion she told him that she was pregnant.

It was at this point that Simon decided to take a break in his life to rediscover the peace he had lost in the course of the preceding six years. He made his decision known to the world at a party he gave for his friends at the restaurant Stephan à Porta in Copenhagen. The guest list was composed of young businessmen, politicians, artists and army officers who demonstrated their contempt for the past by smashing champagne glasses against the walls, eating beluga caviar and Russian peas with their fingers and brawling with the waiters and each other. At one point only did they quieten down and that was when Simon made his speech; but then, on the other hand, you could have heard a pin drop in the room.

"There are," said Simon, "three stages along the way to total control over life.

"The first leads out of the nursery. From infancy the world bends over us in the form of a woman: mothers, wet nurses, maids and governesses endeavour to block our path to life. The first prerequisite for freedom is, therefore, the ability to say: I will do as I please with my own person. It is to this point that we are attempting to bring the masses. A man cannot march if he is still lying in the cradle. There is no way the necessity of war can be discerned from a nursery.

"But then comes the next stage, where one finds the politician and the soldier." (And here Simon let his eye fall on those politicians and soldiers in attendance.) "This is reached when we become capable of infecting others with our own enthusiasm and then steering them in the right direction; when we have dominion over life and death; when we can do as we please with other people.

"Then there is a third stage: for my own part, I have given the world six years of my life. I have quelled all wishy-washy deliberation and rolled light and dark into one, and played my part in raising the waters that are now washing over Europe. I have given the world an art form that is akin to a slap in the face."

Here Simon made a pause during which he eyed every single member of the company, feeling that his words had got through to them like a sudden attack of sobriety and that it was no longer clear whether they were his guests or his victims.

"Now," he went on, "the world has become accustomed to this slap in the face. If I were to stop for a moment, it would come crawling to me and grab me by the throat with one hand while with the other begging me to give it a sound thrashing. And so I have made up my mind that during this seventh year I will rest, and this I have decided to do in order to show that I can do with the world exactly as I please."

Three weeks later, Nina and Simon set sail from Svaneke harbour. It was the first day of winter, and from the south there blew a wind so cold that it seemed to come straight off some icy waste. The town of Svaneke is built atop rocky cliffs that slope steeply down to the harbour and the cauldron thus formed caught the chill winds and swept them down over the quayside and the white mailboat and the reporters who had pursued Simon, every one of whom felt it as a reminder of their own mortality. They had made the journey on behalf of their newspapers and their readers, to write a piece about Simon's departure and his birthday, but for the moment all of that was forgotten. By now they were chilled to the bone, worn out and greatly preoccupied with the war in Europe. A number of them fully expected on their return to be sacked for some unspecified reason, or to be posted overnight to distant war zones, and every one of them feared for the future, every one of them was haunted by just one question: "How will it all end?" And suddenly, this morning on the quayside, it seemed to them that this celebrated, pale-faced agitator ought to be able to answer that question. But Simon waved them away, roughly shoving back one of their number who was rash enough to follow him up the gangplank. They have been sent, he thought to himself, by the life I am about to leave behind, to prolong the leavetaking, but for me, for the new man, taking leave of the old life is a pleasure. And he turned his back on them.

As they sailed out of the harbour the reporters ran along the pier, keeping up with them like lost children.

For as long as the town was still visible off the boat's stern, the sea was sluggish, menacing and of the same hue as solidified pewter. Then Simon shut his eyes and made his mind go blank. Only now does the world come into being, he thought. Then he felt warm sunshine on his eyelids, as though the boat had sailed into summer. And to say that in especially hot summers the seas around Bornholm store up the warmth of the sun and create an unnatural postponement of winter would be a feeble rebuttal to the sense of omnipotence with which Simon was filled as he gradually opened his eyes, creating first the season and his own hands on the rail in front of him, then Nina's silhouette, then – with triumphant awareness of his sex as a mighty brush – the child in her belly, and finally the blue sea under the sun and, sitting on the horizon, the two tiny islands: Christiansø and the even smaller Frederiksø and, like a tenuous black thread, the bridge connecting them.

He noticed that Nina had her eyes shut. "You're dreaming," said Simon. "It's the way of the world: women dream and men act." Nina look at him, sharp-eyed. "Don't you dream?" she asked. Simon thought fleetingly of his pictures. "Even my dreams are actions," he said and immediately felt that he ought to follow up such an astute remark. He glanced round at the other passengers, trying to judge whether this might be the right spot for an impromptu speech.

Suddenly Nina was standing very close to him and when she spoke she was grave as he had never seen her before.

"We went to school on Frederiksø," she said softly, "and there we learned about Bjarke's dreams. During the battle at Lejre Bjarke slept while a fearsome bear fought in his place. They tried to wake him but he said: 'Leave me to dream.' Nonetheless they forced him to come with them and at that the bear vanished. The bear was Bjarke's dream."

Full of incredulous wonder, Simon realized that for the first time ever Nina had given him a warning. But of what he could not tell.

"The dreams of women," he said coolly, "are not bears." And on that note he would have liked to end the conversation, but it stuck in his mind like a bur, like a prophecy he did not understand.

By the time they had been on the island for two days Simon was admitting to himself that everything around him was totally alien to him and that Nina had come home.

He had always thought of himself – and often painted himself – as some fiery natural phenomenon, as an uninterrupted volcanic eruption, setting light to everything around it without itself ever being touched by its surroundings. He had always been of the opinion that it was he who spoke to mankind while it, in turn, kept its mouth shut and listened. Now, for the first time in a long, long while, he found himself passing unrecognized in the street. Not only that, but on this little island, which one could stroll round in an hour, there was not so much as a street on which he might be recognized, only dirt tracks. On these tracks they bumped into people who remembered Nina. They greeted him kindly and asked after his health without knowing or understanding that before them stood a world-famous painter and eminent philosopher. Then they turned to talking to and about Nina. In his unaccustomed role as listener to a story with a central character other than himself and as spectator to a day-to-day life in which he figured as a welcome but anonymous guest Simon noticed that there was something wrong with the vision of the people round about him. Their life, he now saw, lacked perspective. The men were fishermen who would now and again stare down into the deeps and now and again into the heavens, but more often than not kept their eyes on the tools in their hands. As for the women, as a rule they gazed into the cooking pots and occasionally up at the religious samplers on the walls and sometimes down at the children but no one, thought Simon, neither man nor woman, ever looks straight ahead; here, he thought, the horizon wraps itself so closely around them that even their questions do not stretch beyond the bare necessities of the daily round they follow with such short strides that they have no hope of ever getting on in life. He felt very lonely, and in his loneliness he caught himself missing the upturned faces of his audiences and his picture in the newspapers and the feverish chatter of private viewings, and it occurred to him that possibly, just possibly my public has given me something after all.

While Nina, he realized, had come home. As soon as she set foot on land she had been transformed and become one with the island. She put away the clothes he had brought her from Kurfürstendamm and went around instead in a blue dress he had never seen before and which, together with the scarf she bound round her head, made her look like any of the other island women. She seemed to remember everyone they met and everyone remembered her. Her stride shortened, her gait slackened as she led Simon around, showing him the places where she had played as a child, and she would sit quite still for hours on end on the sun-warmed granite boulders while restlessly Simon paced off his prison.

On the morning of the second day he announced to her that this was to be their last day on the island. He saw how her face fell, but she bowed her head in resignation and he had expected nothing less. These days it would never have occurred to Simon that anyone might gainsay him.

That afternoon she asked him to take a walk with her. He sensed that she had something she wished to say to him, but they walked in silence along the water's edge. Beside the bridge over to Frederiksø they sat down on a bench. On the other side of the narrow stretch of water separating the two islands stood a tall tree. In this tree perched two sea eagles, an adult and a fledgling, their backs turned to Simon and Nina. "That's the male bird, there in the tree," said Nina, and pointed to where the female was but a distant, lazily wheeling pinprick far off in the sky. "That pair of sea eagles have been here always," she said. "My grandfather told me that once, when he was a boy, a visiting hunter caught one of the young in a bird trap. Grandfather said that when the trap snapped shut the adult birds were so far away they might never have been there at all. But just as the hunter bent over the young one to break its neck so as not to ruin its plumage, they plummeted out of the sky like a couple of stones. Before taking to his heels he fired a few shots at them, but the blood ran into his eyes and he didn't hit them. Ever since then, though, the adult eagles have been deaf." She fell silent for a moment, casting her mind back. Then she said, "Grandfather set the young one free. The adult birds knew him, so they didn't touch him."

Sideways on, Simon observed her. She was wearing no shoes that day and as she sat there next to him, her feet buried in the grass, there was no way of telling where the island left off and the girl began. Under other circumstances, Simon would have been enthralled by the story of the eagle, king of birds, which he regarded as a fitting and wholesome symbol of the new Europe. But on this particular day there was, it seemed to him, a depth to Nina's story that he could not plumb.

"It can't possibly be the same birds," he said. "A sea eagle can't live to be a hundred," and without warning he gave a loud, piercing whistle. Over on Frederiksø the young sea eagle slowly turned its head, cocked it to one side and looked at Simon. But the adult bird kept its eyes fixed on the sea as if it had not heard a thing.

After this they sat quietly for a while. "Time here," said Nina finally, "is not the same as in Copenhagen. You've done a lot of travelling and most of the people I have met over there have been all round Denmark. With the possible exception of the more remote parts, places like this. But here . . . here you'll find only a handful of people who have ever seen Copenhagen.

"Oh yes," she went on, nodding at the island facing them, "some people spend their whole life over there, without ever crossing the bridge to the other side.

"My grandmother," she said pensively, "never once crossed over to Christiansø and once, when someone asked her why not, she simply replied: 'What business would I have there?'"

Just then, seemingly as an appendix to Nina's words, a young girl in a long green dress broke out of the shade of the tree and slowly started walking across to the windmill. Simon stood up and grasped the handrail of the bridge. "This is what we are up against," he thought sourly, "such resistance to change is precisely what stands in the way of the new era."

He shut his eyes, then eased them open again, and as he did so he was struck by an idea: "I'll have an enormous canvas taken across that bridge," he thought, "and I'll paint them a picture over there the like of which they have never seen, the like of which no one has ever seen; a painting depicting the history of man as a frenzy of longing; a painting containing the hiss of steam, the pounding of pistons and rifle shots; and finally, right in the foreground, with a flash of all-consuming white fire, a painting that reaches out and grabs the public by the throat. And for a public it will have that girl in green and those intransigent men and women, and this picture will change their lives; it will hurl them into the future and inject a substance into their veins, forcing them to run away, forcing them to pour across this bridge and off and away. It will be," he thought to himself, "the ultimate painting, a work of art capable of depopulating an island."

His idea having thrown him into a fever of excitement, he took a pace backwards, as if he were in fact working at his canvas, and in his mind's eye he began to paint, strong in the ecstatic conviction that he was the creator of the universe and in the service of a higher cause.

At that moment he became aware of some form of resistance somewhere in the universe and it was brought home to him that Nina had risen to her feet and was now standing directly in front of him. She eyed him most intently, then said: "Really?"

Initially the shock stopped Simon in his tracks. He knew that not one word had escaped his lips and yet the woman was now talking to him as surely as if she were inside his head. He bent over until his eyes were level with hers and in a soft, steady voice he replied: "Really!"

Just for an instant she seemed to recoil. Then she appeared to bring all of her being to bear on one single point. "We could give it a try," she said.

Anger, unexpected and intense, welled up in Simon's mouth like warm blood, leaving him incapable of speech, but without giving it a second's thought he nodded in assent.

"Well, remember," said Nina, her words coming now as a whisper, and she pressed her swollen belly into Simon until he felt as if her and the child's joint heartbeat were forcing him backwards, "remember to say when you've had enough."

And she stepped away from him and things slid back into place. Against the blue lacquer setting of the sea, the red granite sparkled under a yellow sun, the scent of seaweed and grass hung all around them and on the dark-green bushes huge, matte-black blackberries were ripening. Simon shook his head, not sure whether this conversation really had taken place and whether it could possibly be true that his Nina had challenged him to a duel.

"We're dreaming," he said and started back towards the inn.

But he did not take Nina's arm. Although he had no idea of how it had come about he knew that between her and him a battle such as he had never experienced before and for which as yet he had no words was now being waged.

* * *

That night, Simon slept heavily and fitfully. He dreamt that a bear was sitting on his chest and he woke up fighting for breath. At Nina's request, they slept in one of the small fisherman's cottages next door to the inn. The house consisted of just one room with one window and through this window the moonlight streamed, catching as it fell the streamers of seaweed that hung from the eaves and throwing their shadows across the floor like the rusty iron bars of a prison. His mind in a turmoil, Simon set foot on the cool floor and crossed to the window. From far off in space the full moon viewed him with the impassive alertness of a card player. The world wants something of me, he thought, and the next moment he knew what it was: out of the blue, for the very first time, it dawned on him once and for all that the woman lying behind him was going to have his child and the recognition of this fact made him rigid with fright.

Prior to this Simon had regarded his child – as much as he had given it any thought at all – as yet another work of art, as a *mot juste* that had fallen on fertile ground, as a parallel to the inspired frame of mind in which, on a night in March ten years earlier, he had painted his first picture. Now he looked at the woman in the bed and knew beyond a shadow of a doubt that with this child an inscription would be etched into the universe that could not be painted over like a canvas, nor forgotten or rewritten like some unsatisfactory speech. From far away, from the woman's womb, the nethermost level of humanity cried out to him, calling him to account, and Simon staggered under this burden as though struck by a blow.

Only momentarily, though. Then he shrugged it off and got dressed. He reeled about like a drunkard, bumping into the furniture, but in the bed Nina slumbered on, all her being seemingly focused on sleep. In the doorway he stopped for a moment and considered her: "Nothing," he thought, "can waken a woman."

The night was warm and perfectly still and in the moonlight the dark rock acquired a lustre, for all the world as if the island were one enormous black pearl.

Simon felt happiness surging through him, he was filled with power, he stepped out smartly, with no thought for where he might be headed, and when he found himself standing facing the bridge over to Frederiksø he was under the impression that the world around him was shaping itself in accordance with his wishes and that the night would vouchsafe him an answer.

A woman was crossing the bridge. Simon thought he recognized the slender figure of the girl he had seen walking towards the windmill. She moved slowly but purposefully and as she drew closer, in the moonlight which on this night was strong enough for him to make out colours, he saw that under her jacket she wore a green dress. She was carrying a suitcase and a bag and when she came face to face with Simon she set these down and looked him in the eye.

Even Simon, even the great Simon Bering – a man who had urged nations to act spontaneously – had never failed to falter when confronted with a woman. But this night he felt himself to be in possession of all his best qualities and he grabbed her hand and kissed it. It was the first time in his life he had ever made such a gesture. Her hand was cold, but she looked at him intently and when she tilted her head to one side and smiled Simon experienced a giddy sense of recognition, as if he had seen her before. As she walked past him, going down to the water's edge, he was suddenly aware that this was the first time she had ever crossed the bridge, that she was leaving the island and that it had to have been his presence which had prompted her departure. "She's about to sail over on a fishing boat, to catch the morning ferry to Copenhagen," he thought, "and somewhere on Zealand a job as a housemaid awaits her." All of this he sensed, knowing it as surely as if he were inside her head and without a word having escaped her lips.

He did not take the straight road back, choosing instead a path that crossed the island by another route, and as he walked the certitude of a moment before drained out of him.

One year earlier, in Berlin, Simon had been awarded that city's most prestigious municipal art prize. To mark the occasion his portrait had been painted, the intention being that his motto should be added to this painting. The matter had been brought up by the Chancellor himself and Simon, in no hurry to reply, had silently asked himself why he did not have a motto, and had answered himself by saying that it was because his aim in life had been so self-evident that he had no need of any such linguistic crutch on which to lean. Having thought this far he looked the Führer in the eye and declared out loud: "My motto is '*Ohne Zweifel!*'" and the little man facing him had nodded and returned his gaze and said: "A fine motto for a painter!"

Nevertheless, on this night Simon was visited by doubt. As he was walking away from the bridge, he suffered another attack of the breathlessness with which he had woken. Around him the universe seemed to stretch into infinity and yet he had no room, no *Lebensraum*. For the first time in long enough he felt fear in the form of a sense that something was lying in wait for him in the darkness; felt, too, that he did not have the answers to the riddle with which he was faced but would have to draw them from outside of himself: he had the feeling that the black yet reflective granite surfaces were absorbing all of his strength, so he took to giving them a wide berth. He looked up at the stars and wondered what it was that the Chancellor had whispered to him that time in Berlin about his constellation; he focused his attention on the firmament above him in order perhaps to evoke an answer from up there, until it dawned on him that he was staggering along like a drunk man, that he was about to lose his dignity.

At this his anger returned and he stepped up on to a large, flat rock, feeling as though he were standing in a boxing ring. He was struck by the certainty that on this night he was leaning against a force unlike anything he had ever before encountered, and one which alternately accorded him and deprived him of his self-assurance. But now he was going to fight back and, shoulders hunched, he shifted this way and that atop his rock.

So smooth was it that it reflected both his own shadow and a blurred mirror image of the moon's face. Simon shut his eyes, then slowly opened them, wanting to come up with his own answer to his own future. The white face at his feet turned into that of the girl by the bridge and he realized that he missed her, her and his freedom, with a longing nothing could be allowed to stand in the way of. He broke into a run, running back to the harbour.

Out on the sea he thought he saw white sails moving away from the island, but this left him undaunted. For now that he had made up his mind nothing could possibly go wrong. As he bounded down the steps to the quayside he caught sight of a boat. With just one small foresail hoisted it came scudding across the water from Frederiksø, making for the harbour mouth. Simon laughed out loud. He had never doubted that this very boat would be right here. He waved, the boat swung in alongside the quay and he leapt aboard. "Over to Bornholm," he laughed and fumbled in his jacket pocket for a wad of notes which he held out to the figure on the aft thwart. The boat pitched and headed out of the harbour and it occurred to Simon that money too can be both palette and brush.

There was only one person on the boat and in the darkness Simon took it to be an elderly man. He sat with his hand on the rudder and a rug over his legs, so that there was no way of telling where the boat left off and the man began. Once out of harbour he hoisted the mainsail and the vessel heeled over and shot forward like a bird over a calm sea and beneath an unfathomable star-studded sky. With one thought Simon embraced both the woman behind him and the woman ahead of him, fancying that from the one to the other he was running a silver thread along which the boat was now sailing, and he sensed that the time was right for making a speech.

"As a sailor," he said to the fisherman, " I'm sure you would agree with me that for anyone who has seen something of the world there are three joys that surpass all others: the first of these is the joy of departure, the pleasure inherent in finding that, for the free spirit, as for the birds, gravity does not apply.

"The second joy is that of arrival, of finding that we can go anywhere we please and say: At this moment – and perhaps only at this moment – I belong here, wherever I lay my head."

At this point he fell silent for a moment and thought: "What a pity that I only have this one stunted spectator and not a proper audience, or at the very least someone who could have taken this down in shorthand." At the same time he felt that above his head his words spiralled upwards on broad wings towards the glittering stars and he stood up, grabbed hold of the mast, waited till he had regained his balance then flung wide his arm.

"The third and greatest joy," he said, "is to leave one's mark on the place to which one has come, to feel that one could, if one wished, drop down on the world with such tremendous force that one would never, ever be forgotten, either by people or by places."

He stood there for a while with his eyes closed. The fisherman remained silent but this silence did not bother Simon, who had learned long ago – with or without applause – to congratulate himself on a splendid solo. It did, however, cross his mind that the old man might be slow-witted. "But in that," he said to himself with a wry little smile, "he would be no different from every other member of the general public."

While making his speech he had had his back to the direction in which they were sailing, something which did not altogether fit with his theory on the glories of departure and arrival, but which had been necessary in order that he might be facing his audience. Now, as slowly he opened his eyes, he saw the Christiansø light flashing, not astern of the boat as it ought to have been, but a fair bit to starboard. "We're sailing the wrong way," he told the fisherman, dumbfounded.

This remark was followed by a lengthy silence, during which Simon felt bound to conclude that his travelling companion was a mute.

Then the fisherman spoke.

"My hearing's not so good," he said in a husky voice in which Simon recognized the origin of Nina's dialect. "Well, actually I can't hear a thing. But I get by with 'aye, aye', that being what everybody would rather hear anyway.

"The night," he added, "we're going to catch salmon."

The rage with which Simon was now filled came not from the fact that they were going the wrong way nor from his being mistaken for an angler. It arose from the fact that the man opposite him had not heard a word he had said.

"Ashore," said Simon, bringing his face right down to the fisherman's and spitting the words at him, "I want to be put ashore."

The fisherman looked along his outstretched arm and nodded. "Aye," he said, "it's the haar."

Simon raised his eyes in disbelief. Where before the Svaneke lighthouse had flashed there was now darkness and over this darkness hung a luminous, milky band. Again he pointed frantically at the spot where Bornholm had been, but the fisherman shook his head. "There's no fish there," he said, "and besides, the wind drops when the haar comes down."

Again Simon thought of the girl in the green dress sailing on ahead of him, bound for land, and again he felt as though the universe were barring his way. Just as he took a step to stern, intending to lay hands on the tiller, the mist descended. It enveloped the boat like a cloak falling over it; sky and sea disappeared, the wind died down, the air shone with an opalescent light and just a few feet in front of Simon the fisherman's silhouette grew hazy. A hush fell on the boat. It was, thought Simon, as if the two of them were sitting in a tiny room, as if the universe had wrapped itself so closely around them that they were now all alone in the world. "Tonight," he said to himself, "I am by turns liberated and confined."

Across from him the fisherman fed a line strung with an endless succession of hooks over the side. "Here, right under us," he explained, "the cliffs plunge straight down and the water's deep. The fish hover there – like birds," he added thoughtfully, "high above the sea bed."

There then ensued a long silence during which Simon strove to understand what had gone wrong. Then the fisherman spoke.

"It's mild the night," he said. "Me, I'm only a deaf auld cratur but I had the feeling that you were telling a story a while back. Well, now I'll tell you one, a story about a cold, cold night."

The thought crossed Simon's mind that ever since he had set off to do as he pleased with the world, the world had been forcing him to listen as never before. "And now to this old dodderer as well," he thought.

"There was this one time when I was stranded on an ice floe," said the fisherman. "I was on my way to Greenland – the how or the why of it is neither here nor there – and I travelled some of the way on the good ship *Ragna* of the Greenland Trading Company. But the ice blocked off the sea lanes and in the end it forced the ship down and closed over it. There we sat, twenty men besides myself. Some were suffering from tuberculosis – we laid them off to one side, by themselves. The rest of us paced up and down alongside the black waters wondering whether our hour had come. I fell in with a man dressed partly in Greenlandic fashion who walked to and fro and sang as though he were already off his head. We were joined by a young man who had caught my eye because of his sorry attempt at growing a full beard. Back then I still had my hearing so I heard both the madman's singing and the young man's story of how he was a scientist who had left his wife and children because, unlike the rest of the world, he did not believe that women and children were necessary to guarantee a man eternal life, and because he had heard that anyone who fetches up in the polar regions has found their way both to Heaven and to Hell.

"He told us that what he prized most in life was solitude and silence. I have a notion that he came over to join us and told us all of this in the hope that together the three of us might prove to be three times as solitary and three times as silent. So I made him no answer. And the madman burst into song once more.

"All that night and all the following day – which, by the way, in that part of the world at that time of year was but one long, dark hour – he stood there, singing out across the water. At one point I heard the young man ask him why he sang and he replied that when an Eskimo prays for something, he sings a song in honour of the gods. 'Do you believe in all that?' the young man asked him incredulously. 'In that old wives' tale!' retorted the other, 'ach, no, I just sing to keep warm.

"'And,' he added, 'because you never can tell.' And he went back to his singing."

Here the fisherman took a break, during which he drew in the line, checked the hooks and threw it out again. "Much later," he said, "I don't remember how much later, but it was long after our supplies had run out and the sick were dead and the healthy now only half-alive, I was walking back and forth along the edge of the floe again, not wanting to die lying down. Everyone else had fallen silent but the lunatic in the anorak was still standing there singing. The sky was so clear that I felt I could see every single star, and the northern lights swept down to the icy rim like bridges of frozen light. I put out a hand and passed it through the light and the beam broke asunder only, a moment later, to run together again. Just then, from somewhere out at sea there came an answering song and minutes later a group of Eskimos were running a boat up on to the floe. They took the sick ashore first, and after them the elderly. I helped the madman down to the boat and just before climbing aboard he turned to the young man. 'In parting,' he said, 'I have three pieces of advice for you.'

"'The first is that you have to have damned good references to get into Heaven.

"'The second is that, as far as children are concerned, we don't have them so we can enter into eternal life. We have them to remind us that one day we shall die.

"'And the third thing I have to say to you is not a word of advice to you but a prayer to God: tonight I will pray to him to bless your beard.'"

For a while after that the fisherman said nothing, then: "I never saw that man again, or at least only at a distance. But while I could still hear, I heard someone say that that was Knud Rasmussen, the great Arctic explorer."

The silence in the boat was now absolute. The fisherman had curled up on himself, seeming, with his tale, to have completed his mission. Even the fishing line hung motionless from his fingers. On the thwart between him and Simon lay a hefty fishing knife. The boat had no engine, but as if from somewhere beyond the mist Simon caught a whiff of a faint breeze. And yet he knew that the deaf man sitting opposite him would not hoist the sail; that on this night, on which his luck waxed and waned as the tide ebbed and flowed, cooped up in this weird, minute and fog bound cell with the fisherman and his yarn, he was encountering a resistance the depths of which he could not plumb. He shut his eyes and on opening them again they were fixed, full of joy and inspiration, on the knife. He picked it up, ran a tentative finger along the blade. He could see now that beneath the rug, the fisherman was slight and sinewy as a bird.

With the knife in his hand, the wellsprings of life flowed freely once more within Simon and he felt certainty building up in his breast. Death had always figured in his painting but he had never witnessed it at close quarters. Even the great war which was supposedly to give birth to the new era, the war of which he had always been a keen advocate and which he had in a sense played out in his paintings, was not something he had ever imagined would affect him in any more personal manner. Rather, he envisaged this apocalypse as a long, cold shower which, while it might well leave Europe in ruins, would also clear and purge the air and waft away the mist. And he would then descend from his railway compartment into the purged air, scent the new growth and speak to the new man.

Now, all at once, he was standing on the battlefield himself. He looked at the knife in his hand and thought to himself, this is also a paintbrush and this will be the ultimate painting. He felt no fear, only a powerful sense of purpose and a vague feeling of regret because not even for this act would he have any spectators. Then he bade farewell to this objection too, and was filled with the great joy experienced by those in whose lives words and action suddenly are as one; and with no petty qualms over the thought that his victim happened to be a deaf man he wrapped one hand round the mast for support and flung out his free arm.

"This," he said, addressing the fisherman's sharp profile, "is a speech to one who is about to die.

"Not that long ago," he said, raising his voice in the hope of perhaps, nonetheless, managing to penetrate the silence that confronted him, "I made another speech, in which I stated that there are three sorts of freedom. The first of these is the ability to go wherever one pleases and this I experienced tonight, when we stood out of the harbour. You too are familiar with this feeling, you must have experienced it when you altered course as I was speaking – seeing as how you must have done so. Without quite understanding how or why, I know that you have deliberately led me astray and taken me where you saw fit.

"Then there is the second freedom, the one we possess when we find ourselves capable of bringing a life to an end, and to that one we will both return in a moment.

"But there is also a third sort of freedom, which lies in the ability to cope with utter loneliness. It consists of being able to act – not regardless of the world around us, since there are many of us who can do that – but with no regard for the world inside our heads, for what is known as our conscience. If one can do that, then one is utterly alone and utterly free."

Here Simon broke off and was conscious of his words winging their way out into the wide world. Then he walked round behind the old man and even while totally engrossed in the moment and in his own actions, with one small corner of his mind he was still able to note his own kinship with the great self-sacrificing figures of history; to feel that he had now become the incarnation of Abraham and Hakon Jarl and Agamemnon and perhaps even God himself, who sacrifices his own son on the cross in order to present his followers and himself with that third form of freedom.

At that instant a gust of wind whisked away the mist, like a curtain being pulled aside. The sun still dallied beneath the horizon, not yet ready to play its hand, but like an interim bid a bright violet glow spread across the sea and the score of fishing boats lying to either side of Simon and the old man – freeboard to freeboard, a little forest of masts, the closest of them only an oar's length from Simon, all hovering like birds over the same underwater abyss and fishing ground. And along the rails, faces, possibly hundreds of them, all totally devoid of expression, turned towards the voice in the mist.

Never had Simon had a more deeply concentrated, more completely attentive audience and never had he had less to say.

"Now I am to be crushed," he thought, feeling as though he were in an arena, held there by a tension that would not even allow him to fall flat on his face. And yet at that moment it was not concern for his own person with which he was filled but the giddy sensation of an unfamiliar impotence, of a defeat that went beyond him personally, and without either willing or resisting it he heard himself, in a whisper so soft that only he could hear it, begging the world for mercy.

At that a tautness seemed to leave the boat, the fisherman across from him drew himself upright like someone who has been asleep, the knife slipped out of Simon's hand and over the side and he saw it glint with a green light as it sank down through the water, heading into nothingness.

On the way in to Christians Simon did not once look back. He knew there would be nothing to see. That as soon as he had begged for mercy both the mist and the fishing boats had ceased to exist. That since he had left his sleeping woman he had been moving through a world dreamt up by someone else. And now, only now, did he recall the story of Bjarke's dream.

He did not even glance at the fisherman. But as they laid to and he clambered up on to the quayside the bird-like profile was there at the corner of his eye, and a shiver ran down his spine. Walking away from the harbour he suddenly turned round, knowing in advance what he would find: boat and man had vanished as if they had never been and high above him the great sea eagle was soaring heavenwards.

Outside the cottage Simon stopped for a moment. Then slowly he opened the door and braced himself against the doorpost to save himself from falling. From the bed the woman stared at him with a wan and utterly exhausted face.

"I've had enough," said Simon.

PITY FOR THE CHILDREN OF VADEN TOWN

Over the course of the last century Denmark experienced an upsurge in that particular form of love referred to as compassion. This had its beginnings among the upper classes, but subsequently spread to the rest of the population, whose heart bled, above all, for the poor, defenceless children. By the turn of the century the Danish bourgeoisie viewed its children in a deeply wistful light; the light, as it were, of an interminable sunset. And in an attempt to comprehend this aching sense of compassion they turned to history and to religion, as if to say: "See, in the birth of our nation you have the history of unparalleled parental love."

The general consensus was that the true discovery of the frailty of childhood had been made only one hundred years earlier and, in Denmark more than in any other part of the world, all were agreed that it was the early nineteenth century which with ever-fearful, never-flagging solicitude had begun the process of taking the young and helpless under its wing and, for the first time ever, had endeavoured through the arts and sciences to give voice to the realization that every child carries within it a little piece of Paradise. It was in Romanticism's firmament that the Saviour had truly revealed himself as a divine mother from whose wounds flowed not blood but milk and at whose call to "suffer the little children to come unto me", Denmark's faithful had risen to their feet and wept: "He means us!" The painters of the Golden Age were the first to capture the divine nature of childish things, depicting mothers regarding their newborn babes with rapturous emotion while at the same time seeming to be searching for something which they themselves had lost for ever.

Compassion gives rise to the urge to protect and the nineteenth century was the age of private enterprise on a grand scale. In the wake of the Napoleonic wars and the war with Germany in 1864, collections were organized to raise money for war widows and their children; schools and asylums were being built and at twilight middle-class ladies would foregather in the window bays of spacious parlours to sew and embroider in aid of the Sudan Mission's drive to convert the children of that part of North Africa. Whatever notions these women had of that continent were dim and disquieting but they felt that every neat canvas stitch drew those distant, dark-skinned children closer to the light of civilization and their own bleeding hearts. And they let their sewing things fall into their laps and thought of the Danish children's writer Hans Christian Andersen and the lines with which he had raised himself above his own tragic upbringing, writing:

You Danish tongue, as soft as Mother's voice is,
With you my heartbeats O so sweetly blend.

With the dawning material growth of the early twentieth century, the altruistic spirit came to pervade every layer of society, becoming a ubiquitous, constantly audible note in the nation's consciousness. It crystallized into monuments, into asylums and children's hospitals, into laws against neglect, into epitaphs to child benefactors from the worlds of art and science and at no time was it ever in any doubt that this was part of an all-embracing material and emotional enrichment of the nation.

There was one place in Denmark, more than any other, which had been the source of a whole succession of those incentives to improve the lot of children and this was the town of Vaden, situated on the shores of Vaden Fjord on the east coast of Jutland. It was from this prosperous market town that the rest of Denmark had for a century drawn its ideal picture of parental love. It was citizens of Vaden Town who, both in the Upper and Lower Houses, had championed those major Bills which from the middle of the last century onwards were to define the laws concerning the maltreatment of children and the exploitation of child labour. And later it was these same citizens, in ministries and on select committees, who with dogged persistence had seen to it that these same laws were put into practice. Among its former pupils, Vaden Academy numbered several of the nation's great medical pioneers, eminent doctors who – in the fight against malnutrition and undernourishment and against the major infectious diseases – had dedicated their lives to those yet to grow to maturity. Many of these returned to their birthplace and when, at the beginning of this century, the tuberculosis sanatorium (the first of its kind for children) was built in Vaden the town could boast a hospital and a health service which were famed throughout the length and breadth of Europe.

As a young man, the educator and hymnist Nikolaj Severin Grundtvig spent a brief spell as vicar of Vaden Town, and although not a true son of Vaden he was to be marked for life by his few years of preaching there. It was here, for the first time, that he lifted himself out of the depression that kept dragging him down, formulated to himself the truth upon which he would later build his life's work: that for the adult there is no path to the heart of oneself other than through the child. And even though this pearl of wisdom, as with most of the great poet's utterances from the pulpit, was somewhat obscure – like the light of truth glimpsed through a thick fog of words – nonetheless the good people of the town had the feeling that, as was the vicar, they too were fired by a fierce inner warmth, and they took him to their hearts. When a stone was erected in the driveway of the sanatorium in memory of those doctors native to the town who had given their lives in the service of medicine during the great cholera epidemics of the mid-nineteenth century, the inscription chosen for the stone just turned out to be three lines of a verse by Grundtvig in which he had voiced the observation that this very spirit of compassion was the true hallmark of the Danish people:

For whether alive or dead
Danish hearts have always bled
But freeze they never will!

It was not, however, for these monumental, official good deeds that Vaden Town was known to the rest of Denmark. Its fame derived from its being a widely known fact that its inhabitants possessed a sensitivity of legendary profundity: the townspeople of Vaden loved their children with a wild, fanatical love which could not bear that anything bad should ever befall them.

People did wonder why the universe had chosen Vaden of all places for an onslaught of such powerful emotions, and there were those who pointed to its prosperity and said the reason people in Vaden Town were so loving was that they could afford to be. The town was never heard to respond to this comment, but only because the answer would have been the most obvious one: that the opposite was in fact the case; that – according to some inexplicable, but incontrovertible law – material growth follows on from tenderness towards the little ones.

Early in the spring of 1929 a soft breeze blew in across the South Fyn archipelago and over Jutland as if wishing gently and sweetly to nudge the countryside into a premature and prolonged summer. With the wind, on course for Vaden, there came a large, black, schooner-rigged galleass. The curve of the hull and the two huge centreboards indicated that the vessel had been built to sail close in to even the most humble of Danish harbours as well as along the German and Dutch North Sea coasts. But its rigging stood tall and the fine sweeping lines of its hull were as glossy and well cared for as those of a royal yacht, and indeed it was flying a red and white "Dannebrog" pennant sporting the Danish arms – a flag reserved exclusively for the Danish monarch.

The ship was moving at speed and from its deck, in the white light of the low-lying sun, Vaden Town looked like a toy village waiting for the moment when it would be allowed to come into its own by being given as a gift to a child. The banks of the fjord stretched out into the sea like welcoming arms and at the head of the fjord the town reared up above its harbour in a profusion of bright, almost laughing colours. At the bottom the fishermen's and skippers' cottages, farther up the grand town houses and merchants' establishments and at the very top the church and the sanatorium. But all around the town the old paving and old street lighting had been preserved and down by the harbour, standing cheek by jowl with the modern storehouses, the old warehouses, too, had been retained. Thus in Vaden Town the past was immediately visible, thus the new grew harmoniously out of the old, as a child from its parents.

The town was still encircled by the old city walls. By dint of extensive restoration work and thanks to a neatly designed system of gates and bridges leading to the outside world the town had stayed held within this embrace of dark-brown stonework, as a symbol of the life it offered its children: the open heart on the inside and the protective back turned to the surrounding world.

The ship was bearing down on the town rapidly and with a confidence which seemed to indicate that no one on board had any inkling that the harbour ahead of it was as closed as the grave; that one week earlier at a meeting in the town square first the town council and thereafter the whole town had unanimously agreed to close the town gate and the harbour and to set the two hundred soldiers of the Sixth South Jutland battalion, recruited from and stationed in the town, to guard these.

There was at that time, in the epidemiology department of the University Hospital in Copenhagen, a consultant physician by the name of Christian Windsløv who had his roots, his grandchildren and his heart in Vaden Town. He was a descendant of Professor Frederik Christian Windsløv, who had from 1810 onwards introduced compulsory smallpox inoculation to Denmark, thereby virtually eradicating this disease from the country. His descendants had retained an extensive knowledge and dread of the disease and over the past hundred years it was to them that the few, rare instances of smallpox had been referred. In the middle of February, two children from different parts of Zealand had been referred to Christian Windsløv at the hospital. Having peered into their fever-glazed eyes he brushed the hair back from their foreheads, looking for the characteristic red spots, but there were none to be seen. Instinct then prompted him to spread the children's hands. In the fork between two fingers he spied a couple of fiery scarlet blotches, beneath which the bones gleamed yellow through the skin, as if already the skeleton were laying claim to what was its by right.

In samples taken from the children's throats and the mucous membrane in their noses the doctor found the smallpox virus. And yet the children's arms bore the marks of smallpox vaccination. All that could be done for these children, the doctor told himself, had been done. What he was witnessing here ought not to be and could not be possible.

As soon as the children had been admitted to the hospital he had had them put into quarantine. On the third day of their hospitalization he noted the spread of the variola to the rest of their bodies. Within another forty-eight hours, these had grown into large, confluent patches of inflammation, which by the fifth day were bursting with white pus. On the seventh day Christian Windsløv watched the children die a death more awful than any he had ever witnessed. The usual debility did not manifest itself; in this instance Nature vouchsafed no form of anaesthetization; the sickness induced a remarkably lucid fever in which, through the morphine and periodic convulsions, the children saw how Death came and sat on their chests and took the life from them a little at a time.

The following week, eight sick children were admitted to the University Hospital. The week after that, twenty more. The next week, another twenty. On March 1st Christian Windsløv locked himself in his office. By then he had not slept for a week; nonetheless he was thinking with incisive clarity. Slowly and deliberately he proceeded to write a letter to his boyhood friend, the mayor of Vaden Town, the merchant Nikolaj Holmer.

"First of all," he wrote, "I must tell you that with this letter I am breaking my professional oath of silence. At the present moment I am the only person in the country who knows that a new and unknown strain of smallpox has cropped up in Denmark. The symptoms of the disease bear some resemblance to the smallpox with which we are already familiar but it develops more rapidly, is far more painful and appears to be absolutely fatal.

"I have tried my best to inoculate using the new virus. But with no apparent success. And as you know we have no other recourse. I fear the disease is incurable; that, despite all our efforts, we are here faced with a curse that is beyond our powers.

"To date, here at the hospital we have seen fifty cases. I have today received reports which suggest there might be as many as two hundred more. And listen to me, Nikolaj: by far the majority of those affected are children. The infection must have originated on Zealand and so far as I can tell it has spread from there to Fyn and then to Jutland. But it has not yet got as far south as Vaden; there is still time. For what I cannot say, I am a scientist not an organizer and consul like yourself. But I feel you should . . . indeed, Nikolaj, I beg of you: use this time, use it for our children's sakes."

Knowing full well that this was the strangest and most crucial letter he had ever sent, the doctor signed it, and as his pen left the paper he felt a faint twinge between his middle and index fingers. Spreading his fingers on the paper before him he saw the two red blotches. At this he was filled with a tremendous rage. Not on his own behalf, for over the past fifty years Christian Windsløv had conversed with Death on a daily basis, distantly and politely, as with a well-matched opponent. No, his rage was for the young, the living, those whom he had seen brought into the world and whom he had carried on his shoulders when they had eaten too much, and to whom he had read aloud, and who were now, nonetheless, under threat from this strange and deadly enigma which was breaking through the safety barrier which he had spent his life – and it seemed was now to die – building. A fierce, maternal instinct it was that now welled up in the physician's exhausted body, prompting him to recall a motto he had shared in his youth with Nikolaj Holmer. With tears in his eyes he leaned over and wrote beneath his signature:

Nec nunc nec unquam – now or never.

Then he calmly disinfected the letter and its envelope with carbolic powder and on going out to post it held a rubber glove between the paper and his infected hand.

Nikolaj Holmer received the letter one afternoon. He had never been a man to balk at doing whatever he deemed necessary and as he read the letter his friend had written he sensed that these words were coming to him from the grave. By the time he summoned the town council to a meeting that very evening his mind was already made up as to what would have to be done.

He read the letter out in the assembly hall, then let the horror grow. It was the vicar who put the thoughts of everyone present into words in saying that this was a case of a punishment of sorts being meted out to the rest of the Danish house of the dead, a punishment for which Vaden Town's land of the living was now quite unjustly to suffer.

Then Nikolaj Holmer got to his feet. "Vicar," he said, "if I might put a more secular interpretation on your words and on this infection. Of one thing there can be no doubt, and that is that where this sickness is concerned it all comes down to hygiene and care. The reason it has struck other parts of the country first is that the rest of Denmark does not have our sewers, our standards of domestic cleanliness, our solicitude for children and young people. It would be madness for us to have to pay the penalty for the negligence of others. It seems very likely that Denmark is facing what could be the most widespread and most appalling epidemic in our country's history. Our children must not perish in this Armageddon. I hereby propose that we shut the town gates, that we set the men of the Sixth South Jutland battalion – all of whom are sons of our town – to guard them, and that we then keep them shut until a vaccine has been found or until the epidemic dies out. Do you understand what I am saying, gentlemen? I am proposing that we show we have the courage necessary to put the rest of Denmark in quarantine."

Even while Nikolaj Holmer was still speaking his fellow burghers had grasped that there was no other way. To a man they shared the conviction not only that Vaden acted as a reservoir of sensibility for the rest of the country, but that their town represented the heart of Denmark, and it now seemed to them both sensible and right to cut off the blood supply to this body which had so neglected itself. "If thy right hand offend thee, cut it off," thought the vicar ecstatically, only then to be struck by the thought that man does not live by grand sentiment alone. But Nikolaj Holmer beat him to it. Slowly he walked over to the tall windows overlooking the town and with one wave of his hand took in the grain silos, the storehouses and cargo ships. "Holmer & Son," he said, "will feed the town. And it will not be just one meal. And not only loaves and fishes." He paused. Then softly he added, "Now or never."

The following evening at a meeting in the town square the rest of the town endorsed the town council's decision. During this meeting Nikolaj Holmer made it clear that the Danish constitution made no provision for such a public gathering, nor for the decision at which it had arrived. "But," he added, "I say this merely for form's sake. To me, this meeting is no different from the popular assembly in Athens; we are now the ultimate decision-making authority here. From now on I do not consider any law to apply in this town other than the right of any man to defend his family against a deadly threat from the outside." And so strong was the sense of solidarity among those present that everyone remained perfectly silent and instead of applause the mayor was met by a hushed wave of resolute accord.

This wave also touched Nikolaj Holmer's son, Kristoffer, where he sat surveying the town from a hatch at the very top of the warehouse building in one of the four wings of his father's establishment on the hill. Kristoffer was the only person apart from the members of the town council to have known in advance what the meeting was about. The afternoon on which he received the letter from his boyhood friend, Nikolaj Holmer had sent a telegram recalling Kristoffer from the boarding school he had been attending for the past three years. Kristoffer was the merchant's only son and his hopes for the boy's future constituted the true cornerstone of the merchant himself and of his business. What Nikolaj said to the people of the town in the square he said, at bottom, for his son's sake. And yet here was Kristoffer, looking out unseeing across the roofs of the town, his heart filled with dull, black despair.

For two hundred years Nikolaj Holmer's forefathers had been well-to-do merchants, creating, maintaining and gradually increasing the family fortune by means of small, carefully calculated business deals. Behind this restraint lay a deep fear of the poverty of which the Holmer family had a daily view from their rooms overlooking those lower-lying parts of Vaden. In no member of this family was this fear stronger than in Nikolaj, but in him it manifested itself very early on as a distrust of moderation. Hardly had he learned to talk than he was lifting his head from the thin gruel for supper to say to his sister: "When I'm big I'm going to have cake for supper, and eat it too!" He was not whipped for this presumption, since folk in Vaden did not beat their children, not even for such bumptiousness. But he was sent to bed and his mother came upstairs and sat down beside him and sang in a cracked voice:

Seek out the lowliest places
in the dust, where the Saviour wails
and there you will see Baby Jesus
for the roses grow in the dales.

Against this humility Nikolaj hardened his prickly little heart and turned his face to the wall. He had come to understand that the Saviour, like his own forefathers, had been a failed pedlar, roving dusty highways and byways to hawk a ware on which there was no profit to be made and which had brought him nothing but a fame that came too late. And from when he was very small,

Nikolaj knew why. It was because the Saviour had encouraged laziness. Wherever he showed up people had downed their fishing nets and tools to follow him and hear him preach the gospel of idleness, asking what did it profit you to gather into barns and gain the whole world when, as the birds of the air eat, though they sow not and neither do they reap, so shall you also eat.

On this sermon, which could not possibly lead anywhere except to sure and certain bankruptcy, Nikolaj turned his back, wanting to find a way that led upwards. And so he formed his own ascension fantasy. In this he envisaged an angel appearing and giving him a sign, after which they would rise up together.

He was seventeen years old when, one day, he saw the angel playing ball on a lawn behind the town's private school for girls. Across the lawn floated a number of other heavenly beings all dressed in long blue skirts and white blouses, but there was only one angel and when she departed that spot Nikolaj followed her, keeping his distance – not because he was afraid, but because of the great awe with which anyone who has seen God is filled.

The girl's parents owned a mercantile establishment that was bigger and situated higher up than the Holmer property, and where his family was prudent, hers was renowned for having attained their position by dint of a breathtaking parsimony that had allowed nothing to slip through its fingers, least of all a daughter. These people had always been capable of getting their own way in everything; they had raised up other families or cast them into the abyss; they had influenced governments and given Danish history a direct shove, but it soon became evident that such was the love between their daughter and Nikolaj Holmer that, hand in hand, these two young people met head-on any and every obstacle, in order either to be crushed against it or wipe it out. They set up house together in two poky rooms down by the harbour, and one day seven months after they had first met the girl donned a loose, white dress, pinned a gold dahlia in her hair, took Nikolaj's arm and paraded her pregnant state up through Vaden Town.

Prior to this, Nikolaj had not given any thought to money. Befuddled by love as he was, for seven months the world had appeared to him as if the only question of any significance related to love and a roof over one's head, and he was not sure whether it looked this way because his emotions had immersed him in a heavy stupor or because they had lifted him up to a higher and clearer point of view. But on the day that his parents and hers learned she was pregnant both families announced that they would sever all links with the two young people. And Nikolaj had a fleeting glimpse of his wife and his child as something he might lose; before his eyes the image of the angel dissolved and he saw living creatures who could be struck down by illness or starvation. This nightmare haunted him for only a very short time before the families relented, it being the way in Vaden Town that whatever children and young people have brought together shall no adult put asunder, especially not when, as here, it happened to be an advantageous match for both parties.

But by then it was too late, by then Nikolaj Holmer had been hurled back into his family's fear, his own childhood fear of poverty. He had looked at the woman in his life and said to himself: "I must give her security."

His was one of the most meteoric rises Denmark had ever seen. From his family's fund of experience Nikolaj knew everything there was to know about trade and commerce. Now this knowledge was combined with a new fearlessness, bordering on recklessness, and in this state he invested the family savings in what had all the makings of an act of financial suicide: a private company building, in Rostock, an immense sailing ship, a steel-hulled full-rigger designed to take up the battle of sail versus steam – a battle which had been lost before it even started – and take part in the annual race from Europe to Australia to collect the first, precious grain crop. In its first year the ship, the *Vincent*, completed the trip round the Cape of Good Hope in two hundred days and the sale of the grain in London provided its investors with a return of seven thousand per cent, the largest profit ever made in that market. The next year proved better still. The year after that the ship was lost off Madagascar, but by then Nikolaj had withdrawn his money, by then he owned his first merchantmen. Two years later, he took over the property on the hill and he and his wife and their son Kristoffer moved into the big white house that formed one of its four wings. That same year Nikolaj ordered the building in Helsinki of the full-rigger *Kronos*, the world's largest sailing ship which, one year later on the same grain route to Australia from which he had taken off on his financial ascension, beat the famous tea clipper *Cutty Sark*'s old speed record. Two years later he had extended the fundament upon which his family's security rested far beyond the shores of Denmark, to branches in Bergen, Stockholm and Riga. And from vast storehouses in Cuxhaven at the mouth of the Elbe the company gazed thoughtfully out over the North Sea.

Although during these years Nikolaj Holmer saw his wife every day, he lived in a different world from her; a world of inventories, shipping lists and calculations. And from the solitude to which her husband had abandoned her she began to hear voices. A vague echo of these voices filtered through to the merchant when he began to detect a new, hunted look on her face. He realized that in some way she had need of him and with his practised eye for future prospects he reckoned that in five years at most he would have made his family secure, in five years he would be able to make time for love. But the voices could not wait that long and one spring day they talked her into slashing her wrists. It was Nikolaj himself who found her in her bedroom. In a last attempt to show consideration for those she was leaving behind, she had ordered things in such a way that the blood ran down into one of the huge porcelain vases he had had one of his ships bring her from the Far East and not a drop had been spilt.

Confronted by his wife's body Nikolaj saw that she truly had been an angel, inasmuch as she had succeeded in taking her beauty with her to the other side of the dividing line between life and death. Then it occurred to him that he must have made some mistake, since he had been deprived of all reason for living. He had no idea what this mistake might have been but he responded to his grief with the only answer known to him: work. Even though Kristoffer was only seven years old at the time, he changed the name of the company to "Holmer & Son" and ten years later, when the town of Vaden shut its gates, it was one of the largest commercial enterprises in Denmark and he himself the possessor of one of the biggest private fortunes in Denmark.

It seems unlikely that any other town in Denmark could have done what Vaden Town did. No other place would have been allowed to get away with cutting itself off from the main body of society. But week after week went by and the town remained hermetically sealed.

This could be put down partly to the town's powerful influence, the respect which wealth and position engender, and partly to the fact that thirty members of the Upper and Lower Houses and four government ministers had been born in the town. But most of all it had to do with the reaction of the rest of Denmark to the news of an unknown and fatal disease.

When the University Hospital made the news public, the country was left stunned and for week after week it languished in a state of numb desperation. It was as if the very thought of the disease, the dreadful notion of what those two hundred cases might develop into, was in itself infectious. As if the country's doctors, hospitals, maternity homes and disinfecting plants, every bit of that splendid instrument for the promotion of physical health, had become a failing in itself. As if the nation could no longer live with the knowledge that they had not succeeded in conquering death.

How could anyone possibly react to Vaden in such a state? There was not one member of the government, hardly a soul in all Denmark who could honestly say they had not entertained the thought that Vaden's lofty isolation represented the only sensible option in the face of the anarchy of this ominous disease.

During the time for which the town was closed off, only once did it admit outsiders. On the fourteenth day of the blockade, from his lookout post Kristoffer watched the big galleass anchoring outside the town and signalling for a pilot to be sent on board. None appeared. Instead the blue and white signal flag for "No" was run up the harbour flagstaff, after which the town of Vaden slowly and unmistakably spelled out its refusal. At that, a launch was lowered into the water from the galleass; a small, lustrous barque of polished mahogany with a canopied cuddy at the prow and a steam engine of burnished copper and brass in the stern. At the outermost breakwater this vessel was met by the harbour master, Nikolaj Holmer and four armed soldiers, and even Kristoffer was surprised when the tiny boat was not sent packing there and then. Instead it turned about only after lengthy debate, following which one of the Vaden pilot boats put out from the harbour and towed the galleass in to the quayside, thus committing an incomprehensible breach of the town's isolation.

Her pennant notwithstanding, the ship did not belong to the Danish royal family. Her name was the *Alanda Gleim* and on board she carried the animals, artists, artisans and management of the "Circus Gleim", the most magnificent circus Europe had ever seen. At the close of the previous century, at a special performance given in Fredensborg Palace for Christian IX and the whole of the Danish royal house's extended European family, the King had given permission for this circus which travelled around Europe by sea to fly the royal family's own flag, in recognition of the fact that the circus itself was a seafaring kingdom of sorts, a Noah's ark for the only art form beloved of all walks of life.

The manager of this circus, Mr Gleim himself, had been one of the launch's two passengers. The other was an old man with a grey moustache and sensitive features. He was a dwarf, only four feet high, but according to the circus poster – and the Circus Gleim posters were not given to exaggeration – his reputation ranged from the Cape of Good Hope to the very north of the Gulf of Bothnia. This was that clown adored by all the world, Monsieur Andress.

Monsieur Andress had succeeded in combining the popular appeal of the circus clown with the utmost European refinement. Born to wealthy Hungarian exiles and raised in southern Europe, he had grown into a true cosmopolite. He had received a classical education, had early on decided to become a priest and had by all accounts almost completed his studies at the Jesuit college when an irresistible attraction to music had led him to some of Italy's most celebrated conservatories. Despite his short stature he had proved to have a stupendous voice. A number of composers had written pieces especially for the dwarf's countertenor – until, that is, he left the opera to take up conducting and it became apparent that from this small but perfectly formed body there emanated a musical magnetism which moved the Vienna Opera to offer him the post of musical director which had fallen vacant on the death of Gustav Mahler. But Monsieur Andress said no. From what was – to the rest of the world and his family in particular – some unfathomable corner of the universe the certainty had come to him that he should be a circus clown. And when he stood in the ring for the first time it was plain for all to see that this idea must have come both from the good Lord himself and from his own generous heart. Until then it had never occurred to anyone that this musical dwarf could be funny, believing as they did that he had been born to receive the applause of a vast concert-hall audience while clad in a diminutive dress suit and a child's patent-leather shoes. But from the moment he set foot in the ring for the first time it was so obvious that this was the way – in shoes that were several sizes too large and enveloped in the reek of stables while the world laughed and cried by turns – *this* was how the universe fulfilled its purpose with Monsieur Andress. Without losing any of the clown's touching simplicity he took up its mask, refined it, amplified its childlike quality, dispelled its traditional malevolence, until he was entering and leaving the ring a study in irresistible childlike gaucherie.

It was with such a past and such fame behind him that Monsieur Andress – from the tiny boat, looking down the barrels of the soldiers' rifles – now directed an appeal to Nikolaj Holmer.

For three months, the clown told him, the circus had been touring the Baltic coastline. Sailing down the Baltic they had run into a fierce winter storm; rolling heavily, the flat-bottomed ship had been forced to heave to and thereafter try to ride out the storm. In winds that were continually shifting direction they had drifted now south, now back to where they had started; with horses screaming in terror they had been swept along at twelve knots with all sails furled. Visibility being so poor they had lost their bearings, and when the first rays of sun appeared and land was sighted off the port bow this turned out to be Ærø, one of the islands in an archipelago so hazardous that only skippers thoroughly acquainted with the area are capable of navigating it. The ship had in fact been bound for Kiel, but for the sake of the animals and, more particularly, the children – children who were terrified and weak from having been unable to eat anything for such a long time – the decision had been taken to run before the wind towards Vaden Town.

Faced with the prospect of having to turn away sick children, and confronted by this old man – the very heart and soul of the European circus tradition, whom any head of state would have welcomed with gratitude – Nikolaj Holmer decided to relent, to make an exception and to bid them welcome. "For," he thought to himself, "like us they too have been cut off, they too seek protection for their weakest members, for the women and children."

In the Circus Gleim the emotions that had been unleashed in the town of Vaden found the focal point they needed.

Among the members of the town council there were those who feared that this unusual state of affairs, the town's unilateral breakaway from the rest of Denmark, would lead to individual lawlessness. Their thoughts had turned to tales of towns in the Middle Ages which had closed their gates against the plague and whose inhabitants had then begun first to burn their candle at both ends and, later, to burn themselves out in a blazing inferno of debauchery as they endeavoured to squeeze an entire lifetime into the short span they had left to live.

In Vaden things took a different turn.

On the surface life carried on as if nothing had happened. Each morning the adults rose and went about their business and the children attended their schools, and yet nothing was as it had been. Because, unlike the madness which had caused those mediaeval burghers, faced by the plague, to dance until they dropped, the adults and children of Vaden had been visited by a new and boundless patience, which sprang from their feeling that they were going to live for ever. The reason they found it possible to go on taking part, day in, day out, in a daily round the premises for which had altered completely, was that all at once this life had been shot through by a fresh clarity. From various points around the town it had been possible to survey the lush countryside round about, to survey Denmark. With the closing of the gates this outlook seemed to vanish. The people of the town quite simply stopped looking down a street, over the town wall towards the farms in the south. Simultaneously with the non-arrival of the newspapers, thoughts winging their way towards the larger towns and cities or across the sea quite spontaneously came to a halt. Although there was no way of telling who had made the decision, there came a day when the telegraph counter at the post office was closed and from that day on it was as if the rest of Denmark ceased to exist. To children, only those things which are near at hand have any existence, things remote tend to fade into obscurity. This was how the adults in Vaden now began to view the world. Not that they ever said anything to one another, but they did wonder why they had not isolated themselves long before this, why it should have taken an epidemic for them to tumble to the fact that the essence of security lies in raising barriers.

So powerful was this new sense of immortality that it led people to gather every day at the town square, on the spot where they had, so to speak, democratically voted themselves into eternity; and it was here, outside the town hall, that Nikolaj Holmer and the other tradesmen of the town arranged for the daily distribution of food. And the Circus Gleim, and above all Monsieur Andress, became the new spirit of these gatherings.

It began with a performance to be held in the Town Hall's main assembly room; this location, however – due to an overwhelming turnout, with the whole of Vaden wishing to attend, together with the early and surprisingly warm spring breeze which was blowing over the town – being shifted to the square, into the open air, under a bright afternoon sky which, as the performance progressed, paled, turned blue and grew dark.

They did not present the whole programme, since the town's intensely portentous air of solemnity would not have lent itself to the Circus Gleim's grand, international gala performances. Just three acts, that was what the inhabitants of Vaden saw, were captivated by and went on to demand every evening. A tall white-clad Mongol presenting, without the aid of whip, six Lipizzaner stallions in a freestyle dressage programme; a strong and pliant girl performing serene, introspective acrobatics while suspended from a rope and, finally, Monsieur Andress, the big little clown.

Everyone felt that with him a king had entered the town, with him the universe had sent them a sign that what they were doing was right; because what this dwarf had done was to unearth the child inside the adult and then turn it into God. He always made his entrance in the same fashion, without make-up, in a velvet costume just a little on the big side. He was accompanied, to begin with, by a twelve-year-old boy with whom he commenced to play, and during this game the ancient vanished, during it the years evaporated and out of the old man's body sprouted the boy inside all of them, *puer aeternus*, a radiant symbol of that for which every member of the audience had been willing to give his or her life: the love of childhood.

During his first two weeks in the town Monsieur Andress simplified his act a little with each day that passed, until finally he dispensed with his assistant and entered the arena alone. He was always introduced by the manager of the Circus Gleim, who had grasped before anyone else the professional potential inherent in this audience's blend of warm-heartedness and selflessness and who made his point early on by introducing the great clown in a manner which no outsider would have understood. Each evening, ringmaster Gleim flung wide his arm and said: "Ladies and gentlemen. I give you the musical clown, Monsieur Andress, in Vaden Town. A heart within a heart within a heart!"

Every one of these performances constituted a religious service, from which people made their way home moved, dazed, with shining eyes and the clown's voice still ringing in their ears, a voice which apparently spoke all languages, including a beautiful, soft Danish.

And just as deeply moved was Kristoffer Holmer, on leaving that spot after having passed by, quite by chance, one day, and somewhat reluctantly caught a performance.

The terms in which the town of Vaden perceived its day-to-day life were those which pertain to trade, craftsmanship and shipping. Even that religion which was preached every Sunday in the town churches was geared to their industrious daily lives. No one in Vaden Town was in any doubt that what the Saviour had preached was that those who seek shall find; always provided, that is, that they have risen at half-past five, six days a week, and gone to work. Everything else, everything that smacked of philosophy or recreation, was considered by and large to be superfluous. When the inhabitants of Vaden wanted to look through everyday life at the golden kingdoms lying beyond it, they looked at their children. Even so, most of them would have had an answer on the tip of their tongue if asked how a prince would look. They would have replied that a prince would look like Nikolaj Holmer's son.

Kristoffer Holmer had always been a strapping lad; the fastest runner and with the best eye for a ball of all the boys his age. Not only that but there was a gravely dignified side to his nature which, even before he turned seven, made adults listen to him. He could play the piano from the minute he was first set down at that instrument; he could draw as soon as a pencil was put in his hand and yet he shrank from displaying his accomplishments, seeming to gloss over them, as if wishing to apologize to life for everything which had come so easily to him. He had dark-grey, deep-set eyes which endowed his whole face with a somewhat reticent quality. The women of Vaden thought Kristoffer had the look of a saint and they wreathed him in a halo of pity at the thought of his losing his mother at such a tender age.

People had always agreed that there could be no more worthy crown prince of the firm of "Holmer & Son" and his formative years proved fully to live up to the trust the world had put in him. Even his grief at the death of his mother appeared to have been transformed in the small boy into an early maturity. Without doubting his son for a second, when the boy was fourteen years old Nikolaj Holmer sent him to one of the country's finest boarding schools. During the years Kristoffer spent there father and son saw one another only during the holidays, and each time they were reunited it seemed to Nikolaj Holmer that his son had grown still closer to the outside world's and his own dream of the perfect son and heir.

When Kristoffer was summoned home by his father's telegram and the two met one another for the first time in six months, the merchant could tell that something was wrong, for Kristoffer showed up looking more distant, of a more withdrawn cast of mind and with a more deep-seated, scrutinizing gaze than his father had ever remarked in him before.

Nikolaj Holmer was no great judge of character. To be sure, no one knew better than he how to expose a rake-off or a falsified account, or how to break an embargo. But that part of the human heart not taken up with buying and selling remained, as far as the great merchant was concerned, a closed book. At the counter and across the negotiating table his competence and authority were beyond question. Now, evening after evening, he sat at the dinner table, across from the one person in the world he loved and with whom all of a sudden it had become impossible for him to exchange the simplest pleasantries, and this left him feeling confused, humiliated and angry. They ate in total silence, after which Kristoffer stood up and left the room, the merchant usually not seeing him again until breakfast the next day.

What had in fact happened was that just before he had been called home, Kristoffer had made the discovery that in all probability he himself did not exist. This truth had been brought home to him in the gym hall of his school, during a fencing lesson, striking him out of the blue.

Ever since its founding in the eighteenth century, the school had given special priority to fencing and had always made a point of recruiting the best international teachers in this discipline. On first seeing Kristoffer testing the weight of a foil in his hand and, later, on giving him his first lesson, the school's French fencing master discerned in his new pupil the combination of psycho-physical balance and lightning-quick, stinging menace which is the essence of fencing. For this sport Kristoffer seemed to conceive an abiding passion. That very April, after three years of training, the school had allowed him to take a week's break from his studies and, at the end of those seven days of intensive preparation, under the supervision of his French teacher he had won the Danish national championship ahead of army captains fifteen years his senior with curling mustachios and ten years of tournament experience under their belts.

This was just around the time when the twentieth century's wave of interest in sport was reaching new heights in Denmark, and in the boy from Vaden the country spied a new hope for the next great Olympiad. Kristoffer's training was now geared towards this challenge and it was in the midst of this training programme, with his championship win only a few weeks old, that he found himself overcome by despair. During a bout against the only other pupil at the school capable of giving him a run for his money, for the first time in his life Kristoffer found himself looking inwards.

Up to that point he had always viewed himself through the eyes of others. In the surrounding world's upturned, trusting and admiring faces he had caught his own reflection and understood that he was indeed that Kristoffer who was destined to set off on a journey and discover for himself and for others some hitherto unknown part of the world. This was something of which his teachers and his schoolmates had assured him, something he had also seen in his father's eyes. But on the fencing piste, behind the wire-mesh mask, one's opponent's face is hidden from view and all at once it occurred to Kristoffer that he was actually fighting himself. And from there his gaze slid backwards, into himself. He knew what he ought to have been able to see. He ought to have seen a boy bursting with resolute self-confidence, a fine sportsman, a wealthy young man in the midst of the most splendid formative process, an ever-so-slightly gauche and, for that very reason, an irresistible lady-killer and lover and an eminent businessman in the making. He found nothing of all this, only an echoing, black void, surrounded by the frail shell which people erroneously imagined formed the exterior of Kristoffer Holmer's flawless character. So he lowered his foil and turned his back, thereby exposing the white point denoting the target, and did not notice his opponent's thrust and hit. He strode off, passing between the raised arms of the corner judges, unmindful of the stunned faces – knowing as he did that all of these sentiments applied to a mask. Of the real Kristoffer Holmer, if he were to be found anywhere in that void, the world had never so much as caught a glimpse.

It is a terrible thing for a person to see their own life or that of others threatened by extinction. But it is a far worse thing to know that one is most likely already dead and may possibly never have been alive, while one's fellow men carry on as if one were still moving among them. This was how things stood for Kristoffer when, in March 1929, he came home to Vaden and heard the gate slam behind him, that he might be protected from a threat from outside, a threat which he was bound to consider as far less harmful than the death he carried inside himself.

His father's telegram had reached him while he was still benumbed. Back in Vaden, during the first weeks of quarantine, he had the chance to reflect upon his situation and his thoughts turned, in the first instance, to suicide, revolving around this tempting option only eventually to abandon it. Suicide presupposes some unbearable emotional stress from which it is hoped that death will bring release. Kristoffer had been stricken by something quite different. He had been seized, he felt, by a sense of despair so profound that it went beyond death. He was not religious but he was convinced that were he to do away with himself, all he would leave behind him would be his worthless mask, while that inner emptiness would follow him and laugh at him and shroud him in its terror on the other side of the grave.

He had once tried to explain how he felt to his father. Nikolaj had listened attentively and then he had nodded. "I know just what you mean," he said. "It has crossed my mind, too, when faced with some sure-fire deal, to get up and leave because I felt the time wasn't right to rake in the chips. What matters, Kristoffer, is not to win every time. What matters is to know that, any time you liked, you could have won."

After this conversation Kristoffer had roamed the streets in a state of utter hopelessness and it was then that he had come past the square and had seen Monsieur Andress perform – a performance which had moved him deeply. Not that it made him happy, it had not offered him any hope, but it reached into his heart of hearts and told him that he was not alone, that on this earth, not to mention in this town, there was someone who knew the same pain as he, someone capable of giving it expression.

Kristoffer's first impulse, when the show came to an end, was to fight his way through the crowd, to clasp that little hand, perhaps even to kiss it and, if nothing else, to assure the clown that *he*, Kristoffer, had grasped perfectly and absolutely – had been the only one in town to grasp – the bewilderment of a child in an unfathomable world which the old man had been conveying. But he stayed where he was, restrained by the air of respect surrounding the artist. No one, apart from the mayor and a handful of town councillors, ventured any closer to the old man than the distance between the edge of the ring and the front-row seats, everyone feeling as they did that the warmth which existed between themselves and the dwarf during the show must not be pursued; that it represented the manifestation of a greater truth for which the dwarf acted as some kind of medium. When the performance was over they watched him walk away without daring to follow him and if they happened to bump into the diminutive, neatly attired figure on the street they would make way for him, the women automatically curtsying with the respect instinctively accorded by people to a high priest. And yet Kristoffer felt certain that he could have broken through this circle, as all his life he had got away with doing things no one else was allowed to do. When he now turned away from the square anyway and made his way homewards it was because he had been struck by the thought that he had nothing to offer. How could he walk up to someone in possession of such inner riches when he himself did not actually exist?

From the quadrangle formed by the four wings of his father's property he climbed aloft, to the top floor of the tall warehouse and, once there, opened the hatch overlooking the yard, sat himself down on a sack and looked down on his boyhood home and beyond that, out over the town. Over the past few weeks he had got into the habit of sitting up here, because this was the one place where he could be alone with his emptiness; and because he had played here as a child. Now the view and the unique atmosphere of the loft seemed redolent of a very faint whisper from the past, telling him that his life had, nonetheless, had its meaningful moments.

During the previous century this loft had been used as a storeroom – until, that is, the development of modern cranes and the trade in perishable goods had rendered it redundant. In ranging so far afield the nerve endings of the big mercantile concern, so sensitively attuned to the slightest fluctuation in the stock markets of Great Britain and the United States, had lost touch with those things closest to home. The company had quite simply forgotten this loft. Coming upon it as a small boy Kristoffer had instinctively sensed that, unlike other secrets which had a tendency to grow big and bright when shared with others, this one would fade away were he to mention it, and by dint of the sort of thoroughgoing discretion with which adults never credit children, he had succeeded in keeping this place to himself. In those days he had kept the hatch shut for fear of being discovered but now, when he had been opening it every day, it had dawned on him that no one in Vaden Town, not even his own father, ever looked up; that their thoughts were channelled horizontally and, in his father's case, spanned every one of the seven seas, but were at no time directed up the way, at a point right above his head.

The loft still held the carefully packed remains of a forgotten past, from the days when Vaden was still establishing its reputation as a shipping town. Sacks containing a pungent spice from Sumatra to which no one had been able to put a name either in English or in Danish and which, it transpired, induced hallucinations and had therefore proved impossible to sell and so, for want of anything better, had been stowed away up here, well out of the way. Finely worked wooden boxes containing sextants from the days when compass roses, ornately decorated though they were, gave no more accurate reading than the four corners of the world. Metal caskets filled with charts of parts of the world with coastlines offering little in the way of harbourage and on which the interior of continents had been illustrated with pictures of mythical beasts. From this room Kristoffer now watched the sun setting and a fierce storm brewing.

It started over land, as a dull, pulsating glow that seemed to have nothing to do with the evening sky. Then every ounce of colour drained from the sunset, the sky grew quite dark and a coal-black veil drifted in over Vaden like the shadow of an as yet unseen and unimaginably enormous body descending upon the town from outer space. At first this shadow looked to be a long way off, then it gathered speed and in one great swoop it was on the town. One minute the houses and the sea at their feet were lying in the last narrow band of daylight, the next Vaden was enveloped in darkness, as though an inky mantle had been cast over it. A cloak which was then riven by the first bolt of lightning. For an instant an elongated, snaking streak of white light rent the night, chiselled out of the blackness, then it was gone, taking with it the electric lighting and plunging the town into deepest darkness, as if the rest of the world was of a mind to revenge itself on Vaden and pay it back for its defiance.

The dying of the light left the yard beneath Kristoffer black as pitch. Next this blackness was torn apart by a different sort of lightning, lightning unlike anything Kristoffer had ever come across before, a long-drawn-out, agonizing discharge of white energy. And then came the rain, as yet no more than a foretaste of what was to come; an exultant, rapid-fire drumming of water culminating in a distant clap of thunder.

At this Kristoffer was filled with an irresistible urge to pray for help to the black heavens above.

As a small boy he had made catapults. Down on the shore he and the other boys had tried to see who could sling a pebble highest. He had always viewed other people's prayers as just such sling-shots at Heaven. If there was one thing of which you could be sure in this world it was that pebble and words always found their way back to you – his own pebble some time after the others' – having had no effect on the universe other than to confirm once again what everyone already knew: that Kristoffer Holmer could shoot the highest. Even so, he was conscious now of how, without moving a muscle, he tucked a smooth, round pebble into his sling and, knowing full well that this action contained no small amount of madness, he catapulted his words out into the void, in the form of a wish that for him, too, life must hold some meaning; that there had to be a grain of humanity lodged within Kristoffer Holmer's shell. And he strained all of his senses, listening for the sound of an answer or of the echo which would betray that the pebble had merely fallen back to Earth.

His wait was cut short by a clap of thunder. When the next flash of lightning lit up the yard below him, a figure stood in the gateway. And in the volley of lightning that followed, in one long, continuous run of flashes, Kristoffer recognized this figure. It was the dwarf, the great Monsieur Andress. He was standing out of the rain but in such a way that his form was floodlit by the bursts of lightning. He was looking around, like an actor who has just made his entrance, and the darkness between the flashes made him appear to be moving his head in a series of rapid jerks. It seemed inconceivable to Kristoffer that the little man could have seen anything at all against a sky that alternated between inky blackness and dazzling brightness, and yet for a moment he had the notion that the dwarf was staring straight at him. Then everything went dark and an ear-splitting crash made the room around him vibrate.

In the ensuing hush he caught the sound of footsteps. The measured stride of someone small. Someone had obviously lit a paraffin lamp, and this the dwarf must have lifted on his way up, because now its light came flickering up the stairs and spread into the loft.

Then Monsieur Andress was there in the room.

Kristoffer had been brought up to be polite and to anticipate and be prepared for the unexpected. So, as the clown's steps were drawing nearer, in his head he was planning a fitting reception for him. He saw himself taking a couple of paces forward, sinking to his knees – an act which would bring his head level with that of the new arrival – speaking his name, then going on to improvise some sort of welcome.

Instead, what happened was that he sat where he was, stock-still. In one hand the clown was carrying a violin case, in the other a lamp, but the wavering light that now illuminated the loft emanated, to Kristoffer's mind, from his face. This appeared to be lit up from within; through the fine network of wrinkles and the bushy moustache there radiated a light that seemed to come from some brightly burning, incandescent source of warmth and humanity which shattered Kristoffer's plans, turning them to naught. Moving slowly and with dignity, the clown set the lamp down and divested himself of his cloak, beneath which he still wore his costume of loose-fitting white material. This done, he stepped across to the hatch and looked out.

A fresh burst of lightning blazed over the darkened streets, momentarily throwing up an image of the shining, rain-drenched roofs as rows of tombstones sitting on black earth, and Kristoffer remembered that the town lay entrenched against death.

When the dwarf spoke his voice was like threadbare velvet, overlaid with the delicate patina of all the linguistic regions through which his long life had taken him.

"When you're my height," he said, "it can be quite pleasant to look upon the world *von oben* like this."

It struck Kristoffer that since the day he was born the clown's stature had perhaps not only kept him below others' eye level but might even have consigned him to another world; that the pain which he had recognized in Andress' act might have something to do with an experience not unlike his own, inasmuch as both of them, by dint of a definite congenital defect, stood outside the world that surrounded them.

"From up here, it would be very easy to imagine," the clown went on mildly, "that the countryside and the town down there were *morte*, that we were the last people alive in all the world."

This observation slotted in neatly with Kristoffer's most heartfelt dreams and it was from there that he replied.

"Yes," he said, "that would be awful. But there is something even worse than being alone in the world, and that is not to have existed at all."

The dwarf made no reply to this nor, as far as Kristoffer was concerned, was any reply necessary. For at that moment he was experiencing a sense of having been understood. Filled with equal measures of profound gratitude and unease in the face of the unaccountable, he felt that the universe had answered his prayer, that he was here confronted with a higher being capable of seeing right through what, until then, the outside world had taken for Kristoffer Holmer. "Monsieur Andress is also convinced that he does not really exist among other people," he thought, and in his mind's eye he pictured the show's finale, when the clown collected all of the audience's jewellery, put it on, then strutted around the square like a child begging to be loved because it sparkles – and then, the next day, returning these valuables with unfailing accuracy to their rightful owners, this time as if craving their attention for bringing back something which had been lost. Kristoffer felt his eyes fill with tears.

"I don't know whether you noticed me," he said, "but I was down there, in the square, during your act. It was . . ." – for a second his voice failed him – "it was quite splendid."

Reluctantly, almost, the old man tore his eyes away from the darkness hanging over the town and distractedly regarded Kristoffer.

"When I give a performance," he said, "I am never less than fantastic."

Brought up, as he had been, to aim as high as he could, but never to blow his own trumpet, this matter-of-fact self-assessment took Kristoffer's breath away. "Only a saint," he thought, "could talk like that. Only one who has risen above all other human beings, above the never-ending struggle to make oneself worthy of a place in the world."

"I've often seen you sitting up here," the dwarf remarked.

It was a far cry from Kristoffer's feelings of unworthiness to the fact that the man standing opposite had noticed him before. His mind reeled, as it were, in the ray of merciful light that had now rendered him visible. But once again he replied from the core of his being, to which the clown seemed to speak directly.

"I have discovered," he said, "that I don't seem to exist."

"And where," asked the clown, "did you discover that?"

"At school," answered Kristoffer.

A wince of pain passed over Monsieur Andress' face. "All you gain from school," he said, "is nasty . . ." he broke off, then completed the sentence, ". . . is a dreadful headache."

This simple assertion brought the tears welling up in Kristoffer's eyes once more. Again he was aware of the little man making contact with him across the lifetimes of years and experience that lay between them. Of Monsieur Andress, the world at large knew that he had spent twenty years of his life in convent schools, Jesuit colleges and the strictest conservatories in the world. Out of his fund of learning and experience of educational institutions – experience that towered high above Kristoffer's own – he had dredged up this *bon mot* which was now beaming down on Kristoffer as a crystallization of his own chaotic emotions.

"That," he said, with profound gratitude, "is exactly how it began. With a headache."

Across the hatchway, the yellow light from the lamp cast a gigantic magnification of the clown's silhouette, like an immense black wall. Now Kristoffer leaned towards this wailing wall and opened up his heart, and to his great astonishment he found that it was not empty.

"One day in the gymasium, during a fencing lesson, I turned my back on Castenskiold," he said.

"In a fight," said the dwarf, "you should never turn your back."

"It wasn't like that," said Kristoffer. "You see, all of a sudden I realized that it wasn't him I was fencing with. In a way it was myself. Can you understand that?"

The clown moved a step closer to him. "Yes," he said, "that does happen to some. Particularly at school. There was" – he eyed Kristoffer keenly – "there was a voice which spoke to you, wasn't there?"

Until that moment it had never occurred to Kristoffer that there might have been a voice. But now the clown's eyes, which had been gleaming in the darkness in front of him, seemed to shed fresh light on his shadowy recollection and as he recalled the echo of the gymnasium, the sound of canvas shoes on the copper surface of the piste, the clash of foil on foil, he heard the still-distant, but unmistakable sound of a voice speaking to him.

"Yes," he said softly. "There was a voice. But" – he looked imploringly at Monsieur Andress – "it's so faint that I can hardly hear it."

At this the clown leaned forward and suddenly above Kristoffer's head the loft receded and he beheld the beams and wall bars of the gymnasium. And through the words of command he heard a voice that sounded exactly like Monsieur Andress' asking: "Why do you fight?"

Kristoffer got to his feet with a start, as if trying to shake off a nightmare, but the question held him pinned him to the spot. In self-defence he clutched at the first words to enter his head.

"Because," he said, "the important thing is to take part."

He caught sight of the old man's grey hair, on a level with his face, and realized that he was on his knees. He wanted to say something, wanted to turn this conversation on to another tack, but there was a relentless air about the dwarf now.

"And yet you know," said the voice, "that if you lose today, you will make those who are watching even more unhappy than if you had not competed."

"Yes," said Kristoffer.

"So why do you fight?" The voice was insistent.

"To win," answered Kristoffer.

"And if you win," the voice persisted, "how long will you and the spectators take pleasure in your victory?"

Kristoffer did not reply.

"One night, perhaps," said the voice. "Perhaps one hour. Or one minute. Is that not so?"

"Yes," said Kristoffer.

"*Porca madonna*," said the voice. "Such a fleeting moment for which to wear out your youth."

Like a priest who, having blessed the congregation, then turns to face the altar, the dwarf wheeled around. But now Kristoffer would not let him go. With a great effort of will he pulled himself to his feet, using the homespun sack at his side for leverage, then went after the clown, torn between his terror at the thought of his apparent transparency before those bright eyes in the darkness and his need to hear the voice come with its answers.

"What about school?" he asked. "What about going to school?"

With a flick of his hand Monsieur Andress motioned to him to stay where he was.

"Don't they still tell you that you're being fitted for life?" he asked.

"Yes," said Kristoffer.

"And when life begins," said the clown, "they'll tell you that you live to work, and that you must all work for your country and your children. Those children who in school *da gerade* are starting to learn that they are being fitted for life. And so it goes on, thus all of them – *i goglioni* – push life ahead of them, all the while bawling that they cannot catch up with it." And slowly he recited: "*Piu le cose cambiano, piu sono le stesse cose.*"

With an assurance born of knowing the effect of one's lines in advance, Monsieur Andress turned his back on Kristoffer, positioned himself in the hatchway and peered down into the yard. And as if he himself had conjured up an effective underscoring of his own words, a whole string of lightning flashes threw his silhouette into black relief against a sky seething with electricity.

Although Kristoffer could now feel in his blood a thin, cold, coursing trickle of fear of this thing of which he was now a part, nonetheless he was spurred on by the thought that he might never again be presented with such a chance.

"How," he asked, "did you know there was a voice?"

Slowly Monsieur Andress turned. And now when he stepped down to stand beside Kristoffer there was a somewhat cunning air about him.

"There is always a voice," he said. "All one has to do is listen. That is how I work in the ring."

His eyes grew distant and in his mind's eye Kristoffer saw him in the square with his head cocked, listening in the night for a sound that only he could hear.

"I have the audience in the palm of my hand," he said, and his voice was languorous, enraptured, "I've collected their jewellery, I've been out there, mingling with the crowd. And then I hear a voice, far off and quite faint, but still perfectly clear. And it says I am to bring a boy up on to the stage."

He took Kristoffer's hand and meekly the boy followed the dwarf into the centre of the room. For a split second his mind turned to the assistant the clown had once used in his act, who had been the envy of everyone. "Now," he thought, "I have taken that boy's place."

"We are standing on the stage," said Monsieur Andress, "the audience are on the edge of their seats and I feel something grow out there in the night. I hear the voice whispering about a good trick. It whispers: 'You have a boy. Now get hold of a girl as well. And tonight you will do something tremendous. Something to make the bells ring. And they are already ringing.'" He turned to Kristoffer. "When the bells ring," he said, "something momentous is afoot."

"The church bells?" asked Kristoffer, thinking of Monsieur Andress' clerical past.

"No," whispered the clown, with a faraway look in his eyes. "No, not the church bells. It's the cash-register bells that will chime. If we just find ourselves a girl."

It was at this point that Kristoffer became aware of someone making their way up the stairs. Under other circumstances this fact would have filled him with astonishment and sadness at the fact of his hide-out being discovered. But this night, in the grip of the clown's magnetism, without being fully conscious of doing so, he chose no longer to be surprised.

Then the girl was standing before them. Under other circumstances, Kristoffer would have stared at her, but he was not at all sure that she existed. Like the voice which had spoken to him and which was still ringing in his ears, she seemed to him to be a half-illusory prop in some supernatural stage turn. All he saw was that she was soaking wet, so wet that her long hair, which would under other circumstances – if she did indeed exist under other circumstances – have been curly, now hung down over her shoulder, sending great drops of water cascading off her and on to the floor. The utter improbability of her appearance was only added to by the fact that she was barefoot and to all appearances naked. Then Monsieur Andress dragged his attention back to himself, took the girl's hand and drew them both out on to the floor, and when he now bowed to an imaginary audience Kristoffer recognized, from the show in the square, the characteristic salute which, beneath its superficial deference, maintained a firm grip on the hearts and minds of the spectators.

"Ladies and gentlemen," said the clown, "I give you a young girl and a young man."

He turned to face them. "There is something momentous in the offing this evening," he announced in measured tones. "Something that will make us all richer. In experience and in wisdom. My talent lies in picking up this feeling and putting it across to the audience. We, the audience and I, are expecting something quite beyond belief. Granted, I do not know how this will come about, I have no idea. But I am all ears," and he cocked his head to one side, as if listening to the night sky.

Then the girl took two paces forward and uttered a low moan, which sounded at one and the same time like a snarl and the prelude to a bout of vomiting.

Looking straight at her for the first time Kristoffer saw that she was not naked but simply so sopping wet that her dress was plastered to her body. He had been brought up to live in the world of good, solid facts, for which there is a language that is simple, blithe and efficacious. The events of the past few weeks and more especially the last hour had, however, transported him into another and more perilous landscape, in which he found unexpected and fabulous turns of phrase coming into his head. He did not think he had ever laid eyes on the girl before, but he knew she was a princess. Right at this moment, nothing of what he had learned at school seemed to be readily to hand, and he could not place her as coming from any known mythology, but to his mind she resembled a tragic heroine from one of the great dramas. She was pale. Not wan and colourless, but with a throat and face of a lustrous snowy white; a chill wind hung in her clothes and he was in no doubt that with her she had brought some horrendous experience. Where Monsieur Andress had appeared in the loft surrounded by the light of transfiguration, the girl radiated a kind of exalted lunacy.

She took two faltering steps across the floor, and only then appeared to notice the young man and the old. There was no way of telling what chaotic thoughts were running through her head but she seemed nonetheless to have grasped the solemnity of the situation, for slowly she pulled herself erect, as if to deliver the eloquent opening line that was only to be expected of her. She then raised one arm and stared fixedly at Monsieur Andress.

"I know everything there is to know," she intoned, "about cod."

Then she pitched forward, making no effort to save herself, and would have smashed her face against the floor had Kristoffer not caught her.

No sooner did he feel her weight than he too felt the breath of the chill air that surrounded her. It was the wind from the sea and just for a moment he wondered whether she had come close to drowning.

Then he recognized her.

There had only ever been one person in Kristoffer's life with whom he had shared the secret of his loft, and to this person – someone he had never spoken of to another living soul – his thoughts had kept returning, as to a warm rock amid the torrent of pointlessnes she considered his life to have been. This person was Sonja Vaden. She was of an age with Kristoffer, the daughter of a fisherman whose family might well have taken their name from the town, but whom progress had long since driven beyond its walls to a windswept corner of the fjord. Anywhere else in Denmark these two children would have been separated from one another for their own good, and it would have been explained that the social realities which divided them were a fact which it was in no man's power to change. But in Vaden Town no one could bring themself to be that hard-hearted and so the two children went on playing on the shore and on the hills above the town. Sonja had lost her mother at the age of five, a sorrow she had met head-on and without breaking. When Kristoffer's mother turned away from her husband and her child to follow her voices, Sonja offered Kristoffer – wordlessly, but instantly and unreservedly – her companionship and her slight but remarkably strong shoulders, to help him get over this terrible blow. Day after day, for weeks and months on end, Kristoffer wept when he was in Sonja's company; inconsolable weeping which no one but her was ever allowed to see. This had been followed by a spring of which he recalled having hauled his cart up to the highest point above the town and then driven Sonja down the snaking track with the sun and the wind from the sea in his face and a cloud of dust at his back.

And then she disappeared. Throughout her childhood her father had been in the habit of taking her out fishing with him. One October day they had gone out very early in the morning. Around noon the wind had got up and when at long last Kristoffer had caught sight of the little boat from his hatchway the wind had built up into a storm that swept across the sea like a huge, cold scythe, slicing off the tops of the waves and whisking them away across the water as white streamers of foam. Somewhere in that howling gale a sidelong swell had washed across the boat from astern and carried off Sonja's father. The girl then lashed herself to the wheel and steered the boat through the storm towards the shore. The entrance to Vaden harbour was a narrow one and the townspeople had looked on hopelessly and helplessly as the girl in the tiny vessel neared the moles with their cruelly grinning, stony rows of teeth – teeth which, in that boiling sea, were blanketed by white spume. There was not one among them who would not have risked his or her life for a child in distress if it would have done any good, but the storm had now increased to a force which made any attempt at rescue impossible, so they gritted their teeth against their sobs and thought, full of bitter hate for the sea, that they would not forget this, that there would come a day when not even Nature itself would be able to take a child from them.

Kristoffer too had gone down to the harbour. But unlike most of the people gathered there he did not weep. He had walked out farther than anyone else and no one had had the strength to hold him back. Clinging to the harbour's tall, green entrance beacons he had gazed out at the boat and the only water that found its way into his eyes was sea spray. Sonja had taught him that to everything there is a season. There had been a time to weep, but that time was not now. Now was a time to be strong. Immediately outside the harbour entrance Sonja reversed the engine and with remarkable cool-headedness, as if a little of the sea had entered her blood, she held the boat against the wind and the swell. Kristoffer alone knew why. At one point when despair had looked liable to get the better of him she had told him that all the misfortunes in life come in waves. "And Kristoffer," she had said, "you have to keep count, because every seventh wave is smoother than the rest. That's the one you have to try to ride."

Now Kristoffer could see how Sonja counted the swells and just before the seventh she lined up the boat, opened the throttle wide and rode into the harbour on the clean-cut crest of a high and perfectly level wave, only inches clear of the starboard jetty.

Once inside the harbour basin she had collapsed. When they

brought the boat in to the quayside Kristoffer had watched as they lifted her out and she had been every bit as white-faced then as she was now. Just as she came level with him she had opened her eyes, and he was the first person she saw. "Kristoffer," she had said, and Kristoffer had bent over her and she had whispered, so that only he could hear: "Could you take the tiller for a while?"

As far as he could remember, that was the last time he had really seen her.

Not that she had not stayed on in the town, at the home of a reclusive uncle and a careworn aunt, people who had looked for the worst from life, and got it. Their only child had been stillborn, a fisherman's life was a poor and a perilous one and in religion alone they had found bounty and quiet waters. They regarded Vaden Town much as they regarded the sea: reluctantly, fearfully and with the feeling that it was an unavoidable evil that lay in wait for them each morning outside their front door, dogged their footsteps all day long and did not let them out of its clutches until they were back home with the door locked behind them.

Mindfulness of the woes which Sonja brought in her wake weighed them down even more, causing them to turn their backs still further on the world and hover even closer around the girl. They consulted a doctor, and following this visit Sonja was removed from the town's co-educational school and sent to Lady Moltke's school for girls, to which she was escorted each day by her new mother. Her foster parents did not belong to either the drama or the musical society, they did not take walks nor attend the dances held in the town, so from then on Kristoffer only ever caught glimpses of Sonja, who was always accompanied by an adult. For a while he did try to find some way of getting in touch with her, but this state of affairs was a new one to him, and bewildering. He took to going to church every Sunday, being sure that there at least he would be able to see her. But then her aunt and uncle switched to one of the small, intransigent Free Church congregations whose temple lay down by the harbour, a little whitewashed building to which no one gained entry unless his heart had been scrupulously studied and weighed. And feeling that his inner being could never bear such scrutiny, Kristoffer stayed away. Besides which, all the grown-ups in Vaden said that what Sonja needed was to be shielded, and that this was best done by leaving her alone. So, unwillingly and with his longing for her like a flame that never died, Kristoffer abandoned the search for his lost friend.

But now when, suddenly, he found himself holding her in his arms and realizing that he was big enough to carry her and that she had changed to the point where she might have been a stranger to him, he also found himself thinking – of the rest of his life, as it were: "But it's too late now anyway."

Monsieur Andress removed the cork from a flat, delicately curved silver flask and bent over the senseless girl. Kristoffer had seen him feigning to drink from this flask in the arena, then going out to mingle with the audience, ostensibly the worse for drink, but he had felt quite sure that the flask was empty. Now the scent of old rum made his head reel. He said nothing, but Monsieur Andress read his mind.

"To drink from a flask that everyone knows is empty," the clown said, "and then stagger around drunk as a lord, *that* is art. But to drink from a flask that everyone knows is empty and to have a spot of rum in it anyway, do you know what that is?"

"No," said Kristoffer.

"That," said Monsieur Andress, "is divine."

He poured a little of the liquid between the girl's lips. She swallowed without gagging on it, then opened her eyes and stared straight at Kristoffer with a look of instant recognition. Then what might have been a chill draught slithered between them, one leap brought her free of him and on to her feet and, terror-stricken, she shied away from the stairs.

"They're coming," she whispered.

The dwarf gripped her arm and once more Kristoffer was accorded a glimpse of the remarkable strength residing within Monsieur Andress' tiny frame. And when he spoke it was with authority and power.

"If they come," he said, "I will plant myself on those stairs and then . . ." He paused, the actor in him giving careful consideration to an appropriate reception, ". . . then I shall politely but firmly send them packing," he finished.

Seeing Sonja's shoulders relax, Kristoffer realized that the clown's vehemence had broken through to her dazed consciousness. She stared at the clown.

"I found it," she told him, "I found my way here. I've been here before."

Monsieur Andress did not reply, but merely looked the girl in the eye, and it dawned on Kristoffer that they must have met before, that they already knew one another and that what was happening here must to some extent – and in some way that was far beyond his comprehension – have been planned.

Wordlessly, Monsieur Andress handed the silver flask to Sonja. Kristoffer could not imagine her ever having drunk alcohol before, and certainly never straight from a flask. But she took a long, deep gulp then slowly wiped her mouth with the back of her hand.

Up to this point her face had been distant and shuttered, giving the impression that she had come to the loft determined to say as little as possible and preferably nothing at all. But now the alcohol surged through her, manifesting itself as a rich flush, sparkling in her eyes like tears and loosening her tongue.

"The heat," she said, "that drink induces is a false heat. He often said that. But it feels real enough now." She fell quiet for a while.

Then: "Surely it can't ever be a Christian act to kill another human being, that's what I said to him. But he didn't hear me. I could have got those cod. I know all there is to know about cod." She gazed beyond Kristoffer and out into the night. "No one ever listens," she said, "when you need them to."

"Someone is always listening," said the dwarf, his eyes never leaving hers.

"Even now?" asked the girl.

"Right now," answered Monsieur Andress, "right now someone is listening."

The girl closed her eyes and lingeringly recited:

"Hold tight to what you have
That no one shall take your crown."

She opened her eyes. "That's what he wrote," she said, "in my hymn book. It was the text for my confirmation. Well, he *is* a lay preacher. He prepared me himself. And he gave me a gold ten-kroner piece."

She fell silent, as if the act of talking were a pointless waste of effort; and that she then carried on anyway, Kristoffer knew was due to the fact that facing her she had the dwarf with his enquiring expression, assuring her that the world was listening.

"It was a tiny hymn book," she said, "so small that you had to use a needle to leaf through it. That's how they picture Paradise, you see. Very small, very fine leaves." She stared at her two listeners in confusion, as if herself aware of how she was rambling on.

"Be still, they tell you. Only by sitting still can you enter Paradise. It must be a very small Paradise they're preparing themselves for." She paused. "Like Lady Moltke," she said, "she's preparing herself for an awfully narrow Paradise. So cramped that I doubt there'll be room for anyone but her, her and" – her face contorted with disgust – "her French bulldog."

A low, resounding crash shook the room and amid the din Sonja took another long swig from the flask. By the time things had quietened down her thoughts had changed tack. Her eyes were now fixed on Kristoffer.

"Kristoffer," she said, "do you remember the drama society's production of *La Bayadère?*"

Kristoffer nodded.

"Dad took me to see it. When they started dancing," – her eyes shone at the memory – "when they started dancing I wet my knickers. But Dad, he laid his coat under me. And then he whispered: 'You sit on that and you'll soon dry off all right.' And I did. And afterwards I was up dancing at the party. And it didn't show a bit." She giggled with delight. "And you were the only one I danced with."

Kristoffer nodded again.

"And you didn't know anything about me wetting my knickers."

Kristoffer shook his head.

She looked straight at Monsieur Andress. "He disappeared, I'm afraid," she said.

The clown eyed her intently.

"Well, actually, he died," she continued matter-of-factly. "The sea took him. It was no good, that engine. He's told me that many a time since then. 'It happened because we couldn't keep up with the waves,' that's what he says."

"How could he tell you that when he's dead?" asked Monsieur Andress.

The girl regarded him distantly. "Ah," she said, "but he came back, didn't he. You see, every day I would go down to the shore, and one day he came back and he rose up on to his tail and laughed at me, showing all his teeth. He was always bragging about still having all his own teeth."

"He had a tail?" Monsieur Andress asked.

The girl nodded at him. "As much as a week might go by without him showing up," she said. "A long time to wait when you're alone. But he always came back. Well, we had to talk."

"What did you talk about?" asked Kristoffer.

"Everything under the sun," said the girl. "About Uncle and Auntie. And about the accident. And about you, too. To begin with . . ." she paused, ". . . to begin with, we agreed that you would come and get me. Father said you were bound to. One day you would roll up in the cart and we would drive off. But you *didn't* come. You can go on believing in something like that for a while. And I did see you sometimes on the street. But you can't go on believing in it indefinitely."

Kristoffer felt something on his hands and, on looking down, found it to be his own tears. Marvelling, he realized that from that inner being of his which he had deemed to be quite, quite empty, there now poured a spate of weeping which he seemed powerless to stem.

"Hold on to what you have," said the girl. "That's how their minds run."

"Yes," said Monsieur Andress. "I would say that is pretty much how their minds run, *i coglioni*."

"You know, Dad used to take cod from the tank. I would push the lid off for him and he would grab a few. Never a lot. Just enough to satisfy his hunger. Three or four, that's all. Well, we all have to live, don't we? And it worked just fine for a long time. He would lean over the edge and dip his snout into the water and then he would catch them easy as you like. By throwing back his head."

"Was your father a fish of some sort?" asked the clown.

"A porpoise," said the girl.

A bewildered expression crossed Monsieur Andress' face, as if he were losing the thread of all this, and it occurred to Kristoffer that, his many years at sea with the Circus Gleim notwithstanding, the old man's wide experience of the world might not stretch to the creatures found in Danish waters.

"Auntie often said," the girl went on, "that while there might not be that much good to be got from the sea, at least with the bad that comes out of it you know what you're getting. With people it's different. So they let me go down there alone. But that day he must have followed me. It was Dad who saw him. I had just shoved the lid off the tank and he had eaten his fill. He hadn't said a word. But then I notice that he's looking at something. And then he says: 'Hullo, little brother.' That's when I catch sight of Uncle. He's standing right behind me, with his gun held in to his side, so that I don't see it right away, but then he brings it up, easy like. And I say to Dad, 'For Christ's sake, Dad,' I say, 'swim, swim away from here, or Uncle'll hoot you.' But he doesn't seem to hear what I'm saying. He just looks Uncle straight in the face and then he slaps the water and rears up on to his tail and stays there with the water foaming white underneath him, and he shows Uncle all his teeth. And then it dawns on me why he doesn't swim away. He's going to let himself get shot. He thinks that if he runs away, it'll be all the worse for me. He thinks Uncle will do me harm." She shook her head gently. "Stupid of him, wasn't it? To think they could lay a finger on me. He should just have tried. I'd have choked him. I would have got up in the middle of the night and taken a string from the piano." She pondered this for a moment, then – "a C string," she said, "because 'Our God he is a fortress strong' is in C major. And then I would have throttled him. Oh, I know he's bigger and stronger than I am. But I would have night on my side. And it's not easy to defend yourself when you're asleep and there's a C string wound round your neck."

Kristoffer caught himself swallowing and running a couple of tentative fingers over his throat.

"That's when Uncle takes aim," said Sonja. "He'd brought the double-barrelled shotgun. Dad never used a shotgun. He said it was a weapon for folk who couldn't shoot straight. I try to stop him. 'Uncle,' I say, 'those few fish, I'll get them for you whenever you like, just take me out, I know all there is to know about cod.' But he just cocks the gun. And I say: 'Surely it can't ever be a Christian act to kill your own brother, can it?' But he doesn't hear me, he's miles away. And it's as if I'm paralysed. It all comes, of course, from everybody always wanting you to keep still. You lose the knack of doing anything, don't you. But then I see his finger tightening on the trigger, so I shake myself out of it anyway and I take a swipe at the gun and both barrels go off. I must have shut my eyes because when I open them again, Dad is nowhere to be seen and for a moment I think he's been hit, but then I see Uncle lying on the ground and there's blood all over the place and I realize he must have shot himself in the legs. He's still moving though, trying to grab me, but I don't hang around, I just clear off."

Monsieur Andress was considering the girl through narrowed eyes.

"When was this?" he asked.

She wavered for a second, seeming to have lost all sense of time. "Oh, but it was today," she said.

"So," the clown concluded slowly, "you came straight here."

The girl nodded. "Straight here," she said.

Monsieur Andress took a deep breath. "There you have the advantage of age and experience," he said, half to himself, half to the two young people. "Knowing when some tremendous trick is brewing. The first thing that hits you is the power of it, then everything goes blank for a moment. You feel at a loss, *un sentimento di essere abbandonato*; then you prick up your ears and suddenly it's on you and then . . ." – he looked at the girl – "you hear the most amazing things."

Slowly and with difficulty Kristoffer pulled himself to his feet and walked stiff-legged across to Sonja. He knew that the world had now encapsulated him and that it was about to spit him out. Even so, he felt he might be permitted a final few words.

He positioned himself in front of the girl, stretched questing arms out into space, but not a word escaped his lips.

"Why didn't you come?" she asked.

"They said you had to be shielded," Kristoffer replied uncertainly.

The girl studied him carefully, with no sign of reproach, no hint of condemnation.

"Ah," she said. "And after they've been here to fetch me, then they're going to shield me with a vengeance."

Just then, from somewhere in outer space, Kristoffer was struck by the full extent of his own treachery, and it was borne in upon him that emptiness was not the only thing that lurked inside his shell; that behind his name hid someone who had failed the one person without whom the world was inconceivable, and from whom he was now to be parted for ever. Reeling like a drunkard, he spun round on his heel and put out an arm as if wishing to retrieve the emptiness of before, infinitely preferable as it was to the knowledge that every chance had been wasted. At that very moment, above the keening of the rain he became aware of voices all around him, a muttering, importunate chorus, with one voice standing out, more audible and insistent than the rest. Directly opposite Kristoffer, two eyes caught the yellow light from the lamp and it came to him that the voice he was hearing was that of Monsieur Andress.

"Kristoffer," said the clown, tenderly almost, "you could always jump."

A great, warm wave of gratitude washed over Kristoffer; gratitude that once again the tiny sage had looked into his soul, perceived his despair and shown him a way out. And, as with all conclusive rescues, this one too – even as it was being uttered – seemed quite superb and quite perfect.

With one shrug Kristoffer dismissed all his cares and stepped up to the hatchway. Beneath him the darkness yawned like a bottomless, yet welcoming pit. Then Monsieur Andress' voice fell on his ears once more, soft and compelling.

"On the other hand," he whispered, "to jump into Daddy's yard would be to choose a very short and very easy route."

In a nightmarish change of scene Kristoffer found himself back in the fencing hall and, as if he were indeed there, slowly he swivelled round until he stood with his back to the darkness. Behind him, from the pit at his feet, a gentle suction was tugging him back. In the room before him the girl and the dwarf eyed him intently.

"Last time," said Kristoffer, as if it were quite obvious to what he was referring, "I turned and left. And that's what I'm going to do now, too."

The dwarf laughed softly. "Last time you were left somewhat the wiser," he said. "This time you'll simply disappear. That jump, my lad, would be the last and longest retrograde step of your life."

Kristoffer could no longer tell whether the figure of the little man was drawing him towards life or pushing him backwards into extinction. He sensed only that the dwarf had to have been sent from outside, that he was some great, some universal destroyer and tempter. With some difficulty he tore his eyes away from the clown and turned them on the girl. She was looking at him as she had done many times before, an infinitely long time ago, when he had wept: without fear, without reproach, but keenly, almost urgently, as if he were no different from anyone else.

This look moved Kristoffer to climb back down into the loft and collapse in a heap. Silently the girl took her place beside him and clasped his hand.

"This has all the makings of a grand finale," said Monsieur Andress. He turned to face the hatchway, as if addressing an audience. "The time has come," he announced, broke off, listened briefly to the night, then continued, "to declare these two young people – who have been kept apart but whom I, Monsieur Andress, have reunited, for all the world as if I were Almighty God himself – to be betrothed, at any rate on this stage and for this evening. And I should like to express in song a devout wish for their future and for my own, in that voice which has induced a deluge of tears across the length and breadth of Europe."

And, clearing his throat with a lusty "Ahem", he sang:

Lieber Gott
gibt doch zu
dass ich klüger bin als du.

Kristoffer and Sonja had been looking at one another but as the first note reached their ears they looked up. For at that selfsame moment the clown's world-renowned tenor had cracked, turning shrill and tremulous as a bout of falsetto laughter. Then he fell silent and stood for a moment quite, quite still.

"Ah, yes," he said mildly, "the voice is gone. But I am still here."

He raised his right hand, as though making to wave goodbye, and in a gesture reminiscent of a salute he swept his grey mane clear of his head. Beneath the wig bristled a blond crew-cut, through which the scalp shone rosy pink.

"Allow me to introduce to you a young man washed up by a harsh fate on the rocky coastline of the performing arts."

Gingerly, as if trying not to nick himself, he removed his grey moustache. This done, he wiped his sleeves across his face, leaving the remains of what had been the great Monsieur Andress' face smeared across the white velvet. Kristoffer and Sonja were now confronted by a boy who could not have been a day over twelve.

"Christ, I really should do this in the ring some time," he declared triumphantly.

"Who are you?" asked Kristoffer.

"I am the great Monsieur Andress' young assistant," said the boy.

"Where . . ." asked Kristoffer, "where is Monsieur Andress?"

"Monsieur Andress died a week ago," the boy replied. "You see," he added slowly, "he carried that new smallpox strain into the town." He thought this over for a moment, then – "We'd been on tour," he said, "and on the return trip we take a run into Rødby. But they're not interested in us putting on a show there. Which, my dear children, was a bloody pain in the arse, because we were starving." He grinned at the couple before him. "Oh, it may look pretty grand, the Circus Gleim," he said, "but looking that good costs a lot of money. So we were starving." He laughed at the memory of it. "That's life for you," he said, "even the great Monsieur Andress was starving. So then we try to get into Vaden. And hunger fires the old imagination. And Andress, he tells that story about the storm and it's in the bag, we're in port, there's food enough for everyone. And Andress is the man of the moment, he's so pleased with himself, it's all thanks to him. Then one day he's covered in red spots and he gets sick. There's only him and me in the cabin, and he starts having these convulsions that send him twelve feet into the air and land him on the floor, so that eventually I have to tie him down, and in the end he's in such a state that I'm thinking to myself: *Scheisse*, better now for him to die than to live. And then he dies. And what are we to do? *Mann weiss' nicht, und mann* is too polite to ask. So then I put on his wig – he *was* bald, you know – and I make myself a moustache, I *have* learned something after all, and out I go into that arena. All the others can tell right away that there's something far wrong, but they're scared, you see, so they let me get on with it and the audience don't notice a thing, *nichts*." Dreamily he stared into space. "The public, as it happens, adore me," he said. "In fact, I would go so far as to say that there has not been one night when I have been any worse than that old fool."

The young couple stared at the boy in a vain attempt to come to terms with the metamorphosis to which they had just been witness.

"What about you?" asked Sonja, after a while. "Do you have the smallpox now?"

"One doesn't know," said the boy, "and one is too polite to ask."

Just then the force of the rain increased, rising from a steady thrum to a jubilant cascade. Drawn irresistibly to the tumult outside, the three in the loft approached the hatchway. Over their heads the heavens opened, glaring blueish-white in one long, uninterrupted series of lightning flashes, and out of this whiteness came the rain, tumbling down in huge, heavy drops that pelted the warehouse roof then bounced back into the air, to be shattered into silvery foam by the next wave, till the town below them was enveloped in a steaming, pearly mist.

Still holding hands, Kristoffer and Sonja now shared a vision in which they saw right through the storm. For a split second, the luminous watery mists ran together, and up over the town there reared a figure which reached from the earth all the way into the heavens. And they knew that this was Death; an immense, upright, incandescent skeleton, at its very top the skull laughing delightedly at them while the wet, bony fingers played a wild and watery tattoo on the roofs of the town. This vision stood silhouetted against the sky for no more than a fraction of second, then it was gone and the two gazed in terror at the boy standing next to them; looking, so it seemed, for some explanation or at least some confirmation, but that drawn, white face was giving nothing away.

"I'm leaving tonight," the boy announced. "I've found a gate in the wall that can be opened. I've decided to let you two come with me."

"Are we all going to die out there, like they say?" asked Sonja without a trace of fear in her voice, as if enquiring about nothing more serious than the weather forecast for the morrow.

"One does not know," said the boy. "And one is too polite to ask.

" – but Death," he added, after a momentary pause, "cannot be shut out." And pensively he continued: "Those places where I've spent most of my life, people don't get to be more than . . . than," he balked at having to deal with such large numbers, "maybe half as old as they do here. But what's the use of living to be a hundred and fifty with false this and fake that, like they say, if you aren't truly alive?"

"What will we live on?" asked Kristoffer, this being his first objection.

In the light of the lamp the boy opened his violin case to reveal a dazzling display sparkling against the blue velvet. "On *die* crumbs from *der* rich man's table," he said. "Today the women of Vaden Town turned up in their Sunday best to see Monsieur Andress don their trinkets and *bijoux*."

Kristoffer peered out of the hatchway and down at the main building. The big chandeliers were no longer lit but a solitary light could be seen flickering from one darkened room to the next. This, he knew, was his father Nikolaj Holmer standing fire watch over his treasures and over the one person in the world he cared about – his son, Kristoffer, whom he believed to be safely tucked up in bed by now.

"How," asked Kristoffer, this being his second objection, "can one possibly forget what one is leaving behind?"

"Anyone who is truly alive *can never forget*," the boy replied coldly. "Personally, he added proudly, "I can remember every single thrashing I've ever been given in my life. The thing to do is to live, so you don't have to go around whining about the things you remember."

"Do we have to leave?" asked Kristoffer, this being his third objection.

"That," said the boy, "one does not know. And one is too polite to ask."

Then, out of the violin case he produced a wooden flute. The celebrated flute of the eminent clown Monsieur Andress.

"I promised," he said, "to whistle at the windows of a couple of houses where there are still some young folk who would like to join us."

He regarded Sonja and Kristoffer. "Ladies and gentlemen," he said raptly, "see what a show we have performed for your edification tonight, I and my children. Two tales they have told us which – *now don't deny it* – have touched our hearts. And now look at them – he as straight-backed as any soldier, she as lovely as a little doll. And when they were small that is exactly what they played with, he with soldiers and she with painted dolls. But now, ladies and gentlemen, it is the other way round! Thank you and goodnight."

He closed the case, picked it up, flung his cloak around his shoulders and started down the stairs. Kristoffer and Sonja followed him in silence, Kristoffer recalling the manner in which each of them had ascended that same stairway. He himself as if on his way to the scaffold, Monsieur Andress as if ascending his throne. He could come up with no fitting metaphor for the girl's carriage, but he did happen to think of her bare legs in the days when they used to play on the beach.

By the time they emerged from the gateway the downpour had subsided and the town lay glistening in the moonlight. Only now did it occur to Kristoffer that they had received no answer to the real question. With two long, purposeful strides he caught up with the boy. "What do you want with us?" he enquired of the moonlit back. And the back replied: “It is not good for us to travel alone,” and there was no way of telling whether this “we” was in fact the *pluralis majestatis*, the pompous plural adopted by a world ruler, or the shrewd businessman’s attempt to make his company look bigger than it actually was.

That night a little refrain was whistled outside a number of windows in Vaden Town and later a gate in the wall was opened. Through this a truck was driven out and away. No lights showed on the truck and so almost immediately it was swallowed up by the night. Thus the great clown, Monsieur Andress, carried the children away from Vaden Town.

STORY OF A MARRIAGE

It was the night of March 19th 1929 and the young writer Jason Toft was floating through the centre of Copenhagen.

It had been raining and the rain had washed the city bright as a new pin. Above the rooftops the night sky was clear as a glass ceiling and this combined with the surfaces of the surrounding buildings to give Jason the sense that he was strolling through a prism. And, since he was feeling very happy, all the intensity of the universe seemed to him to have been concentrated in this prism.

He did not meet anyone else, but the echo of music and gay voices wafted to him from distant squares, as if to assure him that life is one long party, and all around him the buildings and the street lamps testified to a world of things that never will fade away. Only those spots where the rain had left puddles seemed vaguely unsettling. In these the reflected extensions of the street lamps were transformed into pillars of light plunging into an unfathomable subterranean sky which made Jason's head spin. He would have stepped in these puddles to prove that they were not in fact bottomless, but was stopped by the thought of them ruining his hand-stitched Italian shoes. He had always been very particular about his appearance.

The light which had broken inside him that night was twofold, being both the light of love and the longing for knowledge. It was both the thought of the woman he loved and the certainty that waiting for him at his destination he would find the solution to a mystery.

Although only twenty-five years old Jason Toft was already an extremely well-known young man. Granted, he had only written the one book, but that in itself had been enough. It was a book about a young man growing up in Copenhagen, and the one factor which had led to this book having been widely read throughout Europe was that its depiction of real life had proved the most accurate in the history of literature up to that point. The faithful rendering of the real world, that was Jason's main preoccupation. Where the great European realists who had once served as his models portrayed the world photographically, he had declared to the world at large that it was from sculpture that he drew his inspiration. His aim was to erect a linguistic work of art around which future generations could revolve, viewing life as it really was. To one reporter's question concerning to what extent his book did in fact reflect real life, Jason had replied that "every mirror has its errors of refraction. I hope that is not the case with my works. Every mirror reverses the image, transposing right and left. That, to me, would be tantamount to literary inaccuracy."

Only in the depiction of love in his novel had he trodden warily, and this he did simply because at that time it was something he knew of only by sight and by repute. Even so he had endeavoured to depict it, since it is difficult to present a painfully accurate picture of life without including love. But he had always been one of his own toughest critics and he knew that he had not pulled it off, that something was lacking, both on the paper and in his own life. There and then he had sworn to himself that his next book would be about love and that he would not write it until he knew what he was talking about. Until then he would wait – a big decision for him to make, since Jason was not one for putting things off and the worst wait of all, to his mind, had to be the wait between two books.

For a year he restrained himself, suffering greatly during that time and rapidly descending desperation's downward spiral. Then love made itself known to him, first as a faint glimmer, than as a dawning of hope and finally as the sunrise's tidal wave of light sweeping him along in its wake. On this March evening that illumination was but three months old and any impression that Jason Toft was walking was purely superficial. For his part, he did not doubt for one minute that he was in fact floating.

One week earlier, this sensation of weightlessness had given him the idea for his next book. It had come to him one night when he had taken leave, temporarily, of the woman in his life. She had been lying naked on his bed and there had come a point when happiness had built up a pressure inside him so great that he who had become famous for his mastery of language had been forced to surrender to the forces that now lifted him out of bed to stand on the floor in the moonlight, and moved him to spread his arms wide in abandonment.

"You are an angel!" he had cried.

And the girl had got up and taken his head between her hands and looked deep into his eyes.

"Never forget," she entreated, "that I can never be an angel. At best a butterfly."

And standing there in the moonlight, with this enigmatic warning sounding in his ears, Jason had the idea for his next book.

Jason had first met Helene van Austen three months previously. On that occasion she had told him her name and little else. That, however, had been enough. It would take him the rest of his life, Jason had felt, merely to take in the music of that name, her fair hair and her skin which was the same colour and had the same scent as lightly roasted coffee beans.

Now, however, time had taught him that love is insatiable in its hunger for knowledge. He was convinced that love consisted of the progress of two people towards one another; that and their eventual fusion, and initially he had fancied that this union was bound to be sexual in nature. After having slept with Helene every night for three months and still only knowing her name he had begun to cast about for other ways of getting close to the heart of her. She sketched; on moving in with him she had filled his flat with drawings and Jason had speculated as to whether the mystery of her could be solved by that route. But he gave up this idea, because he did not care much for what he saw. Her pictures depicted figures and creatures which seemed to him to belong to the world of dreams, or more particularly that of nightmare, and not by any stretch of the imagination to the bright, incandescent real world their love inhabited. When she told him she was going out of town to visit some relatives he decided in her absence to use that time to mull over certain elementary questions which he would then put to her: who she was, what she had been and how she envisaged their future together. The night before she was due to leave these questions framed themselves all unbidden in his head as he stood there beside the bed. Not only that, but he realized that these, together with the answers to them, would go to make up a book. The book on love which he had been waiting for; which he was now in a position to write and which would turn out be a monument erected to their relationship.

Jason knew that love has nothing to do with romance, but that it is tied to reality, to the loved one's body, to the lovely home around them, to the career which he laid at her feet, so to speak, as proof of the lengths to which he had gone in order to solve the mystery of her true identity. And this solution, thought he – conscious that he was hovering weightlessly in the moonlight an inch above the floorboards – must lie with those people who have seen her grow up. “While Helene is away,” he thought, “I am going to make a start on a book about my parents-in-law.”

He had known straight away what the title of the book should be. If he could have been content with a photographic impression of real life he might have called it ‘Paragons’. But he wanted more than that. He wanted this married couple, and through them their daughter, to present themselves to the reader with all the depth and force of their characters. By the time he had returned to the floor and to Helene he had made up his mind that his book should be entitled ‘Figures in the Foreground’.

Helene had never introduced Jason to her parents and in all the time he had known her she had never visited them or spoken of them. Under normal circumstances he would have wondered at this, but in this case the circumstances were far from normal. Margrethe and Georg van Austen had long since ceased to be like everyone else. They had become symbols, and by dint of their remoteness from the rest of the world, symbols are obliged to shine; they are approached only when absolutely necessary and then always with reverence. But it was this very fact, Jason told himself that evening on his way through Copenhagen to the couple’s home on Kongens Nytorv, that drove him. The absolute necessity of coming to understand the woman he loved, and the deference inherent in his paying his respects, as an author, to this couple – these, this night, represented his essential and adequate motives.

For two hundred years the van Austen family had run a shipping line, and in this lay the source of the family fortune. Not that wealth had ever been the family’s ultimate objective. For them the money had been no more than a clear oil drawn up through a wick of philanthropy, sponsorship of the sciences and the arts and an exemplary lifestyle to burn brightly for the enlightenment of the land and its people. That light was what the family aspired to.

The van Austens had always been given to large families and in each generation it had been the case that one or two of the boys had carried on the family business, leaving the others to become lawyers, engineers or astronomers. All of them had proved to be loyal supporters of enlightened conservatism and many of them had married actresses or female musicians for, while the torch of art may be wavering and capricious, nonetheless it is a light of sorts. The marriage of Georg van Austen, then managing director and owner of the van Austen line, to Margrethe Banhoff, an actress with the Royal Theatre, turned out to be the wedding of the decade and the event itself a great and comforting blaze in a wartime Copenhagen beset by the blackout and coal rationing.

The previous century had witnessed attacks on the institution of marriage and the gradual disintegration of family ideals, and now the eyes of the general public rested on grand, formal weddings with a weary, faintly cynical, vaguely malicious, but nonetheless expectant gaze. In Georg and Margrethe's case Denmark, to its dawning surprise beheld a happiness that blossomed and went on flourishing.

The couple had twelve children, all of whom were blessed with their father's dark complexion and their mother's spun-gold hair, and all twelve – their other differences aside – shared an easygoing confidence in themselves which seemed to deliver a stream of promises.

Over the first thirty-odd years of this century Georg van Austen expanded and consolidated the family business, and the company's ships, all of them named after members of the family, sailed the world over under the Danish flag, like a fleet of dispatches to the effect that the van Austen family of Copenhagen had discovered the fountainhead of life and prosperity.

At the Royal Theatre, Margrethe van Austen – even while bearing and bringing up twelve children – had enjoyed a dazzling career. She possessed what was, for the theatre, the hitherto unknown courage to say "no", and without ever giving less than her best, without ever trying to curry favour, without ever striving after anything except the essence of each part she played, she ascended a Milky Way of luminescent female characters to the point where she had become the darling of an entire nation, without ever having asked for this love. Then, to everyone's surprise and sorrow, having just celebrated thirty-five years in the theatre, she announced her retirement. Speaking from the stage after her farewell performance, the director of the Royal Theatre said that during Margrethe van Austen's time there the theatre could have spared itself all the expense of stage sets. "For Mrs Austen has the ability," he said, "with the aid of nothing except just enough light for us to see her by, to transport us to any place and any time." And this was not so much a compliment as a statement of fact.

Immediately prior to Margrethe's retirement the theatre had presented her with the keys to its grace-and-favour residence on Kongens Nytorv, a mansion house on four floors sitting directly across from the theatre itself. This brought with it the couple's definitive elevation to the sainthood.

The great thing, as far as the Danish public was concerned, had never been the wonders which the actress performed on stage or the businessman on the seven seas, nor even the couple's twelve offspring. What fascinated the man and woman in the street was not the transformation of water into wine but the force behind this wonder-working. The truly intriguing, staggering, bedazzling thing about Georg and Margrethe was that, as anyone could plainly see, they had never stopped being in love; that their marriage was a happy one. In a world that hungered and wept for emotions that could stand the test of time, their love came as one long peal of joyful laughter, to which the world had listened at first suspiciously, then warily and finally hopefully.

They had been put to the test. As friends of the royal family they had been invited by Christian X to join him on state visits at home and, later, abroad. They had accompanied the King to North Schleswig on the occasion of that duchy's reunification with Denmark and gone with H. N. Andersen, the head of the Danish East Asia Company, to the peace conference in Paris; in speeches and introductions they were referred to as the representatives of Danish commerce and culture. But both they and the world knew that they were more than that. That what they brought with them, first to the royal house and later to foreign parts, was something greater than wealth and refinement. Above all else, they came bringing love, the modern world's dream of a happy marriage. All through the early years they were thought to be only human. The public kept a close eye on them, waiting for them to slip up, to come tumbling down and be forgotten, but over those years Margrethe's name was never linked to any scandal and the van Austen line's story was one of a company going from strength to strength and never putting a foot wrong; and wherever they showed their faces their happiness and respect for one another were unmistakable. So eventually the press granted them immunity – much as one might imagine a sex offender, faced with a divinely beautiful child, thinking twice and then abandoning his undertaking. It was then that the glorification of the couple began. Full of distrust their contemporaries had looked for signs of their own troubles in van Austen and found none, and such is the human race's longing for perfection that it goes half-mad with delight when it stumbles on it. Now Denmark went down on bended knee before the couple. Those performances which Margrethe gave were attended by audiences greater than the theatre could actually contain and the fire department would have protested, if, that is, the firemen had not also adored her. On the stock exchange the value of the shipping line's shares soared, in a remarkable demonstration of how love may be worth its weight in gold. When Margrethe retired from the stage in order to devote her life to her husband; when the couple finally bowed out of public life Denmark did not feel that it had been let down. On the contrary, having absented themselves from the immediate vicinity of the world at large, the couple now ascended instead into Heaven, where their light seemed to burn even brighter and they became the national symbol of happy and enduring wedlock.

It seemed, therefore, only obvious and right that Georg and Margrethe van Austen should go on living on Kongens Nytorv. They could, of course, have moved out to the north of the city, like so many other wealthy individuals. But those who looked up from the tree-wreathed centre of the square at the tall windows flanked by columns knew in their hearts that this had never been considered. Any ordinary person can move around as they please and even popular public figures enjoy a certain amount of leeway. But for a symbol there is no freedom. Just as two celestial bodies are only able to stay each in their own orbit because of the pull they exert on one another, so exalted beings need their votaries. Like another splendid figure of those days – King Christian X on horseback, riding unaccompanied through Copenhagen every morning – Margrethe and Georg van Austen were no longer in a position to bow out. Had they done so they would have broken faith, they would have sucked all the power out of the symbol, and from then on it would have become more difficult, much more difficult, for the Danish people to believe it possible for two people to love one another till death them did part and perhaps even beyond that.

There was never any thought of such a defection. Fully aware of their responsibility the couple moved into the Royal Theatre residence and, as the theatre's director said with such felicity and sincerity on presenting the couple with the keys to the mansion house: the square was now perfectly balanced. With the equestrian statue of Christian V at its centre acting as its linchpin, this fine square had attained equilibrium. On one side it had the theatre where, after many years' deliberation, Strindberg's and Ibsen's profound distrust of the wedded state was now being acted out, and on the other Mr and Mrs van Austen, who put this distrust to shame.

The gentlemen of the press also attended the presentation ceremony and in his speech Georg van Austen announced that this was to be their last public appearance. "From now on," he said, "for whatever time we have left to us, my wife and I wish to devote our lives to each other and to our children."

This wish was respected. With a deep bow the world withdrew. And in return the couple kept up one public ritual. Every Tuesday evening the long white curtains of the grand dining room on the first floor were pulled back and passers-by on the square below would stop in their tracks to watch those two stately figures take their seats at either end of the long dining table. The curtains were then drawn. Two hours later, just as theatregoers came pouring out of the Royal Theatre, the curtains were once more pulled back and by then the meal was at an end, by then the couple were always standing at one end of the table, side by side, and slowly, without a trace of self-consciousness, Georg van Austen took his wife in his arms and danced her gently and lingeringly out of sight. Thereafter, the curtains slid to, leaving everyone who had observed this sight feeling deeply moved. What they had witnessed was a ritual devoid of affectation; all those two people up there had done was to put the strength of their feelings at the service of a higher cause.

From an early age children in the van Austen family had been taught that the supreme goal in this life is complete sincerity. An endeavour which, in the persons of Georg and Margrethe van Austen, seemed to have been brought to perfection. When the foundation set up by the family immediately after the end of the Great War granted a large sum of money to the Danish Dana expedition's research into the reproductive process of the fresh-water eel, the foundation came under attack from ecclesiastical circles for supporting what was in essence a blasphemous attempt to coax an explanation of the wonder of creation out of the Lord. On that occasion Georg van Austen had coolly replied that "God has no secrets. Anyone who finds it necessary to keep something hidden cannot be God."

And then, with typical consistency, he had added thoughtfully: "The same goes, of course . . . for the Devil."

Although they would never have made so bold as to say so in so many words, the same could also have been said of the van Austens themselves. Margrethe's performances onstage had the ring of utter sincerity and each year – in line with a tradition established on the family's own initiative long before the Companies Act of 1919 – the shipping line published accounts which stood above all suspicion. The same was true of the van Austen's private life. Thanks to innumerable photographs, paintings and newspaper articles, the general public knew all there was to know about the couple's home, their children and the circles in which they moved. Their marriage was crystal clear and transparent and the very fact that this was so enhanced it and lent it power. Symbols are never inscrutable or cryptic. They sparkle simply because they are so easily seen through, because they are purer than the world around them.

For this reason Jason Toft found it impossible to accept the thought that for two hundred years the family history had held a mystery which was being repeated in Georg and Margrethe's life and which apparently eluded solution. It was a mystery which the world at large had remarked upon and been magnanimous enough to forget, since people will happily forgive paragons the odd little *faux pas*, but which Jason – obsessed as he was with reality – saw as being an inexplicable and fascinating flaw in an otherwise perfect diamond. This mystery concerned the family's attitude to foreign lands, to what lay beyond the shores of Europe.

The van Austens' first million rigsdaler were earned during the eighteenth century in the Royal Chartered Danish Asiatic Company's trade in ivory, indigo and ebony from the Danish colony of Tarengampadi in the Bay of Bengal. It was with this money that the shipping line set itself up as the biggest Danish trading fleet in the East. For Denmark during the Age of Enlightenment the van Austen line constituted the country's long and stalwart arm stretching all the way to China, outwardly retaining an iron grip on its tropical colony, but inwardly representing a cultivated, loyal, patriotic and benevolent handshake, while at the same time acting as a source of information on the Orient's blend of barbarity and beauty. It was the van Austen family who, in 1770, at its own expense equipped a neat little mercenary army, shipped it out and countenanced its defence of the Company's interests along the Indian coastline with a brutality extraordinary even for those days. And yet it was also the van Austen family which, sparing no expense, brought home the rarest of Chinese and Indian porcelain and persuaded the Royal Copenhagen Porcelain Factory to institute production of dinner services bearing the stylized Oriental motifs which the whole of Europe had come to regard as symbolic of Danish appreciation of the art treasures of the East.

Early in the nineteenth century, with no explanation given, the van Austen line discontinued all trading operations in India and initiated a restructuring programme which as far as the outside world was concerned was to remain forever unexplained. Out of this restructuring there emerged a shipping and trading company which had retained a number of interests in the West Indies and North America, but which was at pains to point out that it was, to all intents and purposes, exclusively Danish. The sole comment on these moves was made by Georg van Austen's great-great-grandfather at a meeting of the Merchants' Guild. At this meeting the King himself, greatly concerned, had asked whether this withdrawal from the rich shores of India could truly be reconciled with the shipping line's policy of enlightened trade. At this van Austen's face had grown shuttered and he had half turned his head away.

"Believe me, Your Majesty," he said softly, "the light that emanates from those shores is nothing but a Bengal light."

From that day forth the family had turned its face inwards, anchoring itself in Danish culture as if it had discovered that its high ideals were only viable when its back was turned on the exotic. All trace of the East was expunged from the family home. Its members furnished their surroundings with the understated classicism of the eighteenth century, but from then on Greece became their *ultima mundi*.

In Denmark, the van Austens were to some extent successful in checking the wave of enthusiasm for the Orient which swept across Europe during the nineteenth century. They opposed a translation of *The Thousand and One Nights*, and in so doing delayed it for a hundred years. Family members were conspicuous by their absence at the staging of Oehlenschlæger's *Aladdin* and the Casino Theatre's lavish production of *The Caliph Goes Adventuring*. It prevented the conservative press from reviewing the French author Gustave Flaubert's exotic novel *Salammbô* and Mozart's opera *The Abduction from the Seraglio* and dismissed a sobbing Hans Christian Andersen from a family gathering when, on having been asked to give a reading, he had launched into his fairy tale "The Emperor's Nightingale". Never at any time did the company foundation sponsor an exhibition of artefacts from, or books about, or trips to the Orient and no daughter or wife of the family ever appeared at any function in any guise that could in any way have been associated with a foreign civilization.

As time went on everyone forgot that things had ever been any different and the van Austen family's nationalistic bent was accepted as a virtue. One of the rare occasions on which a member of the family spoke out publicly on a political matter came in the year 1900 when Georg's father addressed the immigrant problem in a newspaper article. On that occasion he had written that his family looked to Denmark not out of chauvinism but in concentration and for that very reason he warned against the continuation of the previous century's influx of Jews, Poles and Romanies, and against the exodus to America. "Danish culture," he wrote, "is a fluid which it has taken thousands of years of alchemy to purify. Whether we go on incessantly admitting infusions and suspensions of foreign matter, or ourselves have to relinquish powerful salts, this fluid will never achieve the balance necessary to enable us to irradiate it and truly comprehend what it means to be Danish."

When asked, during his last interview with a journalist prior to the move to Kongens Nytorv, whether in the twentieth century the van Austen line was likely to adopt a more open approach to the rest of the world, Georg van Austen had blandly replied that "we have never closed ourselves off from it. We have no fear of foreign lands. We are Europeans and citizens of the world. But above all we are Danish."

Jason had read this reply immediately after meeting Helene and it had struck him as being a lucid and forthright assertion. What *did* surprise him was something else again: a quite inexplicable staffing policy.

For as long as anyone could remember the van Austens had always had one Indian attached to their household, apparently occupying the post of personal attendant and confidant and amid the family's purified Danishness this figure seemed as enigmatically exotic as would a palm tree in P. C. Skovgaard's paintings of Danish beech woods, of which the family had quite a collection.

Word had it that this strange state of affairs dated back a hundred and fifty years and that these servants were always the sons of successive generations of the same family from some unspecified part of India whom generation after generation of van Austens had persisted in bringing to Denmark. It was said that these foreigners were invariably young men who had not yet turned twenty and that they remained in the country for seven years, after which time they returned home and another young man took their place. Whether this was in fact the case had never been confirmed. What the outside world had seen was that these dark-skinned boys with the finely chiselled features and soft lips soon picked up a perfect, unaccented Danish and then – at all times dressed in white tie and tails, as if they were both butler and guest in the house – they placed themselves between the outside world and the van Austen family. And this they did with such authority that one forgot and forgave the fact that their skin was, when all was said and done, the wrong colour. When Jason wrote to van Austen, requesting an interview, and received in response to his application a courteous reply signed with an unpronounceable name, he realized that, like everyone else who had over the past hundred years gone cap in hand to this most Danish of all families, he too would, in the first instance, have to treat with a foreigner.

These negotiations gave him no cause for complaint, but simply because the letters he received were at one and the same time formal, pleasant and faultless, they excited his curiosity. Eager as he was to arrive at a full understanding of the woman he loved before her return some weeks later, every unanswered question concerning her and her family became a weight on his mind. To be told why she never visited her parents; what it was like to be a daughter from a perfect family; why, as doorman of the Amalienborg Palace of their love, Margrethe and Georg van Austen kept a nigger who had more business outside some heathen pagoda. Gaining answers to these and other riddles had become an obsession with him. So eaten up by his own curiosity was the Jason Toft wandering through the Copenhagen night on March 19th, that his thoughts ran on ahead of him, and this they were able to do because he had no worries in all the world to hold them back, because there was no traffic in the streets and because he did not need to concentrate on walking, seeing that he was, in fact, floating.

What was running through Jason's head was the term "narrative". "Soon," he thought, "a few hours from now, I will have the answers. With these answers I can meet Helene. And together, after that meeting we can face the future, in which we will love one another more and more and in which I will write more and more books and become more and more famous, and all of this I will lay at her feet." And he breathed in deeply at the prospect of this self-augmenting cycle in which their feelings for one another, his art and his income would spiral upwards into infinity, up to Heaven, out into space.

At high school Jason had been drawn to the great realists because of their passion for reality. With the ecstatic sensation that it was in fact his own life that they were describing, he had read Zola and Proust and Pontoppidan. And, deeply disappointed, he had turned his back on them on discovering that in the end they always played reality false. It was then that he began to write himself, driven by his urge to tell the world that literary narrative is an illusion. With relish, as a boy, he had identified with those works of European literature that dealt with real people and it had struck him that the realists' discovery that the real world amounted to a handshake, a pearl of sweat, rumbling bellies and a brick façade, rather than the hazy symbolism of romanticism or the obscure stereotypes of religious literature, seemed to be the stuff of perfect wisdom.

Until, that is, at the age of twenty he hit upon the fatal weakness of these writers: that they let themselves be seduced into bringing their reality to a conclusion, that they introduced a narrative.

In the real world, Jason had found, there was no such thing as a narrative. Reality was made up of never-ending cycles of the kind which he was now about to start. Out of obscure beginnings life went on growing into infinity; conclusions, essential as they are to all plots, are an invention.

Both verbally and in writing he had asserted that all the ills of modern literature had begun when Flaubert – who, as it happens, had turned over a new leaf after the excesses of his youth – elected to lead Madame Bovary to an improbably heroic death.

It was such insight, Jason knew, which had now gained him admittance to van Austen. Helene's name had not been mentioned in his letter, he had not wanted them to know that he was their daughter's intended, he wanted to be received as a writer, not as an acquaintance. He had been asked what he intended to write and he had written answering that he wanted to write a book about the three basic reasons for the existence and the future of the Danish nation in what were otherwise such troubled times. He wanted to write about prosperity and love and intellectual freedom and this he intended to do by delineating certain figures in the foreground to represent these three factors. "And if I now approach you before anyone else it is because – permit me to be blunt – the two of you embody all three." He had received a reply in which he was asked what sort of fictional style he had in mind for this work and Jason had replied that if there was one thing he knew about himself it was that he had altered the meaning of the word "fictional". "I do not write fiction," he wrote, "in the sense of 'inventing'. I observe, and in the case of yourselves what I observe are eternal values. I do not intend to construct a narrative. To depict the eternal quality of language as it is – which is to say with no beginning and no end – in that lies my art."

In this letter he had also said that what he wished was to be allowed to observe the couple at dinner. "What I venture to request," he wrote, "is that I may be allowed access to those hours on Tuesday evening when your renowned curtains are drawn."

In reply to this letter he received the ultimate permission.

Outside the door of the theatre's grace-and-favour residence stood a street lamp and in the light of this Jason came to a halt. In his head he had just been putting the finishing touches to a short introductory speech on the need for role models in a democratic society and as the words came flooding to him, in his mind's eye he had seen Georg and Margrethe van Austen. Standing there in the light of the street lamp he was suddenly acutely aware of himself and it occurred to him that the day might not be that far off when he himself would constitute such a role model, a Danish legend. And indeed, to certain sections of the general public, to many of his readers, might already do so. He thought of the respect shown by Denmark to Adam Oehlenschlæger, Hans Christian Andersen, Johan Ludvig Heiberg and his wife Johanne Luise, and Holger Drachmann. He turned to face Kongens Nytorv. The time might well come when such a residence would be placed at his disposal, a place where he and Helene would assume a position similar to that now occupied by her parents. Jason did not consider it at all unnatural to picture the square before him packed with people who had come to pay tribute to him on the occasion of his eightieth birthday, or his golden wedding, or to congratulate him on being awarded the Nobel Prize, and he raised his right arm and waved at the dark square.

Just then he heard a sound behind him and on turning round he found the front door open and standing in the doorway the van Austen family's Indian retainer. He said not a word. A bewildered Jason mounted the two steps to the entrance. Not until he was following the black tailcoat back through a succession of anterooms did it dawn on him that his right arm was still hovering in mid-air in salute.

They came to a large, square waiting room where the Indian asked him to take a seat before himself going to stand over against the wall opposite. There then ensued an interval during which the two young men studied one another.

Jason was a born democrat. One of his earliest childhood memories was of how his heart had sung with glad accord when women and the poorest members of society won the vote. And ever since he had begun to write he had known that through his art he could get through to the people. Nevertheless, he was well aware that democracy applied only to political power and that it could never do anything to assail the fact that some people had a right to the veneration of others. That being the case, he knew that it was only right and proper that he, too, should receive the recognition of the public, seeing that he presented them with a true picture of their lives. And by the same token high-ranking individuals had a right, if not to their employees' subservience, then at least to their respect.

He noted, however, the absence of any such respect in the Indian's demeanour. Even though Jason had grown up in an age in which footmen and housemaids had disappeared from all but the most well-to-do homes, he himself had moved in circles which were quite familiar with the experienced valet's ability to disappear, as it were, into thin air, leaving behind him a string of neatly ordered arrangements which gave the impression of having effected themselves. But the foreigner opposite him did not possess that knack; he stood there ramrod straight, looking directly and intently at the visitor. "And," thought Jason, "no matter what he may have learned, even though he obviously can write and speak Danish and wear a dress suit, he has not yet learned how to blend into the background."

Where any other visitor might have taken exception to this, Jason's heart was large and generous. Not only that, but on this particular evening, it was so full of emotion and expectancy that he could have forgiven anything. When he addressed the servant he did so candidly and inquisitively.

"You must have spent quite some time in Denmark," he said, "to have learned to speak our language so well."

"Just seven years," the Indian replied.

Jason laughed. Only three months ago his life had still been benighted and loveless.

"If seven years is a short time," he said, "how long is long?"

"We Buddhists measure time in kalpas. If all the conversations and thoughts Europeans have devoted to the study of time were put together they would amount to millions of years. And yet that would still correspond only to the shortest sigh before sunrise on the first morning of the first day of a kalpa."

Jason scanned the foreigner's face, searching for some sign that he was being made fun of, but found none. Then he tried visualizing such a space of time, but the thought made his head spin.

"Seven years ago," he said, "the thought of writing a novel had not even entered my head."

He wondered fleetingly whether he would need to explain to this foreigner what a novel was. Then he recalled that it was the man facing him who had written and asked him how he intended to describe his visit.

"Do you read books?" he asked out of curiosity.

"I read the Buddhacarita every day," replied the Indian.

"Some sort of tale about Buddha, is it?" Jason suggested politely.

"Yes," said the Indian, "some sort of tale."

A sudden thrill ran through Jason at being able to talk thus to a total stranger about the one thing closest to his heart.

"I too have heard many tales," he said, thinking of his childhood.

"But this evening," said the Indian, "there will be no tale."

"No," said Jason solemnly. "Tales are for children. Growing up means growing away from tales and into reality."

For a while both were silent and Jason had the feeling that the other man was also thinking of his childhood.

Then: "Most literature," he said, "consists of a handful of different beginnings, a predictable ending and, between the two, a plot. Reality contains none of these."

"My mother," said the Indian, "a woman who knew a lot of stories, said of life that it has a handful of different beginnings and a predictable ending. In that respect it resembles a tale. And that is why the plot is so important. The plot represents one possible explanation of how to get from the beginning to the end. And everyone other than those few who have attained the ultimate state of enlightenment has need of such an explanation."

Jason was mulling over how he should reply to this, but just when he thought he was coming close to the perfect choice of words, the Indian stepped forward and opened a set of double doors. At this Jason had to get to his feet, reminding himself as he did so, however, that he still owed this foreigner a reply. Then he entered Mr and Mrs van Austen's dining room.

The table at whose midpoint he now found himself standing was long, much longer than it appeared from Kongens Nytorv.

At either end sat Margrethe and Georg van Austen, and there they remained, straight-backed, alert and silent.

Armed with his charm, his consciousness of his own genius and the feel of his Italian shoes, Jason strode across the floor, lifted the great actress' hand and kissed it.

When he raised his eyes, two things held him transfixed. The first was his observation that the woman before him – despite being more delicately formed, despite being silver-haired – possessed all of her daughter Helene's fully refined sensuality; the second was that while the woman's pose was relaxed and her expression friendly, the hand he had kissed locked around his like a vice. Smile wilting, he tried in vain to pull his hand away and then, to conceal his confusion, bowed and kissed the white lace glove yet again. Only then did she release him. From the other end of the table her husband's dark eyes were fixed on them both.

Hiding his surprise behind his most dazzling smile Jason walked down the length of the table to greet the eminent businessman. Van Austen's handshake was dry and firm and in silence he too hung on to Jason's hand for a moment. "Almost," thought Jason, "as a pledge of the hours to come."

At the centre of the table a place had been set for a third person and here Jason took his seat. He was sitting in such a way that he was facing the middle of the three tall windows overlooking Kongens Nytorv and even as he remarked on this the Indian drew back the curtains and positioned himself over by the wall. For those looking up at the windows from the square below Jason now formed part of the celebrated tableau.

The food had not yet been brought in, but at either end of the table stood a long-necked wine bottle and now Georg van Austen turned the label towards Jason.

"This," he said, "is Eiswein. The grapes have been left on the vine until they are attacked by *pourriture noble*, a hyphomycete which causes the skins to perforate so that the moisture evaporates and the juice becomes concentrated. The raisin-like grapes are left for the first frost to nip. This results in an exceedingly sweet and exceedingly potent wine. A concentration, if you like, of the suffering the grape has endured. Would that be putting it too strongly, Margrethe?"

"Georg," said the woman, "you are always so precise."

"What is so remarkable about this," he continued, addressing his words to Jason, "is that the final refining process often does not take place until the first frost. Just before the rot sets in, so to speak. As with cheese and beef. Might it be that a similar theory on human life is what has prompted you to contact us?"

Jason grinned broadly at this grand show of wit, and at being given the opportunity to explain himself.

"I can assure you," he began earnestly, "that I have not come here with any theories. I felt it was essential that I should meet you with no preconceived notions. You see, I did not actually come here as an individual, but as an objective recorder. I have come here on behalf of the general public, to write – as I said in my letter to you – a book about figures in the foreground. A book which I envisage as being a guide to happiness. My one conviction is that you two are capable of providing such guidance; my one premise, that you two have found that love is a tree which can be made to flourish and that you have proved there is no reason to believe that it should not stretch all the way to Heaven."

Somewhat out of breath and rather diffidently he sat back in his chair.

"But you speak," said Georg van Austen, "with all the authority of experience."

Jason blushed, partly at the thought that the experience referred to here had to do with this man's own daughter, and partly from pleasure.

"That, perhaps, is an artist's privilege," he said proudly, "to have the ability to gain insight into things he has not experienced personally.

"But," he hastened to add, "nothing can measure up to reality itself. What I was hoping was that this evening I could persuade the two of you to describe that reality. To tell our fellow men how, from this point of perfect balance in your life together, you recall the story of your marriage."

Two pairs of eyes considered him thoughtfully and the thought flitted across Jason's mind that they seemed to be searching for some hidden meaning behind his words. He sent them his most sincere smile, and as proof of his impartiality he placed a little pile of blank notepaper on the table in front of him.

"I think you should know," said Georg van Austen, "that my wife and I rarely, if ever, invoke the past. The fact is that, at our age, memories, traces of the past, tend to be rather like Aladdin's lamp." His gaze rested momentarily on the Indian. "They may appear to be tarnished, perhaps even badly dented. But if one rubs them one risks conjuring up something extremely powerful. Is that not right, Margrethe, that one must tread softly when rubbing the past?

"Nonetheless, Mr Toft," he continued, "we have consented to perform a little retrospective piece for you this evening. It is not, of course, the first time that we have been urged to make our memories public, but we have turned down all previous requests. There are many good reasons why we have said 'yes' to you. Some of these we may well touch on later; others shall be kept secret, just as there are always both covert and manifest reasons for the things people do, and just as you," – and here he contemplated Jason for a moment – "have quite naturally not revealed all the details of your motives for desiring this interview. But, to begin with, I may tell you that precisely because my wife and I so rarely reflect on the past together, this evening holds – for us, as it does for you – the appeal of novelty. All that Margrethe and

I have actually agreed upon is that we will describe things more or less in the order in which they happened; in order, so to speak, to make you a party to the course of events."

He paused and filled Jason's glass. At the other end of the table the actress poured her own wine.

"Cheers," said Georg van Austen and they drank. Jason had tried sweet wine before and it had always tasted to him of alcoholic lemonade. As he took a mouthful of this wine a scent comprised of almonds, currants and unknown spices drifted upwards into his brain and settled there.

"For my wife and myself," said van Austen, "it was love at first sight. Cheers."

"Cheers," responded Jason and they drank yet again.

"We met, we first laid eyes on one another, at the curtain call after Oehlenschlæger's *Midsummer Night's Play*."

Jason was putting his fountain pen to the paper in front of him when Margrethe's voice interrupted him.

"You are mistaken, my darling," she said sweetly. "It was after the first act of *The Fairy Mound*." And with a little smile she added: "Premature senility in men, Mr Toft, is one, just one, of those failings we women have to put up with." Her eyes sought out Jason's. "But I doubt," she said, "that is something a vigorous young man like yourself could appreciate."

A shadow of embarrassment passed over Jason and in order to conceal this he drained his glass.

"On the stage," said Margrethe, "one is blinded by light, so one does not *see* the audience. One experiences them as a force, and for an actress it is a quite wonderful feeling to be filled with this force. But I have always felt it important to *see* what I was being filled with. Can you relate to that, Mr Toft?"

Jason nodded.

"So," she went on, "whenever I took a bow I always walked right down to the footlights, so that I came out beyond the spotlights. From there I could see their faces. And from there, one November evening thirty years ago, I saw Georg van Austen."

At the memory of the theatre and the stage she had risen to her feet, then proceeded to pace down the length of the table. And no sooner had she taken her first step than Jason found himself picturing the intense self-assurance that thirty-five years of treading the boards had given her.

She stopped in front of her husband, put one hand to his face and tilted it towards her own.

"Do you think, Mr Toft," she said, without taking her eyes off the face before her, "it would be in order to write that his eyes burned?

"Like irons," she added reflectively, "like irons left in the coals until red hot."

She turned to Jason. "At your age," she said mildly, "when everything burns with such a clear flame, you must know how eyes can glow red hot."

"Mr van Austen's keen and intelligent gaze is familiar to me from photographs," said Jason.

"Ah," said the actress, "but it was not exactly intelligence your eyes were shining with that evening. Was it, Georg?"

Jason bent his head and scribbled a note, embarrassed at being witness to such intimate rapport between the people across from him.

"Mr van Austen," he said, much affected, "could you tell me how you recall that first exchange of glances with Mrs van Austen?"

The businessman gave this some thought. Then: "As you can see," he said, "my wife has a piercing eye. In those days they used to say that she could see right through a man's clothing . . ." – and here he made a pause during which Jason involuntarily, but discreetly covered his crotch with his papers – ". . . through his garments, all the way past his wallet and on into his heart. I felt those eyes, Mr Toft, running through me."

Jason had a mental picture of his meeting with Helene at an art exhibition. He recollected the babble of voices, the crowds of people and all at once, cutting through this, her eyes and a strange suspicion that the universe might be a jigsaw puzzle, with the positioning of each piece being of crucial importance to the whole.

"Did you feel," he blurted out, "did you, when it happened, feel that you were being guided, if I might put it like that?"

Again the elderly couple regarded him wordlessly. Then, drawing out his words, Georg van Austen said, "Mr Toft, such was my wife's magnetism that in those days, in all the best circles they said that on meeting her for the first time a young man could tell that she was a machine, a divine machine, which one had to penetrate . . ." – he paused – ". . . if one were to win through to art."

For the first time it occurred to Jason that something in the room was perhaps not quite as it should be. He raised his eyes and was suddenly struck by the thought that, in the bearing of both woman and man, beneath the superb ease of manner, there lay an unseen tension. His eye ranged further, taking in the silent Indian behind them, and as it did so, he experienced some slight problem with his vision. For a moment he had the impression that he was in a forest; on a delta; in the thick of a vast jungle; at dawn, the hour when the big cats are on the prowl. Then he gave his head a shake and reminded himself that he had a chronology, that they all had a schedule to keep to.

"How long after this meeting did you marry?" he asked.

"Very soon afterwards," Margrethe replied. "Because you see, Mr Toft, even though it can be hard . . . very hard to imagine now, at that time Georg was a very attractive man."

"I do believe," said Jason, glad of the opportunity to slip in one of the compliments he had brought along, "Mr van Austen wears his years so well that he raises the general notion of a man's prime by a good twenty years."

"Indeed," said Margrethe, "alcohol does have such a remarkably preserving effect."

"Mr Toft," said van Austen, "love is always a compromise between what is necessary and what is possible. In this case the necessary factor was our mutual inclination.

"And the possible," he continued deliberately, "was my wife's career. I'm sure we can confide that to the young man, can't we, my angel? A career, Mr Toft, which at that point was grinding to a halt. But which, with my position and wealth as a – how shall I put it – a crutch, would surely pick up steam once more."

Behind him, a cold and invisible hand came down on Jason's skull and commenced to squeeze hard.

"And my husband," said Margrethe, "had used his head. You should know, Mr Toft, and I think you ought to write this down, that his brain is the one part of his anatomy my husband has employed first and foremost."

Murmuring to himself, Jason bent over his papers.

"You see," the actress went on, "before he met me he had led a very gay life, so gay that . . . his mother had begun to find it a little too riotous for her liking. Wouldn't you say, Mr Toft, that a boy's best friend is his mother?"

"I have," said Jason, "a wonderful . . ."

"So, you see," she continued, "there were many good reasons why Georg married me and one of the best of these was his mother. Are you writing, Mr Toft?"

"All of this," Georg van Austen interjected reassuringly, "is told purely in the interests of the truth and is not meant as a disavowal of the powerful feelings we entertain for one another. I'm sure you understand that, Mr Toft."

"Absolutely," said Jason.

"And now I would ask you to drink with us," said van Austen, and filled their glasses.

Jason was suddenly conscious of how the wine he had already

drunk had settled over his eyes like a bridal veil and his hand came up to ward it off. For an instant van Austen's expression turned quizzical and Jason recalled having heard that as a young man he himself had sailed as first mate and then captain on the company's ships. Meekly he emptied his glass. Van Austen nodded approvingly.

"No one can possibly get to the bottom of our marriage," he said, "unless they have drunk with us. The fact is, Mr Toft, that it is a long time since Margrethe and I have been able to observe one another's vile profiles while sober."

The woman had been drinking while on her feet. Now she put down her glass and stepped into the centre of the room as if needing more space for what was to come.

"Let us not dwell," she said, "on the wedding. That, after all, is now part of Danish history. Let us move on to the years that followed."

"To the children," prompted Jason, like a drowning man clutching at a life belt.

"To the unutterable loneliness," said the actress.

"You see, Mr Toft," she proceeded, and as she spoke the faint note of levity gradually faded from her voice, "I actually did love him. I am, as it happens, a passionate soul, Mr Toft, and back then I loved Georg van Austen to the point of utter distraction."

Only now, with the situation on the verge of slipping out of control, did Jason see the light. Only now did he realize that this must be the first such conversation that this married couple had ever had; that inadvertently, with his petition and his presence he had succeeded in unleashing a natural disaster.

"No one can have any idea," the woman continued, "how I waited. But he never came. He was overseas, or at a launching, or a meeting of the Guild. He was out ensuring his family's immortality.

"You make a home. He takes no notice of it. You give birth

to children. He takes no notice of them. You create your roles. He takes no notice of them."

A spasm of anger surged through her form, contorting her features into a mask of hate. For a moment only, then it was gone and when she spoke her voice was hoarse but controlled.

"In all my years on the stage there was one thing I wished for more than anything else. I wished that just once he would be sitting down there of his own free will, that he would have come to see me. But that never happened. Oh, of course he came. But always because the King was present or because the company had paid for a gala performance, because it presented him with an opportunity to show some foreign head of state his respect. And always his eyes were distant, brimming with the future, brimming with money, brimming with the van Austen family's colossal, world-famous self-absorption."

She drew a deep breath. "In the end," she said, and now her tone was quite matter-of-fact, "in the end one realizes that one is unloved and there is no more truthful moment than that. There is no pain in this world equal to the pain of knowing that by loving another person in vain, gradually and blindly one has poured one's life down the drain."

"The children," Jason croaked.

"The children," said Margrethe, "oh, we had maids to see to them. In the icy waste where Georg and I have fought out our marriage, a child could easily have caught frostbite. Don't you think, Georg, that we ought to be happy that you have not had more to do with the children than has been the case?"

Georg van Austen planted his hands on the table before him and Jason realized that with this action alone he must on countless occasions have dominated the proceedings at many a directors' meeting and in many a boardroom.

"Ah, my darling," he said, "but you did manage to light lots of modest little fires at which to warm yourself."

The woman's eyes met his and their gazes locked, like two wrestlers getting a good grip and then starting to squeeze the life out of each other.

"In this – imaginary or actual – darkness," said van Austen to Jason, "my wife felt moved to take her first lover.

"If, that is, it was the first," he added. "As you wrote in your letter to us, with the majority of scenarios involving a plot there is no knowing where they have their beginning. It was, at any rate, the first affair to come to my knowledge."

The eminent businessman's expression was impassive but Jason noted that the hands which rested on the table top had begun to tense.

"In my family," he said, "a contract has always been regarded as the highest conceivable human bond. *Pacta sunt servanda*, as Roman law has it. Agreements must be honoured. The social contract between the nation and its representatives, and the commercial contract between men of business, are what make the civilized world what it is.

"The essence of a contract lies not in the signatures, not in its stipulations, not in the document itself. The essence of a contract lies in mutual trust. Trust, Mr Toft, is the supreme human sentiment. And, hence, marriage constitutes the ultimate contract, presupposing as it does the most infinite trust."

Slowly the shipowner pushed back his chair and drew himself to his feet. "There is no greater torture in the world," he said, "than to see one's boundless faith in another human being betrayed."

He thought back. "I opened the door into my wife's bedroom," he said, "and found myself as close to the two of them as I am to you now, Mr Toft."

He took one pace forward and a feeling of blind terror welled up inside Jason. Again he had that sensation of being in the jungle, with a huge white elephant bearing down upon him. With a start he leapt out of his chair and edged away.

"There is something extraordinary about the sight of one's wife naked together with another man," said van Austen. "I know that certain religions cite instances of people leaving their earthly bodies while still alive. At that moment I understood what this meant. Do you hear, Margrethe? At that moment I wanted to leave my body."

The woman opened her mouth to say something, but he stayed her with a raised hand.

"In time, Mr Toft," he said, "you will discover that most women have developed an effusive way with words which serves to excuse and explain their breaches of faith. My wife, with her thirty-five years' in the theatre, her thirty-five years training in systematic duplicity, could explain away the Fall itself. But for we menfolk, action is what counts. Wouldn't you say so, Mr Toft?"

Jason took yet another step backwards and drew his chair in front of him.

"And action it was," continued van Austen, "that came most naturally to me on that particular occasion. I fetched my rapiers. From my student days at Halle. You see, Mr Toft, well up into this century duels against the German universities were still quite common."

Van Austen lifted two silver forks from the table. "I give the young man a rapier," he said and handed Jason a fork. "But he seems unable to grip it." Jason dropped the fork. "So I press him," said van Austen, placing the tines of the fork against Jason's throat. "Then I tell Margrethe that if she wishes to see this little cricket survive to go on chirruping through the summer nights then she will have to beg for his life. A generous offer, don't you think, Mr Toft? But she says not a word and from that I deduce that one thing is for certain and that is that she is not in love with him. And so I decide to let him go."

He took away the fork and stepped to one side. Jason lurched past him and stumbled down the length of the table, dragging a candlestick on to the floor in his wake.

"Just as he was on his way out of the door," van Austen carried on at his back, "my wife came up with a most telling remark. Do you remember what you said, Margrethe?"

The woman stared at him, making no move to answer.

"She said," he continued, dwelling on the words, "'I needed someone to lie with.'" He shook his head. "It was then that I decided he should die after all."

He made a quick lunge at Jason and jabbed him in the stomach with the fork. Jason let out a squeal of terror and fell back on to the floor. Van Austen eyed him with interest. "Yes, that is exactly how he fell," he said. "And do you know where I had stabbed him? In the right lung. At Halle we used to say that if you punctured a lung you could hear the soul leaving the body."

Jason pricked up his ears. He could indeed hear something and for a second he thought he really had been wounded, until it dawned on him that it was his teeth that were chattering.

"I know," said van Austen, talking down to him where he lay, "what you, as the objective recorder – isn't that what you called yourself? – are now thinking. You are thinking, what on earth did we do with the body? An excellent question. But you see, there was no body, because the young man survived. His wound was attended to. But never again did he show his face in this house. And that might have had something to do with the fact that for the rest of his life he would have to get by with only one lung. Anyone with only one lung needs to take good care of himself."

With some difficulty Jason got to his feet and sank into a chair. His glass was refilled and obediently he drank from it. When he looked up the curtains of the windows overlooking the square had been drawn. From his position over by the wall the Indian kept his eyes trained straight ahead and just at that moment Jason could not think where to turn for help.

Margrethe laid his bundle of paper in front of him and stuck his pen in his hand. "But you must hear the rest of the story," she said, "if your picture of these events is not to be as imperfect as my husband's. You see, after that incident he never slept with me again. Are you writing, Mr Toft? After that, not once did he ever come to sleep with me."

"The children . . ." said Jason, but the woman did not hear him, bitterness seeming by this time to have eaten away her self-control.

"Of course in your family, Georg," she said, "you have always kept life at arm's length, isn't that so? You've taken the odd sniff at it, given it a little lick now and again, but when it came to the crunch, when it came to living and suffering, you didn't really have the balls for it, did you, my darling? So off you scuttled, back to the safety of Mamma and your family . . ."

"I warn you not to mention my mother's name," said van Austen.

"Mr Toft," continued Margrethe, slowly and deliberately, "do you know what the most striking trait of the van Austen family is? Its formidable gift for abstinence. For abstaining from life. And the greatest form of abstinence of all is this: on no account to forgive. And that you certainly have mastered, Georg, my sweet. You have the ability to hate and hate, you have allowed a little chunk of ice to enter your bosom and there it lies, keeping you cool. And with this sliver of permafrost in your heart you warm your hands on the family, on the thought of the van Austens' bloody . . ."

"But you have children!" ventured Jason.

"Ah yes, the children," said the actress. "Does that surprise you? But surely you don't think, Mr Toft, that a woman like me can live without men."

"Margrethe!" warned van Austen.

The tears began to stream down the woman's cheeks, but her voice remained clear and calculated. "When one has to live without love," she said, "one can always get by on sex. Now don't tell me, Mr Toft, that you had pictured marriage as being a sort of *Christmas at the Vicarage*, hm? Or like Levin's bogus *Within These Walls*? You surely didn't think this was *Little Women*? I found other men, Mr Toft. And I had children by them."

For a second or two she was quite silent. Then she began to snarl, softly and as if in torment. Eventually she looked at her husband. "I cannot cry any more," she said. "Do you hear, Georg? I'm all dried up. Do you know what it's like for a woman to be all dried up?

"Mr Toft," she went on, "write down that every child was for him."

She pointed at her husband with a finger that trembled uncontrollably. "Do you hear, Georg? Every single child was a cry to you, begging you to listen to me. But you are deaf. And you are blind."

She walked right up to him and her voice dropped to a whisper. "But when all is said and done, you're not a man, are you, Georg? Not really a human being at all, are you? If the truth were told you are nothing but your mother's means of descent to the next generation."

At that, van Austen struck her. The blow hurled her to the floor and he eased himself down beside her.

"It's not nice of you, Margrethe," he said, "to force me to wash your mouth out with soap in front of our young friend here. But being the filthy little whore that you are you know you would do well to refrain from mentioning my mother's name."

Margrethe raised her head off the floor and burst out laughing. Her laughter swelled, then broke and subsided into a snigger.

"You there," she said to Jason, "did you get the bit about the unutterable loneliness? You have to put that in. You have to write that Georg van Austen is the loneliest man on this earth. Even his children refuse to own him. How many years is it, Georg, since even one of the children has shown any interest in seeing you?"

Van Austen's hands opened and closed, groping blindly. "You turned them against me," he said, wetting his lips. "And I have never asked for, never wished for, companionship. The company is my life. In that lies my immortality. That and the children. Even if they don't want anything to do with me."

"Even in that you are mistaken," said Margrethe. "As you well know. But surely you don't imagine, Georg dear, that you could possibly be father to any one of them? After all, one doesn't get to be a father by lying down on the job. You know very well that for *that* one has to be on the ball. For *that* one has to be upstanding. But then you've known that all along."

Van Austen swayed momentarily. "The company," he said, "the company and a monument to my memory."

Margrethe was back on her feet and now, as she spoke, she drove him back against the table. "Passé, yet again," she hissed. "When this gets out, Georg dear, you'll find yourself with a monument to your memory the like of which you never thought possible, the sort of memorial that could destroy a bigger company than yours."

"It will never get out," said van Austen. He pointed at Jason. "He lives with Helene. He would never . . ."

"No," said Margrethe, and she stopped dead, straightened her shoulders and inhaled in preparation for the fateful blow. "No," she repeated, "that little worm will never write about all this. And if he did, no one would believe him. But do you know who they would believe, Georg? They would believe me. People would believe Margrethe van Austen."

"You?" said van Austen.

"Me," said the woman. "I have been writing about us, Georg. On those endless nights when I have sat in the dark and felt life running out, I have held back a little. I have saved a few bits and pieces. I have written a play about the two of us. It may not be any good, but the subject is of interest to the public. So it has been read. And accepted. By the Royal Theatre, Georg. Just over there. And it tells the truth. They're going to lap it up, Georg. They'll see that every word is true. There will be no monument to your memory. There will be a pillar to your shame."

For one split second all the power and attention in the room centred on the woman, as if owing their very existence to her. Then van Austen's hands shot out, fastened around her throat, pulled her to him, lifted her off the floor and squeezed. Jason barely had time to feel the hair rise on the back of his neck before the woman's form twitched in her husband's grasp then hung still.

Stunned, Jason was aware of how in those seconds, the processes by which one ages became palpable; how he turned grey, so to speak, from within.

Then the Indian crossed to the curtains, and as it dawned on Jason what he was about to do, a blind instinct to cover up death and everything else of an unseemly nature made him put out his hands to stop him. But it was too late, the curtains slid aside. Below them, brilliantly illuminated, lay Kongens Nytorv, swarming with people in evening dress who had been making their way home, but who had now stopped to look up at the windows.

Slowly van Austen lowered the woman in his arms until Jason saw her loosely dangling feet touch down on the parquet floor. Then it was as though her high heels regained their footing, the muscles of her calves tensed and began to move, and she executed the first steps of the dance. Van Austen's feet followed hers, the step was in triple time, they were dancing a waltz. Jason lifted his eyes to the woman's neck. It rose straight and sure from her shoulders, bared, the skin glowing with a delicate blush, and it carried her head high, tilting her face up to her husband. Her lips were slightly parted and her eyes rested on his face as if she were in a trance. Gently and smoothly, with eyes for no one but each other, yet with somnambulistic assurance they danced across in front of the windows and then off, through the room, over to a distant white door, and then they were gone.

The Indian drew the curtains, extinguished the large chandelier suspended from the ceiling, sat down at the end of the table where van Austen had previously been sitting, poured wine into his glass and tasted it. Now, when he was lit only by the candles on the table, Jason noticed that his skin had the same deep lustre as Helene's.

Having once tumbled to the fact that the woman was in fact still alive, Jason had admitted defeat and now he left the world to carry him wherever it pleased. For a long time the two men held their peace together.

"Have you any idea," the Indian said at length, "what it was that presented the greatest threat to those ships which sailed from Denmark to Tarengampadi in the old days?"

Jason made no reply.

"The greatest threat facing those sailors," said the Indian, "came from themselves. Mutiny and fights between members of the crew.

"I, of course, am only a dirty foreigner. But even so it strikes me that that, perhaps, is how one might describe Europe. As a place where the greatest threat to the individual comes from the individual himself . . ."

He sat for a while gazing into the candle flames. "There was once a captain by the name of van Austen. In those days his family owned but one ship and even that they owned only a share in. This captain was a hard man. He had tried to combat violence with violence, he had tried to ensure a peaceful voyage by having men flogged and clapped in irons and since he happened also to be a clever man he soon realized that this was not the right way to go about it. There was at that time at the court of Naiken of Tanjore a family renowned for telling the most wonderful stories, and for learning everything so fast that a woman of the family who had been in service in the home of the Dansborg commandant had actually taught herself to speak Danish. Captain van Austen conceived the idea of taking this woman on board ship for the trip back to Denmark, to pacify the men. His plan was to present her to a different sailor each night, on the condition that the man in question had been behaving himself.

"However, the captain must also have been a forgetful and unenlightened man, for there were two things he neglected to keep in mind. The first of these was that it is not right to carry away a woman against her will. And the other thing he failed to remember was who the woman's family were. The Buddhacarita tells of how Buddha set off into the forest to gain the ultimate enlightenment. And the text says: '. . . and he was accompanied by the sons of some of his officials, who had been chosen because they could tell good tales.' This woman's father was a direct descendant of one of those men who told stories to the great Bodhisattva. Do you know what that means?"

"No," said Jason.

"It means," said the Indian, "that for the man who uses force on this woman, for him the justice of the high karma awaits.

"The captain came for her one night and took her out to the ship, which then weighed anchor. On the first night the woman suggested trying an experiment. There were one hundred and twenty-five men on board. Instead of sharing their bunks, she wanted them all to be assembled below decks each evening, or at least as many as the weather permitted, and she would tell a story. And so it was. And even though the ship was subjected to the most gruelling journey home, with dreadful storms off the African coast, the woman's stories tamed the sailors – because, being the kind of person she was, they knew that if she had been handed over to one of them just once, she would never again have told anyone anything.

"The night on which the ship anchored in the roads off Copenhagen she told the three hundred and thirty-fourth story and in the year that had passed there had not been one fight on board ship.

"The stories she had told had been the same ones that her family had been telling for centuries. I have heard tell that these later travelled further to Persia and from there into Europe. But in those days the Danes knew nothing of them.

"Later that same night the seamen threw a much-hated officer overboard. And for this the captain himself took the woman by force, not so much because he blamed her for the killing as because she had dared to impose a condition on a white man. Afterwards he had her dragged down under the ship's keel and up the other side by her thumbs.

"This of course left her crippled, but as he told her it was not her hands he had need of from now on, but her mouth and her sex."

"He should have been made to pay for that," said Jason.

"That is how any normal person would have seen it," said the Indian. "That revenge would have been sweet. And, once she had regained the remnants of her health, she could easily, so easily, have pulled a long pin out of her hair one night and driven it through the captain's eyelid and into his dark brain. But that thought never occurred to her. Is not the first rule of Buddhaghosa: 'to refrain from taking any life'. For generation after generation her family had respected the four sacred truths and through many kalpas – you do remember how long a kalpa is? – in her earlier incarnations she had walked the fourfold path and striven to overcome the four obstacles to deep trance, and consequently this woman was virtually transparent. Can you understand that?"

"To some extent," said Jason.

"The thought of revenge was alien to her," the Indian continued. "All she did was to show the universe her mangled hands and this sight rose up through the heavens to the gods in their pure dwelling and the gods decided that in order for the supreme Dharma to be fulfilled, this man and his line and all their incarnations would have to endure ineffable torments for several kalpas in succession."

Again they sat for a while in silence, the Indian lost in his own thoughts, which Jason struggled in vain to follow.

"I am here," the Indian said eventually, "to fulfil an inkling of a beginning to the first phase of these torments. It was the decision of the high gods that this first phase should take the form of a curse on the van Austen family. And this curse should be love. In each generation of this family one will be born who will never be able to break free of the illusion of love but will be doomed to love another human being to distraction. And be loved in return."

"That doesn't sound like punishment," said Jason, "that sounds like a blessing."

"But this is a terrible love," said the Indian. "Because these two lovers, man and woman, can touch one another in one way only: by re-enacting – week in, week out, month after month, year after year – all the torments of an entire marriage in a single night. And these torments shall be fresh every time."

"Who determines the course of these evenings?" asked Jason.

"I do," said the Indian. "Before me it was my brother and before him my uncle and before him my grandfather. The woman whom Captain van Austen had keelhauled was my grandfather's great-great-grandmother. Thus we are the instruments the gods use to administer the justice of the supreme Dharma. That woman stayed with the captain and four times a month she put him through indescribable torment. They had a son, who had a son, and little by little the European blood obliterated our features. But the curse lives on."

Jason took a drink of his wine.

"Six days from now," the Indian went on, "on Monday evening, I will visit their bedroom and describe to each of them the agonies they will have to go through on the following evening. They then have twenty-four hours in which to prepare themselves."

"So what, come Monday, will their next life be like?" enquired Jason.

"That the gods will decide when the time comes," the Indian replied. "Perhaps she will murder one of her newborn infants and be tortured by that killing for the rest of her days. Or perhaps she will catch some incurable disease from him. Perhaps they will have to watch their grandchildren being abducted and mutilated. To the storyteller there is no end to the horrors of love."

"Why don't they just stop?" asked Jason.

"They always do stop," the Indian replied. "Each new generation either sends us home or puts us in jail, and thinks itself free of us. Every son and daughter of the van Austen family throws their hands in the air in triumph and thinks: 'It fell on my parents because they were weak. But it won't fall on me.' Then one day this person experiences love – first as a tiny spring, then as a tidal wave – and he or she rejoices, until they discover that this tidal wave is imprisoned within a sealed iron container which is heated up until red hot from the outside until the two lovers are begging to be released, no matter how. When that time comes we know and we do not wait to be summoned, we are already on our way, that the equilibrium of the world may be maintained."

In his mind's eye Jason pictured Helene, naked on the bed. "Which member of the family will be next?" he asked.

"Who can say?" said the Indian. "The one who first begins to feel their beloved's heart weighing like a millstone around their own neck."

"Is there no way out?" asked Jason.

"Yes, indeed there is," replied the Indian. "Storytelling, that is the way out. We suffer because through incarnation after incarnation we have cast shadows on our lives. Our stories are formed from these shadows. In each story which this family lives through, it lives with its misdeeds. Thus each story sends a ray of light into the darkness. In the end there is no more darkness. In the end there is transparency. And the torment is at an end."

"What sort of justice is it," asked Jason bitterly, "that is ordered in such a way that one has to experience so much misery in order to gain a mere modicum of insight?"

"Now I am, as you know," the Indian said, "only a filthy foreigner, who has beheld but a fold of a tip of a corner of the supreme Dharma which permeates all things. Nonetheless, it has crossed my mind that were one to form a picture of this justice, one might visualize it as a cosmic laugh; a laugh which hides nothing, but is instead so clear that through it one can see not only the skull but the pulsating life within."

REFLECTION OF A YOUNG MAN IN BALANCE

It is with mild indifference that I view the fact that I live in a world which talks so fast that it needs must breathe through its arse. Words no longer make any impression on me. I am an abandoned building – let us just say a forsaken and forgotten observatory. The world blows through my shattered windows without leaving so much as a trace of itself.

It no longer matters whether anyone believes me. You may take this any way you please. As a confession, a *cri de coeur*, as a chill little fable, as a lament. I look upon it as the closest any human being can come to the truth.

The reason I write this is that something has happened in my life which has liberated me, completely and utterly, from what we refer to as feelings.

There cannot be many signals which actually make it out of the universe which I inhabit. Those people whom I have heard claim that they had now risen, once and for all, above all emotion were usually in the process of drowning in the gutter. If, that is, they were not soaring aloft, bloated as bodies washed up on a beach with self-conceit.

I cannot say that my life has been spotless. But since that

night – the night of March 19th 1929 – it has been good as gold. And that no matter how deep one scratches. Since that night my attitude towards love, desire, jealousy and loneliness has been totally different from that of other people. Since that night I have been free.

Of what the world knows as feelings there is only one to which I admit: a faint sense of anger which I foster because it keeps me warm. I have never understood this. Something tells me that now, tonight, I will get to the bottom of it.

I design and make mirrors. As did my father, and his father before him. I am a qualified engineer, they were not. But that is to progress's credit, not mine. The most profound truth about all craftsmanship is that it is a state of mind. And to that state those changes they call advances hold no relevance. In essence, my work is no different from that of my father and my grandfather.

Which is just as it should be. There is nothing we can say or do that has not already been said or done. It is not only when we speak that we repeat ourselves and others. Our actions too are clichés.

If, even so, it makes any sense to call me an artist, then it is not because of what I have accomplished, but because of what I wished to do.

I dreamt of creating a mirror which would reflect the world as it really is. In a way it is this dream which has purified me.

European history holds two views of mirrors; the truth and the dream. Ovid wrote that Nemesis tampered with the surface of the water, thus causing Narcissus to see a shadow which he mistakenly took for a real person.

The image offered by the mirror in the First Letter to the Corinthians was fragmentary, split, incomplete.

In the emblem books of the Middle Ages the mirror is a symbol of *vanitas* – pride, one of the seven deadly sins.

The mirrors of Hans Christian Andersen and Lewis Carroll

are menacing, untrustworthy. In Offenbach's opera, Dapertutto steals the souls of humans by stealing their reflections.

All these mirrors are false. As are those with which we ourselves are familiar. We know that in a mirror we never see ourselves as we are. Depending on our mood we see ourselves as misunderstood and forsaken, or as the darlings of the universe, or as animals hiding behind a thin film of humanity. But never do we see ourselves as we must actually be. As a composite of all these partial truths. To mankind, the mirror is invariably a screen on to which it projects its longing for equilibrium.

The other mirror recognized by history is a dream. It is the fearless mirror in Snow White. It is Shakespeare's mirror, the one behind Hamlet's words to the players about holding "the mirror up to nature". This dream it was which in the Middle Ages led to many Books of Hours being called *specula*, as an assurance of their comprehensiveness and reliability. In the Orient it is the mirror of the historical Buddha, Śākyamuni, as described by the poet Aswaghosha on the threshold of the golden age of Buddhism: "On the second watch of the night he was granted the supreme, heavenly vision (. . .) With this he saw the whole world, which revealed itself to him as if reflected in a flawless mirror." These reflections are totally trustworthy because they are uncompromising. Because *they remain unaffected by what they reflect*.

I was searching for such a mirror. And now, when it is all behind me, I can confess that my craving for reality had something to do with my attitude towards women.

I knew that the worst thing in the world was to be deserted. Sooner or later we all find ourselves deserted. Consequently, separation was something I practised on a daily basis. I walked out on the women in my life to save myself from losing the knack of desertion. I can now afford to admit that I was afraid of them. Women are the only creatures on this earth with whom togetherness is one long process of leavetaking and separation. They grew more and more alien to me with every day I knew them.

There came a time when I began to fear that I myself might to some extent be to blame for this string of departures. At that point I began to think about the Mirror. I wished I could have it, as an unbiased judge, a fixed point and champion of the truth through the night of passion during which the battle of love is played out.

On May 1st 1927 I was asked if I would construct the reflector telescope for the new Nordic observatory being built above Delsjön, outside of Göteborg. I said yes.

I knew that this observatory was intended as a monument to the Nordic spirit of conciliation. Strikes were being staged all over Europe at that time. We knew that an economic crisis on a hitherto unknown scale was in the offing. It was without a shadow of doubt in my mind that I awaited a new world war.

The observatory represented an attempt to allay the fear, by looking at the stars shoulder to shoulder. As with all monumental national illusions this aspiration – as far as those who made the decisions was concerned – was half-conscious, half-subliminal. Right from the outset, I saw the project for what it really was.

I have been asked why, nonetheless, I offered my services.

What was I supposed to say? We know so little about the causes we actually serve. When Kepler published his theories on optics in *Supplement to Witelo* in 1604, he believed he was confirming the existence of God and the constancy of his day and age. History has shown that he took a crucial step along the path that was to alter the world in which he was writing beyond all recognition.

If, even so, people asked again – as some did – why I took part in such a piece of political chicanery, I replied that I did after all have to live.

If anyone questioned me further I threatened to kick their arses for them.

All this happened four years before the building of the reflector telescope for the Palomar observatory. Opinion had it that it would never be possible to produce a mirror larger than the reflector on the Earl of Ross telescope, which had a diameter of six feet and a focal length of fifty-six feet. It was still a moot point whether the future did not perhaps belong to the refractor telescope.

During the summer of '27 we erected the construction shed. That winter, the ceramic oven. The following winter I cast the mirror.

I am not going to describe the research which led to my opting for a silver-coated mirror. Or my development of homogenous types of glass. Or the sleep I went without in order, for the first time in history, to break the rule which for two hundred years has been telling us that the light absorption of a mirror can never be less than fifty per cent. I want to show you the stars, not entertain you with a description of how difficult it is to reach them.

I made nineteen unsuccessful attempts. The last, successful cooling process lasted thirty-one days. Without pride, without anger, without remorse I can say that no one else has ever seen what we saw when we opened that oven.

It was a perfect concave mirror, a section of a spherical surface the imaginary centre of which lay one hundred and seventy feet away. It had an aperture twenty-three feet in diameter. Words cannot describe it. I have no wish to say any more about that sight.

It was around this time that we first heard tell of her. Her reputation had gone before her, as if she were the world's greatest whore or the world's greatest opera diva. She was a glass grinder.

I set out in search of her. I followed the trail of miracles she had performed. Off the Frisian Islands I spied a golden disc hanging over the ship's superstructure for all the world as if the full moon were being hauled down to the deck. It was not the moon, however, but a dazzling white circle of light emanating from a lighthouse ten sea miles off. The beam had not scattered. It measured one and a half feet in diameter, exactly as it had done when it left what must have been an unimaginable, incomprehensible, perfect lens. It was said that she had made a gift of this lens to the Dutch state.

In Vienna I visited the new orangery. For its ellipsoid walls she had ground curved mirrors which reflected the interior in such a way that visitors could hardly be induced to cross the threshold, once they laid eyes on that vast chamber, almost one thousand square feet of it, sliding over into a trackless and limitless forest of orange and lemon trees in which they were convinced they would lose their way.

I never did find her. Always she had travelled on before I arrived, that being the way with women. Eventually I returned to Göteborg. And there she was.

She commanded everyone except me to leave the shed, then she set to work. First of all she undressed. I tried to explain the spherical aberration to her, the flaw in the concave mirror. I do not know whether she was listening. I do not know whether she understood me. She must have been about five feet tall; half-Japanese, half-Italian. They said her ancestors had been among the first to flee from the ban against emigration that had been placed during the Middle Ages on all the glass grinders of Venice. They had fled to the East.

She removed all her clothes with the exception of a long piece of cloth wound round her hips. Her skin was as white as the mixture of beeswax and paraffin wax used for altar candles. Her feet and hands were swathed in white cotton rags and these she sprinkled with a mixture of crushed magnesium and diamond dust. Then she crawled out on to the mirror and began to grind.

I recall that time as a whole phase of my life. In actual fact it cannot have lasted more than three, or perhaps four days. The roof over our heads was of glass and the mirror gathered the daylight to itself. On the pulverized precious stone she moved as if over cold blue fire. Though her movements were languid her body was at all times bathed in sweat. In the cloud of glass dust that hovered above the mirror her reflection hung suspended, like inverted, sinuous three-dimensional fragments of her real self.

One night we slept together. You ask what made her do it. I have no answer to that. I cannot say that I think that much of myself. I put up with myself because I know that we two are stuck with one another till death us do part. But it has never occurred to me that anyone might love me. I have never felt that I had anything to offer a woman apart from my boyish charm and I do not even have any faith in that now. It may have been because of the mirror. In which case she has been disappointed. Artists are always worth so much less than their works.

Be that as it may, she worried me. When she had completed the grinding process I dismissed her.

Only then did I silver the mirror. Then we mounted the telescope and directed it at the heavens. We took a number of photographs. We saw what no human being before us had ever seen. We saw the first quasar. We saw the planet Pluto. We saw a stellar nebula which appeared to be dispersing and which, by the following night, had vanished from the sky. We saw an unaccountable dark body which came as a surprise to all of us. The astronomers believed it to be some heavenly phenomenon foretokening riches and fame. I knew it could only be a foreign body on the surface of the mirror. The next day I examined the glass. I found nothing. On the next batch of photographs the shadow had shifted position and changed shape. This time I spread a fine-mesh grid over the mirror and pinpointed exactly where the grain of dust ought to be. I trained a microscope on the glass. I saw only my instrument's own light source. Encountered nothing but my own reflection.

It was then I realized that the mirror must be alive. I eyed my colleagues speculatively and noted that they seemed perfectly satisfied; I noted how they congratulated me and each other on such an excellent result and how they looked forward to the inaugural ceremony. How, without any ado, they ousted that tiny, roving, amoeba-like shadow from their view of things.

So I set off in pursuit of her. In the third canto of the *Metamorphoses* Cadmus has to travel the world over in search of a woman. Odysseus sets out looking for one and sails home looking for another. And then there is Tristan. And Solomon.

I mention all this simply because I need history to vouch for the fact that I am not the only fool who has been willing to travel halfway round the globe after a woman. At the time I believed myself to be driven by the notion that she, who had breathed life into inanimate glass, must be in possession of the Mirror. Now, with a mind of burnished granite, I can take the liberty of saying that I also missed her.

I caught up with her in Copenhagen. She was setting up an exhibition of her mirrors and lenses in the Tivoli gardens. That night I climbed over the wrought-iron railings surrounding the gardens.

She was alone.

"You have come to see the Mirror," she said. "It does exist then?" I asked. "Yes," she said and proceeded to tell me about it.

"Anyone who looks into a mirror," she said, "sees what he wishes or fears to see. I have always known that, were I to fashion a mirror which showed things as they really are, that mirror would have to be alive, an organism that could sense the mood of the beholder and present an image geared to that mood."

She steered me over to a corner. A rectangular shape tall as a man was propped against the wall, enveloped in a yellow cloth.

It might have been a painting. She removed the covering. To begin with it seemed like any ordinary mirror. Then I saw that in that dim room it glowed very softly, with a light that seemed to issue from somewhere behind the face of the mirror itself. Not only that, but I could see now that it was not altogether static, that around its edge there ran a faint, plasmic ripple. I stepped right up to it.

I say again: no one need believe what I am now about to relate. I do not believe it myself. At night, when I lie awake, I wonder whether my ability to remember has been impaired. Such thoughts keep me from sleeping. But they make some sense of my sleeplessness. First I saw my own reflection as I knew it. As I thought I knew it. But my features were distorted. I put a hand up to my skin, and my touch told me that it was unruffled. I realized that the Mirror knew my self-control was studied. In order to get closer to the truth it was presenting me with an exaggerated image of my unrest.

Then the image started to fluctuate, producing a succession of warped and disjointed likenesses of myself. I strove to catch every one of them. Then they speeded up. I tried to focus on whatever image the Mirror provided of my outward appearance. At this I disappeared from its face and instead past me there swirled a series of tableaux in which I recognized my own most intimate hopes and fears. What I was witnessing was the Mirror's attempt to compensate for the torrent of impressions and feelings that was surging through me at that moment.

I put my hands over my eyes. I endeavoured to stay calm, wanting to make the Mirror stop. I told myself that whatever it showed me I would view coolly and with composure, for I would know that it was the truth.

When I took my hands away, I saw the room in which I was standing. I recognized the rough, broad floorboards and the walls with their combination of gilt and smoke-blackened grey paint.

But I was nowhere to be seen and there was no longer anything lifelike about the room; instead it now spiralled off into infinity.

The Mirror had registered my hopes of the truth. As a counterpoint to this projection it now gave me a glimpse of an undeniable misapprehension.

I had always felt that I possessed a mulish, rustic streak which would forever set limits on my life, but which would also save me from going mad. Now it struck me that this too was an illusion. That I was a player in a ghastly game designed to drive anyone insane.

From the wall I grabbed an ordinary, square vanity mirror and held it up to the Mirror, intending to force it to display the truth about itself. It responded, not with an image of me, not with an image of the mirror in my hand, but by showing the wall behind me and that alone.

I glanced over at the woman and as I did so the Mirror revealed that I would give anything – including the sight of the Mirror – to press my face against her luminous skin. I watched my love laid bare, loathing my own dependence, and it occurred to me that I could kill her. In tune with my thoughts my hands in the Mirror fastened around her throat. I took a step forward, meaning to do away with her, this woman who was the sole witness to my nakedness, but the Mirror saw through me and showed me kneeling at her feet, snivelling with cowardice. I could not drag myself away from the Mirror, but I did turn my back on it. What I had seen had nothing to do with the finicky, insipid reality of a normal mirror. No, this had possessed greater space and depth than anything I had ever seen before. I could no longer have said which was the real world: the one inside the Mirror or that outside of it.

"How can I tell, my flower," I asked her, "that *you* really do exist and are not merely a fabrication of light created by this mirror?"

"That you will never know," she said. "I am not even sure

myself. When I close my eyes I can see pictures from the time when I made the Mirror. But those memories could just as easily have been formed by the Mirror when it produced me."

Since then it has become clear to me that this is the dilemma with which I too will always be faced. Am I a man writing about what once happened to him? Or does this account add something to my life, in which case it would have to be said that I only come into being as I write; that, in a sense, this account makes me what I am? And in what way does it alter me? When Poe wrote about mirrors – as he did in "Von Jung the Mystific", as he did in "The Philosophy of Furniture" – he too grew superficial, glib, apathetic, as if his own words had turned into a mirror. Will the same thing happen to me?

The history of science in Europe has never succeeded in resolving the debate carried on since antiquity between the Aristotelian and Galenic schools of thought. The question as to how far the beholder is passively subjected to an optical impression of reality, and how far he himself shapes what he sees. Standing there in that room facing the woman it was borne in upon me that this dialogue had never made sense, because the question had been wrongly posed. It presupposes that there is a stable reality to be observed. There is no such thing. As soon as we lay eyes on the world it starts to change. And we with it. Viewing reality does not mean making sense of a setup. It means surrendering oneself and triggering an unfathomable transformation.

I turned to face the Mirror. I knew that if I chased its images they would take flight. If I ran from them they would pursue me. Whatever I asked of them they would not deny me. Whatever I feared the most they would ram down my throat. The history of Europe is the history of a boundless faith in the power of will. At that moment I perceived the infinite limitations of that will. Faced with this mirror I had no choice but to place myself before it and submit. Either that or forget the whole thing.

In his autobiography Carl Gustav Jung describes the moment, while seated at his desk, when he made up his mind to give himself up to the images in his head. Perhaps it is fear that makes people let go. Perhaps it is desperation. It is certainly not courage.

For just a second the Mirror showed me my physical form. Then it must have sensed that I had given in, because it dropped me. The room around me vanished. Somewhere on the fringes of this experience stood the woman.

I do not attribute any specific meaning to what I saw. In "El Aleph" Jorge Luis Borges saw all the points in the universe at the selfsame moment. What I saw was on a much, much smaller scale. And it came in stages, like the steps on a staircase. I cannot say whether it led up or down, whether it led towards or away from reality.

I saw a bottomless valley thick with mist. I saw spiralling towers built out of light. I saw a woman with a dark face and a name which, in a Nilotic tongue, brought to mind the blue-grey hour just before sunrise when her mother gave birth to her in a ditch.

I saw a mirror. Then an infinite number of mirrors reflecting each other's emptiness. Then the mirror they held up to the Danish philologist Rasmus Rask's lips to see whether he still lived. Then his body. Then the bones of donkeys on the caravan route from Tamale to Mecca. The two years the pilgrimage took (how does one see two years?). Then the aroma of Vinho Cheiro from Terceira (how does one see an aroma?). A drinking bowl, lacquered three thousand years ago on a rowing boat on the Yellow Sea, three days out from the coast.

I saw the great systematizers and their works. Linnaeus in Lapland with his botanist's box. The last Buddha to date. Thomas Aquinas. His commentary to *De Anima*. Hegel giving his inaugural lecture in Berlin. Wagner. Poincaré, the last polymath of mathematics. The shadow of a man who might have been the Saviour. The paragraph in *De Coelo* – I believe it was number fifty-six – in which Swedenborg writes that the earthly world is a reflection of the divine.

Then came the great cosmological models. The mirror showed me a world in flux. A world in flames. A world composed of elementary particles. Itself a particle of one greater still. A world of concentric circles. A world which is an illusion. There is a plant. A world that is activated by ideas. Activated by people. By gods. By reason. By economic legislation. A world which does not exist, but is dreamt up by a creature which in turn does not exist.

For a moment there was stillness. Then came the emptiness. It did not make itself known as an absence. It made itself known as a presence, as a palpable vacuum which emerged from the Mirror and drew me to itself.

Anyone who is familiar with emptiness will know what I am talking about. A sinking feeling in outer space.

It swallowed me, then spat me out again.

Human beings are infinitely alike and infinitely diverse. Emptiness may be a baptism, a river, a foundation stone, an annihilation, a cross, a new form of algebra. To me, it meant that I was liberated, once and for all, from love.

Though I cannot be absolutely certain, I believe – and this I say quietly and calmly – that I have also been rendered immortal.

Now I knew what those who spend their lives searching are looking for. They must have seen the emptiness, and for the rest of their lives they have been struggling to repeat that experience. Now I understood why Jesus found it necessary to contradict himself in every third sentence, and why Buddha had to resort to miracles, and Mohammed needed to intimidate and Meister Eckhart to insist that his own personal isolation should become common to us all. All of them had beheld the emptiness and longed to return to it.

The great systems which inform the world about truth and life invariably claim to be absolutely truthful and well balanced. In reality they are quaking bridges built out of yearning. All this I saw and it made me pure and clear as quartz.

Sadly, I am beginning to forget what I saw. Of course I have seen it again, she has shown me the Mirror many a time since then, but forgetfulness erases it all.

It is now eleven days, four hours and fifty-three minutes since I last looked on it. I can still recall, albeit with difficulty, the way in which the emptiness is white. But no longer the emptiness itself.

As I write I am aware that I miss her. That my longing for her is driving me crazy. I know that in saying this I am contradicting everything I have written. I have to face the fact that my balance is not superb, nor is it perfect. That I have lost it.

I know now why I am angry. It is because I fear my dependence on her. Life with her would be Hell. Life without her would be worse still. I have looked on something precious, but I am only human, and that is the problem, for humanity is frail, it falls into decay, it forgets, it betrays, it disparages, it devaluates, it is hit by moral and intellectual inflation.

If only I could remember how it felt to be modest and, hence, in command of the situation. But forgetfulness is devouring my humility. I write this with an increasing and fatal sense of self-conceit. I am being puffed up. I take to the skies. I cannot grip my pencil. My love for her is unique, it is colossal. What happened to my composure? My eye for a cliché? My cynicism? My karmic enlightenment? My mirrors? Where is the woman? Help!